TONI MOUNT

THE COLOUR OF MURDER

The Colour of Murder

A Sebastian Foxley Medieval Mystery
Book 5

Copyright © 2017 Toni Mount
ISBN-13: 978-84-947298-5-0

M
MadeGlobal Publishing

For more information on
MadeGlobal Publishing, visit
our website
www.madeglobal.com

Dedication

Mum and Dad,
Joyce and Albert 'Lofty' Botting,
tellers of marvellous stories.

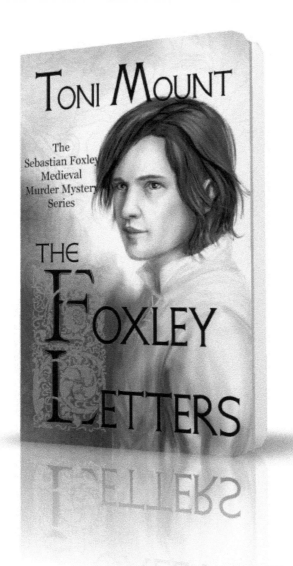

GET THIS FREE BOOK <u>TODAY!</u>

https://www.madeglobal.com/authors/toni-mount/download/

With letters from all the main characters, including Seb, Emily, Jude and even the wonderful Jack, this collection of letters will add to the lives and stories of those involved in the intrigue, drama and excitement of these historical thrillers set in Medieval London.

PROLOGUE

THE CHAMBER beneath the Palace of Westminster was cobweb-draped and thick with the dust of centuries. Few knew of its existence now but these two. The air was dry and chill as the grave. Nameless things had lived and died in this stone vault. They had discovered it a decade before; a place where their late and much-mourned mother had been able to practise undisturbed. A single torch lit the gloom, the light unable to penetrate the arched recesses of this forgotten room but enough to show an open book lying on a table.

He stoked a little brazier to life; she placed a copper dish above the flames to heat a precise measure of rain water.

'This will work, won't it, sister?' he asked, touching her hand in an intimate gesture.

'Have faith. 'Tis our mother's own instructions that we follow. What she has written in the grimoire has never failed us before and will not do so now.' The woman consulted the parchment pages of the book. Murmuring ancient incantations as the water began to boil, she took a handful of leaves from a linen bag. Lance-shaped and rough to the touch, they were dried and crumbled readily as she sprinkled them into the bubbling dish. 'In the name of the Dark Lord and his mistress, Hecate the Wise Woman, I stir this brew thrice widdershins.' She took up an elder rod in her left hand and gently set the water turning in the opposite direction to that which the sun travels by day and the moon and stars by night. An earthy smell arose from the steam. The brazier flames reflected off her silken sleeve as

1

she moved the rod, and glinted on her pale hair, turning it to molten gold.

'Is a single handful sufficient for the task?' he asked. They both knew there could be no mistake in this matter. The future safety, prosperity and happiness of all their family depended upon the efficacy of this potion. 'A few more leaves cannot help but make certain.'

'Be silent, brother. I know what I am about. Our mother taught me well. The leaves of the foxglove are potent indeed. There is enough in this dish to over-try the hearts of my lord husband and all his kin, if we wish to. But for now, one brother will suffice. We cannot afford to attract notice with a sudden rush of dead Plantagenets.'

They both laughed, knowing that time would come.

'No. You are right, sister. I fear I am over anxious about this. So much depends...'

She pressed her fingertips to his lips.

'...Depends upon silence, dearest brother. Now we let the potion infuse until it be cooled, then you may decant it into the wine cask. Be sure to wash your hands after. Now, I must leave you. Edward will require my presence when he greets the French ambassador and I am hardly dressed to play my part.'

'Sister, you are a veritable queen whatever your attire. Go then. Dazzle the fools.'

At the foot of the stair she paused and turned, retracing her steps to kiss him fervently.

'Be careful, brother. May the Dark Lord oversee all our endeavours.' She smiled and he returned that smile, confident now that all would be well.

CHAPTER ONE

Thursday the twelfth day of February, in the year of Our Lord 1478 The Palace of Westminster

RICHARD, DUKE of Gloucester, had been summoned by his brother, King Edward, for a private audience so the presence of others was unexpected. More worrying was the number of the queen's relatives in attendance and particularly so, since he wished to beg a favour of Edward – one he believed the king would be more likely to grant, if they were alone.

Richard removed his fur-trimmed hat and bent the knee before his sovereign as etiquette required, even of a prince of royal blood.

'Up, up, little brother,' said the king, waving Richard to his feet. 'Today should be yet another occasion to please you immensely.' Edward was lounging on a padded chair by the blazing hearth, his feet upon a velvet foot stool.

'Indeed, sire? I thought this was to be a privy audience?'

'And so it is, Dickon, but witnesses will be required.'

'Witnesses?' Richard began toying with his finger ring, a nervous habit of his. Realising what he was doing, he clasped his hands behind his back. It did not do to betray his feelings before the queen's brother, Anthony Woodville, Earl Rivers, nor her sons from her first marriage.

Anthony Woodville stood behind the king's right shoulder, as close as he dared without hindering the movement of the royal arm in raising the wine cup to the royal lips. Impeccably attired in the latest and – to Richard's mind – absurd fashion, the earl's voluminous black sleeves flared from the elbow and almost swept the floor. His pale hair, hanging to his shoulders, was perfectly groomed and trimmed; his pointed chin close-shaven. Some exotic scent wafted in the duke's direction each time the earl gestured with his arms, which was often enough to become irritating. To be truthful, Richard found Lord Anthony irritating in any case; his very presence an annoyance.

As for the queen's sons by her first husband, Thomas and Richard Grey, at a year or two younger than himself, they had made his time at court a misery in his youth, teasing him for his lack of knowledge of courtly ways and who was who. In truth, they had mocked and bullied him as a bumpkin from the shires, making him look a fool at every opportunity. He hadn't forgiven nor forgotten a single one of their humiliations. Now they stood to the king's left hand, bold as pike staffs in their silks and satins, be-gemmed and be-feathered like a pair of gaudy trollops. At that moment, naught would have pleased him more than to slap the smirks from their cunning faces. But retribution would have to wait. Richard could be the most patient of men, when necessary.

The king clicked his fingers and Anthony Woodville handed him a rolled parchment. A servant appeared with a portable writing slope; another with pen and ink; a third with a candle, red wax and a lead seal attached to a ribbon.

'You know what this is, Dickon?' The king waved the parchment.

'No, sire. Of course not.' Here he was, forced to show his ignorance before the Woodville-Grey affinity yet again. Why did the king do this to him?

'You will be most gratified to learn, Dickon, that this writ bestows a peerage title upon your little son.'

'But he is barely more than a babe. Naturally, I am delighted, but is he not overly young for such an honour?'

The king looked up from the writing slope, pen poised. His eyes met Richard's and what the duke saw in those ice-blue eyes caused the hairs to rise upon the nape of his neck.

'I am creating your little lad Earl of Salisbury.'

'Thank you, sire.' Richard could not even pretend to be pleased. This was no honour. It was a gift of blood for the earldom of Salisbury belonged to their brother George, Duke of Clarence, at present residing at the Tower of London 'at the king's pleasure'. To bestow one of his titles upon another could mean only one thing: George's disgrace was not to be reversed. Or worse? Was Edward sweetening a more bitter pill yet for Richard to swallow? Of a sudden, the duke felt in need of a stool to sit down. Instead, he stepped forward, bent the knee and kissed the coronation ruby on the king's great bear's paw of a hand, then watched as 'Edwardus Rex' was scribbled at the foot of the parchment before it passed to the servant, standing ready with the sand-shaker, to dry the ink.

Then Anthony Woodville signed his name as a witness and the Grey brothers, each in turn. How appropriate, Richard thought, that those who so greatly desired George's downfall should sign away what was rightfully his to another. How long would it be before they contrived a similar fate for himself? The heavy seal was affixed by means of a blob of red wax to attach the ribbon and when the wax had set, Edward presented the parchment to Richard.

'When your lad is older, he will be required to do homage to me for the title, of course. Until then, you can enjoy all the revenues and estates it entails.' Edward's smile might have seemed genuine enough to those who knew him less well but Richard recognised it for what it was: a cold, calculated curving of the lips – a warning he understood.

'My lord,' Richard began, 'Edward, by your leave, I would speak with you alone.'

'I'm a busy man, little brother...'

'As I realise, sire, but this is of the utmost importance to us both. I ask permission to visit George at the Tower. He must be so...'

The king, never one for rapid movement, shot from his chair like a man scalded and grabbed Richard's arm in a painful grip.

'No!' he roared. 'I utterly forbid it.'

'But I...'

'I said no. Let that be an end to it.'

Richard was wincing, his upper arm in agony.

'I merely want...'

The king shook him violently.

'You go near him, write to him...' Spittle sprayed with the king's every word. His face was puce with anger. 'You have communication with him in any way whatsoever and I swear, Dickon, you'll find yourself likewise, in the Tower, locked away indefinitely. Do I make myself quite clear on this matter?'

'Aye.'

'What?'

'You do, your grace.' Richard cleared his throat. 'You make yourself perfectly clear, sire.'

The king flung his brother loose from his grasp like a discarded rag.

'You defy me on this, you'll regret the day,' Edward said, turning away, the quiet words more menacing than any blistering tirade.

Belatedly, Richard noticed the faces of Anthony Woodville and the Greys. If looks could slay, he would be a dead man already, three times over. He refused to massage the life back into his throbbing arm while they watched. His humiliation was too great as it was without also acknowledging that physical hurt.

When Gloucester had departed, clutching the royal warrant but having been denied any chance of privy speech with the king, Anthony Woodville stepped over to a side table, strewn with rolls of parchment awaiting the king's attention. Knowing Edward, such attention was unlikely to be forthcoming without someone else's insistence.

Two years older than his brother-in-law, King Edward, Anthony wore his years rather better than his royal relative. Where the king was running to flesh these days, his face heavily jowled and his belly straining his bejewelled belt, Anthony remained lean, his face smooth and unlined, his physique that of a youth half his age of seven-and-thirty. Sober and austere as a monk, he was yet a man of high fashion. The king bedecked himself in damask and velvet of the brightest hues. In contrast, Anthony wore black, in the Burgundian style. Black might seem a sombre colour, true, but its simplicity was all illusion. In truth, it was an excellent way of demonstrating the wearer's wealth and Anthony liked to flaunt the depth of his coffers. Once lavishly scattered with seed pearls and silver thread embroidery, there was naught sombre about such attire.

That's not to say that the queen's brother was a shallow creature much given to show and little else. He was a scholar, a man of letters, a diplomat, a devout pilgrim and a master at the joust, as well as the ultimate courtier.

'I see a certain document here remains unsigned, as yet,' Anthony said, casually moving a parchment roll to the top of the heap. Of course it wasn't signed. The king, poor soul, was encumbered with a conscience, albeit one that might absent itself on occasion, when convenient. But George's death warrant went far beyond convenience. Clarence's death was a matter of survival for the Woodvilles.

The Foxley house in Paternoster Row, London

EVERYONE SEEMED cheerful enough in the workshop this morn. Jude Foxley had arrived – promptly for once – from his lodgings with Dame Ellen in Cheapside, and kissed his betrothed, Mistress Rose, tenderly upon the lips for a good few minutes before settling himself at the binding table where collated pages awaited stitching. Feeling pleased with life, at least for the moment, he was whistling a lively tune. Rose could usually be relied upon to improve his erratic humours.

Taking his cue from Jude, Tom Bowen was grinning as he copied out a passage from the exemplar propped on its stand, enjoying the way his quill formed the letters, smelling the acidic tang of the ink as it flowed. Kate Verney, their new apprentice, was practising her letters at the desk opposite.

'Watch the way you finish the letters, lass,' Tom advised her, 'Else the ink will run into a tail. Hold the quill a little more upright. That's better.' It wasn't so long since Tom had been having the same difficulty but now he was coming to the end of his apprenticeship. One more year and he would be a journeyman, paid a daily wage, but he was good enough already to work without constant supervision from Master Seb.

Kate rewarded his help with one of her bright, gleeful smiles and he thought how much more pleasant she was than her predecessor, Jack Tabor. Not that Jack was gone; just that he was no longer trying to learn the stationer's and illuminator's crafts. A lad who couldn't learn his letters, he had discovered a talent for carving in wood. He was content now – or as content as a moody fourteen-year-old could be – fashioning fine book covers for the Foxley workshop, paid a small wage with bed and board thrown in. It was better for all concerned.

Rose sat by the workshop door, ready in case any customers came in. It was a fact that she drew men like a lodestone drew iron, her pretty face and comely shape attracting admirers to the shop, and they just might be tempted to commission or buy the Foxleys' wares while they were busy gawping at her. In the meantime, she deftly cut and shaped goose feather quills, ready for use. She was a fair scribe herself, though with little training. As the daughter of a glover, Rose was neat, careful and skilful in whatever she undertook. Her eyes kept straying to Jude, busy stitching folios with his back to her. Nevertheless, every glance lit the light of love in her eye and brought a blush to her cheek.

There should have been light and laughter in the kitchen too. Sebastian Foxley, master of the house, sat at the board with his wife, Mistress Emily.

'I've been so longing to tell you, Seb, but it was never the right moment. We were never alone,' Emily said. 'I thought you might have guessed anyway by now, seeing I'm plumper already.'

'Aye, of course I, er, noticed, Em,' Seb lied, feeling guilty for having noticed naught of the kind. If a saint in a Book of Hours had grown a little fatter, he would have seen the change straightway.

'You are pleased, aren't you, Seb?'

'I-I'm shocked, Em. In truth, I thought we might never have children. Are you quite certain? There is no doubt?'

'How many times do I have to say it? Shall I put it in writing for you? Perhaps then you'll believe me. I AM WITH CHILD, husband. I can make it no plainer than that. You are happy about it, aren't you? I might almost think you don't want to become a father.'

'The thought of fatherhood pleases me b-but 'tis a dangerous thing for a woman: childbirth. I be afraid for your health, Em, is all. I love you, so I worry for you. You cannot blame me for being concerned.'

'You don't want our child! I can tell. Well, too bad. A child is coming whether you like it or not, Sebastian.' With that, the tears came and Emily turned to flee up the wooden stairs to their bedchamber and slammed the door after, causing a shower of dust to drift down from the ceiling.

Seb sighed and shut his eyes tight, like one in dreadful pain. He felt close to weeping himself. This was the most fearful thing, the possibility he had been secretly dreading ever since their wedding day almost two and a half years before. As the months went by without any sign, he had begun to hope it was never going to happen but now the worst had come to pass after all and there was naught he could do. He was a fool. He should have told Em the truth afore they were wed and now it was far too late.

The morning was wearing on yet Seb hadn't come into the workshop. More to the point, Jude thought, no ale jug and cups had come either. Earlier, there had been raised voices in the kitchen and Jude decided it was time to discover why no mid-morning ale had been served. And why his brother had done not one iota of work. He found Seb slumped at the board, brooding. His face was pale as ashes; not that he was ever rosy cheeked.

'What are you doing, Seb? Are you sick, or something?'

'No, Jude, nothing like that.'

'I heard the argument. What was that about, eh? You want some ale?'

'Got some, thanks.' Seb's head bowed lower, such that his fine hair hung like a dark curtain, hiding his face from view. It was a pose employed to conceal feelings he knew his eyes would betray.

'Just as well; there's hardly any left in the jug.'

'Have mine.' Seb pushed his full cup towards Jude.

'You don't want it? What's amiss then? Em take you to task for snoring last eve?'

'No, 'tis worse than that.'

'Farting then?'

'This is serious, Jude.'

'Oh lord, you couldn't manage to get it up when she wanted. That's bloody serious indeed.'

'I *can* manage it and that's the problem,' Seb cried. 'That's the whole problem, don't you see? Em is with child!'

There was a long pause as Jude took in the news.

'So? That's good, isn't it? Make an uncle of me, mm?'

'I am scared, Jude. Supposing the babe takes after me? You remember what our Pa said? Birthing me, all twisted and misshapen, killed our mother. What if that happens to Em? I couldn't live with it. I certainly couldn't do what our Pa did: forgiving me for killing the woman he loved and treating me so kindly all those years. Unlike Pa, I'm no saint.'

'Mm. I see your difficulty.'

'What am I going to do, Jude? Should I tell Em about… about w-what I did to our mother, do you think? I don't want to scare her, but… Do you think she ought to know?'

Jude blew out his breath; took a hefty swig of ale.

'I suppose there's no doubt but it's yours?' he asked over the rim of the cup.

'What? What are you saying? You think Em's been with some other? No, not that. Not Em.'

Jude shrugged.

'Well, I don't know. Tell me honestly, little brother, are you capable of-of siring a babe? There. I've said it. I always wondered when you wed, if you'd be able to, seeing the way you were before.'

''Em has never complained.'

'So, I suppose there's no way of knowing, unless you ask her.'

'Ask her what?'

'If the babe is yours. It's not so long ago that she was heart-sick for Gabriel Widowson, is it?'

'Jude! It's mine, I tell you.'

'It would be easier if it wasn't. Then you need have no fear for the outcome.'

'For pity's sake, will you stop this!' Seb thumped the board with clenched fists, making the ale cup jump. 'Everything's going to Hell in a hand-basket and there's naught I can do. I just want peace and quiet. Can I not have that in my own house?'

'Don't take on so,' Jude said, putting an arm around his brother's narrow shoulders, only to be shrugged off.

'Leave me alone.'

'Have it your way then. Just don't forget that the *Sir Gawain and the Green Knight* manuscript needs to be finished, so the customer may approve it and choose a binding for it and – most important, little brother – you're supposed to be at Crosby Place after dinner.'

'Oh, dear God aid me,' Seb groaned, burying his face in his ink-stained hands – the badge of his craft. 'I cannot face Duke Richard, not this day.'

'Just think of the bloody money, Seb. You'll need his lordship's coin more than ever with an extra mouth to feed.'

The Duke of Gloucester's residence of Crosby Place, Bishopsgate, in the City of London

THIS AFTERNOON, Seb was to make the preliminary sketches for a portrait, to determine the most advantageous and complimentary pose for his noble subject. He awaited the Duke of Gloucester in the magnificent solar, where the oriel window, facing to the south-east, let in as much light as possible, that the ladies might see to do their fine embroideries or read. It also gave a view over the gardens, verdant and flower-spangled in summer but now gaunt and colourless, except for the yellow catkins dancing on the hazel trees. Not much else showed any promise of spring as yet.

Lord Richard came from his closet that opened off the solar, leaving the door wide open. Within the little room, Seb could see a carven *prie-dieu* with a dark velvet cushion to spare the duke's knees as he prayed. The indentations were deep and well-worn – a good deal of praying must have gone on there of late. The *prie-dieu* was set before a little altar with a crucifix on the wall above and a pair of slender bees-wax candles still burning. The candlelight glinted on the gold leaf of a triptych – the one Seb had painted for the duke more than two years ago. Those had been troubled times for Seb and Jude, and seeing the figures on the wooden panels now, he wondered that he had managed to give them expressions and poses so serene and peaceful. If the work had been commissioned by any person of lesser degree than a royal duke, Seb knew he would probably have abandoned the project, making his sincere apologies at being unable to complete it and returned the money.

'I thought you would be glad to see that your beautiful triptych accompanies me everywhere as I travel, Master Foxley,' the duke said, smiling. 'Not a day passes that I do not gaze upon your exquisite artistry. It looks very well in the candlelight, does it not?'

'It does, your grace, and perhaps such subtle light is kinder to my work than it deserves.'

The duke laughed.

'Your false modesty is not required, master. It looks as good in the starkest light of day. You should be proud of your skills. Now. Shall we to business? How shall you want me to sit?'

As his silver point moved deftly over the prepared paper – a fine line here; a shading there – Seb's grey eyes flickered from subject to drawing, noting the smallest detail. His dark hair, unkempt as usual, fell over his brow as he worked in rapt concentration. He knew the sketches were good. He shifted his legs for better balance, easing that ever-troublesome left hip, leaning against the casement of the oriel window as he worked. The intricacies of his art served well in diverting his thoughts from Emily's condition.

His subject, Lord Richard, sat upright in a cushioned chair, the light playing on his angular profile as clouds scudded across the winter skies beyond the window. He appeared as easy as he ever did; only his hands in his lap – never quite still – betrayed his true state of mind. Seb had his easel set up by the window. The February light was perfect today: bright enough to illuminate his work but not so harsh as to be unkind to Lord Richard's hard chiselled features. They were alone in the chamber, apart from the duke's great wolfhound lying by the fire, sleeping, flicking an ear as he dreamed. What did dogs dream about, Seb wondered, as he traced the curve of the lord's cheek in a single line.

'Sir Robert Percy asked to be remembered to you, Master Sebastian. I should have told you earlier, but it slipped my mind.'

'That is most kind of Sir Robert, I had hoped I might see him here,' Seb replied, smiling at the memory of a good friend.

'Rob did not journey to London with me this time. I gave him leave to remain in Yorkshire with his wife, Joyce. Sadly, she was brought to bed of a still-born bairn a few weeks back and has yet to recover fully.' The duke used the northern word for a babe. 'I grieve for them: they had waited so long for this child. At least Rob has an heir by his first wife, but Joyce's bairn would have been the seal upon their happiness.'

Seb tried to give his entire concentration to sketching a fold in the lord's robe but his blood ran chill, hearing the duke's words.

'Perhaps, your grace would…' he cleared his throat as the words seem to lodge there, '…would kindly pass on my condolences to Sir Robert.'

'Aye, of course. Rob will appreciate them.' The duke glanced at the artist without moving his head. 'And how is your goodwife? You must have been wed for more than two years now. How is the famous May Queen archeress, your beautiful bride?'

'Emily is well, my lord, thank you for enquiring.' Seb wondered at the duke's excellent memory. God knows, he must have a thousand more important things to remember than the May Day revels nigh three years gone and the more recent marriage of a young woman he had met at the time. But of course the man remembered. That was Lord Richard's way: a man with a long and precise memory indeed.

Seb set aside a completed sketch and affixed a fresh sheet of paper to the board with wooden pegs to begin an outline of the duke's head, in profile this time, moving his easel, rather than troubling his subject to get up and summon a servant to shift the heavy chair.

'And your brother? Jude is his name, if I recall correctly?'

'You do, my lord. Aye, Jude is well but…'

'But?'

'But not as he was. I believe his time in Newgate gaol changed him. He has never been the same since but he has found a good woman of late, God be praised.' Seb drew the details of the gold threadwork collar of the duke's doublet of crimson velvet, fashionably slashed with dove-grey silk. The floor-length robe was of the same luxurious cloth.

'Indeed. Gaol changes any man. I've seen it for myself in my own brother.' Lord Richard sighed heavily and began fidgeting with the ring on his finger.

Seb frowned. It took him a moment to recall that the duke had another brother, apart from King Edward: George, Duke of Clarence, currently lodged in the Tower of London at the king's pleasure. And it seemed the king's pleasure was that he should remain there a long while. Seb didn't know what he could say that wouldn't offend either the king or the duke, so he said nothing. But Lord Richard didn't require a response. His pewter-coloured eyes were focused far beyond the glass of the window, across the rooftops of the city.

'George too is changed,' the duke was saying. 'He, who was so fastidious, now refuses the attentions of his servants and goes unwashed, in soiled linen, beard unshaven, hair uncombed. He hardly eats, claiming his food is likely poisoned, to hasten his end. I saw him last month, briefly, and barely knew him for my own brother. I would attempt to persuade him to allow the servants to tend his needs; urge him to eat. I would beg the king to release him.' Seb saw the duke's shoulders sag beneath the velvet. 'Well, I tried, but now the king has forbidden me to see George again nor even to write to him. And I understand none of it. None of it,' he cried, throwing up his hands.

'I know George has behaved badly in the past,' he continued, 'And the king always forgave him. This time, for some seemingly lesser matter, he is incarcerated. He said the king will have him…' The duke closed his eyes. '…have him executed. I told

15

him that was foolish talk: it will never come to that. And yet...'
He shook his head, further disarranging his hair as it lay dark
on the gold embroidery, but Seb did not remind his sitter to
stay still. The poor man was clearly devastated and speaking of
things a humble artist had no right to hear, his thoughts with
one sibling or the other, in the Tower or at Westminster.

Seb set down his silver point and coughed quietly.

'I have completed the preliminary sketches, my lord. You be
free to move now, if you want to. I will just transfer a rough
outline to the proper canvas, so you may approve the pose.'

'I apologise. What did you say? My thoughts were far away.
Forgive me, Master Sebastian, blathering on.'

'I have near finished for today, sir.'

'Good, good. Shall we meet at an earlier hour come
tomorrow: eight of the clock then?'

'Aye, my lord, and I'll bring my apprentice, if I may. I shall
start working the pigments, laying in the ground colour, and
he will be mixing them for me, if you allow? It will speed
the process.'

'Of course. Friday, then. Good day to you, master, and
thank you.'

Seb draped a cloth over his easel to protect the work, took
up his scrip and bowed out of the duke's presence, well aware
he now knew more than he should of high-born folks' affairs.

The Foxley house

THAT NIGHT, after a day fraught with worry, Seb lay
abed, staring into the darkness, fretting over Em. No
longer occupied with work that might divert his thoughts, every
time he closed his eyes, his father's words of long ago tolled like
the passing-bell in his ears: 'Your birthing killed your mother'.
The news imparted by Lord Richard that Sir Rob's baby had
died did not help matters but at least the man's wife survived.

He thought Em was asleep beside him until she asked:

'Why are you so angry about the babe?' He heard the quiver in her voice; knew she had been weeping, silently.

'I'm not.'

'Well, you're not pleased, then.'

'You don't understand. I can't explain.'

'Try.'

'No. Now be quiet and go to sleep, woman. Let me have some peace at this hour.' So he turned his back upon her, leaving her miserable on the far side of the bed. What else could he do?

St Paul's bell chimed the midnight hour. He could not sleep with worry chewing at his soul like this. There was guilt too, for his unkindness to poor Em who had no idea what she had done amiss. Eventually, he left the bed, wrapped his night robe around himself and went quietly downstairs, to endure his wretchedness alone, without disturbing Em.

In the kitchen, the embers of the fire still glowed and he stirred them to life with a poker and added another log from the basket – an extravagance at this time of night but he was desperate for comfort of any kind. He poured a cup of ale and sat at the board with it but did not drink. Tears ran down his face yet he made no effort to wipe them away. Nessie was snoring in the alcove behind the curtain; there was no one to see him weep.

CHAPTER TWO

Friday the thirteenth day of February
Crosby Place, Bishopsgate

THE BELL of St Helen's church by Bishopsgate chimed eight as they mounted the steps to the magnificent great hall of Duke Richard's residence. Master Seb braced his narrow shoulders and straightened his jerkin beneath his mantle before turning to inspect young Tom. As the apprentice, Tom was encumbered with his master's scrip and tools of the trade.

'Wipe your boots on the scraper, Tom. Don't want you treading dung into his lordship's hall, do we?'

'No, master. Is the duke very fearsome, like they say of the king?'

'You mean does he eat young apprentices to break his fast? Fear not. 'Tis Lent: even the duke foregoes meat for forty days.' Tom looked startled but Master Seb laughed. 'Lord Richard be kindly enough, so long as no man crosses him.

'What do you think? 'Tis a very fine place, isn't it, lad?' master whispered as they followed a liveried servant.

'Aye, master.' Tom gazed up at gilded beams and gorgeous tapestries, wondering how anyone had managed to paint the star-spangled ceiling so high above.

Another servant was in the solar, busy lighting dozens of candles in silver sconces to brighten the chamber on such a dismal day. The oriel window showed the murkiest of landscapes, wreathed in mist, a single wet, yellowing leaf clung to the glass pane. But a welcome fire blazed in the hearth, giving off the sweet scent of applewood, and two additional braziers warmed the space around the artist's easel.

Master Seb rubbed his hands together before the fire while Tom set out the palettes and brushes, the oyster shells, the ground pigments and the basket of hens' eggs on a table.

'Move the table away from the braziers, Tom, else the pigments will dry out too quickly.'

Tom obeyed, glancing at the covered board upon the easel, eager to see his master's work so far. He'd never seen a portrait and could hardly wait to discover how close a likeness of Lord Richard his master had achieved.

'Don't forget to make your courtesy to his grace... and take your cap off, now! Whatever next. Where be your manners?'

'Sorry, Master Seb, I forgot.'

'You don't forget such matters in the duke's presence and don't speak unless you're spoken to.'

'Yes, master.' Tom tried to sound solemn but his excitement was mounting at the prospect of being so close to a royal prince of the blood.

If Tom expected a fanfare of trumpets or the like, he was disappointed. Lord Richard strode in unannounced, accompanied only by the biggest hound in all God's Creation which lolloped over to the hearth and sprawled before the fire, as if it owned the place. And who would dare argue otherwise with such a beast? Tom kept half an eye on those fearsome jaws even as he bent the knee beside Master Seb. Lord Richard came right up close to greet them, his smile warm as the fire-side.

'Welcome, Master Foxley,' the duke said, his voice strong and pleasant. 'And this fine lad must be the apprentice you promised?'

'Aye, your grace, this is Thomas Bowen.' The duke took Tom's hand. Such an honour, Tom swore to himself he would never wash it again.

'You've got an excellent master here, young Thomas. Work hard and learn well from him.'

'I will, your grace,' Tom said, casting another wary look towards the dog.

The duke laughed.

'Oh, don't mind old Boru...' The dog flapped its tail in the rushes at the sound of its name but didn't bother to raise its shaggy head. 'He's an Irish wolfhound and was once a terror indeed, but now he's past his prime, his teeth drawn, but he serves me well, don't you, Boru?' The duke bent to fondle the dog's ears, not bothered that his robe of crimson velvet came away, covered in grey dog hair. 'A short session today, I fear, Master Sebastian, time is pressing this morning.' Lord Richard went to sit in the gilded chair. 'Arrange me however you will, master. I have brought along a book to read. I grew tired of studying bare trees and grey skies from the window and counting the number of slipped tiles on the roof of St Helen's. But if you prefer me not to read...'

'I have no objection whatever, my lord. In fact, it will denote you as a man of learning, if I include it in the portrait.'

'Excellent.'

Tom stared at the image revealed when Master Seb removed the cloth from the easel. Never had he seen anything like it. The duke seemed to sit there, except that the board was only about three feet high, it was like seeing the man through a window. Yet it was naught but a few lines drawn on a whitened board.

'This is the under-drawing, Tom,' Master Seb explained, 'Now we are going to lay in some ground colour. Prepare some yellow ochre and make it thin; it will only be a wash to take out the whiteness of the board.'

Tom did as he was told but wondered why, after all the effort spent preparing the smooth, pristine white surface, master was now going to wash it all yellow. He would ask why, later. In the meantime, he took advantage of the fact he was training as a limner to stare at a royal duke – something few would ever be permitted to do. Lord Richard was fine-looking, Tom thought, his hair like black silk but his complexion pale; straight of nose but the mouth too thin-lipped to be accounted handsome. But it was the eyes that held your attention: impossibly deep like the grey waters of the sea – if that was how the sea truly looked, for Tom had never seen it, but that's how he'd heard it described – and it seemed to be reflected in Lord Richard's eyes.

'Come along, Tom, we haven't got all day to wait upon your mixing,' Master Seb said, though his sigh was more of weariness than impatience.

Tom blended the yolk of a separated egg with the finely ground ochre to produce an even paste before spooning a little into an oyster shell.

'Which brush, master?'

'The large badger hair for this stage. And thin the ochre more… That's better, then you can lay it in.'

'Me, master?'

'Aye, as I showed you in the workshop: long even strokes across the board. Do the whole of the ground, including my lord's head and hands but avoid his shirt, robe and shoes. You do that whilst I make further sketches. And after, you can tell me why I ask you to avoid the ochre wash in certain parts.'

Lord Richard sat immobile as a carven saint whilst his likeness was committed to paper with a silver stylus, yet again: his features, the way the folds of his robe fell in the light, the crease of cloth at his elbow, the exact position of his feet and the shadow they cast upon the floor beneath, even how the curve of his buttocks sank into the hollows of the cushioned chair.

Master Seb spent fully an hour making his precise sketches, taking far longer over considering a line than executing it, as was his way. When he finally turned away from his subject, the duke stood up, stretching.

'I'm afraid I have business elsewhere now, Master Foxley, and must leave you in peace to complete your 'laying in', or whatever it is. Thank you for your time. Stay as long as you wish. You will return on Monday? I shall have more time then.' With that, Lord Richard called to his dog and left, giving them no chance to make their courtesies even to a departing swirl of crimson velvet.

Master Seb sat down on his stool, tired after a night without sleep. He stifled a yawn and rubbed at his eyes.

'Are you unwell, master? I can leave this if...'

'No. Never leave a wash half done, else it will leave a hard edge. The remaining pigment will dry out and be wasted. It is unlike his grace to have arranged other business... he usually sets time aside. Perhaps it is urgent.'

A few minutes after the duke left, a servant came in with a tray, bearing a steaming jug and two pewter cups.

'Lord Richard said you would benefit from something warming on such a cold day: spiced wine. You can serve yourselves, can you not?' The hot red wine, flavoured with spices and sweetened with honey, was something Tom had never tasted before: the potency of the first mouthful almost took his breath away but the second slipped down easily, warming, soothing. No wonder wealthy folk drank so much wine. Master was already getting a little colour back in his pale, weary face – the duke was as good as a physician.

'Don't think we'll get served wine every time we come,' Master Seb said, 'And don't get a taste for this stuff either... so many spices... We can't afford this at home.'

Tom recognised there was cinnamon and anise, which he had taken in a medicinal remedy for a bellyache one time. The apothecary he had once worked for used to have all the spices on his shelves but, though Tom had sniffed and ground every one, he was never allowed to taste such luxuries, 'til now. Ginger? Nutmeg, perhaps? It was delicious, whatever was in it.

'Now, Tom, what have you noticed this morn?' Master sounded livelier now; looked much improved. Tom pulled a face.

'About what, master?'

'You were watching Lord Richard very closely; what did you observe about him? Anything out of place?'

Tom knitted his brows.

'A loose thread? A mole on his forehead?'

Master's expression was grave: he'd failed the test.

'A portrait must be keenly observed: every line, every angle, even though the limner may choose to omit many of them.' Tom craned his neck, trying to see master's sketches of the duke; what had he missed? 'No use looking at those, for I did not draw the particular detail but you should have noted it, at least.'

'I don't know, master. I'm sorry.'

'Well, his grace had a little nick on his cheek, just above the jaw on his right side. I dare say his barber's blade must have slipped when he shaved him this morn. I did not draw it because it will be gone in a day or so, but there can be no excuse for you not seeing it: it was plain enough.'

'I didn't notice it,' Tom admitted, shaking his head, 'But I'm glad I'm not my lord's barber this day; he must have been punished severely for his mistake.'

'Perhaps I should punish you severely for your error, too? Would that make you pay more attention in future?'

Tom stared at the floor: the wretched old apothecary had beaten him mercilessly, but Master Seb never had. Was this to be the first time? 'Back at home, you will draw Mistress Rose, Jack and young Kate over and over: faces, hands, hair, clothing, until I'm satisfied that you are really seeing the subject in detail.'

'Aye, master, I'll do that willingly,' Tom grinned with relief: this was just the sort of 'punishment' Master Seb would devise – something more useful than a birch rod across his back. Besides, Tom enjoyed sketching: dogs and other creatures particularly. People were rather more difficult but he was improving and he would be content to study Mistress Rose all day.

'Now finish the ochre wash and clean the brush and shells properly. Then you can answer my earlier enquiry as to why I bid you omit the yellow ochre from certain parts.' Master sat back, still sipping his wine, sketching the chamber, the oriel window and the view beyond as the mist was clearing. 'By the way, you're making a good job of that wash, did I say? Firm, even strokes... I'm pleased with your work.'

Tom felt pride well up: the apothecary had never praised him. Master Seb willingly gave credit but only when it was thoroughly deserved.

Westminster

RICHARD HAD succeeded, unexpectedly, in gaining an audience with the king. This time, the queen's relatives were not present. A relief, indeed. Only William, Lord Hastings, the king's chamberlain, was in the solar when Richard entered.

'The king is still dressing, my lord,' Hastings said, making a quick bow. He and Richard were old friends.

'So late as this? 'Tis nigh time for dinner. What was he about last eve, Will, to keep him so long abed? Is he ailing?'

The chamberlain turned to the window that looked out across the Thames. Barges, wherries and all sorts of river craft criss-crossed the sullen waters in what seemed a chaotic fashion. Richard joined Hastings to watch. One large, sleek vessel in particular, red and gold and flaunting a silken banner, was forcing lesser boats to make way, its distinctive curved prow cleaving the waves like a wire through cheese. The trumpeter could be heard from here sounding his warning: Anthony Woodville's state barge was leaving Westminster water-stairs. 'Ailing? You might call it that,' Hastings said. 'Last night's whore did not please him. Hence, why no one else is here. They're all avoiding his ill-temper. You haven't chosen the best of days to come, Dickon, I warn you. Naught pleases him at present. This business with George, you understand.'

Richard nodded. He understood full well. Or believed he did.

Finally, the king appeared, shouting for wine.

'Dickon? What in Hell's name do you want, eh? We spoke only yesterday.'

Richard's obeisance was ignored as Hastings handed the king a cup of rich Bordeaux wine.

'I-I would speak with you about George, your grace...' Richard said, still upon one knee.

'Bloody George! I told you no, Dickon. Now get you gone before we both regret...'

'Please, I beg you hear me out, Ned. I have no intention of seeing him or causing you anger in any way on his behalf. Rather, I would do something for his children.'

'His children are perfectly safe and under my protection. You need not concern yourself. Leave us and leave this matter entirely alone. I'll have no more of your interference. I warned you yesterday.'

'Aye. I have not forgotten but I have an idea that may be of comfort to his children in the future.'

'Oh?'

'If our brother languishes in the Tower – and I am not saying he doesn't deserve such punishment as you see fit to inflict upon him,' Richard added hastily, seeing the king's thunderous look, 'But the children are so young and motherless. Now their father is not there to comfort them either. Surely, you do not mean to punish them also?'

'And your point is?'

'The new fashion for portraiture. You have had your likeness set in paint, as has the queen. I too am having a portrait made in my image. I thought if anything should chance to befall me of a sudden, my children will have my portrait to be a consolation to them and a remembrance of me. It occurred to me that a portrait of their father might likewise comfort and remind Margaret and little Edward. Children's memories may be of so short duration and...'

'So you know of an artist?'

'Aye. Master Sebastian Foxley. You may recall he painted the triptych with the likenesses of our lord father and brother Edmund. He is most skilful indeed. A few sketches are all he may need. Please, Ned. Give your consent for this one favour I would ask of you.'

The king finished his wine, picked a fleck of lint from his gorgeous sleeve and tugged at his earlobe, thinking.

'Very well, Dickon. You can have your fellow make a likeness of George but there will be no passing of messages, no discussion with him, you understand? Just a single hour for him to make his drawings. Can he work so fast?'

'Aye, I am certain he can. Oh, Ned, I am so grateful for this benevolence and thank you from the depths of my heart.'

'I'll have instructions drawn up that your fellow must abide by, to the letter, and a warrant to permit access to the Tower and to the, er, prisoner. Any deviation from what is permitted and your artist won't be leaving the Tower – ever. Understand?'

'Of course, sire.'

'I'll arrange it for Tuesday next. One hour is all.'

Redmaine Hall in St Pancras Lane

IT WAS an impressive residence, set betwixt the church of St Pancras on the left hand and that of St Benet Sherhog on the right. Roger, elder son and heir to Giles Redmaine the owner, loved to stand in the lane and admire the fine workmanship of the grand house that would one day be his: the heavy oaken door with its gilded knocker in the shape of a lion's head, the symmetrical windows in all three storeys and everyone of them glazed, the intricate plaster pargetting betwixt the timbers. And then there was the marble image of St Giles set in his own niche above the door. His father's personal saint, of course; it was the one thing about the imposing frontage that he would change as soon as he came into his inheritance. He was sure the saint had even been carved in his father's stern likeness – such conceit – designed to watch his sons' activities beyond the house. Or Roger's, at least. Young William was too meek and mild ever to cause any offence or stray from their father's strictly imposed narrow path of righteousness and sobriety. A path too confining for Roger; he strayed often and widely. Unfortunately, his father had heard of his wayward behaviour and was hinting that Roger might be struck out of the will, that William would inherit all, if he didn't mend his ways. Such a possibility was not to be borne.

'Where were you?' Giles was not one to waste time on loving paternal greetings. He was seated in a cushioned chair pulled close to the hearth. On the table before him, neat ledgers lay open with pens, ink and paper to hand. Giles Redmaine trusted no one else to do his accounting. 'William was in the shop when I stopped by; you were not. What were you about this time, eh? Whore-house? Ale-house?'

'And "good day" to you too, father. I trust you be your usual cantankerous self? And – if you must know – I was at the place of easement: the shit-house, father, if it's any of your business?'

'Don't you speak to me in that tone, Roger. You're not too big that I couldn't take a birch rod to your back as you well deserve.'

Roger laughed. He was nine-and-twenty years of age. Who did his father think he was? But this was just typical of the way he was treated. Always had been.

'How is business faring in Cheapside?' Roger asked. He was ever wary of enquiring after his father's extensive affairs as a leading grocer in the City of London. There was a vast web of foreign contacts too, merchants from distant places: Venice, Aleppo and Alexandria, as well as closer to home in Bruges, Tournai and Lyons. Redmaine Hall was at the centre of a worldwide collection of threads, trading in all kinds of luxury goods, from ambergris to almonds, nutmeg to nacre, zedoary to zithers; and at its heart sat Giles, like a spider, ever alert and waiting. And just as secretive.

'What do you care, so long as there be meat and wine upon the board and velvet and miniver upon your back? You can't even be bothered to attend at the shop when we take delivery of a consignment, can you? As was the case this morn. William had to deal with it all, as usual.'

Roger shrugged and rubbed at his drooping eyelid – a trait inherited from his mother, like his lack of any business acumen whatsoever. He'd had no idea a new consignment had arrived any more than he knew what was recorded in those pristine accounting ledgers and letter books, recording moneys made, debts owed, contracts signed and correspondence received and sent. His father refused to let him into that side of the business and didn't employ a secretary or bookkeeper either. Only God could know what would happen if and when Giles breathed his last.

'Was the delivery from the Levant, father?' He took a stab in the dark, meaning to show an interest at least. He reached out to a volume bound in Cordoban leather.

Giles slapped his son's hand away as if he were a grubby schoolboy touching a valuable manuscript.

'From the Baltic. Amber and furs from Russia, shipped through treacherous winter seas by the Hansa merchants. They should've waited for better weather. We lost cargo when one craft was overwhelmed in high seas. And they've raised the price of beaver pelts, seeing how fashionable beaver hats are become these days. Of course, you'd know about the fashion, though you know naught of how such items are come by and won't bestir yourself to learn.' Giles sighed and took up a silver gilt cup and drank deep. It wasn't fine wine that he took as a restorative. Oh, no. Giles Redmaine never touched any intoxicating beverage. Taking sobriety to the extreme, he drank naught but goat's milk, like a weaning babe.

'I would learn, father,' Roger protested as he always did. This was a frequently rehearsed conversation. 'I want to learn. But all you would have me do is stack boxes at the warehouse and label shelves in the shop. You treat me like an apprentice.'

'That's all you are and all you are fit to do!'

'I'm nigh thirty years of age, father...'

'And behave like a youth half that, so how else should I treat you? You are unsuited for such business and useless indeed. I shall have to summon the notary and rewrite my will, bequeathing everything to William. I mean it!'

Thus ran their encounter, ending in anger for the father and frustration for the son. It never ended otherwise. Roger stormed out, slamming doors in his wake, heading for The Barge Inn to extinguish his fiery humours in strong ale. As he strode along Bucklersbury, kicking at pebbles, chickens and anything else that crossed his path, he fumed inwardly, his father's words churning over in his mind. Why did the old devil always treat him like a child? Precious bloody William, though five years younger, could do no wrong, of course, being the favourite. Was it Roger's fault that *he* took after their mother, a feckless beauty who served little purpose but to spend money and live in luxury, the perfect advertisement for her husband's wares? How dare father threaten to change his will? But just suppose it was more than a threat? Suppose William inherited the house, the business, all their father's wealth – which was vast, he was certain. What then? He, the elder son and rightful heir, might have nothing. Would he even receive the generous bequest of a manor and lands in Kent that were destined to be William's, as the will stipulated in its present form? Precious William might have it all.

Over too many cups of ale, Roger seethed, stewed and began to scheme. How would matters lie if his father died now, before he could draw up a new will? The trouble was, his parent was hale and fit, likely to last another score of years at least. An accident might befall at any time but could never be relied upon. What if William died? Surely Roger, in this case now the only son, would inherit all, even if the will was changed. Unless

William wed and had an heir of his own. Roger knew William was love-struck indeed and was doing all he might to persuade their father to let him wed Jacquetta Haldane, but her father was a humble apothecary in Lothbury, so Giles had forbidden the match. It seemed to be the one point at which William failed to please his parent, having refused to agree to the far more prestigious union Giles was arranging, to the eldest daughter of the mercer, Edmund Verney, a lass named Alice. She was comely enough with a generous dowry.

Roger couldn't understand his younger brother's problem. After all, he'd wed Mabel Tottenham, as his father ordered, without making a fuss. Mabel, daughter of a fellow grocer, had been wedded, bedded and delivered of a child within a year. That both were now lying in St Pancras churchyard, dead within days of the birthing, was irrelevant. Roger had done his duty. One day, he might even repeat the exercise but widowerhood suited him for the present.

But what if William did oblige and wed Alice Verney? And suppose he begat an heir upon her, one that lived? That could not be allowed to happen. Roger began to think how an accident might be contrived to befall his brother but there was a problem. Roger had to admit to himself that, despite jealousy at William being ever favoured by their father, he felt close to him; loved him, in truth. He couldn't plot William's demise. But his father's death? Now that was a spice of a different flavour entirely.

The Foxley workshop

'MANY THANKS for your custom, master,' Rose said as she saw a customer to the shop door, 'I hope your son enjoys the tales.'

'What did you sell to Master Hopwood?' Jude asked, 'The old skinflint never buys anything, just wastes our time.'

'I told him how wonderful were the stories of Master Aesop, the book your brother used to teach me to read. Master Hopwood complained that his son has no interest in studying anything, so I recommended the fables, told him there's a moral to each one, which I think persuaded him.'

Jude pulled Rose close and breathed deeply of the scent of lavender in her hair where it escaped her cap.

'And did he pay full price for it?'

Rose laughed.

'And when did I ever let a customer get away with anything less?'

'Good lass. You make more money than that brother of mine any day. It's a wonder the business survives with him forever making charitable concessions to our customers. When was the last time he charged anyone full price, eh?'

'Master Seb is generous by nature, Jude. Please don't condemn his goodness of heart.'

'He costs us money we can ill-afford. Sometimes I fear we hardly make a living.'

'Jude, I pray you, leave my hair be. Another customer may come in at any moment.'

'So what? You are my betrothed, aren't you?'

'Aye, so you say, and like to remain that and naught more. For nigh a year past you've been promising to post the wedding notices in the church porch, yet you haven't. Why, Jude? Why do you delay so? Have you had a change of heart? Tell me.' Rose looked up at him with those beseeching eyes he could never resist so he turned away from her.

'Things happen, Rose. I told you, money is difficult at present.'

'But Master Seb always pays us our dues every Saturday without fail. I have saved most of my wages for us. What of you, Jude? How much have you saved?'

'It's not a woman's place to ask such a thing of her husband.'

31

'But you're not my husband and I wonder if you ever will be. I love you, Jude…' She touched his hand, his sleeve.

'Don't try beguiling me with sweet words, woman. I've told you: we'll wed when we can afford it and not before.'

Fortunately, two customers entered the shop before the exchange deteriorated further. Rose greeted them with a welcoming smile and Jude went back to stitching and pasting a new binding onto an old book he was repairing, one of a number that had gone mouldy with disuse when the church of St Mary-le-Bow had been closed up for a while, awaiting re-consecration after the Lawrence Ducket affair. As he stitched, Jude cursed the priesthood and one in particular – the one who was the cause of delay in their marriage arrangements. Jude wanted Rose to be his wife with the over-zealous eagerness of a convert to a new religion. Before he met her, marriage had seemed an appalling condition to which he would on no account commit himself, yet it had taken her just a few weeks to change his mind, heart and soul.

But then his past indiscretions had reared up, hideous and vengeful – not that he could recall the particular incident that now utterly thwarted his honourable intentions. He could never reveal the truth to his beloved. How he was ever going to break the news to Rose, he didn't know. Her disappointment would be unbearable. How could he hurt the woman he loved? It would break her heart in twain. He could not do it. He would just have to buy his way out of this tangle of villainy and extortion, somehow.

Jude swore mightily as the needle pierced his thumb and drew blood. That damned priest at St Mary's was out to hurt him at every turn.

'Master Jude? Have you seen Jack?' Kate Verney bounced into the workshop, her dark curls bobbing at every step. 'Dame Ellen brought some wafers for Mistress Em but she says she cannot look at food this day. She told me I could have them but I saved some for Jack. Where is he?'

Jude groaned. Such boundless enthusiasm was too much for a man heartsick and in despair.

'How should I know? Avoiding work, as ever, no doubt? Hasn't Master Seb set you a task to do?'

'Aye, master, and I've done it. Do you want to see it?'

'I suppose so, since he's not here.'

Kate fetched a large sheet of paper and unrolled it for inspection.

Used to Tom's reliable but uninspiring work and Jack's messy efforts with pen and ink, Jude was surprised to be presented with a page of fine script with a number of beautifully executed initials.

'Master Seb told me to write out the Paternoster in my best hand and then to decorate the initials however I liked. Is it good enough, do you think? I'm not sure I got all the Latin right and this curlicue isn't quite how I wanted but...' She waited, watching as he scanned her work.

Jude read the prayer through. The Latin was all correct and he could see naught amiss with any curlicues.

'Mm. It will suffice, Kate,' he said, giving it back. It didn't do to praise an apprentice. It might lead to them becoming over-confident, complacent, even slap-dash in their efforts. 'Look to your letter 'a's for fear they become too small and watch to keep the ending of words in the right hand margin more even. Break words and use hyphens to make every line the same length across the page.'

'Aye, master. Shall I do it again?'

'No. As I said, it will do. Leave it for Master Seb's approval. In the meantime, you can stir that pot of glue on the brazier for me. See if it be liquid enough to use yet.'

That Kate could be trusted with such a task was a measure of her worth indeed. Jude still wouldn't have let Jack near a pot of glue, even after all this time.

Later, with the book covers left to dry, Jude had business elsewhere.

'I'm away to a cock-fight,' he told Kate.

'Cock-fighting in Lent, master? What shall I do while you're gone?'

'Mm. Don't tell Master Seb what I'm about else he'll have a seizure. It's our little secret, Kate, eh? Just betwixt us two.'

The lass laughed.

'He should be back soon from Crosby Place, seeing he'll be expected to attend choir practice at Paul's later,' Jude continued. 'In the meantime, Mistress Rose is in the shop; you can give her company and dust the books for sale. If Jack returns, tell him there are glue brushes and pots to be washed, thoroughly.'

'I could do them, master.'

'Well, Kate, what a wonder you are: an apprentice who volunteers to do a horrible task.' Jude smiled at her as he put on his woollen mantle and hood.

'It will save Jack the trouble. He hates washing pots.'

CHAPTER THREE

Saturday the fourteenth day of February

TOM TIDIED the sketches of people that he'd completed ready for inspection – Master Seb's means of punishment for his lack of observation at Crosby Place yesterday. He was quite pleased with most of them. The image of young Kate was best. He'd caught her bouncing curls and mischievous grin but, somehow, the eyes just weren't right. They looked lifeless, as those of a dead fish. He would have to ask master how to put that to rights. The picture of Mistress Rose almost looked like some real person but, for certain, it wasn't Rose and he just couldn't see why it was wrong. The third image was closer to the truth.

'Who is that supposed to be?' Master Jude had come into the workshop so silently, Tom was taken unawares until the man was looking over his shoulder.

'Er, just a customer, master. The fellow left afore it was finished.' Tom felt his cheeks redden and he hastily hid the drawing beneath his other efforts.

'The poor bugger has my sympathy: hair so sparse and face so lined, otherwise he might be quite a comely fellow.' Jude went over to the collating table and sat before the neat pile of pages, set ready for him.

'Indeed, master.' Tom dared say no more. Thanking the merciful Lord that Jude hadn't recognised himself, he made the sign of the cross as soon as the man's back was turned. Perhaps he shouldn't show that one to Master Seb.

'Ready, Tom? I have the list of items we need here for you.'

'Aye, Master Seb. I'll fetch my cloak.'

'Do not disturb Mistress Em. She feels unwell this morn.'

'Again?' Jude said, checking the matching catchphrases betwixt the next two gatherings of pages, to be certain they were consecutive before he began stitching them together. 'It was the same yesterday and the morn before that, wasn't it?'

'Aye. Apparently, 'tis often the way with women at such a time, so she tells me. I pray that be true and she's not sickening elsewise. She says there's naught to be done but to sip a tisane of camomile.'

'Sounds more like an excuse to shirk her chores to me. I'd tell her to get on with the bloody laundry and preparing dinner and cease moping.'

'I dare say, brother,' Seb sighed. 'You always are so full of sympathy.'

'So I am when there's good cause, but this? 'Tis just fluff and smoke, a state of mind, a woman's fancies. My belly would churn too, if I dolloped the best part of a dish of honey on my soused mackerel.'

'Em did that?'

'Yesterday, at dinner. Made me feel ill to watch her. I wonder you didn't notice; the rest of us did. By the way, a note came from that bloody nuisance of a customer, the fellow you're doing the *Sir Gawain and the Green Knight* tale for. He wants to know if it's finished yet.'

'Not quite but 'tis coming along well. I have two more miniatures to do. You may tell him that much. I'll work on it later, after I have done the Accounts and taken young Kate to see her father.' Seb turned away and did not see Jude wincing, as if he had caught his fingers in a door.

'Ready, master,' Tom said, swinging his cloak about his shoulders. 'And Mistress Em says we need saffron for the supper dish she's making and can I buy it from Master Haldane whilst I'm there, to save her the errand as it's a long walk to Lothbury and she doesn't feel up to it?'

Seb groaned.

'Saffron? Does her dish truly have to have such an expensive ingredient?'

'So mistress says.'

'Ah, well, purchase the smallest amount the apothecary will allow, anything to keep her content. Here, take another three groats for it. More important, we need more yellow ochre pigment – not the cheap stuff; I want the best quality. And white lead. I shall be using that in the highlights in Lord Richard's portrait. Which brings to mind those drawings I asked you to do.'

'I did them, master, as you said. Mistress Rose and Kate but not Jack. You know he never stays still long enough to draw.'

'I'll see them later, lad. But where is Jack?'

'Out in the yard, whittling away. Mistress Em said his wood shavings were blowing into her kitchen every time the shop door opened, so she sent him outside. He's not best pleased, master.'

'On a day so chill, 'tis hardly surprising. But you must be away to Lothbury afore the shop closes for dinner, it being Saturday. Have you got the list?'

'Aye, Master Seb.'

'And we'll look at those drawing when you get back.'

Seb sighed deeply. Another confrontation with Emily was the last thing he wanted but he trudged through to the kitchen where his wife ruled her kingdom.

Emily was rolling out pastry, a dusting of flour up to her elbows, and instructing Nessie to chop the turnips more evenly, to dice them all of a size so they would all be cooked in the same time.

'How are you feeling, sweetheart? Better, I trust?' he asked.

'Are you making a pretence that you care?' she said, scowling at him.

'Of course I care, Em. By the by, I gave Tom a shilling for the saffron you want.'

'You require my thanks in writing? You'll be eating it too.'

'No, Em, I was simply saying...'

'You mean to tell me it's too expensive? Is that it? Don't I deserve a pinch of saffron when I have a great fancy for the flavour?' She brandished the wooden rolling pin at him, scattering flour.

'For certain, you deserve it but...'

'Oh, there's always a 'but' with you, isn't there?'

'Please, Em, I do not want to argue with you. Can we just forget about the saffron: I shall not speak of it again.'

'Very well.' She went back to the pastry but her expression hadn't softened.

'But I would speak of Jack.'

'What about him? What is he saying? That I've taken my broom to him, as he be deserving? Because he's a liar, if he says so.'

'No. He has said naught of the kind but Tom said you sent him to work in the yard.'

'Well, he makes such a mess. I cannot have wood shavings in my pie.'

'But he was in the workshop. How can the shavings get here?'

'There's a draught.'

'Em. 'Tis freezing outside. Jack's carving requires dextrous fingers. How can he do work of a high standard, if his hands be numb with cold? He must come within doors...'

'Not until my pie is made.'

'Nessie, mull some ale for Jack and take it through to the workshop. He will need to thaw his blood.'

'How dare you defy me, husband!'

'You are being unreasonable, Em.'

'I am not. You deny my authority in my own kitchen.'

'Enough, Em. Nessie, mull some ale for your mistress also, to soothe her humours...'

'I don't need...'

But Seb had gone out into the yard to tell Jack to go around the side alley and enter the shop by means of the front door. The kitchen was out of bounds but a brazier warmed the workshop.

Meanwhile, Seb retired to the parlour, to face his regular Saturday trial and penance: the Accounts. How he loathed this weekly chore. He always hoped that Jude would assist – as per their agreement as partners in business – but his brother rarely obliged, always having some other urgent matter requiring his attention on a Saturday after dinner. The Panyer Inn, probably. Seb tipped out all the coins from the bag. Each day, when the shop closed, their takings were put into the leather pouch and, at week's end, Seb studiously counted and noted the incomings, compared them to the outgoings, praying they would tally. They seldom did, resulting in a good deal of sighing, crossing out and head scratching. All of which never helped. Then the profits – usually a few shillings – would go into a wooden box that was kept behind a removable half brick in the side of the parlour chimney. Its hiding place was known only to Seb, Jude and Emily.

The trouble was, this day, the sighs and head scratching helped even less. Despite recounting coins a half dozen times, there could be no doubt that money was missing. Of itself, that was not so unusual. Seb often forgot to record the purchase of a new brush here, or a bag of ground chalk there, or, like today: an entire shilling for saffron. But this was different. A whole five marks was unaccounted for. That was £3 6s 8d. A large portion of their takings that had amounted to only £3 9s 3½d this week. It was impossible. And with bills totalling £2 18s 11¼d and wages to pay, food to be bought, fuel for the fires, more reams of paper needed, a piglet to be purchased for fattening and Jack having outgrown yet another pair of shoes; that meant...

Seb buried his head in his hands. Numbers had never been easy for him but even he could see they'd made a loss this week. That could not be right. A precise sum like five marks had to have gone somewhere. Mislaid, maybe? A purse slipped between the rolls of parchment and boxes of pigments and inks in the storeroom? Had they paid for some expensive item and he'd forgotten it? Five marks could buy a middling sort of horse or re-tile the roof twice over. He would have to look into the matter but how to do it without making himself look foolish or upsetting the rest of the household – especially Em in her present irascible mood – he could not think of a means. Eventually, he threw down his pen, put the stopper on the inkpot and closed the Accounts book with a resounding thud. Perhaps he might later recall having settled some large bill or other. Maybe Em had paid it on his behalf? He refused to despair, straightened his jerkin and prepared to go a-visiting.

'Kate!' he called out. 'Where are you, lass?'

'Here, Master Seb.' Kate appeared, ready booted and cloaked, her irrepressible curls already escaping her hood and her boundless joy of life shining forth like a summer sun at midday. He couldn't keep back his own smile, seeing her delight. 'May I take the drawings I made at the horse sales last week? I think Papa would like to see if my work is improving and horses be a difficult subject, I find – so many long legs, never still for a moment.' She laughed. 'I know Tom has much the same trouble.'

Seb nodded. Tom had indeed found that particular drawing lesson hard. Truth be told, Kate's horses were most life-like, better than Tom's which looked like stilt-walkers wearing animal masks, such as were seen in Mummers' Plays at Christmastide. Tom had seemed distracted at Smithfield that day, more interested in watching a pair of pretty wenches selling hot pigs' trotters than in using his charcoal to best effect. And it wasn't the food to blame. No doubt but he was now of an age when a comely face and fluttering eyelashes caught his attention more than the subjects at hand. Seb had noticed that amongst Tom's most recent drawings – those set as a punishment – the sketches of Rose showed far more eye for detail than others, she being a more beguiling subject for the lad, clearly. He would have to have words. An apprentice couldn't let such thoughts divert him from his work, so the work suffered. But Seb, being Seb, would probably delay the reprimand indefinitely, as was his way, and his deep dislike of confrontation of any kind.

The weather was pleasant for once, the wintry sun trying its best to defeat the veil of cloud as Seb took Kate across the way to Walbrook, to visit her family and make his report upon her progress to Edmund Verney, the maid's father. Her apprenticeship with Seb had come about almost by accident when he, hoping one time to buy some fine cloth to cheer Emily, had discovered the most beautiful textiles at Verney's mercery shop. What he wanted had been far too expensive but the mercer had suggested they come to an arrangement: the cloth at a generous discount, if Seb would consider Verney's daughter's skills as an artist with a view to a possible apprenticeship for her. Emily got her fine cloth – ready-made into a gown befitting a lady – and Seb was pleasantly surprised at the lass's draughtsmanship.

'See how the pale sun changes the feathers of those starlings on the gable, Kate,' Seb pointed out. 'Note how their black plumage isn't really black at all.'

Kate followed his pointing finger.

'Oh, aye, master. I see glossy greens and purples on their backs too, when the light catches them. They're not dull little birds after all, are they? Grand as princes.' Kate clapped her hands and began singing a well-known tune but with words invented in the moment, all about the starlings.

Seb joined his voice with hers, humming along, until they ended the tune in a cascade of laughter. Just then, a shaft of stronger sunlight broke through a gap in the thin hazy cloud, like a beam shone straight from God's hand in heaven.

'Stand a moment, Kate. Look at the tiled roof on St Stephen's church. With the sunlight upon it, do you see how the tiles show countless variations of colour?'

'I see red and crimson, rose, vermilion and so many shades of brown, tawny and russet. I never saw so many colours in a plain old roof before, master. I think your eyes see different to other folks'.'

'Not at all, lass. You noticed them too, once I pointed them out. 'Tis a limner's task to see the details of form and colour, the play of light and shadow in all things that others do not. Practise your art, Kate, all the while, even when you have no pen, brush or charcoal in hand. See there, beneath the church eaves where the shadow lies deepest. Like the starlings, at first the shadows look black, but what colours are they in truth?'

Kate squinted and screwed up her eyes.

'I see darkest blue and, against the stone, a deep brown, like a roasted chestnut. And along further, they seem more greyish, even greenish, like mouldering bread.'

'You have an excellent eye: make good use of it and you'll prosper as an artist, I know.'

'You think so, master?'

'I do. Now tuck your hair away as neatly as you may afore I knock at your father's door.'

The Verney house in Walbrook

'COME IN, come in, Master Foxley,' Edmund Verney welcomed him as a servant took them through to the parlour. 'And how is my little maid? Not vexing you unduly, I trust?' He waved Seb to a cushioned bench beside a goodly blaze of logs in the brick hearth and Kate took her place on a stool. The warmth was indeed appreciated by Seb whose hip was again aching from the chill outside. He eased it surreptitiously while Edmund was ordering refreshment for the visitors, though Kate saw him grimacing. He caught her look of concern and forced a smile to assure her it was naught. He was regretful now, having told her to notice details in all things.

Good ale and wafers were served by a comely young woman, as pale as Kate was dark, yet there was a family likeness. As she came in with a tray, Kate leapt from her stool, barely allowing time for the woman to set the tray upon the side board before flinging her arms around her waist.

'Alice!'

'Kate!' Both Seb and Edmund said together.

'A little decorum, Kate, if you will,' her father added.

'Sorry, Papa, Master Seb, but we haven't seen each other for weeks, me and Alice. Have we, Alice? And I've so many things to tell you, sister.'

'And I you, little Kate,' said the elder lass, embracing Kate tightly.

Edmund clucked his tongue and shook his head.

'You must think I breed such ill-mannered children, Master Foxley. I pray you, forgive their enthusiasm. With your consent, I would suggest we let them withdraw to some secret maidens' nook to chatter away whilst you and I discuss Kate's work, aye, and conduct – or misconduct – in peace, over our ale.'

'But Papa, I'm very well behaved, I swear upon my honour,' Kate protested.

'Go on with you. I shall hear the truth from your master – alone.'

Seb nodded his agreement.

'What a handful she is,' Edmund said when his daughters had made their courtesies and left, 'But I wouldn't exchange them for God's own angels. They bring me such pleasure.' Despite his words, Seb noted that a fleeting shadow seemed to flicker across Edmund's face. 'And Kate,' he continued. 'Well, master, I dare say you've encountered that smile of hers, like to charm the birds from the skies and the worms from the earth. What's a father to do but praise the day she was born?'

'I too can rightly commend the lass: diligent, able and willing to do tasks others prefer to avoid. And she brings light to the dullest of days for us all. Her work shows great promise.' Seb opened his scrip. 'She wanted you to see these drawings she did at the horse sales at Smithfield.' He handed Edmund the sketches. 'You see how she paid every attention to the forms and positions of each beast, in particular the tilt and angle of the hooves which is most difficult to achieve. Yet it is all of a piece: the animal seems balanced, poised but solid enough: flesh and blood upon the move. I tell you, Master Verney, your daughter has great talent.'

'I'm pleased to hear you say that, but I shall be more than relieved if you can say as much for her behaviour in your household. Would your goodwife give my Kate a report so good as yours, master?'

'Oh, indeed she would. If your daughter has a fault, we have yet to uncover it.'

As they returned home, Kate asked:

'Master? Did you give my father a good report of me?'

'I praised you to highest heaven, Kate.'

'You never did. Father didn't look so pleased as that when I returned.'

'I think he was saddened by your leaving.'

'No, he wasn't. You told him I'm lazy, hopeless with a pen...'

'I said naught of the kind.'

'I know, master. I just like to hear you say I'm good.' She was laughing merrily as they turned along Paternoster Row.

'And did you pass a pleasant hour with your sister?'

'Oh, yes. Did you know, Alice is to be wed at the end of Lent? 'Tis all arranged, she told me, and she has a new crimson gown and dainty slippers with bows on. She is so excited and her betrothed, William, is so very handsome, she said, and they'll live in such a grand house in St Pancras Lane. Is that not wondrous news, master? I shall be allowed to go to Alice's wedding, shan't I?'

'I expect so…'

'Thank you, thank you, thank you, Master Seb. I knew you would let me. I'll be so good from now 'til then, so I deserve it.' She grabbed his hand and kissed the back of it. 'You're a kindly man, master. Father said you would be a good master to me.'

Seb made no answer. His thoughts were elsewhere, already back in the workshop, imagining the next colourful miniature required for the 'Gawain' manuscript he was working on. An image of King Arthur's feast would be much enhanced, he thought, if he included Queen Guinevere. Such a figure would be a suitable addition and a vision of Rose, adorned with a jewelled circlet, brought a sparkle to his eye.

The Foxley house

IN THE kitchen, Tom had also returned and was telling his tale:

'Haldane's shop was in such an uproar, Mistress Em, I feared I'd never get served. That's what took so long but I got the saffron you wanted and Master Seb's bits and pieces, in the end.' He put his purchases on the board and shrugged off his cloak.

'So what was amiss?' Emily asked, eager for any titbit of gossip to share in church on the morrow.

'I know not, mistress, but Master Haldane's daughter was running half-demented, though whether with woe or joy, I couldn't tell, upsetting pots and knocking shelves. Two customers left in high dudgeon without speaking to the apothecary at all, so he served me at last, having ordered his daughter to clear up the mess she'd made in her agitation.'

'And you have no idea why she was so distracted?' Emily asked, trying to glean more.

'Well, she kept mentioning a man's name: Walt or Will, maybe, so I suspect it was a maid's usual trouble – love – an excess or lack thereof.' Tom cast a glance at Nessie as he spoke, knowing she was constantly falling in or out of love with every butcher's boy or grocer's apprentice that caught her eye.

Nessie sniffed and put her nose in the air, turning away from Tom. He at least had never been the object of her attentions and was grateful for that.

Redmaine Hall, St Pancras Lane

THAT SAME evening, a few streets away, supper in the Redmaine household was hardly amicable. Giles Redmaine demanded the presence of both his sons to discuss important business matters after the evening meal. William attended as usual. He lived with his father and dined and supped with him most days. But such a command summoned Roger from his preferred activities, whether in a tavern, a brothel or any other abode of disrepute.

'I know not why you insist that I come here, father, you never needed my opinion on your affairs before,' Roger said, washing his hands at the laver bowl and drying them on a snowy linen towel.

Giles was already seated at the head of the table.

'And what makes you think I require your opinion now?' Giles's voice was cold as cracked ice. 'This is a gesture of courtesy, nothing more. Now sit down that we may be done with this meal – with this whole charade. Let us make the pretence at least of being a family.'

The old man reached for a platter of savoury dumplings, little round clouds of sage, garlic, wheaten flour and suet.

'Shall you say grace first, father?' William suggested, smiling.

'I was about to. Don't need reminding.'

'Of course not.' William was used to this, well aware that his parent's memory was not so blade-sharp as it had once been but Roger gave his brother a look, his eyebrows raised in question. He hadn't realised the old man might no longer be infallible. William returned a knowing glance, an exchange of information both understood.

With supper done swiftly – there was never any talk during a meal in the Redmaine household – Giles pushed back his chair, took up his goat's milk, served in a fine Venetian glass as if it was best Gascon wine, and sipped it appreciatively. His sons had to be content with small ale, weak and watery, for strong drink was not permitted at their father's table.

The servants cleared the platters and were dismissed. Once their duties were done, they would leave the premises for the separate servants' dwellings across the courtyard. The old man valued his privacy too much – or trusted them too little – to have them live-in.

'Well? What is it you would say to us? I want to be home before curfew is rung.' Roger was resentful of every moment spent in the old man's company.

'You have no more manners than those street-walkers, tavern-doxies and clapper-dudgeons you consort with. Did I not raise you to have a little courtesy, at least?' The old man wagged a bent rheumaticky finger at his son. 'No wonder you'll never make a half-decent man of business. Manners maketh man, Roger, raises us above the beasts, yet I swear a pig conducts itself better than you.'

'I didn't come here for a lecture on etiquette.'

'Hold now, brother.' William took up the ale jug. 'Have some more…'

'Neither did I come to drink this cat's piss.'

'I'm sure father will get to the point of this meeting, won't you, sir?' Ever required to play the peace-maker since their mother had died years before, William soothed both parties with quiet words. 'Father? Will you not tell us this matter of importance that weighs upon your mind?'

'What?'

'The important matter, father.'

'Oh, aye. That.' Giles finished his milk and set the glass down carefully.

Roger fumed but said nothing, fidgeting on his cushionless bench. His nethers were still somewhat chaffed by last night's over-enthusiastic activities with a tupenny whore in Bankside. The unforgiving wooden seat did not help but he grinned at the memory of damp thighs and hot breasts. To think on such pleasures was the best way of keeping a reign on his temper; else he'd be tempted to throttle the old tyrant with his bare hands.

Giles eased his creaking bones out of the chair and went over to a small oak chest on the buffet, amongst the display of silver-gilt dishes, masers and ornate candlesticks. As he tried to lift it, William hastened to assist, only to be waved aside.

'I can manage. Don't go thinking I'm incapable because I'm not.'

'Forgive me. I never meant to imply...'

'Now.' Giles fumbled in his purse, found a dainty key and unlocked the chest. Once the lid was opened, the pile of parchment documents within seemed to come to life, expanding and unrolling until the top two or three spilled onto the board. He set them aside and lifted out more until he found one with a green ribbon and pendant wax seal attached, in the manner of a royal warrant. 'This,' he said, shaking the parchment roll in Roger's face, 'Is my last will and testament, as I deemed fit to write it a decade since. It leaves the business to you, Roger, as my elder son and heir. However, in the years since, you have proved a grave disappointment to me in all things. You are hopeless in business, idle in your ways and dissolute in your conduct. You could not even beget a living legitimate heir during your marriage, though rumour runs you have a plethora of healthy bastards scattered across the city...'

'But, father, the child's death was hardly my fault...'

'Silence! In short, Roger, you are useless as an icicle to stir a pottage pot. I would be a fool to leave my thriving business in your keeping. It would be in ruins within a twelvemonth. So, on Monday, I meet with my lawyer to draw up a new will. Fear not, Roger, your generous allowance will continue as now and my property in which you currently dwell will be left to you, so you'll not lack for a roof over your head. What you make of your life will be up to you but there will be a condition in the new document that you will not pester the next owner of this business for monies to get you out of any debts you may incur in the future. Understood?'

Roger nodded. In truth, he'd never wanted the tedious responsibilities of running his father's business but he did want to inherit this fine house, the wealth and respect that would be his due when he replaced his father. His present dwelling was large and comfortable but it would never bring him such recognition as being the master of Redmaine Hall.

'So who will inherit?' he asked, doing his utmost to conceal his displeasure. 'William, no doubt?' Precious bloody William.

'Indeed.' Giles smiled at his younger son, showing missing teeth. 'But again, there is a condition.'

'You would have me inherit all this?' William motioned with his arms to encompass the grand chamber.'

'Aye. And both shops and the warehouse by Queenhithe. It will all be yours, *if* you do as I wish.'

'But I never expected so much. As your younger son, my hope was...'

'Never mind your hope. In order to inherit, you must comply and marry Alice Verney, as was arranged. I'll suffer no more delays, procrastinations and prevarications from you, William. You will wed the maiden as soon as Lent is ended, or I'll bequeath everything to your cousins, my brother's children in Brentwood. Do I make myself clear on this?'

'You do, father.' William spoke with a sigh in his voice and a sinking heart.

The wind was blowing from the north-west, such that the matins bell chiming at St Martin-le-Grand Abbey was easily heard in Redmaine Hall. Giles was disturbed from his fitful slumbers. Never a sound sleeper, he blamed St Martin's bell and an old man's bladder, getting out of his warm bed to use the jordan kept in the closet. Relieved, he heard another noise – one which did not belong at such an hour. The sound of banging, wood splintering and metal clattering. It seemed to come from the parlour below his chamber. With no servants to summon, he would have to go down to see what was amiss. Perhaps a window casement had blown open in the wind and an animal had got in. It had happened once before and he'd meant to have the latch mended but forgotten about it. He'd have to remind William to get it done.

As he lit a taper and, armed with his stoutest walking staff, went barefoot down the stairs, he was already bemoaning the damage done, judging by the noise. A light shone under the parlour door. No stray cat, then. He raised his staff and pushed the door open. The place was a shambles. Silverware lay strewn amidst the floor rushes, his chair and the benches overturned but he lowered his stick.

'You? What in Satan's name are you about? Look at this mess. And my chest? Why have you…'

'I wondered how much din it would take to waken you. You're going deaf in your old age. But now that you are here, I shall bid you good night – once and for all.'

Of a sudden, the staff was snatched from his hand and blows rained down upon Giles's head. He tried desperately to defend himself, crouching low, one arm shielding his face whilst, with the other, he attempted to wrest back his staff.

'No! I'll do whatever you ask. No!' he screamed, tasting blood.

But his assailant was stronger, bludgeoning him to the floor. One powerful stroke in particular caught him on the side of his skull. The elderly bone shattered like eggshell. The weight of darkness descended and engulfed Giles Redmaine.

CHAPTER FOUR

Sunday the fifteenth day of February
Redmaine Hall in St Pancras Lane

THE OLD man's body lay sprawled in a pool of crimson blood amongst the rushes, as the dawnlight strengthened and showed the gory scene at its worst. Sickened at the sight, William rushed out to the courtyard and vomited.

The servants were coming from their accommodations across the way.

'Are you ill, Master William?' Walter, the steward, asked. 'Can I assist you?'

William spat and wiped his mouth with the back of his hand.

'Oh, Walter, something terrible has come to pass. My father lies dead in the parlour.' He paused and took a shuddering breath to calm himself.

'Are you certain? Shall I send for the surgeon, to see what may be done?'

'I fear 'tis too late for that. The coroner... oh, and the sheriff, I suppose, would be best to summon. It seems the house was broken into during the night, our belongings taken.'

'Come inside, master. I'll prepare you some restorative. Then we'll see what's to do. But first, I'll order the maidservants to keep out of the parlour. We don't want them to be distressed, coming upon Master Giles all unexpected, do we?'

'You're a good man to have by me at such a time, Walter. I was in quite a panic, finding him. 'Tis not something I ever wanted to see. I know parents usually die before their children but, in truth, I thought – hoped – my father would live many more years. 'Tis an awful sight, Walter, I warn you.'

'I'll send one of the scullions to fetch the coroner. Now come and warm yourself, master, before you take a chill.'

Jude accompanied Master William Fyssher, the deputy coroner, to Redmaine Hall.

'Bugger it,' he muttered under his breath. 'Some old goat chooses to throw his last dice on a Saturday night of a purpose, to drag me from my bed first thing on a Sunday morn. Inconsiderate. That's what it is.'

'It's the job, Foxley. You don't want the work – aye, and the wages – I'll find someone else to assist as my clerk.' The coroner pulled at his wagging grey beard.

Jude was always of a mind to give the shovel-shaped thing a good tug, it annoyed him so, for some reason he couldn't name.

'Not at all, sir. But my bed was warm…'

'And filled by some comely whore, no doubt?'

'Most certainly not. You mistake me, sir.'

Fyssher laughed. He had known Jude for some while now.

'Given 'em up for Lent, have you?'

'No. I am to be wed. I would not be unfaithful.'

'But you're not wed… yet.' Fyssher said with a meaningful look.

They reached the grand door of Redmaine Hall. Jude gave the lion doorknocker a hefty thump that was answered by a well-dressed servant of middle years. He looked immaculate and efficient, even at such a God-fearing hour.

'Show me the deceased,' the coroner ordered. 'I don't have time to waste.'

Jude gave the servant an apologetic nod. Fyssher never paid the least mind as to whether the family or household might be sorrowing at the death he came to examine.

'This way, sirs. I'll fetch Master William from the kitchen. He was so distressed by what has happened. The parlour is this way, if you would follow me?'

Jude gazed around at the exquisitely carved balustrade on the stairs, the Flemish tapestry hangings in the passageway, the sheer number of wax candles burned down in the cressets. The servant halted by a door.

'In here, sirs. If you require anything, just call. I am Walter, the steward, at your service.'

The room was in chaos, furniture flung anyhow, fine silver-gilt platters and drinking vessels lay dented, embroidered cushions and parchment rolls scattered about. A cushion of blue velvet, fringed with gold tassels lay soaking up a puddle of blood. The victim lay open-eyed, staring up at the coffered ceiling, beside the cushion, as if he'd meant to use it as a pillow but had missed it when he fell.

'Is this how the body was found, lying just so?'

Fyssher addressed his question to a young man, hesitating at the parlour door.

'N-not quite, sir,' the man said, a tremor in his voice. 'My f-father was lying face down when I found him. I turned him over t-to see whether I could aid him… i-if he breathed still.' He broke down, sobbing, and was comforted by the steward who stood close at hand.

'And you are?'

'W-William Redmaine.'

'Master Giles's younger son,' the steward added, which comment earned him one of Fyssher's infamous scowls. The coroner didn't appreciate folk who spoke without being asked, especially servants who ought to know their place – as this one clearly did not.

Jude, however, did know his place. Thus, he kept silent concerning the open casement with a drooping latch that he noticed; the scuffs upon the window frame. He looked out of the open window. Down below was a muddy patch of earth, probably where the servants emptied the laver bowl after the diners had finished washing their hands. If Fyssher noted such matters, he would duly write them down, as was his task as clerk. If Fyssher said naught about it, then it wasn't Jude's place to record it.

'And was anything stolen?' Fyssher asked.

'I don't know, sir, I couldn't bear to look,' William replied.

'Well, look now, make an inventory.'

'I'll do it for you, Master William, shall I? Seeing I polish the silver every week,' the steward offered, overstepping the bounds of propriety once again, setting the coroner huffing with disapproval.

'The best candlesticks are missing, I can see that straightway, master, and the covered maser. But all else seems to be here.'

'Note that down, Foxley. I'm done here but you will stay and make a list of any other valuables taken. See to it.'

St Michael's Church

JUDE MANAGED to finish the inventory in time to attend High Mass with Seb, Emily and the household. More importantly, with Rose who looked as delicious as ever.

'There's a case you might be interested to hear of, Seb, over at St Pancras Lane,' Jude said by way of a greeting.

Seb was frowning up at the Rood, high above them, draped in plain linen for the Lenten season.

'Did you hear me, little brother?'

'Oh, good day, Jude.' Seb turned his attention to his footwear. No doubt but the mud on them was quite intriguing.

'What's amiss? You and Em had another falling-out, eh?'

'What? Sorry. No. I'm just worried about her.'

'She looks well enough to me. You still fretting about whether the babe be yours or not?'

'No, Jude.' Seb said, a spark of anger giving an edge to his voice and making it over loud. Other members of the congregation looked at him, staring. 'No,' he said more softly, taking Jude's arm and turning away from the gawping eyes of neighbours. 'That's not in question, as I told you afore. I'm concerned for her at the birthing time; what the babe might do to her, if 'tis misshapen as I was. I think I need to speak with Father Thomas on the matter.'

Jude couldn't help but bark out a laugh.

'And what do you suppose a celibate old codger like him knows about childbirth? You'd do better to ask Nell Warren over there.' He nodded towards one of Dame Ellen Langton's fellow gossips, a woman with five sons and four daughters of her own, all flown from home nowadays, but she still acted as the neighbourhood midwife.

'I cannot speak to a woman on so privy a matter.'

'Oh, well, that was my best suggestion, take it or leave it. Now, I have more important things to concern me.' With a shrug, Jude pushed through the gathering congregants to where Rose was standing with Tom, Kate and Jack. The latter had grown so much of late, he looked like Paul's steeple, towering over the others. Jude realised the lad must be nigh as tall as Seb these days – a little urchin no longer, aye, but still a bloody nuisance along with that damned dog of his. 'Rose, my dearest heart.' He embraced her, kissed her with a resounding smack of lips on lips, uncaring who tut-tutted at such a show. He'd kiss her naked flesh before the altar, given half a chance.

'Jude, behave yourself, you lusty knave.' Rose sounded severe indeed but the glint in her eye did not elude him. 'Later,' she whispered, close in his ear.

The warmth of her breath had an immediate effect. He knew he could now pay no heed to the words of the mass, his thoughts on more worldly deeds. Carnal deeds, if Rose permitted, never mind that it was the Lord's Day.

'I suppose your brother will be expecting an invitation to dinner, as usual?' Emily said. They were kneeling in prayer on the chill tile floor but his wife's thoughts had turned to her household chores.

'If 'tis no trouble,' Seb said. The cold through his best hose was making his hip ache. He wished the prayers might be done with swiftly. Women were fortunate in all those layers of shifts and kirtles and over-gowns they wore, shielding their knees from the unforgiving ceramic tiles.

'He is always a trouble to me, as you well know. I hoped I might be spared his company upon just one day a week, but no. Whatever sins I may have committed, your brother is my daily penance for them. Now, what was this I heard? Dame Ellen said there is a rumour of murder over in St Pancras Lane? Is it true?'

'Aye. It seems rumour travels faster than fire in a hayrick,' Seb replied, keeping his voice low as Father Thomas continued with the mass.

'Who died?'

'I know no details. Jude mentioned it is all.'

'Dame Ellen said that Mary Jakes told her that she'd heard it was Giles – or was it George or Geoffrey? – Redman or some such. Wasn't that what Jude was telling you about? He must know, working for the coroner.'

'But I do not, Em. Let us attend our prayers, as we ought.'

Despite Emily's 'penance' and no meat permitted until Easter, the household enjoyed a good dinner of whiting, served with white bread, cole worts and last summer's crop of alexanders pickled in verjuice and ginger. She was proud of her fine stock of preserves and knew this was one of Seb's favourites – not that he deserved to be spoilt in the least, he had so begrudged her the saffron yesterday, as if they couldn't afford it.

Last week, she knew the shop had done well because Rose told her how good the sales of books had been – and she should know, having sold more than Seb and Jude together. Seb's gloomy face after he finished those wretched Accounts the day before was just a ploy, so she would not think they had coin to spare. Oh, aye, she knew her husband's ruse well enough and wasn't to be fooled. He kept the purse strings tighter than a fat friar's girdle. Thinking of which, with her belly already showing, she would likely need a longer girdle soon. One of red silk with a silver buckle would be lovely.

Redmaine Hall

'WHAT REASON can we give for our visit?' Seb asked Jude as they approached the grand doorway of Redmaine Hall.

'That the coroner has another question or two, of course, and you are my assistant,' Jude said. 'You can note down the answers this time but you'll see why I think there's more to this death than a thief in the night being disturbed by the householder.'

'Mm. You mentioned a loose window latch. That would be invitation enough to some felon, would it not? Particularly if they were aware the family was quite wealthy.'

'Aye, and knowing that, if *you* were a thief, what would you bring along with you?'

Seb thought whilst Jude made use of the lion knocker for the second time that day.

'A sizeable bag to carry away my ill-gotten gains, I suppose.'

'Precisely.'

Seb shook his head, wondering at Jude's meaning, as the steward led them along a grandly furnished passageway to a small room that overlooked a courtyard.

'I'll inform Master William that you are here – again,' he added significantly.

'Is this where it happened?' Seb asked when they were alone.

'No. It took place in the parlour. We passed the door on the other side of the passage. It overlooks the street at the front and the entrance to the courtyard on the side of the house. But I'll tell Master Redmaine that we need to examine the chamber once more. See what you think.'

'Does Master Fyssher have doubts then?'

'Him? Not likely. He wouldn't query the sighting of the Virgin Mary in a brothel. But I do and I want your opinion.'

The man who entered the room a few minutes later was around Seb's age or a little older, fair complexioned and good looking in an unremarkable way. Seb noted his pale colouring was somewhat at odds with eyes of such a dark hue as to appear black.

'How may I assist you, Master Foxley?' he asked Jude, smiling. 'Walter said the coroner has more questions?'

'Indeed, Master Redmaine,' Jude replied, 'And he wished me to look again at the scene of the crime. By the by, this is my assistant. Ignore him. He's only here to make a few notes at my dictation.'

Seb gave Jude a sharp prod in the ribs with his elbow as Redmaine led them across the passage to the parlour.

'Thank you for that gracious introduction, *sire*.'

'Well, I don't want him taking too much notice of you as you go poking around his parlour, nosing into nooks and crannies, do I?'

The parlour was a splendid chamber but marred by a dark stain upon the floor and the tang of blood in the air.

'The soiled rushes have been swept out,' Redmaine explained, 'But the scouring of the floorboards cannot be done on the Lord's Day. The servants will attend to it upon the morrow. Now what questions do you have? I shall be pleased to do anything to assist in the apprehension of my dear father's killer. You will understand how deeply grieved we all are.' The young man dabbed at his eyes with his sleeve.

'A list of all those who were present in the house last eve would be useful,' Jude said.

'That I can provide in an instant: just my father and me. As I told the coroner before, the servants sleep elsewhere because my father has – had – so little liking for company.'

'And you were both sleeping upstairs?'

'That is so. My father's chamber is above us here,' Redmaine pointed up at the decorated ceiling, 'My bedchamber is above the room where Walter had you awaiting me.'

'And you say you believe your father heard some disturbance down here which awakened him and he came to find out the cause?'

'I think that is a reasonable assumption, Master Foxley.' Redmaine toyed with lacings on his doublet, winding the ends around his fingers.

'Yet *you* did not come to investigate the noise? You left that to your elderly father?'

'I was asleep. I heard naught.'

'Truly? Your youthful ears be less sharp than an old man's?' Redmaine laughed.

'If your chamber was as close as mine is to my father's, like me, you would always slumber with pillows pressed close at either ear. My father snores like a rolling ale cask full of pebbles, grunts like a sow in farrow and curses like a captain of archers – all whilst sound asleep. I tell you, I heard naught through such barriers of duck-down and feathers. Now, do you have any other questions I may help answer?'

'I should like to look in the chambers upstairs, if I may? The coroner had some concerns…'

Left alone in the parlour, Seb looked around. The buffet still displayed a fine collection of silver-gilt and polished pewter tableware. If theft had been the motive, the miscreant – as Jude had pointed out earlier – must have come without a bag to carry off his ill-gotten gains, else why was so little missing? He glanced at the notes Jude had given him: candlesticks and a maser had been taken. Not much of a prize with so many valuable items on open display. Still, the old man had disturbed him. Perhaps the thief, having beaten the poor fellow to death, had little thought for taking more silver and fled with what he had.

Seb then began a closer examination of the window casement. The latch was loose – that was noted already – but it was on the inside of the frame. If it had been opened from outside, perhaps with a knife blade, there might be some sign of it. There was none. But the bottom of the window ledge was scuffed, showing new wood and a raised splinter or two, just as Jude had said. Outside, below the window, was a patch of wet earth. Seb gauged the height from the ground to the ledge. It was quite a high window.

Then, on hands and knees, Seb looked at the floor beneath the window. It was unfortunate that the rushes had been removed. It meant he was unlikely to find any trace of mud on the floor – if there had been any. Easing himself up, having to use the buffet to aid his aching hip in taking his weight, one of the doors at the bottom swung open a little, its catch not having been closed properly. He had not intended to pry but a collection of parchment rolls tumbled out. He would put them back and yet, as he did so, one felt sticky in his hand. He found a gobbet of blood and grey matter… and then more. These documents had been close at hand when the old man was attacked and then hastily hidden in the buffet.

There was just time for Seb to read the bold heading on one of the documents when he heard footsteps coming down the stairs and Jude thanking Redmaine in a loud voice to give him warning. He returned the rolls to their hiding place and shut the door. It was not inclined to stay closed since the foot of a candlestick was in the way and he debated whether to put the catch across to keep it shut. Would Redmaine notice if the catch was not as he'd left it? No time for debate, he shoved everything back inside, closed the catch and got to his feet with a gasp of pain as his hip made protest.

'My thanks once more, master,' Jude was saying when he saw Seb mouthing something silently at him. Jude frowned back.

'Master Coroner required you to ask about the will, most humbly begging your pardon, sir?' Seb said, playing his part.

'Oh, aye, about the will... No doubt your father had drawn up his will, Master Redmaine?'

'Indeed. Father would never leave such things to chance.'

'And you, as his heir, are the main beneficiary?'

'No. That will be my elder brother, Roger. I sent him word of father's death first thing, but he was not at home. I had not really expected him to be so. Roger has his preferences concerning how best to pass a Saturday eve and a Sunday morn – if you take my meaning. He should be here to deal with all this.' Redmaine sighed.

'Do you have a copy of the will?' Jude asked, aware that he was going well beyond his authority to ask but Redmaine did not seem to wonder at the request, only sighed again.

'There is a copy, probably buried amongst father's ever-multiplying piles of paperwork. I haven't had cause to enquire about it since it was written, years ago. I dare say I could uncover it, if you need to see it? But that would rightly be Roger's place to do so, would it not?'

'Aye. It would.'

'Otherwise, Master Foxley, if I may assist the coroner or your good self in any way at all, you need but ask. Anything in my power...'

'Indeed, Master Redmaine, you've been of great assistance to us. Thank you and farewell.'

Outside the house, Jude went to turn right, along St Pancras Lane towards Soper Lane and Cheapside but Seb pulled him to the left and ducked into the entrance to the Redmaines' courtyard. There, he examined the mud beneath the parlour window and the wall above it.

'Can you reach the window ledge from here, Jude?'

'Bit of a stretch. Step aside can't you, out of the bloody way?' Jude moved to a position beneath the window. He could just grasp the ledge above with his finger tips. 'A ladder would help. Oh, now, look at my Sunday-best boots! You owe me, little brother. I'll leave you to clean all the damned mud off them. Bugger it. I was going to wear them when me and Rose walk out later.'

Seb wasn't listening.

'A ladder, aye, yet there is no sign that one was propped here in the mud. No footprints but yours, Jude, either. And no scrapes of mud on the wall, if the thief managed to climb up, and the latch showed no sign of scratches from a blade having been used to lift it from outside. Apart from the scouring on the window frame inside which, I suspect, may be deliberately done afterwards to purposely mislead us, otherwise there is no evidence that anyone gained entrance to the parlour by that means. I misdoubt that William Redmaine is telling us the whole truth.'

'I got the same feeling,' Jude said as they trudged past the church of St Mary-le-Bow, taking time to make a rude gesture in the direction of the priest's house.

Seb did not ask why, his mind on the matter in hand.

''Tis not just a feeling but a fact,' he said, pausing for a moment and wincing.

'Your leg hurting you?'

'A little. It matters not. As I was saying, Redmaine was not being truthful, about the will especially. He knows full well where it is and it was there, perhaps lying upon the table, when his father was slain.'

Jude whistled out a breath.

'Well, I hoped you would agree with my thoughts about the thief coming through the bloody window – of which I was doubtful – but how do you know about the will?' At that moment, Seb stumbled as his hip gave out but Jude caught him up. 'Almost like times past, little brother: you needing me to hold you up.'

'I trust not. 'Tis just the cold has got into the joint. A warm fire will soon ease it, and some of Em's liniment.'

'You'll stink like a bloody tanner's tub for a month, you use that stuff: stale piss and dog turds. Is that what she puts in it?'

'I don't know but it helps.'

'And so does mulled ale and it smells far better. Come on, Seb. The Panyer Inn is closer and more welcoming than that wife of yours. They have a good fire within and you can tell me all about Redmaine's will and how you know.' Jude pushed the door open and helped Seb over the threshold.

'I believe Master Fyssher should question the elder son,' Seb said as they waited for their ale to be heated and served.

'I agree but he won't; too bloody idle for that. If Roger Redmaine is to be asked for his account of the matter, we will be the ones doing the asking.'

'But the law requires...'

'Bugger the law, Seb; the law is meaningless. Haven't you learned that much in recent times? The law sent me to the gallows, Gabriel to the stake and poor Lawrence Ducket to a grave in a ditch, and half the time the so-called upholders of the law were among the guilty parties. And the law would have allowed the devil who tried to kill my Rose to get off with the slight inconvenience of a damned penance. No, little brother, the law is just an idiot's set of rules. What we need is justice.' Jude thumped the board with his fist. 'Justice for that old man and he won't get it from Fyssher.'

'Well, that was quite a speech, Jude. When did justice come to mean so much to you?'

'As I said: that bastard, Weasel, would have killed my Rose and got away with it. Justice is more important than the law. Ah. Ale at last. Get that down you, Seb, that'll warm you through.' He poured generous measures from the pewter jug into their cups. Steam arose, scented with herbs, sweetening the sour stink of the customers at the Panyer.

As they sat over their cups, either side of the board close by the hearth, it was a concern to Jude how grey and drawn was his brother's face. His leg hadn't bothered him so much in a long time. Hoping to distract him from his discomfort, he asked about the will.

'So, did you find the will? Was there time enough to read any of it? Who's the beneficiary? And how do you know where it was when the old man was killed?'

'It was in the bottom of the buffet. I saw it when the door fell open. There were blood stains upon it, still fresh. As William Redmaine told us, his brother, Roger, gets most of the business and estate, from what little I had time to read.'

'Could Roger be impatient to inherit, maybe? Not content to wait for his father to die of natural causes, he hastens things along?'

'Perhaps.' Seb moved awkwardly on his bench, biting his nether lip and screwing up his eyes.

Beneath the Palace of Westminster

'WELL, SISTER? Tell me what the dice foretell?' Anthony Woodville could not conceal his impatience.

Elizabeth raised her hand.

'These things take time and cannot be hurried. Now hold your peace, keep silent and allow me to give the dice my full attention.' She shook the dice in their little oaken pot, three vertebrae from some creature unknown and older than time itself, before casting them upon the board. Foretelling the future by means of dice was no simple art. It took years of practice and an excellent teacher. Elizabeth had been an apt and eager student; her mother, Jacquetta of Luxembourg, an inspiring tutor, had taught her well.

By the light of two black wax tapers, the Queen of England studied the small bones. They were stained brown with age – or ancient blood – each about the size of a silver penny. How they fell in relation to each other, as well as which carven symbols Fate decreed should be uppermost upon them, were the crucial elements.

'Come Hecate, Wisest of Women, grant me sight to read,' she murmured, as if in prayer.

'What do they say?' Anthony asked again.

'You confuse things,' Elizabeth said, swatting him away like an irritating fly. 'The dice have fallen strangely. I cannot tell.'

'Cast them again.'

'No! Fate cannot be rewritten. My eyes are unable to see; my mind cannot interpret.'

'You are weary, sister. Leave the dice as they are and look again later, when you are rested and refreshed. Come, I'll see you to your chamber.' He made to take her by the hand.

'And leave these for any prying eye to see? Don't be a fool. I must read them now or not at all. Light another candle then step well away. Do not distract me again with your idle words and interruptions.'

Anthony obeyed her, as he always did, not because she was the queen but because he knew retribution would come, if he did not. Elizabeth's true power was fearsome and had naught to do with being the first lady in the land – an occurrence brought about in any case by the artistry of Elizabeth and her mother – but everything to do with her knowledge of earth magic, her closeness to the Dark Lord, to Hecate, Wisest of Women and Lady of Witchcraft, and to the Fates.

Eyes closed, Elizabeth moved her hands over the dice, palms downward, in a circular motion, widdershins, the jewels on her fingers glinting in the light, all the while breathing deeply of the scented candle smoke. She opened her eyes. Her vision cleared and she peered at the dice through the smoke. Gradually, the symbols seemed to grow in size, come alive and move into some semblance of order. Now they made sense; spoke the truth and revealed the future.

'Tuesday's eve,' she said, her voice echoing in the silent vault beneath the palace.

Anthony jumped at the sound.

'So soon? But Edward has not signed the death warrant as yet.'

'And we shall so kindly spare him the trouble, the heartache of signing away his own brother's life. It must be done, Anthony, for our safety's sake. I leave the arrangements in your capable hands.'

'You are certain the potion has stood long enough? It must be potent…'

'Cease your questioning. The Fates decree that Clarence will die late upon Tuesday eve and we are to be their agency in this. I have done my part. The rest, brother, is up to you. Tuesday. See it done. That is my final word on this matter. We will not speak of it again except that we must play the part of grieving family afterwards.'

CHAPTER FIVE

Monday the sixteenth day of February

THE CHILL dampness of sleet was in their faces, carried on an easterly wind that sliced through woollen mantles, padded jerkins and linen shirts to wound the flesh beneath like a sword blade. Even the stench of the middens was frozen such that, for once, it didn't assault the passers-by with its foul airs.

They weren't late but hastened all the same, eager to reach Lord Richard's hall and the promise of warmth. Seb gritted his teeth to keep them from chattering as he shivered. His fingers, benumbed within his gloves, would needs be thawed again so he could take up his brushes with any semblance of skill.

'I hope they serve us more of that mulled wine, master,' Tom said, his breath puffing like smoke as he spoke. 'We will need it on such a day.'

'Aye, but I warned you not to expect such luxuries. It was a great kindness on the duke's part but not to be relied upon. Hard work will warm us just as well.' Despite his words, Seb too was hopeful.

In the solar, a servant was adding more charcoal to the three braziers set around the oriel window where Seb would work: one beside the duke's chair, one by the easel and another by the mixing table for Tom's benefit. An elderly fellow was stacking apple logs in the blazing hearth, across the room. For certain, the chamber was far warmer than outdoors but there was a definite draught from the window and icy shards of sleet pattered against the glass panes.

Tom got his wish: mulled wine was served and they relished every drop, feeling it restoring life to cold flesh, as Lazarus resurrected from his tomb.

When Lord Richard arrived with his loyal wolfhound, he was smiling, a light in his eyes warmer than the brazier's glow.

Seb smiled in return as he and Tom removed their caps and bent the knee but quickly realised the joyous expression had little to do with their presence. Rather it was because of the man who followed half a pace behind the duke. Broader, taller by a head of red-russet hair, grinning hugely, there was no possibility of failing to notice Sir Robert Percy's entrance.

The northern knight strode towards Seb, arms outstretched in welcome.

'Well met, Master Sebastian Foxley, my dear friend,' he said, the laughter clear in his voice. The chamber seemed even warmer of a sudden. 'I trust you are well and prospering?'

'Sir Robert.' Seb bowed. 'Indeed we are, thank you. And you also?'

'As ever. My lord keeps me busy indeed about his affairs.'

Richard, seating himself in his chair, chuckled.

'Not so busy as that, Rob, that you don't have time for taverns and eyeing fair maidens.'

'You wound me, sir.' The knight clutched his breast in a theatrical gesture. 'I'm a married man with responsibilities, as you well know. I haven't eyed a fair maid since, er Saturday last, when we left Grantham.'

The duke laughed.

Even Seb appreciated the jest, knowing well enough that Sir Rob was faithful to his beloved wife, Joyce, and would remain so to the grave.

'Now. To work,' Richard said. 'Arrange me as you will, Master Sebastian.'

Seb did so, consulting his earlier sketches so the velvet robe draped to best effect as it had last time. Once settled, Richard opened his book at random but did not read.

'Do you object if I remain?'

It took a moment for Seb to realise that Sir Rob was asking his permission, not Lord Richard's.

'Of course not, sir.'

'I've never watched an artist at work. Will it distract you, if I look?'

'No. Once I begin work, I shall not notice you, sir.'

Sir Robert laughed heartily at that. Going unnoticed wasn't something he experienced often, except by blind men in the dark perhaps.

'Tom, prepare some vermilion, thicker than a wash but of a consistency to flow smoothly. Mix it with the white of egg. I shall lay in the ground colour for Lord Richard's robes. Remember, last time I told you not to wash that area with yellow ochre. Have you worked out the reason why?'

'I think so, master,' Tom said, carefully separating an egg, tipping the yolk into an oyster shell and the white into a slightly larger dish. 'The same reason we mix vermilion pigment with the white, not the yolk, 'tis so we get a true red colour and no taint of tawny from the yellow ochre beneath. Which brush shall you want, master?'

As Seb removed the cloth from his easel, Sir Rob took a long, considering look at the portrait in its earliest form. He stood with his head on one side, like a thrush listening for worms in the ground, stroking his jaw and frowning a while. Then he nodded approval and grinned.

'He's caught you precisely, my lord, as you might have expected. A good likeness already. Now, with your permission, I have taverns to visit and maidens to inspect...'

Lord Richard waved his friend away with smile.

The chamber seemed to cool with his departure but Seb was too deeply engrossed with his painting to heed the change, stroking the fine lustrous pigment upon the image with the care of a new mother for her firstborn.

'An azurite wash next, Tom, to darken the shadows,' he instructed, pausing to compare his work with the sitter before him, adding a brush-stroke to further define the edge of the robe against the chair behind. Satisfied, he handed the brush to Tom for rinsing out and leafed through his earlier drawings to remind himself of a detail; how Friday's somewhat better daylight, once the mist had lifted, had illumined the velvet folds, highlighting parts and deepening the shadows. This day, the dour, sunless light cast no shadows.

'I have another commission for you, Master Sebastian,' Lord Richard said unexpectedly. 'An urgent one, if you be willing to take it on, that is. 'Tis a sensitive one, mind, but I will pay you well for it. If you agree, it must be done tomorrow's eve.'

'Another commission, my lord?' Seb queried. He wasn't really paying attention, too concerned with the work in hand. 'But this is far from finished.'

'I know, I know.' Forgetful of maintaining his pose, the duke shifted in his seat to face the artist. 'I'm not much of a one for begging favours, Sebastian, but if you be willing to oblige me in this matter...' Lord Richard took a shuddering breath and dabbed at his closed eyes with his sleeve. 'Forgive me...' The wolfhound, sensing his master's distress, bestirred himself from the hearthside and came over to nuzzle and lick Richard's hand. The duke ran his fingers through the dog's wiry coat and succeeded in a measure to calm himself. Seeing he now had Seb's full attention, he continued: 'Would you be willing to visit the Tower, to draw my brother of Clarence imprisoned there, in order to paint his portrait? I shall quite understand if you wish to refuse but please, grant me this...'

They ceased work for dinner and no more was said of the matter. Seb and Tom dined in hall at one of the lower boards. Sir Rob rejoined Lord Richard at the top table. Separated though they were, Seb and the duke were both considering the same question: was Seb willing to visit the Tower of London and construct a likeness of a condemned man, a royal duke, no less?

The Tower had first been raised by William the Conqueror to intimidate the Londoners, to forever remind them that he had defeated them. Down the centuries, it had been maintained, repaired and vastly expanded, swallowing up and devouring the entire London parish of St Peter in Chains, for the most part at the cost of the citizens' own purses and their enforced labours. No matter that it was a sumptuous royal palace, it was a fortress, a prison and a contemptible affront to every right-minded Londoner, and none would venture through its grim portals willingly without a very good reason to do so.

In their previous discussion in the solar, it seemed Lord Richard believed a goodly weight of coin could overcome any such reluctance. Perhaps, if Seb had been any other citizen, the duke would have been correct.

Seb's hesitation had naught to do with the Tower's history, nor its buildings. After all, he was not a Londoner born and his family had no generations of connection to the city, so far as he knew. Rather it was the circumstances in which Lord Richard wanted him to go there, the situation he might find. It was not so long ago that his own brother had been imprisoned in Newgate Gaol and condemned to die in a hangman's noose. Remembering the horrors of that time and place, Seb wasn't sure he could face an encounter with another man's brother in a similar squalid dungeon, likewise with his life in grave doubt. Even if he went, would he be able to work with such evil thoughts filling his head? Simply visiting Jude in prison, the visions had tormented his nightmares for months after. Could he contemplate repeating the experience? He knew what Jude would say: 'Think of the money, Seb.' But money hardly compared with peace of mind, did it?

'Will you do it, master?' Tom asked, mumbling through a mouthful of manchet bread and thick pottage.

'I don't know, lad, to tell you truly.' Seb took a spoonful of the pottage and sampled it warily, uncertain whether he could eat or not.

'Master Jude would.'

'Aye. Master Jude would be persuaded by the coin but I am not he.'

'They say the Tower's a horrible place. Full of ghosts of dead traitors and strange beasts.'

'The strange beasts, no doubt, are the denizens of the Royal Menagerie. As an apprentice, my master, Richard Collop, got permission to take me there one time, to sketch the creatures, but the lions looked so sorry and woebegone we never went again. As for ghosts, I suppose unquiet spirits may lurk anywhere but I be sure they rarely, if ever, molest good Christian folk. I dare say 'tis safe enough to visit the Tower for a short while.'

'So you'll do it then, Master Seb?'

Seb sighed and moved his pottage bowl away.

'It seems I have talked myself into it, lad, so, aye, I suppose I will, though it be against my better judgement after the last time.'

'You mean those sorry lions?'

'No. I refer to the camel which spat at me such a disgusting gobbet of foul phlegm, I could never rid my mantle of the stain and I do swear the stink, or the memory of it at least, lingered nigh as long.'

Tom hiccupped with laughter.

'Just as well then, that Lord Richard doesn't want a picture of a camel to grace his chamber.'

'He wouldn't get it from me for any price, that be certain.' Seb retrieved his pottage bowl and, decision made, ate his meal with pleasure.

Redmaine Hall

WHILE SEB was working at Crosby Place, Jude was overseeing the workshop – or that was how it was supposed to be. Rather, it was Rose who was dealing with customers and Jack and Kate got on with their appointed tasks as best they could.

In truth, Jude was over at St Pancras Lane, still asking questions, supposedly on the coroner's behalf. This time, the elder son, Roger Redmaine was also present.

'So, Master Redmaine, I – upon the coroner's instruction, that is – must ask where you were last Saturday eve?' Jude tried to be courteous, though that wasn't much in his nature, and Roger's attitude was surly and aggressive from the first moment. Jude had been confronted in the passageway by the new owner of Redmaine Hall and left standing. There was no invitation to enter the reception room or the parlour, and Roger stood in the doorway of the latter, arms folded, scowling at the coroner's clerk.

'I was commanded here to supper by my father. That was the last I ever saw of the miserable old miser living – praise God – then I had business elsewhere. Which is none of yours, so don't ask.'

'And there are witnesses to this business elsewhere?'

'Probably but I shall not name them. I most certainly wasn't here, as William will vouch for, beating the old devil's brains out, much as I should have enjoyed doing so at many a time past.' Roger blinked a few times. His right eyelid drooped somewhat, making him seem half asleep. Jude wondered if the lazy lid was a permanent thing. 'My parent hated me and the feeling was mutual,' Roger continued, 'To the point where he had decided to cut me out of his will. Ah, but Fate saw to it that he never had the chance.'

'Your father was about to change his will?' The conversation had become more interesting of a sudden.

'Aye. He was intending to speak with his lawyer this day. Won't happen now. But don't you go thinking that gave me cause to kill him because it didn't.' Roger wagged an angry finger in Jude's face, forcing him to step back. 'I don't want his wretched business, hanging like a millstone round my neck. I'd have been content for Will to inherit it and have the dismal responsibility. As it is…' Roger sighed, 'It's my damned burden after all, curse his soul.'

Jude scribbled Roger Redmaine's words in his note book as fast as he was able.

'Now. I have nothing more to say to you,' Roger said, going to the front door and opening it wide. 'Don't annoy me again.'

Jude bade the unpleasant fellow farewell with a show of polite manners he begrudged. His foot had hardly touched the top step when the door of Redmaine Hall was slammed behind him.

'And God's blessings be upon you, too,' Jude muttered, deciding the nearest tavern would be the best place to re-write his notes. They needed to be in a legible hand he would still be able to comprehend later, adding items of information he hadn't recorded at all as Roger Redmaine's words poured out in a torrent. Words that illumined the death of Giles Redmaine with a bright new candle.

.

The Foxley house

SUPPER AT Paternoster Row was a lively affair. Jude, delighted to hear of yet another lucrative commission from the duke, required to learn the details, so invited himself to stay for supper. He was eager, too, to tell Seb what he'd learned at Redmaine Hall.

Emily demanded to know more of the dinner served at Crosby Place. What went into the Lenten pottage? What kind of bread was provided for the lower tables? And, most important, how did the cooks' art compare with her own?

Seb, with the undiscerning palate of a dung-carter, as Emily said, was of little use in guessing the ingredients of the pottage, except to say it 'tasted very well', but Tom, having served a few years as an apothecary's apprentice, had more idea of the spices and pot herbs that might have gone into the dish.

'With parsnips and nutmeg, you think? I'll have to remember that,' Em said. 'I am tired of eating leeks, leeks and yet more leeks. 'Tis a pity we had such a glut of the wretched things last season.'

'Any chance of anuvver 'elpin', mistress?' Jack muttered, offering up his well-scoured platter, only to be ignored as Emily signed to Nessie to clear the dishes.

'I thought they were your favourite dish, Em? Wasn't that why you planted so many?' Seb said. 'And that plum tart was delicious,' he added, licking his spoon, hoping to keep in Em's good books.

'They are not my favourite and never were. And as for the plum tart, that was made with dates and figs: a special treat but I could have saved the expense, since you cannot tell one from the other. Tomorrow, I'll spare my purse and serve you bread and water, husband, see what you make of that!'

Seb gazed down at his pigment-stained thumbs. He should know better; keep silent. These days, whatever he said to Em seemed to upset or annoy her. Without looking up, he sensed her scowling at him. Aye, and Jude grinning like a gargoyle at him, no doubt.

'So, little brother, tell me, what does the duke want you to do at the Tower? Such a bulging purse as he has promised must demand something out of the ordinary?' Jude leaned forward across the board, as eager to hear as Seb was to tell of something other than their supper repast.

'It does not sound so arduous a task, except for the subject matter.'

'Wot's 'ardius' mean then?' Jack asked, out of habit more than interest.

'I am to make the preparatory sketches for another portrait,' Seb continued, 'Within the space of an hour, no more, which is possible, if there be no distractions. If I sat here and drew you, young Kate,' Seb smiled at their exuberant apprentice who tossed her dark curls and beamed at her master, 'Without interruptions, I could have more than enough material in that time to complete a portrait from them. But my subject will be his Grace, the Duke of Clarence.'

His audience gasped as one. Even Jude's eyebrows raised in surprise.

'Clarence? The one who was but lately condemned?'

'Indeed, Rose. The same. And who can say whether he will be obliged to sit for me? I know not whether his permission has even been asked or if he knows to expect me? It may take that single hour to convince him that his brother Gloucester has sent me, that I come with good intent and not to mock a man in his misery. I agreed to do it because – truth to tell and Tom will vouch for it – Lord Richard was nigh in tears over it, all but begged me to do it, but I fear it will not go well.'

'Don't b'lieve that, do we, Beggar? Dukes don't weep, do they?'

'I assure you, Jack, a duke is a man with feelings like any other.'

'I'll come with you, Seb, see you safe...'

'No, Jude. I fear the king's warrant – 'tis sealed or I'd show you – is for me alone and no other is to accompany me beyond the gate.'

'Then at least I shall go that far,' Jude insisted, 'Since your hip has been so poorly of late and the ways are icy underfoot. I can wait for you at the gate.'

'I suppose there can be no objection to that. Thank you, I'll be glad of your company there and back, at least. The hour is specified precisely and it will be near dark by the time I've completed the task. I don't expect it will be a merry one, in any case. You'll be able to cheer me after.'

'Why is the duke so set on having the portrait done?' Emily asked, seeming to have forgotten Seb's blunder over the fruit tart.

'He says it will be for Clarence's children to remember their father, if he should be, well, executed. Lord Richard never used that word but his meaning was clear, was it not, Tom?'

'Aye, that's what he meant,' Tom agreed. 'But keep a look out for ghosts, master.'

'That Tower's 'aunted fer sure, ain't it, Beggar? Ev'rybody says so, don't they?' Jack concluded glumly, giving the remains of the date and fig tart a morose stare, as though it had no right to sit upon that platter when it should have been filling his belly.

'Well, Jude. You said you met Roger Redmaine today and that what he said changes everything?' Seb settled back on his stool, taking his ease in the warmth of the kitchen fire whilst Em and Nessie scrubbed and washed pots and platters and Rose and Kate dried them off and put them on the shelf. Women's work. Tom and Jack were playing fox and geese, moving pieces on the board according to the fall of dice. Seb hoped the game wouldn't end in argument and ill-feeling, as was too often the case with the lads these days.

'I tell you this, Seb, the elder son is naught like the younger,' Jude said. 'Bloody discourteous and rude and reluctant to answer my questions.'

'Were you honestly there on Master Fyssher's behalf, as you told Roger?'

'Course I bloody wasn't but if I told him that, he'd have refused to say anything. Whereas William was polite and helpful to a fault, this Roger has the manners of a bloody goat. Admitted plainly that he hated his father... Hey, Em, any more ale, woman?' Jude held out his empty cup.

'No. Fetch it yourself, you idle dog. Or better yet, go buy it at the Panyer. I'm busy.'

'Rose, you wouldn't deny a thirsty fellow, would you, my dear heart?' Jude wheedled.

'Mistress Em says no, so don't you try playing us off one against the other, Jude Foxley.' Rose could look as fierce as Emily, when she had a mind.

'Bugger it. Jack! Get me some ale, now.'

'Don't see why I should. Tell Tom t' do it. 'Sides, we're in the middle of a game, ain't we?'

Seb groaned as he eased himself stiffly from the stool.

'And where are you going?' Emily demanded.

Seb didn't reply but the ale jug in his hand gave answer enough. He went out to the yard, where the ale barrel stood under cover of the lean-to, swathed in canvas to stop the tap freezing up, but to keep the ale cool enough to last a week without going sour. He refilled the jug and returned to the warmth of the kitchen. He could feel Em's eyes upon him, disapproving and angry, but refused to look at her.

Jude was almost embarrassed to see his brother, clearly pained by his hip, yet doing tasks that others should do, just to keep the peace.

'I'd have fetched it myself, little brother, except 'tis no longer my place here, to do as I wish. You could have said 'aye' and I bloody would have, to spare you the trouble.'

'No matter. I was stiffening up as I sat, not moving. Help yourself then tell me the rest.'

'Where was I?' Jude poured icy ale for them both.

'Roger hated his father...' Seb prompted.

'Oh, aye. Well, more than that, his father had arranged to see a lawyer this very day, to change his will and cut Roger out of his inheritance. A motive for murder, if ever there was one, don't you agree? Besides, he's a disagreeable bastard.'

'Does Roger have an alibi for Saturday eve?'

'He says so but refuses to name names or give any details.'

'It seems you may have solved the murder, then, Jude.'

'Aye, so let's drink to that!'

Yet Seb was frowning.

'But what of the valuables that be missing? Why should Roger take what would shortly be his, since his father could no longer change the will?'

'To make it look like a bloody robbery, no doubt?'

'And how did he get back into the house? We've determined that no one came in through the window, as was assumed to begin with, so how could Roger gain entry? Unless someone within unbarred the door for him?'

'You think he may not have acted alone? Walter the steward could have been in on the bloody plan, couldn't he? Or maybe Walter is the killer? Perhaps he was stealing the family silver and old Giles caught him in the act? Oh, Seb, I thought I'd solved it, but now you've put us back in the bloody dark as before.'

'I will not apologise for doing so. We have experienced at first-hand what can come to pass if guilt be apportioned too readily. I don't think we have finished with the questioning as yet. I'm not convinced that Roger is a killer, simply because of his incivility.'

'Wot's "incitivily" mean, master?' Jack asked, stifling a yawn.

'It means, firstly, that you should not be listening to conversation that doesn't concern you and, secondly, that it be time you put away the game and went to your bed. You also, Kate and Tom. Hasten now. Do not fail to say your prayers of thanks, remember, and at least one Paternoster and an Ave on your knees beside your bed.'

That night, afore bed, Seb had a good many prayers to say. In particular, prayers beseeching the Almighty to keep Em safe and in good health. He also asked for divine aid at the Tower upon the morrow, having not the least idea what to expect in that forbidding fortress. The thought of it scared him more than he would admit.

CHAPTER SIX

Tuesday the seventeenth day of February

DESPITE THE February chill, there had been plenty of customers at the shop in Paternoster Row. Once again, a commission from Richard, Duke of Gloucester, had brought the Foxley name to the notice of folk with money to spend and new orders ranged from cheap little Books of Hours to be decorated with just a few red ink capitals to a pair of portraits of an ex-Lord Mayor and his wife. As well as the just completed 'Gawain' that now required collating and stitching, heraldic coats-of-arms, tavern signs and an illuminated version of *The Decameron* would keep Seb busy for months to come. So, with few qualms, Seb and Jude decided to close the shop early, to prepare for Seb's engagement at the Tower of London at three of the clock.

His scrip laden with fresh paper, a stout board to rest upon, supplies of charcoal, red chalk and his favoured silver point, Seb had what he needed to draw the subject of his next portrait: George, Duke of Clarence – if the duke was willing to oblige him, which was uncertain. He checked yet again to be sure the king's warrant was also in the scrip.

Swathed in their woollen mantles of dishwater grey – Seb's – and peacock green – Jude's – and wearing winter boots, the brothers were ready.

'I hope the duke is in a kindly humour for you,' Emily said, kissing Seb's cheek in the doorway. 'I'll have a fine supper ready to warm you when you come home, so don't be tardy.'

'The king's warrant permits one hour only from the hour of Nones,' Seb reminded her, 'So I shall be done by four of the clock, then the time it takes to walk back. We shan't be late, shall we, Jude?'

Jude shrugged, uncertain whether the promise of supper applied to him also. It would depend upon Emily's mood of the moment which could be fickle indeed. He hefted Seb's scrip onto his shoulder, knowing the weight would likely unbalance his brother's less than sure footing on the icy ways.

They took the short cut through the transepts of St Paul's and turned into Watling Street, crossing Bread Street where they had to make way for a laden cart that crept past at a snail's pace. Its load was covered by a canvas sheet but the stink identified it all the same: barrels of stale piss destined for the tanneries. The carter was just emptying the bucket chained outside Allhallows church for the use of passers-by who thereby donated their contributions to the leather-makers beyond Aldgate. An unsavoury task indeed. The stink made them both catch their breath. Seb wrinkled his nose and hastened into Budge Row.

Passing by Edmund Verney's house, the Walbrook was especially treacherous where the stream gurgled and splashed in its channel. Swollen by last week's snowmelt, it spat water far beyond the boundary of its deep gutter, creating a slick of dark ice. Outside St John's church there, Seb slithered and slipped, losing his balance. Fortunately, Jude's strong arm proved his saviour.

'Thank you. I was nigh fallen there.' Seb steadied himself betwixt his brother's grip and the wall of a house.

'Can't have my little brother meeting royalty with a muddy arse, can I?' Jude chuckled. 'The name of Foxley would never live down the bloody ignominy. Come on, else you'll not get the whole hour for your drawing.'

They trudged past Londonstone, along Candlewick Street, East Cheap and into Tower Street. This way was sloping up towards Tower Hill and some unthinking housewife had lately emptied her bucket, quite missing the central gutter that would have carried the water away. Seb almost came to grief a second time on the expanse of ice that was too wide to step over. Jude caught him up but his leg twisted awkwardly, sending a lance of pain through his bad hip. He winced but gritted his teeth, saying naught of it but thanking Jude for his timely aid once more.

Outside the main gate into the Tower, there was a tavern. Its hanging sign proclaimed it to be 'The Royal Lyon' but the beast shown there was far from being either royal or even a lion. A scrawny creature with a sharp nose, pointed ears, long neck and a horse's tail was as far removed from being lion-like as Seb could imagine. An unfortunate bird-dropping had half obliterated one of its blue eyes, giving it a definite squint. Jude pulled a face when he saw what Seb was looking at.

'I hope their ale's better than their bloody artistry,' he said. 'I'll tell them you'll paint them a far better sign for a decent price – one that looks like a bloody lion, at least. I'll wait in here for you. One hour, aye?'

'One hour,' Seb confirmed, envious of a sudden that Jude would be sitting in the warmth of an alehouse whilst he ventured into that notorious fortress across the way.

'Watch your step, little brother. Remember what I said about getting a muddy arse.'

'Fear not. I shall indeed watch my step – in every way.'

Jude gave Seb's shoulder a reassuring squeeze as he handed him the scrip.

'You'll do well enough.' Then he pushed through the tavern door, leaving Seb alone before the gateway.

Seb rummaged in his scrip so he had the warrant ready in his hand, King Edward's seal uppermost, as he approached the gatehouse. He squared his shoulders and walked, head up, towards the two men who guarded the royal precincts. One was tallish and well-built but slovenly in his dress, leaning on his pike-staff, picking at his nose. Seb wondered whether the king was aware that his guard made so poor a first impression. He doubted it. Perhaps a long, cold spell on duty was excuse enough. The other was neatly garbed and looked somewhat more alert but neither man challenged Seb.

'God give you good day, sirs,' Seb said, holding out the warrant for inspection.

The neater guard hardly glanced at it.

'You know where you're going?' he asked, sighing and folding his arms.

'No, sir. I was instructed that I should have an escort, sir.'

'Hal! Shift yerself, yer idle bugger,' the fellow yelled.

A lad ran from the gatehouse, pulling on his jerkin, boots unlaced, hair capless and flying in his haste.

'Aye, sir?'

'Escort this, er, visitor, to the Lieutenant's Lodging.'

'Aye, sir. This way, master.'

The lad scampered ahead, passing beneath the great stone vaults of the arched gateway. Seb had no hope of keeping up, not trusting the smooth cobbles underfoot that might send his boots slithering sideways at any moment. Once into the daylight again, Seb saw the youngster was waiting for him by a fence that marked off the area of the Lion Tower, where the Royal Menagerie was housed. A long mournful roar issued from one of the wooden cages and Seb pitied the creature that made a sound so sorrowful.

'You ever seen the beasts here?' the lad asked as he turned through another portal that opened onto a wide sanded space.

'Aye. When I was about your age,' Seb replied, happier to be walking on sand than cobbles.

'They're a fine sight.'

Seb kept his thoughts on that matter to himself.

'Is it far to the Lieutenant's Lodging?'

'No. 'Tis there, across this yard – what they call 'the Green', though it's not green at all.' The lad was pointing at a fine new house. 'They use this sanded ground for weapons practice. And over there – see them sparks flying? – that's where they cast new cannon. I like watching 'em 'cos it's warm by the furnaces. And farther along is the Royal Mint where there's more furnaces but they don't let us in there, fearing we might help ourselves to the coins. And that's St Peter's church... Get away, you!' He clapped his hands to scare off an inquisitive raven – the Tower was famous for the great black birds – that had come to investigate the visitor.

Seb shuddered, hating the creature, knowing they were believed to be foretellers of death.

'Here, master,' the lad said. 'Shall I knock the door for you? The lieutenant won't be in cos he never is, but somebody will be.'

The door was opened by a grandly dressed somebody wearing parti-coloured hose and a ruffled neck cloth. He did not speak but raised a questioning eyebrow. Seb held out the warrant. The man accepted it but held it betwixt finger and thumb as though Seb's touch had soiled it beyond bearing. It was so ill-mannered. Seb was left on the doorstep, the door closed against him.

'I'll have to leave you now, master,' the lad said and scurried off, back they way they had come.

Alone, Seb waited, blowing on his chilled hands and stamping his feet, wondering how much of his precious hour would be wasted, lingering like this, becoming ever colder. Or would only his time in the duke's presence be counted? His fingers might well be too numb to hold his charcoal by then and naught could be drawn in any case.

Somewhere close by, a dog howled. It was not a comforting sound. Seb shivered and the hairs on the back of his neck prickled. Eyes were watching; he felt sure. The dog howled again. A shout was followed by a whimper. This place was full of cruelty. He was tempted to leave now. No doubt, he could think of some explanation to give to Lord Richard for his failure to complete the commission but it would be a lie and he had no skills in deceit.

At last, a toothless fellow appeared, encumbered with the largest set of keys Seb had ever seen. They looked of a size to open the gates of Hell itself.

'This way, if you must,' the gaoler muttered so Seb hardly heard him above a sudden great clatter and hiss from the direction of the cannon founders. 'Devil take the king's idiot whimsies. Drawings? What's that in aid of, eh?'

'A portrait of his Grace of Clarence,' Seb explained.

'A what?'

'A likeness, if you will.'

'Madness, that's what it is. Well, he's in here.'

The Bowyer Tower at the Tower of London

WHEN THE gaoler unlocked the door into the prison chamber, the stench near sent Seb reeling and gagging. Used to the smells of London, he was all but overcome by the foulness of the chamber. It was overwhelming, eye-watering, akin to the foetid stink of the tanner's cart earlier. But he managed to control himself and went in. As the gaoler announced him by name and the purpose of his visit, Seb removed his cap and bent the knee, remembering he was in the presence of royalty, however revolting the place.

A man stirred within. He was seated at a cluttered table strewn with odds and ends of bread, dirty linen napkins, spilled wine, candle wax and unwashed spoons. A book lay open, its pages rumpled and soiled with crumbs and wine stains. Behind him, a meagre fire burned in a hearth deep in ashes, giving out little heat. The chamber was hardly warmer than the castle bailey outside. In the far corner, a latrine bucket – from whence came the worst of the stink – was near overflowing.

The gaoler went to remove the obscenity.

'Out, damn you!' the duke roared. 'I won't have you in my presence, you espier, you Woodville-lover. Get out!'

The man obeyed, cursing his royal prisoner as if he was less than a butcher's cur. Seb felt himself blush at such foul words. The gaoler slammed the heavy oaken door and Seb suffered a momentary panic upon hearing the key grate in the lock, imprisoning him with the duke.

Seb had seen George, Duke of Clarence a few times from a distance, usually about Warwick's Inn, one of his fine houses in the city. He'd gained the impression that Clarence was like his brother, the king: well-built and mayhap inclined to put on flesh. Unlike the lean, wiry Gloucester. Yet now there was not an ounce of spare flesh on Clarence's frame. He looked to be starving despite bowls and platters strewn about the chamber, many still piled with food mouldering and rotting away.

Remarked for his style and perfection of grooming, the once-handsome duke now wore tattered, grubby clothes that looked and smelled as though he had worn them ever since his imprisonment the previous summer. Unshaven, unwashed, his blond hair hung lank, long and dark with grease. His doublet was unlaced and the shirt of once-fine linen bore so many stains and so much filth it was no longer possible to know its true colour.

'What do you want? You come to espy upon me too, or just to gawp at the chained bear, his teeth drawn? I won't have those people in here. They say they would clean the place but I know that's not their true intent. They're not to be trusted. Well?'

'Your grace, the Duke of Gloucester has arranged for me to...'

'Dickon? What does he want? Blood, no doubt. They're all the same. Scavengers waiting for my corpse. I know that's all they want of me.'

'Not at all, my lord. I have come to record your lordship's likeness for a portrait – with your permission, of course.'

'An artist, then?' Clarence poured himself some wine from a large pitcher, splashing the book's open pages.

Seb felt the urge to retrieve the ill-used volume. Books were precious. But he restrained himself.

'I like to think of myself so,' he said, watching the wine soaking into the parchment like a blood stain. 'I have brought my drawing stuff for the purpose.'

'What purpose?'

'To capture your likeness, as I said. To make a portrait of you. My Lord of Gloucester would have it so. I have been granted a single hour with you, sir, if you allow?'

'You sure the bloody Woodvilles didn't send you?'

'Certainly not. Richard of Gloucester, in his great kindness as my patron…'

'Great kindness?' Clarence snorted. 'What is he? A damned saint? Listen to me, you, whatever your name is? Dickon is no more a candidate for sainthood than I am. He grants a favour; he wants something in return. What is it he wants of me now?'

'Naught, my lord. An hour of your time is all.'

'A whole hour? When my entire remaining lifespan can probably be measured in days, not weeks? You ask a great deal.' Clarence drained his cup and refilled it, stared at Seb, considering. 'Well, you better get on with your task, master artist, while I still live and breathe, hadn't you? Wouldn't want to disappoint dearest Dickon, now would we?'

All the while Seb sketched, the Duke of Clarence prattled on, somewhat drunkenly. As a man deprived of company for nigh half a year, he seemed to be relieved to hear his own voice.

'Good to have someone to talk to, other than those damned servants Ned has sent to espy upon me. That's what they do, whatever your name is?'

'Foxley, my lord. Sebastian Foxley.' Seb concentrated upon drawing the duke's eyes. They seemed barely focused. He might have to paint them a little otherwise than they appeared.

'Aye, well. So who did you say sent you?'

'The Duke of Gloucester.'

'Why does he bother?'

'Because he cares about you, my lord. He pleaded your case to the king, so he said.'

'Huh! That's a fine jest. Nobody cares about me. They can hardly wait until I'm dead afore they share out the spoils: Ned, Dickon and those Devil-cursed Woodvilles. They're the cause of all this, I know that. Woodvilles… I spit on the whole pack of them, filthy, low-born, self-seeking leeches. I'd hang the lot of them.

'You say Dickon sent you, master artist?'

Seb frowned at a curve he had drawn, delineating the duke's broad forehead. It was somewhat amiss and he began again. His subject was making him nervous.

'With King Edward's permission. To draw your likeness, aye.'

'Why?'

'My Lord of Gloucester believes your children will take pleasure in seeing your portrait, if ever they cannot, er, s-see you in person.' Seb chose his words carefully. He took a fresh sheet of paper and pegged it to his drawing board. 'He truly does care, my lord.'

'My children?' Clarence asked, suddenly animated, a light in his eye. 'Do you bring a message from him then, about my Meg and little Wardy? How do they fare, my little ones?'

'The king's grace expressly forbade that I carry any message in the warrant I was granted. I am sorry for it. I know naught of your children, my lord.'

'Oh. The king forbade it?' The duke wiped his eyes on his sleeve and sniffed.

Seb's heart ached for the poor man, kept from the children he so clearly loved.

'The bloody Woodvilles, you mean.' Clarence brought his fist down with a crash upon the board. 'The so-called queen and her venomous kin. They rule England now. Did you not know that? Ned is their puppet, does as they say. That's why I'm here, looking Death in the face. If you hear I'm dead someday soon, and not by the headsman's axe, be sure my demise will have the colour of murder about it and the Woodvilles will be behind it. You remember that, whatever your name is.'

'Foxley, sir.'

'They must have me dead, see? I know too much… privy to their dirty little secret. Doctor Stillington. You know him? Bishop of Bath and Wells he is now. You know why? His high office is a bribe to keep his silence. But he told me. Course, he was just a humble priest at the time, when it happened. When Ned's over-lusty prick got him in trouble the first time. Lady Eleanor Butler, daughter of the Earl of Shrewsbury she was. Me and our Dickon were far too young to know of it but our lady mother knew everything. She'll speak out one day, if she has courage enough. Well, clearly, I can't tell anyone now… except you, whatever your name is. You're nobody, so you don't count but the day will come, mark me, when the truth will out. Those bloody Woodvilles will fall into Hell's mouth, as they justly deserve.

'She bewitched him, you know, that woman who calls herself queen.' The duke took another good swallow of wine and set the cup down. He ran his thumbnail through the cold wax dripped from a candle on the table, scraping it off the wood. 'Eleanor should have had the nerve to speak out, foolish woman, to make it known she was already Ned's wife when he wed the Woodville witch. Course, she's dead a few years since. Too late to cry out now but Ned's children are all bastard-born, all the same. His son can never be king. Just another Woodville bastard. All of them.'

Clarence caught his cup as he knocked it with his elbow.

'You'll join me in a cup of wine, master artist? I'm sure there's another cup here somewhere. So much rubbish. You see, I can't eat the pig-slops they call food.' He tapped the side of his nose with a grime-encrusted fingernail. 'Poison. They taint my food, those accursed Woodvilles, but I won't make it easy for them. I don't eat it.' The duke was now upon his hands and knees, rummaging through the debris beneath the table, disturbing a couple of sleek, well-fed rats that scampered away.

'May I assist you, my lord?' Seb offered. It hardly seemed right that a man of noble birth should be grovelling on the floor like the lowliest scullion.

'What?' Clarence resumed his seat at the table but continued searching, throwing napkins, spoons and platters to the floor. 'The wine's safe enough though. I'm allowed to have it sent in by my favourite vintner. Ah, here's one for you,' he said, discovering a cup beneath a heap of soiled napkins. He picked up the pitcher, shook it and peered inside. 'Oh, no matter. Only enough wine for one last cup, anyway. Mine.'

Seb smiled and nodded, relieved he wasn't going to be forced to drink from a filthy cup. He was not much of a wine-drinker anyway.

Just then, the door was unlocked again, the key grating, setting Seb's teeth on edge. Two lackeys rolled a rundlet barrel across the filthy floor and set it upon a stool.

'Malmsey wine,' one fellow announced, 'A gift from a well-wisher, my lord.'

Clarence's face split into a smile that showed a semblance of the handsome prince he had lately been.

'And a timely one, too. The jug was empty. Malmsey, you say? Excellent.'

When the men had gone, locking the door behind them, Clarence grabbed the empty jug, tripping in his haste to refill it.

'Shall I do that for you, your grace?' Seb offered, feeling it was wrong that a royal duke should be forced to serve himself.

Clarence gave no answer but held out the jug.

Seb obliged. The faucet leaked somewhat and wine dribbled across his hand. Having filled the jug and replenished the duke's cup, Seb licked the wine from his fingers. He had never tasted malmsey afore and, with a grimace, decided he had no wish to do so in future.

But Clarence seized the cup and drank it down, pulling a face as he set the cup on the board.

'Not the best I've ever drunk,' he complained, 'Still, 'tis better than naught. Pour some more and have some yourself.'

Seb obeyed, wondering how Clarence could drink it down so fast. Drowning his sorrows – which must be legion, poor man – he supposed. Warily, he sipped his own drink, just a finger's span in the bottom of the cup, but even that amount was more than he wanted. It tasted quite peculiar.

The distant Tower clock chimed, denoting the passage of Seb's allotted hour. The bleak daylight of February was fading fast. Fortunately, he knew Jude had thought to bring a torch that might light their journey home. He packed up his paper and drawing things, into his scrip, and asked the duke's permission to leave.

Clarence shrugged indifferently.

With relief, Seb heard the keys jangling again and the lock turning. The gaoler stood in the doorway.

'Out, you. Your hour's done.'

Seb made a parting obeisance with an effusion of thanks, both of which went unacknowledged as the duke sought solace in his cup. Then he stepped out into the darkening bailey of the Tower of London.

'You know your way,' the gaoler said as he relocked the door of the Bowyer Tower. 'I've got better things to do than escort you.'

Seb nodded. He could but hope he remembered the way out afore the gates were closed and locked for the night. Jude was waiting and Em would be angry if he was late for supper and, if he was locked in, her wrath would be unbearable. It wouldn't do to upset her, now she was with child. He must hasten but in which direction? He had come by way of the Lieutenant's Lodgings, to show his royal warrant and explain his purpose. Now, he simply had to find the main gateway, wherever it was in this maze of stone towers and walls.

A thin, sad snow was falling in the bailey. Seb trudged southward, skirting the outbuildings which, by their scent, were probably bakehouses and brewhouses. Passing a stable block, he could hear a horse whinnying. A groom, coming out, bade him 'good eve' and Seb returned the greeting, touching his cap. The forbidding outline of William the Conqueror's massive keep, the White Tower, loomed out of the half-light. Seb did not want to think of what might have come to pass behind those white-washed walls down the centuries. With a shiver, he hastened on. Torchlight flickered on the grand Coldharbour Gateway that gave entrance to the Royal Apartments, kept privily beyond an inner curtain wall. A fellow passed him by without acknowledgement, trundling a two-wheeled barrow, piled with faggots, struggling with its weight up the slippery slope.

The path led Seb down towards the Garden Tower on the right hand and the curving wall of the Wakefield Tower to the left hand. The snow was heavier now, sent swirling and cavorting by a rising wind off the river and he pulled his hood forward to keep the hard little flakes from his eyes. Beyond lay St Thomas's Tower and the Watergate where he would turn right and follow the way to the main gate, passing the Lion Tower where the king's great beasts gave off a sour stink, unique in London.

By the Watergate, Seb saw a stately barge, rocking gently in the slack, slimy water of low tide at the bottom of the water-stairs. It rode without light or lantern, showing no livery, but Seb knew the shape of its elegant prow, curving swanlike, a blacker outline against the fading dusk. Her cargo discharged, she waited. Her crew were shrouded in darkness, their voices no more than sibilant whispers, like the wash of wavelets on the Thames gravel.

Then he heard the sounds of a scuffle, blows landing, a muted cry, a curse. Then a thud.

Never a man of violence, he hesitated, not wanting to become embroiled in someone else's fight. Looking around, he could see no way of avoiding the scene other than to wait until it was over, so he retraced his steps a little, seeking shelter from the snow in a doorway. As the snowfall eased for a moment, he could make out a dark form sprawled in the slush. A man was lying wounded – or worse. Discretion was most certainly the better part of valour in this case and, if he needed any further reason to withdraw, the glint of a naked blade provided it. He had no intention of adding his own corpse to their affray and kept to the deepest shadows beneath St Thomas's Tower, remaining still and silent, clutching close his scrip, full of his most recent work. Frozen hands and feet, as the biting February wind blew in from the river, were preferable to a knife at his windpipe.

'Is-s this-s the man you s-saw with Clarence?' Seb heard someone say. The words were hissed. A pause. 'You know what my lord did command: no witnesses.'

'Nay, I think not but we must find him, whoever he be.'

Seb's hip became cramped with waiting; he eased his stance, his foot grating upon a pebble.

'You hear that? Is-s that him returning?'

'Mayhap. I think someone lurks there, by the wall. See anything?' The speaker's position became obvious for his words made puffs of white fog in the gathering gloom.

Seb edged back, feeling his way along the stonework. Finding a doorway, he withdrew into its deeper shadow. The voices came closer. He groped for the door latch behind him. It yielded so readily, unexpectedly, that he nigh tumbled backwards into the room beyond. Of course, those who would seek him must have heard the door rattle and seen, briefly, the wedge of torchlight that showed where their quarry had gone. He found himself in a grain store, sacks of wheat, oats and barley piled high, but there were voices here also. Someone had lit the torches in their sconces and left a barrow just inside the door.

'Are yer aidin' us or 'inderin', eh? Cos yer not much 'elp, are yer? Now take that barley t' the barra or step aside, can't yer?'

Seb had to hide behind the wheat stack as a wisp of a lad dragged a sack towards the barrow, puffing and struggling.

The door opened.

'You s-see anyone come in here?' demanded the fellow who hissed like a serpent.

'Nay, sir,' the lad wheezed, 'On'y me an' Wat. Them cooks ordered...' A slap sounded and a gasp, followed by a sob.

'He's here s-somewhere. I can s-scent the bugger; s-smell his fear. S-search this hole. He can't have gone far.'

From his hiding place, Seb caught a glimpse of them in the torchlight. Both were heavily built, broad shouldered, one tall, the other – whose words hissed like a serpent – more compact but still intimidating, a long-bladed knife in his left hand. The taller fellow had lank hair and an odd face, frog-mouthed. He too was similarly armed.

Seb eased into a narrow gap behind the sacks, pressed up against some ancient, worm-ridden wood panelling. The wheat dust rose to tickle his throat and nostrils but he dared not cough nor sneeze. He swallowed hard and held his nose until the urge to sneeze subsided. A torch burned near at hand and he feared it would illuminate him if they looked his way. Squeezing into the space as tightly as possible, suddenly the wood panel swung away, revealing an opening barely of a size for a child to pass through. But the artist's frame was slight, almost skinny, and he grabbed the torch, breathed in and disappeared into the gap.

Beyond the panel, he found a passageway, the walls rough hewn, the roof low, but with knees half bent and head down, he could walk well enough. The torch lit a tunnel that sloped a little in what he believed to be the direction of the river, then a few steps down. Perhaps there was a way out. Escape! The gravelly surface of the packed earth floor crunched beneath his feet and the flickering torchlight cast his shadow to dance and leap along the walls and roof. The air was cold and clammy, musty smelling as old woollen clothes long since discarded, and the unmistakable stench of accumulated rat droppings.

As he hastened along, the roof became a little higher and he could walk upright, which was somewhat of a relief for his aching hip. He shifted his scrip to his other shoulder to further ease the weight on that side. Then the passage turned sharply to the left and just in time for, behind him, he heard voices, cursing. It seemed his pursuers had discovered the loose panel and were squeezing their bulky selves through the gap, into the passage. He broke into an ungainly run, his hip protesting at such ill-use but he ignored it. His life depended upon it.

The passage continued fairly straight which made his flight easier but also meant that as soon as the men behind turned the corner, they would see his light. Then, up ahead, the way seemed to end at a blank wall. Bathed in sweat, his mouth was parched as the sands of Araby. He would have to face them and die like a dog. But no, his time had not yet come for the passage actually branched to both left and right. Which way? He went right, thinking that was towards the river again, if he hadn't lost his sense of direction completely, and since the ground began to slope down once more, it seemed he was correct.

It was becoming damp, then muddy underfoot. The stink of rats and rotting filth was stronger at every step. A sure sign that he was nearing the river where the underground tunnel must end, hopefully, in an unbarred doorway to freedom. Certain that he was now deep underground, he could sense the weight of the earth, of the massive stone structures above pressing down upon him. His breath came in shallow, tainted gasps of pain, as though a great mass bore down upon his chest, threatening to suffocate him. He paused to catch his wind, leaning back against the cold slimed stone. As his breathing eased and quieted, he heard distant footfalls and muffled voices.

He ran on, trying to keep his tread silent, but there were now puddles on the floor and his boots sloshed through the water. They would surely hear it. The voices came again. Closer now. He had to get out of sight somehow. There appeared a gap in the wall, as if another passage had been intended and then long ago abandoned. He darted in, pressing into a far corner but, of course, he could not conceal the flaming torch he carried. He had no choice. With grave misgivings, he plunged the light into the puddle at his feet. It hissed, spat and spluttered out. The darkness swooped down like a midnight crow, wrapping him round in a hellish shroud, the ultimate blackness of a dead man's grave.

He listened. The footsteps came. And stopped right there. Torchlight flickered across his hiding place but did not penetrate. He held his breath, willing his thudding heart to beat more softly.

'I told you he must have turned to the left. No one in their right mind would keep heading for the river. This passage is turning into a damned bog beneath our feet.'

He recognised the voice of Frog-mouth.

'We ought to s-split up,' said the Serpent.

'Not likely. We only have the one torch. I say we go back and search that left hand tunnel. Together.'

The footsteps retreated, fading, taking the light – the only light – with them. The terrible darkness closed back behind.

Never had he known a lack of light so absolute. He closed his eyes, trying to convince himself it was no worse than being abed on a moonless night, the blankets drawn over his head. But it helped not. Panic stirred in his belly like an awakening demon. He had gone blind; would never see again. Were his eyes open or closed now? He couldn't tell. His hand before his face was invisible. And the silence. London was never so quiet as this, even in the midst of the night. At home, he could hear the wind in the apple tree in the garden, the mice behind the wainscoting, the patter of rain, sparrows roosting 'neath the eaves, dogs barking, babies wailing, neighbours laughing or quarrelling. The night hours were never silent, 'til now.

He shivered as his sweat cooled, drawing his mantle and hood closer. His boots were soaked through. He was exhausted. Sleep was tempting. There would be no need to open his eyes at all. But then what? Did he expect to be rescued? No one knew he was down here, deep in the earth's bowels, but for those who desired him dead anyway. They may as well leave him to his fate. That's what would come to pass: he would die in this subterranean hell of hunger, thirst, cold, whichever happened first. Or of madness? Could a man die of insanity? His mind was already conjuring nameless horrors to torment him in his blindness: monsters, devils, Old Nick himself.

'Lord Jesu, I beg aid of Thee,' he prayed. But this was hardly the realm of angels and saints and beings of the light. This was Satan's kingdom. Was this to be his tomb? Buried alive? Hot, salt tears coursed down his face. He should have surrendered to the Serpent and Frog-mouth. Better a quick end on a knife blade than a slow death in this Stygian silence, utterly alone.

But why were they out to slay him? He had done no wrong. Apparently, he was a 'witness' but to what occurrence he did not know. A state barge moored at the Tower's Watergate stairs: what of that? Where was the harm in it? What had he seen that condemned him to this fearful end?

He opened his eyes, though it made no difference, and pushed himself away from the wall. To hell with the Serpent and Frog-mouth, he cursed them aloud, his words bouncing back at him from the stones. He would defy them. He would live!

Feeling his way, hands groping along the wetness of the wall, he stepped into the unknown, the unseeable. The very thought of the excruciating weight above him grew worse, pressing down upon him, his guts knotting themselves into agonising tangles of panic. His heart beat thunderously, as if attempting to break out betwixt his ribs. The dark was a tangible thing, like an invisible curtain that hampered his movements, threatening to trip him, strangle him, bind his arms. He lost count of the times he stumbled, falling against stones or into mud or stinking water, sobbing as he went.

He stopped to calm himself, wiping away the wasted tears, speaking aloud encouraging words, insisting that all would be well. Taking heart somewhat, he seemed to be making fair progress along a winding passage, having lost his sense of direction long since, when his out-stretched hands found a solid barrier ahead. It seemed to be a pile of rubble and his newborn determination was gone in a moment. The roof had collapsed. Could he go no further? Was this the end? He moved his hands with care, touching everything within reach. Mayhap he could get around the fallen stones. Or could the tunnel lead off in another direction? He couldn't face having to retrace his steps, having come so far. The tears began again, in frustration this time, as he pictured just a few yards beyond the blockage an open door to blessed daylight.

Was it even daylight? Time meant nothing in this terrible place. How long had he been here? Hours? Days? Did it even matter? He would never know.

He felt so very thirsty. His heart was pounding a wild drumbeat, as if it would escape his chest, if it could. Tremors racked him; waves of nausea and dizziness afflicted him. In the world above, the real world: in God's own miraculous and beautiful creation, the sun would be rising, shedding its life-giving light. Would he ever see it again? He choked on a sob. He was so tired. Did it matter if he died here or elsewhere in this unholy blackness? The rats would gnaw his bones clean in a few days wherever he lay; a sorrowful skeleton to be discovered centuries hence, perhaps, and wondered at.

He sat upon the rubble and began to pray. Pointless, of course, in this Godforsaken pit but what else could he do? If he didn't pray, his thoughts would wander where it was better not to let them stray, so he recited aloud the Paternoster, the Ave Maria and the Credo, over and over, like a man demented until he fell into an uneasy sleep, his head resting on his leather scrip held close upon his knees.

CHAPTER SEVEN

Later, that same evening,
Tuesday the seventeenth day of February
The Foxley house

'WHERE ARE they?' Emily demanded of Rose, hands on hips, scowling. 'Damn the pair of them. I told Seb I'd have a good supper ready. If they're drinking themselves witless in some tavern or other, I shall beat them both to a mush with my broom, so help me. They're the most thoughtless, inconsiderate bone-headed rapscallions in London. Well? Don't all stand there, gaping like dead fish. Nessie, serve the supper. No reason to waste good food or for us to go hungry just because the wretched Foxleys cannot take the trouble to arrive home when they should. Jack, have you washed your hands?'

'Aye, mistress.'

'Well, it doesn't look like it to me. Wash them again – properly.'

Supper was nigh eaten by the time Jude arrived, breathless and dishevelled, at the kitchen door from the courtyard.

Emily left the table to confront the brothers. She took a breath, about to take the pair to task for their tardiness, but then saw Jude was alone.

'Where is that husband of mine? I have words to say to him.'

Jude shook his head.

'Is he not home already? In truth, Em, then I know not where he is. Rose: some ale, lass, if you will. I ran all the way from the

Tower, near came to grief with the bloody Watch of Bread Street ward, thinking I was up to some felonious intent.'

'You were supposed to wait for Seb,' Emily said, standing betwixt Jude and the ale cup Rose was offering him. 'You said you would accompany him, so where is he?'

'Believe me, Em, I awaited him, just as we arranged, but they closed the bloody gates of the Tower and still he hadn't appeared. I thought I must have missed him, somehow. I asked the sentries if they'd seen him. They answered that they'd seen him go in earlier but that was all. A lad told me he'd escorted Seb to the Lieutenant's Lodging and left him there. I could make no other enquiry as the Tower was being locked for the night. Hell's bloody name, Em, he must also be locked in that place now 'til morning. Something must have delayed him.'

'He could have slipped, fallen and broken his neck and you just abandoned him!' Emily screeched, beating Jude with clenched fists, hammering at his chest.

'Hold off, sister. I did no such thing.' Jude grabbed her wrists. 'I waited, enquired after him, then came here in all haste for fear we missed each other, somehow. What else could I do at this hour? In the morning, I'll go back, bribe my way into the Tower, if needs be, and find that foolish brother of mine. He was probably so deeply engrossed in his bloody drawing of the duke, he forgot the hour, reached the gate and found it already closed. You know Seb as well as I do: such is all too likely, is it not?'

'Aye, I suppose so, but to spend all night in that awful place...' Em dried her eyes upon her apron.

'I know the Tower has a reputation but 'tis hardly a place of lost souls, now is it? Ordinary folk dwell within; there are taverns and a church. Someone will give Seb food and lodging for charity's sake. He'll do well enough for one night and I'll be there to meet him when the gates open at dawn. Now, cease your tears, woman, and give me some food, if you have an ounce of Christian mercy in your heart for a man half-starved.

Save your anger for your idiot husband when I bring him home tomorrow.'

Tuesday night or Wednesday morn, the eighteenth day of February

Beneath the Tower of London

SEB JERKED awake of a sudden, finding naught but darkness, thinking his eyes had failed to open. Then he recalled the horror of his situation. This nightmare was real. But what had awakened him? If his pursuers had returned, he would make himself known to them this time. He shouted out but his words echoed and died, unanswered in the blackness. He called again and again but no feet came hastening, no light showed. Only the drip of moisture and the scurry of unseen rats. And then he felt it and knew what had roused him from his deathly slumbers: a cold draught stirred his hair and brushed his cheek. It carried the river's taint still but it smelled fresher. He was right: he was that close to freedom.

He turned so the draught was full upon his face, shouldered his precious scrip and, hands out before him, moved towards its source. The rubble heap stood resolute, so far as he could tell. It was in his path but the draught crept through it, so it could not be an impenetrable obstacle. He began to climb, dragging his scrip after. Loose stones fell away beneath him, sending him slithering back down, but he tried again, finding purchase for first a hand, then a foot, inching his way upwards. A sudden cascade of rubble showered upon him, setting him coughing and scrabbling for a hold. The roof might collapse utterly at any moment but that hardly seemed important compared to the chance of escape.

He climbed again. The top of the mound levelled out but there was a gap of barely a hand's breadth betwixt rubble and roof. Perhaps not a roof fall then but an intended barricade, thrown up to prevent pursuit. He scraped away at the stones, enlarging the space, breaking fingernails and gashing palms, wriggling forward an inch at a time. Then he lost his footing and slipped back in a deluge of stones which clattered down around him. He shielded his face but was struck and felt the trickle of hot blood run down his cheek. His hands were sticky with sweat, or that too might be blood.

Back up he went, clawing his way over the top. There was no question of stopping now for the draught was stronger and sweeter, drying the blood and sweat upon his face. And then he was through, tumbling down the far side to land in a heap, his foot caught up in the strap of his scrip. After all that had happened, he would not lose his bag now.

Untangling himself, he clambered to his feet. Bruised and hurting, he had hoped to be rewarded, to see that proverbial blessed light at the end of the tunnel. Instead, there was just more of the same unrelenting darkness. But the draught was nigh a breeze now and he stumbled along, feeling it ruffle his mantle and lift his hair. Was it his imagination or was the wall curving away from him as he hastened towards the scent of fresh air? Or was he so unbalanced on his throbbing hip that he listed like a drunkard in favouring it so? Then he saw it – or thought he saw it – a greyness afar off, a subtle lessening of the dark. It was real: it had to be. Heart hammering, he limped towards the faintest glimmer of light, joyous at seeing salvation. And that was when it happened.

Of a sudden, there was no longer a floor beneath his feet. He stepped into the void. A nothingness as terrifying as the darkness and far more dangerous.

A crimson sea of pain engulfed him. The light, though feeble, pierced his eyes like splinters. His head was pounding like an anvil beneath the blacksmith's hammer. Every bone ached. Seb squinted, trying to see without letting the blades of light strike his eyes. Groping about, he felt stones and gravel beneath him. He lay awkwardly, his body twisted, so he attempted to sit up. It was a mistake.

Lightning flashes of agony lanced through him. His heart was thudding so painfully, each beat was an axe blow. It hurt to draw breath.

Slowly this time, he moved a hand, an arm. That limb seemed to work well enough, though the fingers were sore indeed and the elbow hurt. His other arm, his right, was another matter. It lay bent beneath him, under his back, and he was unable to move it. A leg then. His right leg obliged him, moving a little, but his left seemed weighed down. He made to look, to see what held it and his head was again struck by lightning, so it seemed.

He lay still to recover. So that was it: an injury to his head. A knock. An accident, a mishap had befallen him. But he had no remembrance of it. And where was this place? A cave? A bear-pit? Carefully, one-handed, with his fingers he explored his face, his skull, feeling for damage. He winced, gasping as he found a tender lump above his right ear, sticky and hot. Blood.

Well, it was no use lying here in this cave. Help would not be forthcoming unless he fetched it himself. Inch by inch, oh so gradually, he untangled his limbs and eased into a sitting position. Sweat poured from him. His heart galloped like a racing horse. He had to stop, overcome by nausea. But it passed and he moved again. His right arm, mercifully, was not broken, only quite numb because he had been lying upon it all the while. His left leg too was fairly whole, though the ankle was swollen as a pig's bladder and bound about by the strap of his scrip. Behind him, a stone stairway had crumbled and fallen away but he used it as a prop in an attempt to stand. The walls spun dizzyingly and his ankle gave out beneath him. Oddly, the world seemed jaundiced, a strange yellowish-green light made all the colours wrong somehow. Unable to stand, he would have to crawl.

After what seemed hours, on all fours, sobbing with pain and weakness, pulling his scrip behind him, Seb came out into the wane winter's daylight. He fought his way through brambles and briars, thorns tearing at his clothes and flesh, until he lay exhausted on an open pathway, staring up at a milky grey-green sky. No one came by to aid him. Just a crow perched, cawing on a gatepost. That might be his salvation. Crawling through the icy slush, he dragged himself along, making for the gateway betwixt a hedge and a bare tree. He could do no more.

St Katharine's Hospital by the Tower

'SISTER AGATHA found you', the nun explained, leaning across the bed to pull the sheets straight, 'When she went to sweep away the slush from the gateway afore it froze again. So slippery, it was, we don't want folk to fall, do we? But too late for you, young man. That was quite a fall you must have taken.'

Seb blinked a few times, trying to see the dark shape above him more clearly. It resolved itself eventually into a woman of middle years, swathed in a black habit and pristine wimple but still everything was tinged a yellowish green. What was amiss? Was it the light at fault or his own eyesight?

'Where am I?' he asked.

'St Katharine's, outside the city. Do you not recall?'

'How did I get here?'

'As I said, a lay sister found you lying at our gate. I know no more than that but I doubt you walked here on that ankle. 'Tis severely wrenched, you know, but Sister Charity has bound it up for you. Rest should mend it in a few days. As for that gash upon your head, we are awaiting the surgeon to tend it. It'll need stitching, most like. Ah. Here is Sister Magdalene with your food. I'll leave you in her capable hands.'

Wednesday morn

Crosby Place. The duke's private chamber

'I WAS MUCH in need of that exercise, Francis. Thank you. You worked me hard indeed.' Duke Richard had removed the bassinet that he wore for arms practice. The linen coif beneath was damp with sweat. He unfastened his gauntlets that protected his hands and reached for the towel his squire held out. 'My thanks, Geoffrey,' he said, mopping his face and peeling off the coif. A cascade of dark hair fell in moist tendrils to his shoulders.

'You near broke my damned wrist.' Francis, Lord Lovell, winced, flexing his hand. He pulled back the sleeve of his arming doublet to reveal a bruise already turning purple.

'The way you came at me, what was I to do but defend myself? You played the part of a most formidable opponent. You were not holding back. For a moment I thought you had forgotten we were but practising.'

'You didn't hold back either.' Francis sounded testy. He had lost the bout in the practice yard. Richard had sent his blade flying from his hand and the man himself sprawling in the dirt. Such humiliation was not to be taken lightly.

'You think not? Yet I turned my sword to catch you with the flat of the blade, not the keen edge, else you would have more to bemoan than bruises. Here.' Richard handed Francis a cup of wine before pouring one for himself, the latter judiciously watered, despite the presence of their squires who should have performed the service.

Such behaviour by the duke always annoyed Francis who was ever most conscious of the meaning of rank. Even a baron – soon to be a viscount, as he hoped – did not pour wine for himself, let alone for others.

'My gauntlet came loose. That's your damned fault, Brandon,' Francis yelled at his squire and cuffed him sharply over the ear, 'I could have lost my hand, you accursed bloody fool. What do I keep you for, eh? I ought to send you back to your father, you useless whelp.'

'Did you not check the strap yourself, my friend? In battle, your opponent would have shown no mercy. 'Tis a mistake that could cost you dear.'

'Don't lecture me, Dickon. I was trained as well as you. Of course I bloody checked it.' He hadn't and the oversight rankled.

'I apologise and am heartily sorry for having injured the right hand of my right-hand man. I beg forgiveness.' Richard grinned and held out his hand in a gesture to restore their long-standing friendship but Francis took it warily – in his left hand. 'Yet you do not trust me?'

'I don't trust anybody these days. 'Tis safer thus.'

The two men were, by this time, stripped down to their shirts, their armour removed when the steward came to the door.

'Matthew, I am in disarray, as you can see. Can this wait until I am decent?'

'My apologies, your grace, but a messenger has come from the king.'

'Surely even he can wait until I'm clothed.'

'Indeed, my lord, but… but…'

'But what, Matthew?' The duke was seated on a stool, pulling on his hose, but looked up at the elderly servant hesitating at the door.

'The messenger is wearing a ribbon tied about his arm, sir. A black ribbon.'

Dear God in Heaven. A mourning band.

'Help me with these points, Geoffrey, quickly. Get them tied, lad. Hasten. Fetch my gown; no matter which one.' The duke stepped into his shoes but didn't bother to fasten them, swung his gown about his shoulders and was still organising his attire as he flew down the stairs to the great hall.

The royal messenger fell to his knees before Duke Richard.

'Stand, sir. You have a letter for me?'

The messenger stood up.

'No, your grace, no letter. 'Tis but a verbal message from my Lord Hastings. He thought you ought to be informed.'

'Informed? Of what, sir?' Richard plucked at the black ribbon tied around the man's sleeve. 'For pity's sake tell me who has died?'

'Your brother died in the small hours of this morning, my lord.'

'The king? It cannot be…'

'No, my lord. Your brother of Clarence, at the Tower.'

'He has been executed? Without due warning? No, sir. You must be in error.' Richard groped blindly for the chair of estate upon the dais but found the foot stool instead and sat down heavily.

'There is no error, my lord. I am sorry to be the bearer of such tidings.'

'But why in the middle of the night? Tell me – and I would have the truth, sir – did the headsman make a clean job of it? Did my brother meet a swift end? Please God that he did. Did he have the services of a priest? He did, didn't he? Tell me true.'

'I know not, my lord, but Lord Hastings is as shocked as you. He said the king's grace had not signed the death warrant as yet. It lies still, awaiting his signature. Mayhap, it was not an execution but a death from natural causes? I am but casting in the dark, my lord. In truth, I know no more than I have told you.'

'Aye. My thanks.' Richard stood up, wandered across the dais. 'Someone pay the man,' he said, waving his hand in a vague gesture. 'See he has refreshment.'

Later, Francis found the duke in the privy garden, hatless, no cloak, shoes still unfastened, walking aimlessly along the gravel path, trailing his hand through the colourless winter twigs of lavender and rosemary bushes. He plucked a frost-browned sprig of rosemary and held it to his nose. It had no perfume now it was dead.

'So, George is gone at last.' Francis caught his friend's sleeve. 'I hope that be an end to all this trouble for King Edward. He must be relieved. Are you listening to me?'

'Rosemary for remembrance, aye. He has not seen fit to tell me.'

'Who hasn't?'

'A messenger from Will Hastings but no word from Ned. Does he even know? Perhaps he hasn't yet heard. That must be it. No one has told poor Ned. He will be devastated.'

'What are you rambling about, Dickon? You'll freeze your bollocks off out here without a cloak. Come indoors. I'll send for mulled wine to restore you.' Francis made to lead his friend back inside and he came willingly enough but seemed hardly to know what he was doing or saying.

Back in the solar, Richard sat silent beside the fire, a cup of mulled wine going cold in his hands. Francis had ordered furs to be brought and wrapped about to warm him, the fire to be built to a blaze but his friend seemed not to notice. The sprig of rosemary lay in his lap.

Then the trumpet sounded, summoning the inhabitants of Crosby Place to dinner in the hall. The blast jolted the duke from his reverie and he blinked like a man awakening from a deep sleep.

'Take this away, please,' he said, having realised he was holding a full cup. 'Aid me, Geoffrey, I seem quite entangled here.' Richard was attempting to fight free of the pile of furs swathed about him. 'Was that the call to dinner I heard?'

'It was, my lord.' The young squire pulled the last fur coverlet aside and began folding it neatly.

'The morn has quite flown.' As he made for the door, Richard paused by the oriel window where the artist's easel stood, the portrait resting, cloth-draped, awaiting the next stage of painting. 'Was Master Foxley not coming to continue his work this day?'

'He was, my lord, but there has been no sign of him. And perhaps it is as well?'

'Odd though, Geoffrey. Master Foxley has always proved most reliable.'

'Aye, my lord, he has. Perhaps he is unwell? I could make enquiries, if you wish?'

'Mm. What hour is it, Geoffrey?'

'The dinner hour, sir. Shall we go into the hall?'

The duke wandered from the solar and was about to take his seat at the high table upon the dais when the clatter of hooves and jingle of harness could be heard outside in the courtyard.

'See who that is, Matthew. Ask them to join us at meat, if you will.'

The steward returned within a few moments, a huge smile deepening the creases on his wrinkled old face.

''Tis Sir Robert Percy, my lord, may God bless him.'

'Amen to that. Robert!' The duke hurried outside to greet the new arrival. 'Hold dinner until he be ready,' he ordered.

Francis huffed and groaned inwardly. Bloody Saint Robert Percy. Dickon idolised the wretch as if he were the pope's candidate for canonisation. Still, Rob couldn't have come at a better time. Let *him* deal with Dickon in his half-demented state. *He* could cope with their friend's witless wanderings. Francis had better things to do than coddle the grief-stricken. And if he hadn't, then he'd invent something of pressing importance – an engagement with a juicy whore or a cask of fine wine – at his house in Ivy Lane.

Dinner was a strange affair. Robert Percy noted straightway that Dickon seemed distracted. His platter went ignored; he tied his napkin in knots and asked repeatedly how Joyce Percy was recovering from the loss of their child. Rob had answered fully when first he had arrived two days before, yet Dickon asked again as the next course was served, enquiring as though he hadn't asked nor heard the first time.

'What's amiss with our Dickon, eh, Francis?' the tall Yorkshireman asked when he managed to catch the baron alone for a moment. 'He's not himself.'

'George died.'

'Oh, no. When was this?'

'Last night, so they say. And good riddance say I.'

'You are heartless, Francis. You know how deeply Dickon feels about family, even the black sheep.'

'The world's a better place without George of Clarence and the sooner Dickon comes to see that... How many times did that ungrateful wretch betray his brothers, plotting treason, trying to get his greedy claws into everything that was rightfully Dickon's... even his wife? Dickon should be celebrating, not mourning his passing.'

'You know he won't be doing that. For all his brother's faults, Dickon loves him. Loved him, I should say.'

'Then he's quite mad and belongs in bloody Bedlam with the rest of the insane idiots of London.'

'On Monday, Dickon was telling me that the king wouldn't sign the warrant for George's execution. I suppose he must have misjudged Edward.'

'No. He was right – as always. The king didn't sign. George wasn't executed, apparently.'

'How did he die, then?'

Francis shrugged and sent his squire to fetch his cloak and have his horse saddled.

'Who knows? Broke his damned fool neck? Heart gave out? Who cares? He's gone, thank God. Now. I have business elsewhere, Robert, so I'll leave Dickon and his misery in your capable hands. Farewell.'

The Foxley house, Paternoster Row

'BUT WHERE can he be? There must be places you haven't made enquiries, people still to ask, corners of the city not yet searched.' Emily, pale and dishevelled, mustered her troops in the kitchen. 'Jack, have you made enquiries of all the gate-keepers, like I told you to?'

'I done Ludgate, Newgate, Aldersgate, Cripplegate and Moorgate, like wot yer said. Nobody remembers seein' Master Seb go in or out yesterday nor s'mornin'.'

'What of Bishopsgate, Aldgate and London Bridge? Have you asked there?'

'Weren't time, wos there?' Jack's voice became a childish squeak of indignation of a sudden. He cleared his throat and it returned to a more manly timbre. 'Yer said to be back 'ere at eleven of the clock, so I wos.'

Emily sighed and nodded, feeling the tears threatening again.

'Tom, did you go to Crosby Place as I said? That was where he should be this morn. They might know his whereabouts.'

'I did, mistress, but I couldn't ask anyone. Something's afoot there. Folk creeping about on tip-toe, no one speaking above a whisper and I heard them say the duke was not available to see anybody. They were all wearing mourning bands too...' Tom let the sentence dangle and stared at his boots. Such information would hardly be welcome.

'I see. A-and you, Rose?'

'So far, I have asked at every ale-house, tavern and inn along Cheapside, Poultry and Cornhill as far as St Peter's there. Next, I shall go north, visit such places betwixt St Martin's and Guildhall.' Rose tried to sound hopeful but felt she might as well be searching for a lost halfpenny in the Thames river mud. It was no easy task to describe Master Seb in any way that might single him out from the crowd: young, dark of hair, slim, tallish, plain of dress. Saying he had a slight limp didn't help much either, not when so many folk had worn down shoes, gouty toes or lame legs anyway. 'I know we'll find him, mistress. I'm sure the snow last eve meant he had to find shelter. You know he hates walking out when the ways be slippery. He's safe somewhere, I'm certain, just waiting for the slush to melt afore he makes his way home. Better that than a bad fall.'

'Aye, I suppose. But he could have sent me word. He must know I would worry so. He is so thoughtless... Merciful Mary, if aught has befallen him. Oh, Rose.' Emily buried her face in her apron and Rose hastened to put a comforting arm around her. After a few moments, Emily composed herself. 'You,' she said, turning to Nessie the maid servant, 'Take money, here,' she delved into the purse that hung from her girdle, 'Take this and buy us all a cookshop pie for dinner. I have no time to prepare anything else. Kate, get back to the shop and don't forget to ask every customer that comes by if they have seen Master Seb. Accost them in the street, if they would pass by without coming in.'

The little apprentice – such a sweet lass, bobbed a courtesy and left the kitchen.

'And what of Jude?' Emily asked Rose. 'I might have known he would absent himself the one single time he is needed.'

'He went back to the Tower, as he promised – no sign, though. Now he's gone to see Master Fyssher, the coroner.'

'Working?'

Rose shook her head slowly.

'No.' She reached out and took Emily's hand. 'To make enquiries, just in case...'

'Asking the coroner... about my Seb?' Emily gave a shuddering sob. 'That cannot be.'

'Of course not. 'Tis just a, er, precaution. Come, mistress, let us set the table. Nessie will be back with our dinner soon. Tom, Jack, go wash your hands.'

'I washed 'em this morn, didn't I?' Jack muttered.

'Do as you're told or no dinner. The choice be yours, young Jack,' Rose said, putting on her stern face – which was hard indeed for one so pretty. 'You're not sharing a platter with anyone unless your hands be clean.'

'Don't come clean no more, do they. All that ink wot I bin makin'.'

'Then scrub them.'

'Yer knows it don't bloody come off.'

'Language, Jack. You know master won't have you using such words.'

'Master Jude says stuff all the time, don't he. Wot diff'rence does it make, any'ow?'

Of a sudden, Mistress Emily's broom caught him across the backside.

'Cease your arguing, Jack Tabor, and do as Rose tells you,' Emily cried, her patience at its end. It mattered not that these days the lad was now taller than she by half a head. He wasn't so big that her favoured weapon couldn't still do its task.

'She ain't me master.'

The broom came down harder this time.

'If I didn't need you to make more enquiries this day, I swear, Jack, I'd throw you out on the street to beg your bread as you used to.'

'I ain't never begged in me life, I ain't.'

'I got us a pie, mistress.' Nessie came in from the yard, laden with a cloth-covered basket. 'Eel, cockle and mussel pie, as it's Lent.' She pulled a face. Lent was but two weeks old and already she was tired of fish. And still almost another thirty days to go 'til Easter. She would die of fish-poisoning long before that, she was sure.

Emily nodded.

'Set it down then. No doubt but everyone is hungry. We won't wait upon Jude.'

Jack slunk off to wash his hands as best he could. The ink stains though, were indeed permanent, as he'd said, and would only wear off with time, as every scrivener knew. Why did women have to make such a bloody fuss over clean hands, anyway, he wondered? And now there were two women telling him what to do. Bad enough when it was just Mistress Em but now there was Rose as well. And even a maid as an apprentice in the workshop! Mind you, she wasn't so bad but, in truth, there were too many damned women everywhere. The sooner they got Master Seb back home, the better.

But what if they didn't? What if he never came back? What then? Master Jude would probably be in charge, always cursing him and beating him. He wouldn't stand for that. No. He'd run away, far away. Get on a ship, like Master Gabriel did a year since. No women on a ship. Aye. And maybe he'd find Master Gabe: he always liked him. Well, if he was going to run away, he'd better eat while he still had food put before him, even if that meant he had to scrub his hands raw. So be it.

'You know, mistress,' Nessie said as she dished out the eel mixture onto the platters, 'There's rumours everywhere. In the cookshop they was saying the Duke of Clarence is dead at the Tower.'

'Oh.' Emily had more important matters to think on but the lads were interested – as youngsters often are – in any lurid tale.

''Anged was he?' Jack asked, shovelling eel and shellfish into his mouth.

'Beheaded because he's of noble blood,' Tom said, eager to show off his superior knowledge. 'That's what they do to dukes. They use a great axe to cut through the neck.' He chopped the table with the edge of his hand. 'Bam! Like that.'

Nessie jumped.

'Urgh, that's horrible,' she squealed.

'I bet there was blood flyin' all over, wasn't there?' Jack said, still chewing. For once, they were talking of something interesting instead of business, quill-pens and paper supplies. And the newest matter that was yet more tedious: Mistress Em's babe. 'I seed a fella wiv his brains bust open one time when a cart ran 'im down. Blood an' grey stuff sprayed out.'

'Jack! Enough.' Rose had seen Emily turn pale. 'Do not speak of such things, especially not whilst we're eating.'

'Why not? I wos just sayin' wot 'appened, wosn't I?'

But it was too late. Emily fled out to the yard, a napkin pressed to her mouth.

'Now see what you've done with your vile story. We don't want to know of it. Eat your food in silence, as Master Seb would tell you.' Rose left the table to follow Emily outside, to see if her friend needed her aid.

The eel pie was just a fading memory and a scattering of salt-crust crumbs by the time Jude arrived.

'Dinner is done with,' Emily told him as she folded the napkins and set knives and spoons by the wash bucket. She still looked pale but had otherwise recovered.

Jude shrugged.

'I had dinner with the coroner. Another helping of Fyssh, if you take my meaning. Where is everyone?'

'Where do you think? Scouring the streets, as you should be, if you cared one jot for your brother.'

'That's what I've been doing, you foolish woman. Unlike you: sitting here by your warm fireside, wallowing in self-pity.'

'How dare you say that! Someone has to be here in case he returns. He may have been set upon by thieves, broken his neck in a fall, taken by a seizure, an apoplexy... anything. Believe me, I'd rather be out looking than here, tearing my hair and chewing my nails to the quick. Oh, Jude... brother... what has become of my poor Seb?'

Jude almost reached out to touch her but thought better of such a demonstration of concern.

'Well 'tis unlikely he's dead,' he said, helping himself to ale. 'The coroner had only a couple of corpses to see since yesterday: a beggar woman froze to death and a child kicked in the chest by a mule, so definitely not him in either case. I've been down to Queenhithe and Billingsgate. No human bodies washed up on the last two tides, only a dead cow and a badger from upstream.

Unless he's decided to take holy orders and become a bloody monk, I'm short on ideas of where else to look.'

'Thank you. I am truly grateful to you, Jude. Sorry I was short with you before. I just don't know what's to be done.'

Well. He had never had an apology from Em before, ever. She must be worried indeed. Or mayhap, being with child was making her stony heart a little softer?

CHAPTER EIGHT

Wednesday, after dinner

EMILY SAT on their bed – their marriage bed – running her hands across Seb's pillow. She had cried so many tears, she could weep no more. Remembering how she had once loved him secretly, how she used to slip betwixt his still-warm sheets when she should have been making the beds, those times when he'd been Dame Ellen's lodger, the scent of him upon the linen had made her heart dance. Yet a few years of marriage and her heart danced no longer. She clutched his pillow close and breathed deeply. The scent of him was too faint, or had she grown so used to it, she no longer noticed it? Where had the magic gone?

Her fingers strayed to an amber pendant that hung upon a silken cord, nestled at her breast and worn in secret, hidden beneath her shift, against her heart. It had been another man's gift to her, delivered with a letter from Gabriel Widowson, their one-time journeyman. Seb knew of the warm, golden stone but was unaware that she wore it most days in remembrance of Gabriel. In a sudden flash of guilt, she unfastened the cord and set the pendant aside, vowing she would not wear it again.

Seb. Oh, Seb.

Where was he, that foolish creature? He made her so angry nowadays. Why had he changed so, from a gentle, caring man to an inconsiderate, selfish oaf? His every thought was for his work with not a moment left for her. She did everything expected of a goodwife, tended his needs, the needs of the household, and what did she get in return? Naught, except for a husband who couldn't be bothered to come home when he should, nor even take the trouble to send her word, so she did not fret over him. He just did not care enough even for that, the wretch. If he lay dead in a ditch, then serve him right; she wouldn't waste another solitary tear upon him.

But what if he truly was dead? What then? What would become of them, of her and her unborn child?

Emily fell on her knees beside the bed. Oh, most holy Virgin, she prayed, let not my child be born an orphan, his mother a widow-woman already. Care for my Sebastian and let him come home safe. If it be the Lord's will and he return to me, I swear I'll be a better wife to him. I shan't be shrewish to him but sweet-tempered, even though his constant foolishness makes me angry.

She grabbed a handful of bedsheet to muffle her sobs. I do love him still and want him, Holy Mother, truly I do. I realise that now. Just let him come home... please...

'Mistress Em.' There came a knock at the bedchamber door. 'Mistress Em!'

Amen. Emily ended her silent prayer in haste and made the sign of the cross.

'What is it, Nessie? Can it not wait?'

'No, mistress. There's a visitor. Sir Robert Percy – you remember him – has come to ask why Master Seb never turned up this morn to paint the duke, like he was s'posed to. What shall I tell him?'

'Tell Sir Robert I'll be there directly. Show him into the parlour.' Emily clambered to her feet. What must she look like? Cap awry, apron crumpled, eyes swollen with weeping, tear-stained face: hardly a suitable condition to meet a man of such substance. What would he think? Hurriedly, she did her best, straightening her clothing and rinsing her face in the laver bowl, but there was naught to be done about her red-rimmed eyes. It was too bad. And was the parlour made ready for visitors? She couldn't recall how it had been left after yestereve's distractions and all the comings and goings this morn, with no time for housewifely duties. Was the hearth swept and the fire laid for lighting? Were there fresh candles in the sconce? Had the rugs been beaten, the settle cushions tidied? Oh, sweet Jesu, why did Sir Rob choose this moment to come?

'Sir Robert Percy.' Emily made a deep courtesy, taking the opportunity to cast her eye over the parlour. Fresh kindling had been laid and logs stacked by the hearth, though the candles were but stubs. The rugs didn't look too dusty. Perhaps a man might not notice the faults.

'Mistress Foxley, I trust you are in good health?' the tall knight said, removing his hat and releasing his oh-so-red hair.

'Indeed sir, well enough, I thank you for asking. Will you take ale? We have no wine, I fear.'

Sir Rob laughed. It was a heartening sound.

'I always prefer ale, dear mistress. Like Lord Richard, foreign wine is not so much to my taste as good English ale. But in this case, I will not impose upon your kind hospitality. Crosby Place is in mourning, after news was brought – you have heard of what came to pass at the Tower last eve?'

'Aye, sir, about his Grace of Clarence?'

'Ah. So you know of it. Was that why your husband did not come to continue his work on the portrait this morn? That was most tactful of him.'

'Tactful? Sebastian? No, sir, you are mistaken. My husband never came home last night. He went to the Tower, bearing the king's warrant to make drawings of the Duke of Clarence, and we haven't seen him since. We know not where he is. Young Thomas went over to Crosby Place to make enquiries as to whether my husband was there but all was in turmoil and he found no one to ask. Seb never arrived then?'

'No, mistress. 'Tis most perplexing.' He noticed the young woman's lip quivering, saw the glint of tears in her eyes already puffy with weeping. So that was the reason. 'If I may be so bold as to change my mind, mistress, I would appreciate a drop of ale.' Fetching it would give her a few moments to compose herself. He had to learn more of what had been going on. It occurred to him – a worrying possibility indeed – that Clarence's death and Seb's disappearance might be connected, somehow. Best not to speak of it here with his wife, and she, if he wasn't mistaken, being with child.

By the Church of St Mary-le-Bow

JUDE HAD an urgent matter requiring his attention that Wednesday that had naught to do with searching for an errant brother. And, for once, it wasn't the Panyer Inn, either. He stopped at the priest's house by St Mary-le-Bow and hammered his fist upon the door.

'Thornbury! You mangy mongrel, open this damned door.'

When, at last, the cleric obliged, there had been time enough for Jude's ill-temper to become inflamed.

'Oh, 'tis you,' Thornbury muttered and stood aside so Jude could enter his house.

'You keep me waiting on the doorstep where every bloody rumour-monger can see me and invent some damned scandal about me. I ought to wring your scrawny neck and be done with you.'

Although Jude had told Em he was going to see Coroner Fyssher again – which he had – to ask for another list of bodies found, washed up by the Thames or lying in gutters, that had taken a few moments only. None were Seb, God be thanked, but Jude did have to visit a priest, though not to make his confession nor to post notices about his future union with his beloved Rose, although that did have to do with it.

St Mary's church was lately re-consecrated, having been boarded up for a year, following the murder within its sanctuary of a local goldsmith. The repercussions had but recently played themselves out with the exile of a number of important citizens. Of course, Seb had got himself embroiled in the mess but Jude had never expected to suffer any consequences, until now. With the church closed and, therefore, no income, the priest had had to find some other means of gaining a living. Which he had. And now Jude was paying the price. Or another instalment, at least.

'Don't threaten me, Foxley,' Simon Thornbury said, 'Or the price of my silence will cost you more dearly than at present. Where's the money?'

'Here.' Jude gave a small coin bag to the priest who tipped the contents into the palm of his hand.

'This is not the sum agreed.'

Jude shrugged.

'That's all there is. The dice have been running against me of late and the coroner is tardy in paying my wages.'

'So, gambling to raise the cash hasn't worked for you? There must be other means.'

'You've already had every penny our business can spare!' Jude roared, 'Be content with that. There is no more.'

'The woman demands another fifteen marks as compensation for your breach of promise, else this case goes to the Court of Arches, as it should have done already. You swore to Marriot Clearwater that you would wed her and now you intend matrimony with some harlot...'

Jude backhanded him across the mouth. Thornbury stumbled sideways, dabbing at his split lip.

'How dare you insult my betrothed. Rose is worth fifty of your damned Margaret or Mary, whoever she is. I never promised the bitch anything.' The trouble was, there had been times in the past when he might have been too drunk or so insane as to make a promise of marriage just to get a woman into bed and not remember it. In truth, he had no recollection of this Margaret or Marriot or whatever her name was but that didn't mean he hadn't made this promise to her.

'Now the price goes up, Foxley: twenty marks! And don't think your lame excuses will soften my resolve. Twenty marks by Saturday next or we'll see you in court.'

Two days! Just two days to raise another twenty marks when he had already borrowed five marks upon Friday last and another five yesterday morn from the business. The leather pouch kept in the parlour chimney had weighed perilously light when he returned it to its niche. A good thing Seb only did the Accounts on a Saturday. Of course, he would pay back every penny, eventually, but at some point his little brother was going to notice the missing coins and ask questions – questions Jude neither could nor would want to answer.

But what if Seb was never going to be there to question him? That sorrowful thought brought him back to the even greater matter of urgency: where was Seb? Best make certain the daft idiot hadn't arrived home in the meantime.

The Foxley house

ALMOST AS if he smelled the ale being poured, Jude arrived.

'Any news?' Emily asked, even before introducing Jude to their important visitor.

'The coroner has heard naught of him, so that must be good news. Ale! Thank God: my belly fears my lips have been sewn up.'

'Sir Robert, you may remember my brother-by-marriage, Jude Foxley?' Emily said. Having served ale to the knight, she passed the second cup, hers, to Jude.

'Of course. How could I forget?' Sir Robert set down his cup, untasted, and gave a little bow.

Jude touched his cap and nodded.

'You find us all out of kilter in the workshop, I'm sorry to say, if you wish to buy a book or place an order, sir?' Jude drank down his ale in a few gulps and handed the empty cup to Emily to be refilled.

'That was not my purpose, Master Foxley. I came because Lord Richard wanted assurance that your brother was well, since he didn't come to Crosby Place this morn, as arranged.'

'Oh, I understand. Has Emily told you of my brother going missing?'

'Aye, Mistress Foxley has informed me. This must be a cause of great anxiety for you all. I shall not intrude further upon your time but I will make enquiries concerning your brother, if you permit? It may be that Lord Richard's name and his badge upon my sleeve will open doors and loosen tongues at the Tower of London, he being Constable of England.'

Westminster

'SOMEONE ELSE was there, with Clarence? You imbecile!' Anthony Woodville was quivering so his hands twitched – hands that of their own accord should close around the fellow's neck and choke the breath out of him.

'Forgive me, my lord,' the wretch hissed, 'We couldn't know the duke'd have a vis-sitor, when the king s-said nobody could s-see him.'

'What did I tell you? No witnesses! You should have made an excuse not to leave the barrel as soon as you saw the visitor. Who was it? Steps may have to be taken...'

'I don't know, my lord, never s-seen him before. He was-s doing drawings-s of the duke; a mere artis-san of s-some s-sort.'

'Well, find out his name, damn you! This-this artisan may need to be silenced. It is as well that it was no person of any consequence. Now, you offend my eyes; get out of my sight! And don't return until you know his name. Then I shall determine what must be done – with him and with you, you fool.'

'Trouble, dearest brother?' Queen Elizabeth swept into the chamber. She was alone, Anthony was relieved to see, having dismissed her gaggle of ladies who otherwise trailed in her wake, like minor moons, doing their best to reflect her glorious light.

'Naught of any consequence, Bess.'

'You are certain? I heard the word 'witnesses'. You said there would be none. If our plans founder, Anthony...'

'Fear not, my love. All will be well. Clarence is no more: that is the important thing. We are free of his threats, now.' The earl took the queen in his arms and kissed her. But this was no act of brotherly tenderness. She returned his kiss, eyes closed. 'One day, Edward will be gone too,' Anthony whispered, 'Then we shall be free of all the accursed Plantagenets.'

'Except one.'

'Gloucester? He is naught to us, Bess.'

'You forget: now Clarence is gone, Gloucester could be dangerous. If he ever suspected he is now Edward's rightful heir, though he be ignorant of the fact...'

'And shall remain forever so. Do not worry, my love, my queen.' He kissed her again and, as the softest snow, warming, she melted and surrendered to him.

St Katharine's Hospital by the Tower.

'AS I said last time you asked: Sister Agatha found you by our gateway. Do you not remember?' the nun said, sighing.

Seb shook his head, then winced and gasped at his mistake. Blinding green and yellowish lights flashed before his eyes. Pain seared his skull like hot irons.

'Where is this place, mistress?' he asked when the pain eased a little.

'I told you that also. Do you not listen? And you should address me as 'sister'. Sister Veronica. You are in St Katharine's

Hospital, outside the city. More to the point, young man: who are you?'

'I am… My name is… Sweet Jesu have mercy, I-I cannot say. I do not know.'

'You don't know your own name?' Sister Veronica frowned. 'Or you refuse to own it? Are you a felon running from the law? Because if you are, I shall report you to the Master of St Katharine's. He is Lionel Woodville, younger brother to the queen? He will know how to deal with your sort.'

'Please, Sister Ver-Veronica?' The woman nodded. 'Do not be so quick to confound me. I am no felon… at least, I don't think I am. If I could only remember…'

'Rest. Sleep. That's what you need.'

Another, younger, sister tip-toed into the infirmary. For the first time, Seb noticed other beds, other occupants, snoring, moaning or lying quietly.

'Perhaps this may assist our patient's memory,' the newcomer said, smiling and laying a heavy leather scrip upon the bed.

'Sister Charity, I don't see how this bag of nonsense will help. He needs sleep; naught else.'

''Tis the bag that was in his grasp when he was found. It may remind him. Do you know what is in it?'

Seb wasn't sure if she was asking him or Sister Veronica.

'It's up to you, I suppose,' Sister Veronica muttered and stormed off, not bothered whether her stomping feet roused other patients from needful slumber.

'Does this bag look familiar to you?' Sister Charity asked him. She had kind eyes and a soft smile that reminded him of someone, though he knew not who that might be. What colour were her eyes? Green. But then everything looked green. He fingered the well-scuffed leather and picked at a thread of the stitching. It was in need of repair. At one end, the long shoulder strap was tearing away from the bag. There were smears of mud and other stains.

'I do not remember it. I'm so sorry, but I don't.'

'No apology is needed. Shall we see what is inside?'

Seb forestalled her, putting his hand over the ties that fastened it. A sudden fear that the bulging bag might contain the ill-gotten gains of some nefarious activity, as Sister Veronica had suggested, set his heart pounding like an angry drummer again. Sweat broke out upon his forehead.

The nun nodded and patted his arm.

'Too soon, perhaps.' She took a cloth from a bowl beside his bed and wrung it out before using it to wipe the perspiration from his face. Her touch was gentle, the cloth smelled of rosewater. 'Sister Veronica is correct. You need rest above all. Sleep well, friend.' She plumped his pillow and settled him, removing the bag but leaving the flower-scented cloth to cool his brow.

Seb closed his eyes on the strange green world, wondering what secrets the bag enclosed within. Gold plate and jewellery? No, not so weighty as that. And it rustled rather than clanged like metal. Stolen documents, maybe? Lawyers' property? Church papers? Praying that was not the case, that he was no thief, he drifted off to sleep.

Crosby Place, Bishopsgate

'SEBASTIAN IS missing, you say?' Richard's voice was hoarse with alarm. 'What have I done, Rob? I commissioned him to sketch George for a portrait; naught else. Yet I sent him to the Tower. Can it be a coincidence that he goes missing the same night that George dies? Is there a connection? I fear there must be.'

'Be easy, Dickon. Seb Foxley wouldn't harm a fly, never mind do murder.'

'Did I say he would? You mistake me. I meant if one man dies all untimely in a chamber, then why not another who is with him?'

'You think your brother was killed and whoever slew him might have killed young Foxley also?'

'If he witnessed something untoward, it may be so. How may I ever make recompense to his family for their loss? Why did I ever think to send him upon such a mission, putting his life in jeopardy?'

'Dickon, you couldn't have known George would die that same night. You sent young Foxley with the best intentions. Whatever befell either of them at the Tower, 'tis not your fault. You cannot blame yourself.'

'But I do and ever shall. I sent an innocent man to his –'

'You don't know that. Seb is a resourceful fellow. He is probably hale and hearty as ever.'

'Then where is he, Rob? Why has he not returned home to his wife? Answer me that.'

'I have no answer but I shall find one. Give me a warrant and I'll go to the Tower. I told Jude Foxley your authority as constable could get at the truth where his enquiries earned none. Would you do that, Dickon?'

'Of course, if you believe it will do any good. A writ of mine cannot outweigh one of the king's by any means but I suppose it may be better than naught at all. I have pen and parchment here... I shall do it now.'

The Royal Lyon tavern

THERE HAD been a time when Sir Robert had aided Seb greatly in saving Jude's life, as Jude well knew, but otherwise, their acquaintance had been slight. Seb always spoke highly of the knight and now it was Jude's turn to ask his aid to rescue his brother.

Even armed with Gloucester's warrant, Sir Rob and Jude had learned nothing new at the Tower.

'The lad at the guardhouse seemed honest enough,' the knight said as they sat in the Royal Lyon tavern, sharing ale and information.

'Aye, but I misliked the look of that gaoler: too shifty by half.' Jude scowled over his cup. In truth, since his time in Newgate, he had hated every fellow who owned the office of gaoler, anywhere. 'He would put a knife in your gullet without a moment's pause, seems to me. He could have slit the duke's throat and my brother's. Seb wouldn't put up much of a fight.'

'The official report given out by Anthony Woodville as the King's Coroner a few hours ago says naught of any injury to the duke, no knife wound or other hurt. I read the copy sent to Lord Richard myself.'

'How did he die then?'

'According to Woodville's investigation – such as it was and brief by any measure – Clarence drowned his sorrows in malmsey wine to the extent that his heart was awash and gave out. A peaceful end, he reckoned.'

'And what do you and Lord Richard think of that conclusion?' Jude licked his finger, absent-mindedly, and dipped it in a little heap of crumbs he had brushed together on the board. Having missed dinner, he popped them in his mouth, then regretted it. God alone knew what he'd just swallowed: mouse droppings, other folks' spittings out. Poison. Now that was a fearful thought.

'What can we think? I suppose we have to accept it. There was no evidence of foul play mentioned.' Sir Rob rolled his ale cup betwixt his palms, hoping the drink might improve in flavour if he warmed it.

'Suppose the wine was tainted, poisoned even?' Jude let the question hang, dangling like an unused noose. He watched the knight's expression: first surprise, then doubt.

Sir Rob shoved his cup away. The very suggestion was enough to put him off drinking such a dubious brew.

'I don't know, Master Foxley. Could wine be of such poor quality to prove fatal? I doubt it. Besides, Clarence wouldn't drink any but the best.'

'He'd been imprisoned for months,' Jude pointed out. 'In straitened circumstances a man may not be able to choose. Any wine, however bad, might be better than none.'

'Surely, no man would drink stuff so dreadful that it might kill him?'

'If he was aware it might, I agree. But what if it tasted well enough? Or if it was a wine he had never tasted before, so knew not what flavour to expect? I've no idea what bloody malmsey wine should taste of, so a poisoner could catch me out.'

'You have a point, master. Malmsey was the duke's favourite wine. He drank it all the time. However, it is a very sweet wine with a distinctive taste, such that a taint might go unnoticed. But the report does not mention any likelihood of poison as the cause of death.'

'Just because it's not mentioned doesn't mean it isn't a possibility, does it? I've worked with Master Fyssher, deputy coroner, for long enough to know he gets a first impression, the look of the scene of death, and that's sufficient for him to record, as often as not. He isn't always right. Why, at this present time, me and Seb are looking into the death of Giles Redmaine... or at least we were 'til now. Our suspicions don't matter much anymore, not to me. But none of this helps us find my brother. And this ale is bloody awful.'

'I heartily agree with you there but what next to do in our searching, I don't know.'

'Will Lord Richard's warrant carry any authority in other places? Though I hate to suggest it, if Seb was out after curfew last eve without a torch to light his way, the Watch might have thrown him in some gaol or other, thinking him a ne'er-do-well of some kind. We could make enquiries...'

Sir Robert nodded and pushed back his stool.

'A definite possibility, Master Foxley, if a most unsavoury one. I would suggest we split the task with so many prisons to visit but, since we have but the single warrant, we must go together. Perhaps any gaol that lies betwixt the Tower and your home should be first on our list?'

'Aye, but our time grows short. 'Tis nigh bloody dark already. We'll also need a torch or we may join my brother in prison.'

'In which case, at least we will have found him,' Sir Rob said, grinning.

St Katharine's Hospital by the Tower.

SISTER VERONICA was lighting a few tapers around the infirmary. Supper would soon be served to the five patients there but already the gloom of night was settling over St Katharine's. Seb was feeling better after a good sleep but he kept his eyes shut. Every burning taper wore a weird green halo, like some off-colour saint, and he preferred not to see them so strangely.

'How are you faring? Has your headache improved?' Sister Charity asked him as she held a cup of sweet water for him to sip.

'Much improved, sister, thanks to you and your meadowsweet tisane, although my sight is still peculiar, my heart no longer slams against my ribs like hammer blows every time I move or even breathe deeply.' He took another refreshing sip. 'Tell me, does the light in here seem greenish to you?'

'No. It is the same as ever: just the tapers' glow and the last dregs of winter daylight through the window.'

''Tis not stained glass tinting the light?'

'Bless you, no. St Katharine's is not so wealthy a foundation that the infirmary can be glazed. Oiled parchment fills these windows to keep out the wind and rain but let in the light – what little there is in dreary February. That blow to your head must have nudged your sight askew. I'm sure it will improve.

Now, before Sister Magdalene brings the supper bowls, shall we look into your bag?' Sister Charity giggled like a mischievous child. 'I confess to being most curious as to what is in it. It feels, er, interesting.'

He half expected his heart to start thudding, as it did the last time the nun had made the suggestion but it didn't. He was feeling stronger so, still with grave misgivings, he agreed they should open the bag. It was like teetering on the edge of an abyss, not knowing what might be discovered, whether he would be able to step back. A Pandora's Box containing who knew what.

'Papers,' he said, taking out a handful and spreading them on the bed.

'Drawings,' said Sister Charity, sorting through them. 'Drawings of a man. I wonder who he is? Not you, for certain. A sorry-looking fellow but a good hand drew them, I think. They look very lifelike. Did you draw them?'

'I do not know.' In truth, he didn't care whether he had or no. Relief: that was all that mattered. Naught to incriminate him, God be thanked. Exhausted, he lay back against the pillows but Sister Charity was still looking through the bag.

'All kinds of stuff for doing the drawings,' she said, laying out chalks and charcoal on the bed, unmindful of the marks they made on the pale blanket. 'Ah. What is this? It looks most important. Well, I never! A grand seal indeed.'

Seb heard the crackle of new parchment being unfolded. The sound seemed familiar somehow and reassuring. He sat up, leaning forward and took the document. He squinted at the inky scrawl, frowning to make out the words.

'I cannot see it well enough to read it,' he said, tossing it on the bed.

Thinking he was too embarrassed to admit he didn't know how, Sister Charity offered to read it to him. Her eyebrows rose so high, they near disappeared into her veil.

'This is from the king,' she said in a whisper. 'King Edward himself signed it… a few days ago.'

'Tell me what it says,' Seb said, eager now.

'It says:

From King Edward, this thirteenth day of February in the year of our Lord Jesu 1478 written at our palace of Westminster in the county of Middlesex.
To whom it may concern at our Tower of London, greetings.

Let it be known that one Sebastian Foxley, stationer and artist of Paternoster Row in our said city of London and citizen of the same, in the employ of our brother of Gloucester, bears this, our royal warrant, to the effect that he and none other has been granted, by our royal prerogative and pleasure the space of one hour for the purpose of committing the likeness of our brother of Clarence to paper for the purpose of portraiture and none other. The time and day to be specified herein and none other. To whit Tuesday the seventeenth inst from the hour of Nones one hour only proceeding.
This is our warrant signed and sealed upon the date above aforesaid.

'A royal warrant indeed, well bless me!' Sister Charity crossed herself. 'So tell me: are you this stationer, Sebastian Foxley? Is that your name?'

'I do not know. How can I be sure?' Perhaps the bag wasn't his. He may have come upon it by accident, lost, and meant to return it to this Sebastian fellow, whoever he was, in Paternoster Row. Or worse: he might have stolen it. Was he a common footpad or a clapperdudgeon or some other rogue, robbing innocent passers-by on the road?

'There is a means of finding out,' the nun said.

'How?'

'Let us see if you can draw. If you can, then 'tis likely you are Sebastian Foxley of Paternoster Row.'

'And if I cannot? Then you'll know me for a thief.'

Sister Charity made no comment but found an unmarked sheet of paper in the bag, a wooden drawing board and a piece of red chalk. Then she left him to do what he might to prove he was an artist – or a criminal.

A bowl of pottage was brought to him but it went cold upon the tray. Sister Veronica fussed over the waste of it, chiding him, coaxing him but the pottage remained untouched, as did the pristine paper. When she returned to snuff the tapers and remove the drawing board, the paper was still unmarked.

There was no drawing because he was no artist. Certain of it, he lay down, pulling the blankets over his head so that he could sob in secret, knowing he had stolen another man's possessions and committed who knew what other crimes that could be laid at his door.

CHAPTER NINE

Thursday the nineteenth day of February
St Katharine's Hospital by the Tower

SEB'S BED was closest to the altar at the eastern end of
the infirmary chamber. A priest had just finished intoning
the litany for low mass so quietly that the squabbling sparrows
in the eaves almost drowned his voice, but the religious order
here intended that if your life could not be saved by healthful
treatments, at least your soul would be rescued from Satan's
clutches. Yet the sorrowful face of Christ upon the rood hardly
seemed to promise eternal joy in return for present suffering. Seb
sighed deeply, inhaling an excess of incense smoke that made
him cough. He supposed he should be grateful that it disguised
the reek of sickness, medicinal infusions and boiled cabbage that
otherwise scented the air.

Sister Veronica had berated him for failure to eat his breakfast
bread and now Sister Charity remained unimpressed by his
excuses for having drawn not a single line since last eve. These
nuns were harsh women, Seb decided. Now he sat upon the
hard infirmary bed with the wretched drawing board upon his
lap and a red chalk in his hand, wishing he had never seen the
artist's scrip that now hung from the peg beside the bed, nor its
contents which were certainly not his.

'Just try!' Sister Charity demanded, exasperation carving
lines into her face that might otherwise be comely.

'I am not an artist. Please, let me be.'

'Then who made those fine drawings of the Duke of Clarence, if not you?'

'This fellow, Sebastian Foxley, no doubt, but I do not know him.'

'You vex my patience, young man. Simply move the chalk upon the paper: see what happens. Look. I'll make the first attempt.' Sister Charity took the board and chalk from him and began to draw.

'You waste too much time on him,' Sister Veronica told her. 'The office will begin shortly.' She had hardly said the words when the summoning bell, calling the nuns to church, began to chime.

'Just try, can't you, if only to humour me?' Sister Charity abandoned the board, put an expression of quiet piety upon her face and tucked her hands into the voluminous sleeves of her habit before braving the chill of the cloisters.

'She's a goodly soul, that Sister Charity,' said the ancient fellow in the next bed when the sisters were gone. He had coughed and wheezed half the night, keeping all the patients wakeful but sounded sprightly enough this morn. 'Mind you, young 'un, it don't do to cross her, if you want kindly treatment here. Just do a drawing for her, for all our sakes, else she'll be venting her spleen on everyone. Sister Veronica is sour enough, without Sister Charity adding verjuice to the pottage, if you take my meaning? Draw something, can't you, just to please her?'

Seb sighed and picked up the board. The nun had drawn a bird. At least it was recognisable as such, if a lopsided, tail-heavy creature that could never take to the air might be called so? A sparrow, may be? He saw exactly how it was amiss. The beak too sharp, the neck overlong and the creature seemed to have a waist that might wear a girdle belt, and the tail had too many feathers. He could correct it or redraw it?

Instead, he took the chalk, drew a small circle, four straight lines coming from it, two dots and a short curved line within the circle. A stick figure. He was right: he was no artist and there was an end to it! He threw away the chalk, not caring where it went, dropped the board on the floor with a clatter, wakening the occupant of the bed opposite who cursed him with most unchristian language. His head ached, his ankle was throbbing, the world still looked green and all he wanted was to be left alone.

He must have slept for a while. Upon waking, he saw the board had been tidied away and the scrip was gone from the peg. He should be relieved, he told himself. Relieved, aye. And yet he felt more a sense of loss. He leaned over the edge of the bed to see if it had fallen. After all, the strap was much damaged and could have broken. He cast aside the blanket, noting the red chalk marks of yesterday on the pale wool, and eased his feet to the floor. His ankle was heavily bandaged and he wondered if it would bear his weight. It was painful but they had said it wasn't broken, so what harm could it do? He took a tentative step, testing it. It would serve.

He limped around the infirmary, looking under beds, opening the aumbry where the altar vessels were kept, and searching shelves. It was the task of a few moments only for the infirmary was sparsely furnished and there were few places to look.

The ancient fellow coughed and spat into a basin by his bed.

'If you're wanting that leather bag, a brother took it away, since you said it weren't yours,' he said, still attempting to clear his throat. 'And your drawing proved you're no artist, as you surely told them.'

Seb didn't reply. The walls were beginning to spin and his knees turning to water. Sweating, he groped his way back and fell onto the bed.

The Foxley workshop

MISTRESS EMILY had told Tom to direct Jack and Kate in their appointed tasks in the workshop. She and Master Jude were too concerned with the search for Master Seb to have time to deal with apprentices. As an apprentice of sorts, not an official one, Jack decided there was no reason why he should take kindly to such an arrangement.

'Don't see why you get to tell us wot to do. Yer only a 'prentice after all, ain't that so, Beggar?' The little dog licked Jack's hand to show he agreed.

'But not for much longer,' Tom said. 'Come summer's end, I'll be a journeyman, earning a wage. Then you will have to do as I say, Jack.'

'Only if Master Seb keeps you on. If it wos me, I'd send yer packin', wouldn't I, yer big know-it-all?'

'And I'd kick you out on your skinny backside, Jack Tabor, you useless good-for-nothing jackanapes.'

Jack left his carving of a new book cover and the two lads sized each other up across the workshop.

Kate abandoned the far too easy exercise in letter forms that Tom had set her to do, skipped off her stool and ran into the shop.

'Mistress Rose!' she called, 'Come quick.'

Tom and Jack were ready to go hand to hand. Tom was stocky and strong but, of late, Jack had overtopped him in height and what he lacked in flesh, he made up for in agility and a longer reach.

By the time Rose had bidden a customer 'good day' and come into the workshop, Tom had a bloody nose and a split lip. Jack was cursing and rubbing a kicked shin and Beggar was running in circles like a thing demented, barking.

'Stop this! Both of you,' Rose shouted but, in truth, the fight was already done. 'How dare you behave like ruffians? You ought to know better, especially you, Tom. What would Lord Richard think of you, if he learned of this? He'd bar you from ever visiting Crosby Place again. You want that?'

'He started it,' Tom said. A poor excuse indeed but one common enough in such circumstances. He wiped a trickle of blood from his nose with his sleeve and sniffed loudly. 'He broke my nose, I reckon.'

'Serves yer right for calling us a useless good-for-nothing jackanapes when I ain't no such fing. I work 'ard, don't I, Beggar? Carving wood's not easy, is it?'

'Make your apologies and give each other the kiss of peace,' Rose ordered.

Tom scowled. Jack turned away.

'Now!' Rose folded her arms, waiting, tapping her foot.

'I'm going out to fetch more paper,' Tom said, taking his cloak from the peg behind the door. Rose grabbed him by the back of his jerkin.

'You aren't going anywhere until you and Jack have reconciled,' she said.

'Reckon-wot?' Jack asked.

'Made your peace. Now exchange the kiss... I'm waiting, Tom. Jack, stop looking so sullen. A kiss won't kill either of you.'

A token of peace had never been given more grudgingly nor more insincerely meant since those sworn enemies, Queen Margaret of Anjou and the Duke of York, had exchanged kisses in their grandfathers' days. But Rose was determined this scuffle would not escalate into war as had happened then.

'Now embrace as firm friends,' she told them.

'Wot? Never. Come on, Beg, we've got fings to do.' Jack stalked off, the dog trailing behind him.

'He's an idle good-for-nothing...'

'Tom! Cease your complaints about Jack. He does what's asked of him, as we all do,' Rose said.

'And his carving is beautiful,' Kate added. 'I think he's very clever at it.'

'He's just a damned monkey in a midden – naught but mess and trouble.' Tom grabbed at the nearest thing he might fling across the workshop. Tragically, it happened to be a pot of ink. It hit the wall above the pristine collating table. The pot shattered. Ink rained down, splattering the pages of a finished book awaiting stitching and pooled across the table before dripping on the floor.

Rose, Tom and Kate stared in silence. Black blood. That's what it looked like and just as horrifying. The besmirched pages were Master Seb's most recent exquisite work, the fine illuminated manuscript of the tale of *Sir Gawain and the Green Knight,* ordered as a betrothal gift by a wealthy tailor. Now it was ruined utterly. Rose stood with her hands covering her mouth, as if to lock in a cry of dismay. Kate was sobbing into her apron. Tom seemed turned to stone, not moving, not speaking.

A shriek brought them to their senses. Emily was returned. She had been making enquiries of every acquaintance she could think of who knew Seb, who might have seen him. No one had. And now she came home, frustrated, footsore and exhausted, to be greeted by this scene of disaster.

'Who did this?' she asked, speaking softly to hide the tremor in her voice. 'Who did this? Answer me, someone.' Her voice broke. 'Who has destroyed my husband's beautiful work?'

'I-I never meant to...' Tom looked like a soul facing the Day of Judgement.

'You? Why? Why would you? His best work. Perhaps... his last ever...' Suddenly, Emily flew at Tom, striking him, pummelling him 'til his nose bled afresh. 'You heartless monster, you unforgivable beast.'

'Come, mistress, come to the kitchen.' Rose took hold of Emily, pulling her away from Tom. 'Calm yourself. Think of the babe. You shouldn't upset yourself so.'

'How can I not, after what he's done? Seb's last ever work.'

'Don't think that. Master Seb will come home and do other works just as fine, better even. You'll see.'

'But that's just the case, Rose: nobody has seen him, anywhere. What if he never comes home?'

Kate came through to the kitchen. Her hands were ink-stained as was her apron.

'Mistress Em?'

'What is it, Kate?' Rose asked. 'Can you not see Mistress Em needs to rest quiet a while?'

'Aye, but there's a monk in the shop, asking after the Foxleys. He says it's important.'

'I'll deal with this,' Rose said.

The monk was tall and thin, a nose like a heron's beak. He was leafing through a little book of poetry that was displayed on the counter.

'May I help you, brother?'

'Brother Andrew, mistress, and I'm hoping rather that I may help you. Is this the Foxley household?'

'It is.'

'So you are Mistress Foxley?'

'No, sir. Mistress Foxley is indisposed at present but I live and work here. Rose Glover, sir.'

The brother nodded.

'And would your master be known as Sebastian Foxley?'

'He would, sir. Have you found him? Is he safe?' Rose forgot all formality and etiquette and grabbed the brother's hand. 'Please say you know where he is, I beg you.'

He drew back a little but not too much. Rose's eager, lovely face was hard for any man with blood in his veins to resist.

'Perhaps. But first, I come to return this.'

Rose hadn't noticed until then the battered leather scrip lying on the floor at his feet.

'That's Master Seb's. I'd know it anywhere. Where did you find it?'

'It came to us at St Katharine's Hospital by the Tower. It was brought in with a patient, a man injured.'

'Master Seb! It must be him.'

141

'Well, there lies our difficulty, Mistress Glover. We learned that this bag belonged to Sebastian Foxley, an artist of Paternoster Row, because there is a royal warrant bearing that information within. The Master of the Hospital, the most worthy Father Lionel Woodville, in his kindness and consideration, sent me to return his belongings. But you are saying you know not the whereabouts of Sebastian Foxley?'

'He never came home on Tuesday eve, sir. We are so worried... but is he not the patient you spoke of? If he had the scrip, then surely...'

'You might assume so, yet the man denies that this bag is his. He says he is not an artist, as Master Foxley clearly must be, and the name means naught to him.'

'Then why did he have my master's bag?'

'Perhaps he found it?'

'Master Seb would never leave his scrip. 'Tis as precious as life to him.'

'Stole it, maybe? Snatched it away?'

'Oh, please don't say that. But who is the patient; what is his name? We may know him.'

'He refuses to tell us.'

'What does he look like?'

'Like many a young fellow. Ordinary enough. I wish I could tell you he has some uncommon feature that you might recognise, but he has none.'

'Does he have a slight lameness in his leg?'

'Most certainly. A severely wrenched ankle would make any man lame for a while but it will heal, so I'm told, by those who tend him.'

'Is he dark haired; grey of eye?'

'Mistress, I saw him for a moment only, when I fetched the scrip to bring it here. He was sleeping, muffled in blankets. I know only that his head and ankle have required treatment. Now, I have completed Father Lionel's errand and must return

to St Katharine's before Sext. I bid you good day, Mistress Rose
Glover. I pray you may find your master.'

'Thank you for returning the scrip. Good day to you, Brother
Andrew. Oh. I wonder: could I visit this patient? He may know
something?'

'Close relatives only.'

'But if you don't know who he is, then who's to say I'm not
his sister?'

'Do you have a missing brother?'

'Not that I know of, but you see my point? How will you
learn his name unless someone recognises him? And how can
that come to pass if you allow no visitors? A few minutes are all
I ask, brother. I'll get my cloak.'

While Rose departed, Brother Andrew scratched his tonsure,
deciding he needed the services of a barber – and a confessor.
What a woman! And such admirable logic. She would beguile
a saint into temptation. She'd certainly wound him around her
finger like yarn on a spindle. He ought to leave now, before she
returned with her cloak, but he knew he wouldn't.

St Katharine's Hospital by the Tower

AT FIRST, Rose did not recognise the man in the bed
closest to the altar, his head so swathed in linen bindings,
they concealed much of his face.

'Well, there's a welcome sight for my old eyes,' said the man
with the cough.

Seb looked up and half turned his head to see who had
entered the infirmary, who might be so pleasing to look
upon. Aye, a pretty lass, indeed. He wondered who she had
come to visit.

As he turned, Rose saw the less injured side of his face and
knew him at once, hastening to his bedside.

'Master Seb!' Relief and joy spilled over in tears. 'Thank the holy Virgin that you are safe. Whatever befell you, my dearest master? Mistress Em will be so relieved, as will we all be.'

Seb looked at the lovely woman before him, smiling through her tears. Who was she that called him "dearest master"?'

'Forgive me, mistress. It seems you know me but I fear I know you not. I do not recall your name, if it was ever known to me.'

Rose stopped short, about to take his hand. She stepped back a little.

'But I am Rose, Rose Glover. I work in the shop. I'm betrothed to your brother and am friend to your wife. Surely you remember?'

'He remembers naught, mistress,' Sister Veronica bustled over. 'You should have been warned.'

'You say I have a brother and a wife?' Seb asked. His senses were reeling again. So many questions.

'Aye. Jude and Emily. Then there are the apprentices, Tom, Jack and Kate, and Nessie the serving wench.' Rose frowned, cocking her head to one side. 'Do you not recall anything, master? We have been searching the city for you. You are Sebastian Foxley of Paternoster Row, the best artist and illuminator in London, commissioned by the Duke of Gloucester. You must remember that.'

'No. None of it. You must mistake me for some other. I am no artist. Please, leave me be. I am not the one you seek.'

'You must go,' Sister Veronica ordered. 'You are causing him distress. The surgeon instructed that he must remain calm. Such agitation will undo all our good work.'

'But he is Sebastian Foxley. He must remember something,' Rose insisted. 'Let us take him home. Familiar people and surroundings will remind him, won't they? His memory will return, won't it?'

'Such head wounds are chancy things,' the nun said as she escorted Rose to the gate. 'He may begin to remember gradually or all at once or, perhaps, never. There is no certainty over these matters. We cannot see what hurts have been done inside his skull. Rest and quiet are all that can be advised to aid his recovery.'

'When can we take him home?'

'Sister Charity and the surgeon will decide that, probably depending on whether he is fit to be moved and whether he can be cared for appropriately.'

'Of course he can be cared for. Mistress Emily and I know how to nurse the sick. We can send a cart for him at any time. Master Jude and Jack are strong enough to lift him.'

'Come back tomorrow,' Sister Veronica said and shut the gate.

'Thank you, Sister,' Rose said, speaking to the blank wooden gate with its heavy iron latch as she heard the bolt rattle home in its hasp on the other side.

Rose hastened home, eager to report that she knew Master Seb's whereabouts and that he was safe and cared for. However, by the time she was hopping over the puddles of melted snow in Carter Lane, about to enter the precincts of St Paul's to take the short cut through the transepts, she slowed her pace. Telling Emily that her husband's person had been found was one thing but how could she explain that his memory was still gone astray? How to tell a wife that her husband had quite forgotten her very existence?

On her way through the cathedral, Rose stopped to light a candle for Seb, to pray for his recovery in mind as well as body, and a second to beg aid in breaking the news to Em with the least possible harm to her and the unborn babe.

The Foxley house

HAVING REHEARSED her speech in her head with words as gentle as may be, Rose discovered Emily was not at home. Jude was alone in the kitchen, looking tired, dispirited and dishevelled from hours of searching the streets for his brother. His soaking wet boots lay discarded in the midst of the floor, his cloak in a heap upon the table. Jude was slouched on a stool, half asleep over his ale.

'Em and Nessie have gone a-marketing, so I helped myself to ale,' he said, stifling a yawn. 'The youngsters are in the workshop, though I doubt there's any work being done. I can't be bothered...'

'I found him,' Rose said.

Jude came fully alert and leapt from the stool like a man stung by a wasp.

'What? You found Seb? Where is he? Is he alright? Is he safe? Tell me. Where is the bloody fool so I can wring his stupid neck, causing us so much worry?' He held Rose in such a fearsome grip she had to protest.

'He's at St Katharine's by the Tower. In the infirmary. He was injured but is now quite safe. The sisters are tending him...'

'The imbecile. What has he done? Broke his bloody neck to save me the effort? Oh, Rose, how is he? How did you find him? Have you seen him?'

'Calm yourself, Jude. Drink your ale and I will tell you everything I know – what little that is.' Rose began her tale, shocked to see Jude wiping his eyes occasionally with the back of his hand. She had never seen him weep before.

By the time Emily and Nessie came home and then Sir Robert arrived to see if there was any news, Rose's story was well and thoroughly told in every detail but one.

'There is something I have to tell you about Master Seb. Although his wounds are healing... I know not how to say it...'

'What? I'm his wife. I have the right to know everything.' Emily sounded angry but still Rose hesitated.

'You see... I fear... well, the truth is... Master Seb doesn't remember anything.'

'You mean, he can't recall how he came to be in the infirmary? Well, that's hardly important now. I want him home.'

'No, Em. He can't remember anything at all: his own name, who he is or any of us…'

There were looks of disbelief exchanged around the kitchen.

'Of course he can. That's just Seb being obstinate,' Emily said, wringing her hands in her apron 'til it looked like a dish clout.

'I fear not. I'm sorry, Em. I don't think he's being stubborn. He just doesn't recall. He didn't know me at all. When I mentioned you and Jude, the names meant naught to him. I'm so sorry.'

'He will remember as soon as he sees us. I know he will.'

Rose nodded.

'I hope so.'

'We shall all pray for him at Crosby Place. Lord Richard will insist upon it,' Sir Robert said as he took his leave. 'When Seb is fit to come home, send us word. Lord Richard has a litter kept for his lady's travel. I know he'll be pleased to allow the use of it. It will be more comfortable than a cart on uneven streets.'

'I'm sure Seb will appreciate the honour,' Jude said, a hint of mischief returning to his smile, 'Travelling like some bawdy courtesan will please him mightily.'

Sir Rob gave him a look.

'My apologies, sir, I never meant to imply that the Duchess of Gloucester was anything but a most honourable, noble lady.'

Sir Rob laughed.

'Fear not. My lips be sealed. I have my own opinions on the Lady Anne, not all of them especially charitable.'

Westminster

FATHER LIONEL Woodville bowed low as he was admitted to the presence of the queen, his sister. His eldest brother, Anthony, was there in the bedchamber with her. Lionel was not a party to his siblings' unusual relationship, nor did he want to know. Likewise, though aware that these two dabbled in certain arts, as their mother had, but having ambitions in his chosen career in the Church, he would not involve himself. Nonetheless, he was a Woodville with the same blood in his veins.

'Ah, Lionel, welcome,' the queen said, helping herself to a sweetmeat from a silver dish. 'How are matters at St Mary's?'

'St Katharine's,' he corrected. 'Well enough, your grace, I thank you for your concern.'

'Should we be concerned?' The queen fed another marchpane delicacy to Anthony, as if he was a favoured lapdog.

'No, my lady, except that something strange has occurred at the infirmary.'

'Oh? Do tell. Some noble woman in trouble with a stable lad, is it? Or a monk seduced one of the sisters?'

'Nothing salacious.'

'Mm. Pity. So what is this strange occurrence then, Lionel? We are all ears.'

'It's just that being aware that King Edward forbade any visitors to the late Duke of Clarence – God assoil him – it seems odd that a patient in the infirmary had in his possession a warrant signed by Edward to the effect that he might spend time with the duke and make drawings of him, in preparation for the painting of a portrait. I wondered if you knew of this, my lady?'

'When was this?' the queen asked, her voice giving no hint as to whether she knew of the warrant or not.

'The man was brought in, injured, on Wednesday morn. The warrant stated that he should visit the Tower for one hour upon Tuesday eve. I have it here.' Lionel handed over the parchment bearing the royal seal. 'And since his bag also contained pictures of Clarence, it would seem the warrant had been used as specified.'

'Who knows of this?' Anthony asked, quiet until now.

'Not the man concerned, that I can vouch for. His memory has been obliterated by a serious blow to the head. Apart from that, my secretary, Brother Andrew, and two of the sisters. One of the nuns, a crotchety old biddy who has her uses, will say naught. The other... if I command her silence, will obey.'

'And the man,' Anthony consulted the warrant, 'This... what is his name? This Sebastian Foxley. Is he like to die of his injuries?'

'He seems to be recovering.'

'What of his memory? Will it return?'

'I cannot say, Anthony. I am a priest, not a prophet.'

'It might be as well if he suffered a relapse – permanently,' Anthony said.

Lionel's jaw fell open.

'No. No. I want no part in your schemes! I am a man of God. I will not...'

'Hush, brother,' the queen murmured, 'We ask nothing of you. We are grateful for this, er, intelligence. You may leave us. Go back to your prayers at St Mary's.'

'Katharine's.'

'Wheresoever.' Queen Elizabeth waved her hand in dismissal and Lionel bowed out.

'That husband of mine, the Devil take him, is the most cretinous imbecile. What does he mean by signing this warrant? Is he quite mad?'

'He must be, Bess. Who knows what Clarence may have told this Sebastian Foxley fellow? All our efforts to conceal our secrets may be for naught. What is more, see here, the warrant states the fellow is Gloucester's man. If he tells Gloucester, the outcome doesn't bear thinking upon.'

The queen chewed her thumbnail.

'We have no choice, dearest. Whether Lionel likes it or not, this man must not recover. He must have no opportunity to regain his memory – if indeed, he isn't just playing the part – he must never speak to Gloucester.'

'I agree. Shall you make a waxen image or a potion?'

'No, there is not time for subtlety; the Dark Lord cannot be summoned upon a whim. You must send one of your men first thing on the morrow. Sebastian Foxley must be silenced. Forever.'

Friday the twentieth day of February

The Foxley house

SEB'S ARRIVAL home in an elegant horse-litter drew the neighbours out in numbers. The Panyer Inn was briefly devoid of customers as everyone poured into the street, craning their necks for a better view of the fine personage who was visiting the Foxleys in such style – a countess, at the very least, a status that was swiftly raised to 'duchess' when the Gloucester coat-of-arms was recognised.

Imagine the groan of disappointment when the occupant of the litter was lifted down by Sir Robert Percy and Jude and turned out to be none other than their own Master Seb, bandaged, grubby and obviously bewildered. He was hastily assisted into the shop, out of view without answering a single question posed by the inquisitive on-lookers: where had he been; what had occurred and how come he travelled in such royal fashion? But Seb could not have told them since he was as ignorant as they.

Sir Robert dismissed the grooms who turned the horses around – no easy task in the narrow way but they were skilled in the art – and returned to Crosby Place, as did the knight, having received every assurance that the duke's protégé needed no further aid and lacked no comfort.

Once settled in a cushioned chair in the parlour, beside a good fire, Seb was given over into the hands of the women of the household. His single muddy boot was removed, the other could not be worn over his bandaged ankle, and a padded footstool provided. A fur-lined counterpane was tucked around him and a pillow put behind his head. The finest items had been sent by the duke in an effort to assuage the lord's self-imposed sense of guilt as having caused the artist's predicament, yet Seb had no idea whether the deep carved oak chair or the matching stool or the fur coverlet were usual or not.

'When you're rested, we'll get you to your bed upstairs. You'll be more comfortable there with less to disturb you,' said the woman wearing the concealing cap of a married wife. His wife, he wondered? The man called Jude had mentioned a wife. Or was she Jude's wife, maybe? It was all too confusing: so many people and so many names that meant naught to him. But he remembered Rose, pretty Rose from yesterday. He gave her a weary smile of thanks when she held a cup of ale for him to sip. At least he knew two names: Jude and Rose and he hoped he would learn the others in time. The wife and the plain-faced wench. He closed his eyes and let sleep banish his anxieties for a while.

He was awakened by some activity which involved rolling a great washtub into the parlour. Did the women not wash their linen somewhere other than in this well-appointed chamber? The tub was set upon a sheet spread before the fire and draped with more sheets before a low wooden stool was put in the middle of the tub.

'Ah, you're awake at last,' said the wifely one. 'We're going to bathe you. So much dirt, we cannot have you lying upon clean sheets. How did you get so filthy in an infirmary?'

'I know not, mistress,' Seb said. 'They told me I arrived all muddied indeed. I cannot tell you how.'

'Don't call me, mistress. I am Emily, your wife. You call me Em, mostly. You can remember that much, can't you?'

'Emily. Em. Aye, I'll remember that. Emily.' Seb tested the word on his tongue; the feel of it and the sound of it in his ear.

Was it familiar to him in any way? Emily. He couldn't be sure. So, this woman was his wife. She seemed most efficient but stern, ordering Rose and the younger wench to fetch and carry. The wench came in, struggling with a steaming bucket in each hand. Then a tall, skinny lad brought two more, followed by Rose – pretty Rose – with another and a basket of washcloths, sponges and a collection of stoppered bottles and pots. Under Emily's direction, the bath was prepared. Pleasant flowery scents wafted up as she added rosewater and a few drops of violet oil to the hot water. Violet oil. He recognised the odour and remembered it was good for treating bruises. Was his memory improving? He hoped so. If only his green-tinged eyesight would do the same, although he was becoming used to the women's no-doubt snowy linen head covings, their aprons, even their hands and faces having this strange unworldly hue.

'Come now,' Emily said, 'Let's get you out of these dirty things. We'll have to remove your bindings from your head and foot too, if we're to get you properly scrubbed but we'll be so gentle.' She undid the fastenings on his leather jerkin, then the lacings on his linen shirt. Both were the worse for wear and it would take a deal of work to get them clean and wearable again. Seb sighed, thinking of the bother he was causing these women, the additional efforts. Emily – Em – and Rose eased him out of his clothes. He heard their muffled gasps at the state of him. He glanced down at himself, so bruised, battered and grazed. The bruises were darker now and more extensive than yesterday, when Sister Charity had smeared salve upon them. Em unwound the bindings from his foot, revealing a misshapen ankle blacker than a soul condemned. He winced as it was unsupported.

All three women took his weight as they helped him into the bath and eased him down onto the stool. At first, the hot water was a shock but it soon began to soothe his myriad hurts. They bathed him with soft sponges and wadded up a linen towel to

serve as a pillow, so he might take his ease for a while. He could
have slept. More hot water was poured in.

'I'm going to unbind your head, so we can wash and tend
your face,' Emily told him.

He lay back with his eyes closed so did not see her expression
of horror and dismay at what she found beneath the bandage.
He could not know that his face above his left eye bore purple
bruising like a wine stain upon a tablecloth, nor the gash behind
his ear, though neatly stitched, was stiff with dried gore. 'We
won't wash your hair for fear of disturbing the stitches,' she said,
'But we can tidy you up somewhat.' His face was bathed with
such care he was near unaware of Emily's ministrations. Her
touch was less than the brush of a feather.

Even so, the effort of being bathed had tired him
immeasurably. The women had to summon Jude and the tall lad
to help lift him from the washtub. His mumbled apologies were
waved aside. An entire pot's worth of daisy salve was smeared
upon his cuts and bruises, the bindings were replaced with fresh
linen strips on his ankle, though they left his head unbound,
and he was dressed in clean nether clouts and a warm night
robe. Although Emily had said they would take him to his bed,
he was so exhausted she relented and allowed him to sleep the
afternoon away in Lord Richard's fine chair, sent from Crosby
Place that morning by cart for Seb's ease and comfort.

Seb had said little since his return. A man of few words at the
best of times, he truly wasn't himself and no wonder. Even Jude
had been shocked by his brother's sorry state, worse than he'd
ever seen after a drunken tavern brawl, bar a blade in the ribs.
Seb's only complaint – though it seemed a strange one indeed
– was that everything looked green to him. Refusing to leave
her precious patient, Emily had asked Jude to visit Haldane's
apothecary shop, to buy more salves and to ask whether there
were any eye drops or such as might aid Seb's weird vision.

In the meantime, certain Seb would not be doing the weekly
Accounts come Saturday, Jude had helped himself to another

three marks – that was all there was – from the leather pouch secreted in the parlour chimney even as his brother slept a few feet away. He'd had to be quick. Emily had only left Seb in his charge whilst she made a hasty visit to the privy – something a woman with child had to do more frequently, apparently. Jude couldn't care less but seized the opportunity. It would mean another visit to that thieving priest at St Mary-le-Bow but it was on the way to Haldane's shop. Anything to get out of Thornbury's clutches and marry Rose, at long last.

His purse lighter by that precious three marks and his head still buzzing from the fierce exchange of blasphemies, curses and slanderous words with that wretched priest, Jude arrived at Haldane's shop in Lothbury to find himself standing outside in the street at the end of a lengthy queue of customers. A plump woman with ruddy cheeks, looking in rude good health herself, informed him that there was an epidemic of chesty coughs and cases of quinsy, such that the apothecary was having to brew more potions and physics while they waited.

'I want treatments for neither,' Jude told her, in no mood to linger in the cold, his temper still riled from his meeting with the damned priest. 'Let me through.' His attempts to elbow his way to the front of the line earned him no merit whatever as goodwives and others shoved back at him, telling him to wait his turn like everyone else, though their language was more colourful than the sentiment. Jude even heard a vile term that was new to him – a rare thing for a man who knew such a wide repertoire of tavern slang – but he would remember it for his next unavoidable encounter with Thornbury as it suited the devil well: an incubus. Whatever it meant, Jude was sure it described the man perfectly. Planning his collection of apt phrases for future visits to St Mary's passed the time until he finally entered the shop.

Master Haldane was flushed and sweating, trying to deal with so many customers. It was hard to say who was more frantic: the apothecary or those in need of his medicaments to treat sickly babes, wailing children, ailing spouses and failing ancients. Jude wrinkled his nose at an excess of the usual stinks belonging to such a place, enhanced by so many sweaty, clamouring bodies swathed in wet woollen cloaks.

'Jacquetta!' the apothecary shouted at his daughter, 'Cease swooning over that so-called soul-mate of yours and aid me with these customers, you silly wench. Trade doesn't stop because you're moon-sick over some foolish fellow. Now pay heed.'

'But papa, Will Redmaine promised he would come this day. He says he loves me.'

'Then he has still fewer wits than I gave him credit for but perhaps he has seen sense in not coming. Even if he did, you'd have no time to waste in speech with him. Now fetch me that next distillation of almond oil, it should be ready by now. Come on, move yourself.' Master Haldane clapped impatient hands and shooed the wench out of his way. 'What can I do for you, mistress?' he asked, turning to the next customer who was being vexed by a whining toddler, pulling at her skirts.

'Wait, Nathan, mama is just getting you something to soothe you, now stop it, you'll tear my apron. I'll take some almond oil, as soon as you have it, master. Anything to relieve this son of mine and earn me a respite from his everlasting moaning. Takes after his father, though that man complains whether his throat be inflamed or no.'

'Jacquetta! Get a move on with that oil. Decant it now.'

'I can't. We have no more pots nor bottles nor vials to put it in,' cried a petulant voice from the stillroom beyond a curtain from whence the assorted smells emanated. A scent like marchpane was especially strong and more pleasant than most.

Haldane sighed loudly.

'Then douse a clean cloth with it, let it soak in briefly. That will suffice.' He turned back to the customer. 'That will be one halfpenny. Anoint his neck with it, where the throat is most sore within, as often as need be. If you supply your own pot, I can fill that in the morning.'

The woman shoved a half-coin across the counter, took the almond-smelling rag and departed without a word of thanks.

'Good day to you, mistress. Who's next?'

An old biddy was so busy looking at a shelf of intriguing bits and pieces, from snake-stones to Thor's thunderbolts, Jude pushed past her to the counter.

'Tch! Daughters. What's to be done with them, eh? If only my wife had given me sons, I wouldn't have such troubles. Now how may I help you?' the apothecary asked, turning to Jude. 'If you want something for sore throats or coughs, master, you'll need to bring your own pot now.'

'I'm not certain my father – God rest his soul – would agree with you about daughters.' Jude grinned. 'He had two sons and I'm sure we were troublesome enough, my brother and me. As for stuff for winter ills, I need neither. Daisy salve for cuts and bruises, violet oil and, if there be such a thing, something to remove greenness from the eye.'

'Salve. That will be a halfpenny for this small pot, tuppence for the larger one on the shelf there. Help yourself. Jacquetta! Bring a vial of violet oil. Tuppence also for that. Now, what is it you want? To remove greenness from the eye? I'm sorry, master, but if you are born with green eyes, that is God's will and cannot be altered.'

'No. You mistake my meaning. My brother has taken a blow to the head and now says that everything looks green to him. I wondered if eye drops of some kind might help him.'

'I have never heard of such a symptom following a head injury but my eyebright ointment will certainly aid surer sight, though whether it will remove this greenness, I honestly could not say. I have only read of such a strange occurrence – this greenness – as a symptom of foxglove poisoning but you say your brother suffered a blow to his head, so a case of poison doesn't seem likely.'

'I suppose it's possible,' Jude said, opening his purse and taking out a few coins – a precious few. 'He was in an infirmary, so who knows what evil mixtures they might have forced upon him.'

'There is a way to be certain, master: ask your brother if he has suffered severe heart palpitations. That is how foxglove juice kills. If he was poisoned by such a means, he is fortunate indeed to have survived. But, having done so, I believe the discoloration he sees will fade gradually. The eyebright will help.'

Jude parted with more coins, reluctantly, adding the eyebright ointment to his purchases at the exorbitant cost of a whole groat. Four pence for a miniscule vial of the stuff. At such a price, he hoped it would work.

St Katharine's Hospital by the Tower

THE LIGHT was already fading on this short winter's day when the sisters attended the office of Nones at three of the clock. No one saw the unexpected visitor pass through the Master's privy gate using a key, skirt the Master's house, cross the cloister garth and enter the infirmary. Silent as a serpent, he approached the bed closest to the altar, as instructed. The occupant slept soundly, as did the other patients. He lay upon his back, snoring and wheezing on every breath. A pillow lay unused on the empty bed next to him and the visitor took the pillow and pressed it over the sleeper's face. The patient began to struggle but the visitor was strong and the victim weak. The fight was soon done. The elderly fellow with the cough would disturb nobody's slumbers again. Having replaced the pillow on the vacant bed, the visitor left as quietly as he had come, to return to his lord and report the task accomplished.

Sebastian Foxley, once the possessor of a royal warrant, was a threat no longer.

The Foxley house

WHEN SEB awoke, he felt greatly improved. The bath, though tiring, had proved an excellent restorative. Better yet was the merry smile of the lass who sat upon a stool, watching him as he slept. Her eyes were bright as a bird's.

'How are you feeling, Master Seb? May I fetch you some ale? Mistress Em said I should do whatever I might to make you comfortable. She left me to watch over you whilst she prepares supper.'

Seb eased himself more upright in the chair. The lass leapt to straighten the cushions at his back.

'I'm well enough, lass, and lack for no comfort. I think the king can be no better served than I am. You are all so kind to me, er ... Do not tell me... You must be Kate. Do I have your name aright?'

Kate clapped her hands in delight and laughed.

'You do, Master Seb. Indeed you do. I am Kate, Kate Verney, at your bidding, sir.'

She made a little courtesy, still laughing. 'You remembered.'

Seb did not tell her that Jude had spoken of their young apprentice, Kate, whose sunlit nature cheered everyone. She could be no other than this happy lass.

'Are you content here, Kate?'

'Oh, master, I truly am. You are teaching me so much about how to improve my drawings and how to make beauteous illuminated manuscripts. One day, I hope to be as skilled at artistry as you, master, if I work very hard. The last work you did was so wondrous, far better than anything I've ever seen elsewhere.'

'Was it so?'

'Aye. It is the tale of *Sir Gawain and the Green Knight*. Shall I show it to you?'

Without awaiting reply, Kate bounced out of the parlour but returned swiftly with a few loose pages from a manuscript. 'This is the Green Knight here with his fiendish face and bloody axe. See how his demon's eyes seem to be looking straight at you. You did that, master.'

'I did?'

'Of course. None other could do it so well. This is my favourite miniature.' Kate showed him another page. 'See here, Gawain is riding off on his quest to find the evil knight. The horse is so lively looking, it could nigh leap from the page. I love horses, master. And all the spring flowers here, around the edge. I can almost smell their scent. And the little birds perched on the branch. It's very well done, isn't it, master?'

''Tis rather, er, green.' He wondered if that was true or if it was just his eyesight still at fault.

'Aye, to represent renewal and rebirth, so you said.'

'Did I?'

'You said that was what the story was all about: the death of the old year and the coming of the new, the turning of winter into spring and the circle of the seasons, round and round.'

'I said that?'

'And you sang a song while you painted this. Do you recall it? 'Tis all about the summer. *Summer is a-coming in, loudly sing cuckoo! The seed it grows, the meadow blooms...*' Kate had a lovely voice and Seb found himself joining in:

'*The wood all springs anew. Sing cuckoo!*' It came as a shock to discover not only that he remembered the words but he had a fine voice too. They repeated the song, singing it as a round, one after the other.

Their singing and joyous laughter brought Emily hastening from the kitchen.

'What's to do?' she cried. 'What's amiss? Seb? Are you in pain?'

159

'By heaven, was our singing so bad as that?' he said, still laughing.

'No, but unexpected. What is this?' Emily picked up the manuscript page that lay upon Seb's lap. 'Kate! How dare you show this to Master Seb after what occurred. He is not to be vexed or annoyed in any way. Get you gone afore I fetch my broom to you. And take these with you.'

'Oh, Em, do not be so hard on the lass. She was cheering me, giving me cause to laugh – the best medicine, I warrant. She did no harm. In truth…'

'In truth, she overstepped the bounds of her instructions. She could have undone all my good work so far in restoring you.'

'As I was saying, in truth, far from vexing and annoying me, I believe young Kate has aided my remembrance of things considerably. I am grateful to the lass. Please do not be angry with her.'

'Is your memory truly returning?'

'I've remembered how much I love you, Emily Appleyard.' He drew her towards him and onto his lap. Then he kissed her softly.

'I love you too, my dearest husband.'

Seb's smile grew, little by little, transforming his bruised face: Emily loved him still; that was all that mattered. They kissed again.

'Ah, so, making a swift recovery, are we, little brother?' Jude said, entering the parlour at precisely the wrong moment.

'You always have to spoil everything, don't you, you wretch?' Emily said, flying off Seb's knees as if they were white hot.

'I bring salves and eye ointments, as you demanded of me, your highness,' Jude said, sweeping off his hat and making a ridiculously low bow, such that he near overbalanced.

'Don't you mock me, Jude Foxley. I'm not in the humour for your kind.'

'What kind is that?' he said, sounding all injured innocence.

'You know full well. Now cease your antics and be gone.' Emily began trying to move Jude to the doorway but he evaded her.

'I would speak with my brother. I have thought of things that might shake loose his memory.'

'He has no need of them. His memory has returned without your aid.'

'Is that true, Seb? That's marvellous, indeed, little brother. Do you recall everything? All that happened to you at the Tower? We know you saw the Duke of Clarence because we have the drawings you did of him.'

'I cannot say, Jude. How can I tell what I don't remember?' Seb sighed and frowned. 'I fear I still don't recall the Tower. You mean the Tower of London?'

'Where else? We were there upon Tuesday last. You had the king's warrant to gain entry. I waited for you in a tavern nearby. The Red Lion it was, I think. Oh, no, the Royal Lyon. That was it. You remember now?'

'No. I'm sorry. I do not.' Seb closed his eyes in an attempt to concentrate his efforts but then shook his head. 'Forgive me but I cannot recall it.'

'Leave it, Jude,' Emily said, pulling him aside. 'Have you not eyes to see that you are overtaxing him? Let it be, for pity's sake. Come away. Let your brother rest until supper be ready.'

After taking a fine supper of a white fish pottage flavoured with saffron, served with pickled alexanders – his favourite, so he was reminded – and fresh bread, in the kitchen with everyone else, Seb returned to the comfort of the chair in the parlour. Emily was a fine cook, the food far more tempting than that at St Katharine's, but the effort of eating it and being duly appreciative of all the attention lavished upon him was tiring indeed.

The fire was warm, the cushions welcoming and he soon began to doze, only to be roused by a deal of noise.

'Master, now yer betterer, I need you to tell us if I'm doing this right, don't I? See, I ain't sure this pattern's right. Look.' Jack pushed forward to show Seb a piece of his carving.

'Step aside you. I'm the proper 'prentice. I should be first.' Tom was brandishing a sheet of fine vellum, hardly taking care with the precious piece. 'I've been waiting since Tuesday, master, to ask you how you want this page ruled up. You were going to give me instruction but then you went off to the Tower, so it still isn't done and you said it was urgent.'

'I asked first, you great loon. Get outta me way.' Jack elbowed Tom aside but Tom stuck his foot out, tripping the taller lad so he nigh pitched into the fire. Jack grabbed at the nearest thing to save himself: the arm of the chair but, on the way, he caught the vellum in Tom's hand.

'You useless dog turd, you've torn the vellum now.'

'That wos your fault, you fat arsed roisterer.'

'Enough! I beg you both,' Seb said, holding up his hands as if to ward off an assailant. 'Please. I cannot deal with both at once.' He sighed and ran his hand across his brow, realising his forehead was wet with sweat. 'The morrow will be soon enough…'

'But that's Sunday, master,' Tom said.

'Monday, then.'

'I might want t'work on my book cover afore then, though, won't I?' Jack protested.

'You can't. Not on the Lord's Day,' Tom said, snatching the carved board. 'This is rubbish, anyway.'

'No it ain't, is it, master?'

Before Seb could give any opinion, the lads were exchanging blows and kicks there in the parlour. There was the sound of cloth ripping and Tom overbalanced, falling on top of his master. Only when Seb cried out as an elbow knocked the stitched wound on his head did the squabble cease abruptly.

The lads both apologised to Seb. Jack looked sheepish but Tom seemed more sullen than truly sorry.

'What are you two about?' Emily demanded from the doorway. 'Did I not say that Master Seb wasn't to be disturbed? And what of this?' She held Jack's arm to examine the ragged tear in the sleeve of his shirt. As she looked up into his face, she noticed a speck of blood on his lip. Turning to Tom, she saw the red welt of a blow to his cheek. 'Have you been fighting again?' Em exploded with anger. 'Outside, the pair of you! You're going to feel my broom 'til you can't sit for a month and this night you can sleep in the lean-to. I'll have neither of you under my roof and it's bread and water all next week for both of you. You're not to be trusted, even in your master's presence and he a sick man. I'm surprised the remembrance of what happened the last time you two had a spat wasn't enough to deter you. Now, out!' She shooed them from the parlour. She was still breathing heavily as she straightened Seb's cushions, tucked the coverlet more securely and fussed him generally. 'I'm so sorry they disturbed you. Did they vex you greatly?'

'No, not really. But what did happen that should have deterred them from quarrelling?'

'Naught to concern you now, husband. You need to rest. And I must give them a thorough taste of my broom but I'll do it in the yard so as not to disturb you further.'

'No, Em. They're just being lads. A bit of a squabble. High spirits is all. I shall speak with them upon the morrow concerning their behaviour.'

'And say what? "Don't do it again," in your sternest manner? They don't listen, as you well know. A beating will have more effect and sore backsides be a fine reminder that lasts longer than your few words of reproof, which they'll forget as soon as you cease to speak. Save your breath and let me deal with them my way.'

Seb hated the thought of corporal punishment being used on anyone but criminals but was aware that few folk agreed with him. He felt there was an excess of pain and suffering in this world as it was and couldn't see how inflicting yet more pain could improve anyone's lot in life, or their manners, come to that. But Em seemed determined and he was too weary to argue the case. He hoped she wouldn't be too severe with them.

'Are you truly forcing them to sleep out in the lean-to this night?' Seb asked as he lay abed, waiting as Em disrobed by candlelight. ''Tis far too cold for that, wouldn't you say?'

'It's what they deserve.' She was unpinning her cap, pushing each pin into a little felt cushion to keep it safe.

He watched as she loosed her hair so it tumbled free. It was the colour of autumn leaves: the light brown oak, the golden willow, the coppery shade of beech. It glinted in the candlelight as she combed it out. He reached over and lifted a strand, letting it slip through his fingers like molten moonlight.

'I wouldn't want either of them to fall sick with a chill,' he said, stroking a lock of hair that hung wayward across her pale shoulder.

'Do not concern yourself, husband. You worry over much.' Emily folded her kirtle neatly and set it on the linen chest.

As she moved around the bedchamber, he saw how the candlelight caressed the curves of her luscious breasts, her belly rounding with their unborn child. Holy Church forbade such thoughts during Lent and with a woman already with child but Seb couldn't help what inclinations filled his battered head. Aye, and afflicted his loins.

Emily slipped between the icy sheets with a shiver.

'They're sleeping in their beds, aren't they?' he said. 'You aren't so harsh a mistress as you make out.'

'Aye. I couldn't bear the thought that you'd worry about them all night but I doubt they are sleeping. They're too sore for that.'

'Thank you, Em, for your consideration. I'm grateful indeed. Now, come, let me warm you.' He rolled towards her and drew her close.

'But your injuries… you must lie still and rest.'

'I shall fully comply, afterwards. In the meantime, I promise neither my head wound nor my bruised ankle will put to great effort. Unless a kiss be overwork?'

'Sebastian Foxley, you are an unworthy sinner.'

'I know. Holy Church will despair of me.' He kissed her neck, her shoulder.

Emily sighed.

'We should sin more often,' she whispered.

Hours later, in the depths of the night, Seb awoke, bathed in sweat and gasping for breath. It was dark as Satan's maw and the nightmare wasn't ended. He had been running through such blackness, fleeing for his life. His pursuers were close behind and gaining: he could feel it. He beat his way through echoing silence, unseen walls closing in on all sides. They would kill him if they caught him, he knew. Was he awake or was this a fearful dream? He could run no more, groping like a blind man.

He reached out. Felt fresh laundered linen, then warm soft flesh. Someone sighed and moved beside him. He sighed too, relieved, wiping the sweat away with the edge of the sheet. His breathing steadied. He clasped the work-worn hand in his, lacing his fingers with hers, and drifted back to sleep.

CHAPTER TEN

Saturday the twenty-first day of February
The Foxley shop

THE THIN wintery sunlight just took the edge off the chill as Seb sat by the shop door, watching the world go by. A few yards farther along Paternoster Row, the long shadow cast by St Paul's great spire lay dark upon the shops and houses but here, Seb could close his eyes and feel the sun's warmth softly healing his bruised face. Emily had suggested that he sat out here, swathed in Lord Richard's fur-lined coverlet, reclining like a nobleman in the fine carven chair, and Seb had a feeling she wanted all the neighbours to see the evidence of the duke's high favour by showing off the singular piece of furniture with its velvet cushions.

A cluster of children came clamouring and squealing along the street, playing throw-and-catch with an ox's hefty thigh bone. Seb draw a sharp breath that hissed through his clenched teeth, awaiting the thud and cry of pain as the bone flew towards a little lad's face but the cry did not come. The youngster deftly caught it and flung it back, end over end, laughing. Seb smiled at their joyous antics. Had he ever played such riotous games? He thought not. He could only recall how he'd often watched Jude and others but was never asked to join them. No. With his misshapen shoulder, as it was in those days, his lame leg and need of a staff for support, running and throwing games had never been for him. A sharp memory stabbed him in that moment: some child calling to him, or rather to Jude 'Where's that three-legged, hunchbacked toad of a brother of yours?' Words that had wounded him deeply then and could hurt still.

A horseman rode by on a spirited mount, scattering the children and splashing mud. Seb grabbed up his coverlet in an effort to protect it from the rain of miry filth. What would Lord Richard say if it was ruined? What would Emily have to say upon the matter? But his concern was displaced by delight when he realised the man's cloak, now disappearing into Cheapside, was a true crimson red – not in the least dulled by any tinge of green. His sight was much improved, God be praised for His great mercies.

Emily came to the shop door, bringing him a cup of ale.

'My thanks, Em,' he said, taking the cup in one hand and lifting her apron close to his face with the other.

'What are you about, husband?' she said, pulling it from his grasp and straightening it.

'Your linen is a proper white.'

'Of course it is. I take a deal of trouble to see that it is so.'

'What I mean, Em, is that it looks white to me now. I believe my eyes are becoming better. The light no longer seems greenish to me.' He gazed up at her, looking deep into her dark sapphire eyes – a colour that had captured his heart long ago.

'That is good news, Seb. Soon you'll be able to get back to your work, what with your memory returning and your sight improved. And you have Lord Richard's portrait to complete and the Clarence picture also and plenty more tasks besides.'

Seb sighed at the prospect. The thought of so much work was intimidating. He said naught to Em but one thing that had not returned was the least conviction that he was an artist. He stared at his hands. They bore the ink and pigment stains of the craft but did not look capable of creating the illuminated miniatures Kate had shown him last eve. So detailed and precise; could they really have been done by a pair of hands so ordinary? The only answer was to try, yet still he dared not. As with Sister

Charity at the infirmary, he had this dreadful fear that all the drawings were feigned, that someone else had done them, and somehow folk were mistaking him as the creator of such images. He would be found out for certain as soon as he took up a pen or charcoal. How could he explain his utter failure when they all believed in him?

Jude came and leaned on the jamb of the shop doorway.

'How now, little brother? Taking your ease as usual?'

'Aye. I wish to thank you, Jude. Either the passage of time or the eye ointment you bought are working well. My sight is clearer this morn.'

'It had better be the ointment that's doing you good at that bloody absurd price,' Jude said, waving to one of his tavern-dwelling cronies off to the Panyer Inn even so early. 'And I meant to ask you last eve, but Em wouldn't allow it, about palpitations of the heart. Haldane told me, when I mentioned about your eyes seeing green as a result of that blow to your head, that it was a most unlikely symptom. He said, so far as he knows, only one thing can cause it: the poisonous juices of the foxglove plant. I don't see how you could have been poisoned – unless by some gruesome potion given you at the infirmary – but Haldane said the one definite symptom of foxglove poisoning is severe heart palpitations and 'tis those that kill the victim. So, have you been afflicted thus?'

'I'm not sure. I may have been,' Seb said, racking his brain, trying to remember. It was more like a bad dream – a nightmare – when his heart had beat so violently against his ribs as if it would splinter them and flee and he could hardly draw breath for the pain of it. Had that been real or just the imaginings of an injured mind?

Last night, his sleep had been disturbed by vague horrors aplenty that were difficult to name and impossible to describe. Running through a blackness so intense, pursued by demons that he only knew were chasing him by the echo of their footsteps, pounding behind him, ever closer. He had awakened, sweating and shivering in fear, a half dozen times during the night, disturbing Em from her slumbers. Eventually, he had willed himself to stay awake, to dream no more, yet he had slept again, dreamless, until the dawn. He supposed such an injury was more than likely the cause.

Jude had to step aside to make way for a customer, a well-to-do tailor, to enter the shop, squeezing past Seb's chair. The brothers touched their caps in courteous greeting.

'Ah, good day to you both, Master Sebastian, Master Jude. I've come as we arranged. You said the pages of my 'Gawain' would be completed by the week's end and that I could approve it and discuss a suitable binding for it. I am so eager to see it: a betrothal gift for my godson.'

Seb frowned, thinking.

'Er, aye, sir,' Jude stuttered. 'The 'Gawain' you say? Ah, indeed, well, as you can see, my brother is not able to work at present and, anyhow, I be certain he said *next* week's end for your approval of the work. Did you not, Seb?'

'I truly cannot recall,' Seb admitted, shaking his head which only served to make him wince and did naught to restore any knowledge of such an arrangement.

'Nay, sir. I fear a blow to the head and a spell in the infirmary have quite addled my brother's wits. Whatever he said to you before has quite escaped him. I can but beg pardon on his behalf for your grave disappointment.'

'I would have you know, Foxley, I closed my business early this day so I could get here before you shut shop, just to see how my book is progressing. And now you tell me I mistake the day.' The customer wagged a bony finger perilously close to Jude's face. 'This isn't good enough, such ill-service. I shall inform the guild.'

'No, please. My brother cannot help his misfortune. Your book will be ready for viewing and binding by, er, Wednesday next, shall we say?'

'And I have your word on that?'

'Indeed you do, sir.'

'I shall hold you to that, both of you,' the customer said, glancing at Seb, then back at Jude. 'See to it or the guild master shall hear of your malpractice.'

When the customer had gone, Jude blew out a breath.

'Bloody hell, Seb, you'll have to put this to rights. We can't afford to risk our reputation this way.'

'What did I tell him, in truth? Did I say *this* week's end?'

'Aye, but it can't be helped.'

'The 'Gawain'. Kate showed me some of the pages last eve. Could we not have let him see those, at least? They looked well enough to me.'

'That is but a single gathering from the midst of the book.'

'But most surely, I must have begun at the beginning? What of that and the rest of it? Would I have arranged for him to come this day, if the work was hardly started?'

'So Em hasn't told you.' Jude said, turning away to tidy some little booklets upon the shelf that were neat enough already.

'Told me what?'

'About the manuscript. How it was ruined beyond redemption and needs be done again.'

'No, she said naught of it. What came to pass?'

'Tom and Jack bloody quarrelling is what came to pass. I'm sorry, Seb. A pile of pages was soaked through with ink. There was no saving it by the time I knew of it. Somehow, that one gathering escaped the mess. I know not how you'll redo it all come Wednesday.'

'How much was lost?'

'Seven gatherings: two before the one we rescued were sitting, soaking up the puddle of spilled ink. The five following were doused as the pot shattered, so they said. I would have given those lads a bloody good birching but by the time they confessed, I was more concerned about you going missing. But they've not escaped punishment. Rest assured, I'll get around to it. They well deserve it, the buggers.'

'That won't restore the lost work, though, Jude, will it? Sore backsides will not aid them in ruling up new pages for me. I be certain they've learned their lesson. Em gave them a thrashing last eve for some misdeed and I'm sure that will suffice. They can begin preparing the fresh gatherings after dinner, whilst I construe the Accounts. It is Saturday, is it not? I confuse the days. They shall lose their usual afternoon of freedom. That will be punishment enough.'

'Never mind the bloody Accounts, Seb. I'll do them,' Jude offered. 'Though the takings were few enough this week, what with us all chasing across London, searching for you, since Wednesday.'

'That be most thoughtful, Jude. My thanks for that.' Seb seemed to recall that something was said about them sharing the task of checking the finances each week, when they first took over Matthew Bowen's old business more than two years ago, and that Jude had assisted him with the Accounts – never mind doing them by himself – no more than a handful of times since. 'In that case, I shall spend an hour or two looking over the damaged manuscript. Mayhap something more than a single gathering can be saved. I pray so, for I know not how much can be done afresh in time, otherwise.' He did not add the words 'if at all', but that was his great fear. That he was no longer able to do any work of that kind.

Seb looked up as the sun disappeared. It was not a passing cloud that dimmed the light but the deep shadow cast by the cathedral spire. It would be an hour at least until the low sun reappeared to warm him again, so Seb asked Jude to assist him by taking Lord Richard's chair back to the parlour. As he folded up the coverlet, he noticed a courting couple across the way, arm in arm, laughing and kissing. Was that not – what was his name? Was it William Redmaine? What was he doing on this side of the city?

'Am I remembering it aright, Jude? Is that not the younger Master Redmaine, he that be betrothed to Kate's sister, Alice?'

Jude looked up.

'Aye, and that's not she. I know that wench. She is Jacquetta, Master Haldane's daughter. I saw her yesterday at her father's shop and, if I remember, she was bewailing the non-appearance of that very fellow, calling him her soul-mate, or some such bloody silly nonsense. Oh, well, I wish them good fortune of each other.'

'But what of Alice Verney?'

Jude shrugged.

'What's a few wild oats sown here and there? He's not wed yet, is he?'

'No, I suppose not but it doesn't seem right somehow.'

'You know your trouble, Seb? You're a bloody saint. We can't all be like you.'

Seb was grinning, or as near as maybe with his face so bruised.

'What?' Jude asked, seeing his brother's expression. 'What? Ah! I understand.' Jude laughed aloud. 'So you're not so saintly after all. Well done, little brother. I wonder you could manage it, with so many bruises.' He clapped him on the shoulder. 'Come on, let's see what your Em has contrived to fill our bellies. I'm starving and I'll need all my strength to do combat with those damned Accounts later. And you too must need feeding up after that.'

After dinner, Seb set Jack to preparing sheets of vellum, sizing them with smelly rabbit skin glue – a sticky task indeed the way Jack went about it – and whitening the surface with powdered chalk. Kate was keen to offer her help to Jack but Seb sent her to the kitchen, saying this was not her punishment but the lads'. Tom was to prick and rule up the pages. It was tiresome but had to be done accurately, so no point in asking Jack. Seb looked in dismay at the remains of the 'Gawain' manuscript. So little was left undamaged that to cut out and paste any parts onto fresh vellum was going to be so painstaking and probably result in something worse than a beggar's patched breeches that it was as well to begin anew. If he could.

With the troublesome pair thus engaged, Seb did something he had never done before. With a candle stub, stool and drawing equipment, he secreted himself in the tiny storeroom and shut the door. Privacy was a rare thing but just this once he had to be alone and certain that no one saw what he was doing. He could well imagine the lads would already be exchanging whispered speculations as to what he might be about behind the closed door. Too bad. He could think of no other way.

Having put the candle where it gave the best light without endangering the stacks of paper and rolls of parchment, he made himself comfortable upon the stool, pinned a fresh sheet of paper to the drawing board and selected a piece of charcoal. Then he closed his eyes and waited.

He changed his mind about the charcoal and took up his silver point instead. His head was aching somewhat. Perhaps he should go and ask Emily for some of her meadowsweet remedy. Seb had never been a man who put things off until the morrow yet now... For pity's sake, draw something – anything – he told himself. He returned to the charcoal and drew a hesitant line, not knowing what it was meant to be. He drew another, so forcibly this time that the charcoal snapped. It was no good. He stared at the paper and watched as, one after another, tears dripped and soaked in, spreading, blotching the lines. He turned the board on its side. Now smudged, he could see the lines might almost make the profile of a face. A man's face, wearing a cap at a jaunty angle. It could be Jude, if the nose was better defined, the brow a little less severe.

Within a matter of minutes, the likeness was done and, aye, it was Jude to the life now. The tears came more copiously than ever but this time they were tears of relief. Seb Foxley was most definitely an artist!

Meanwhile, in the parlour, the subject of Seb's drawing was having less success. Jude wondered how he could disguise the lack of coin in the leather pouch when the day book, kept mostly in Rose's neat hand, showed good sales on Monday and Tuesday. He frowned over the numbers. Those two days alone had seen more profits than the few coins remaining. He understood bookkeeping, just about, enough to know that you added up the incomings, then the outgoings and the difference betwixt the two should be the amount of money in the bag. Of course, it wasn't and was never going to be, not when he was borrowing such sums as that bloody devil-damned priest was demanding of him. In the past, he'd occasionally taken a few pence here and there, to tide him over when he lost at dice. But now he was taking out three marks, five marks at a time. It had gone too far. He would have to confess to Seb, tell him about the whole wretched business with Thornbury and the woman whose name he could never remember.

But not yet. Seb's recovery was still in its early days. Best not to tax him with such ill tidings. Best not to worry him with his health somewhat precarious. Aye, better to wait another week at least. Perhaps the priest would drop dead at God's behest and solve all his problems. Perhaps, more likely, the bugger wouldn't. Jude was never a man upon whom Fortune liked to smile, unlike Seb, who had a smile as wide as London Bridge as he came into the parlour.

'Oh, Jude,' he sang out, 'I am that happy, I hardly know how to tell you: I can draw!'

'Whoever said you couldn't?' Jude closed the heavy Accounts ledger in haste and used its bulk to conceal the leather pouch which, conversely, weighed so little. 'I'm not quite finished here.'

'No matter. I just wanted you to know that I can still draw. Look, I've done a sketch of you and I so feared that skill was lost to me.'

Jude took the drawing of himself. His appearance was rather fine, he decided.

'You thought you couldn't draw any longer? Whatever made you believe that, little brother? I've never doubted you.'

'Well, I doubted myself. I had forgotten so much. I could not think that I had done those drawings of the Duke of Clarence I was shown, nor the 'Gawain' miniatures. Or, if I had done them, whether I still knew how? I was that uncertain. Indeed, I admit, I was even scared to try for fear of discovering my talent too was utterly forgotten. I was so afeared, Jude.'

'But now you've proven yourself and need doubt no longer. So, shall we adjourn to the Panyer Inn and celebrate?'

'Shall I help you with the Accounts afore we go?'

'No.' Jude shoved the bookkeeping to one side. 'No, I'll put the coin bag away for safety's sake. I'll finish the construing later.'

'Very well. I'll fetch our mantles...'

Just then, Tom came bounding in, all breathless, arms flailing like pennants in a gale.

'Masters! I caught 'em, masters. The pair of them, behind the pig sty. I saw them!'

'Calm yourself, Tom,' Seb said, taking a hold on the apprentice's arm.

'But I saw what they were doing.'

'You saw whom doing what exactly?' Jude asked, turning swiftly away from the chimney where he had hidden the money bag. He hoped Tom was too distracted to notice that which he ought not to know.

'Jack and Kate. I caught them kissing and... and fumbling behind the pig sty.'

'Bloody hell, Seb, we can't have that going on on the premises – it'll get us a bad name in no time. What are you going to do about it? A damned good beating's deserved, that's for sure. We can't be known for such slack discipline among our bloody 'prentices, can we now?'

Seb's joyous countenance of a few moments since was gone, sooner than a flower touched by frost.

'Shall I tell them you would speak with them, masters?' Tom's face was flushed with anticipation – delight even, relishing the prospect of Jack's punishment.

Seb sighed, his shoulders sagged.

'Aye. I suppose I must speak with them upon the matter.'

'And you'll be strict with them, won't you, brother?' Jude insisted. 'Any birching to be done, I'll oblige, if you're not yet feeling up to it. We can't let the buggers off lightly.'

Jack and Kate came in together. Jack was staring at his boots and refused to look up. Kate seemed overly solemn but met her master's eye.

'Leave us, Tom,' Seb said, closing the parlour door behind him. A gloating witness was not required. 'Sit, both of you: Kate on the settle and you, Jack, on the stool.' Seb took his seat in Duke Richard's grand chair, hoping it might supply some lordly confidence in him. He could sense Jude hovering by his shoulder; the power behind the throne, as the saying went. 'Well, Jack, let's begin with you. I would hear your side of the story.'

'Wotever Tom said we did, it ain't true, is it, Kate?' Jack said, scuffing a muddied boot on the edge of the hearth stone. 'He's tellin' lies.'

Seb held out his hand, signing Kate to remain silent.

'Then you tell me what is true, Jack. Were you and Kate behind the pig sty?'

'S'pose so. Aye. Wot of it? We wosn't doin' nuffin, wos we?' The lad continued to scuff the hearth with his boot and still refused to look up. 'Kate got mud on her shoes. I wos 'elping t'get it off, wosn't I.'

Seb glanced at Kate's footwear. Her shoes looked clean enough though damp from the grass behind the sty. The hem of her gown was also moist as might be expected. Naught was out of place in her dress otherwise – no loosened lacings or unwarranted staining from the wet grass. That was a relief, indeed.

'Is that the case, Kate? Speak truly now.'

'Mostly, Master Seb... except we...'

'Don't say nuffin, Kate!' Jack cried, suddenly raising his eyes to beseech her to keep a still tongue.

'It's too late. Tom's already said...' Kate met her master's gaze. 'We kissed, me and Jack. That's all it was. Just a kiss... to see what it was like. We wondered and wanted to know.'

Seb ran his hand across his brow. Was Kate being truthful? He wanted to believe her. For certain, his headache had returned with a vengeance. He would hear no more of this from choice but dared not leave the matter to Jude who'd take a rod to them both without a moment's hesitation.

'And this was the first time ever?'

'Aye. We've never done it afore, have we, Jack?'

Jack shook his head but didn't speak.

'And you'll promise me you'll never do the like again? Else I shall have to report such behaviour to your father, Kate.'

'Oh, no, master. Please don't tell him. I swear – we both swear, don't we, Jack – we'll never do it again, ever. Please forgive us, Master Seb.'

'Aye. And don't abuse my trust again, either of you.' Seb considered a while, unknowingly rubbing at his temple.

The miscreants waited; so did Jude. Kate was winding her fingers in her curls. Jack chewed at his nether lip 'til he tasted blood, thinking of that far sweeter taste of Kate's soft mouth against his. Jude tapped the back of the wooden chair, impatient to hear the verdict and the sentence. It was a pity Seb was master here with the right to decide, for Jude had no doubt as to what the decision ought to be: a damned good hiding.

Seb spoke at last:

'Tis bread and water for supper for you both, and the same to break your fast on the morrow. And you will each say the Paternoster five times, aloud, at table, to end your frugal meals. Do you understand?'

'Aye, master. Thank you, master,' Kate said.

'Then you may go to the kitchen and help prepare supper. Tell mistress that you won't be eating a proper meal and why.'

When Kate was gone, he turned to Jack. The lad's expression was sour and sullen enough to turn milk.

'I'm hoping you didn't urge Kate to such behaviour, Jack.'

'I never!'

'Whether that be true or not, whoever seized the initiative...'

'The inny wot?'

'Whoever started it, there will be no more of it, you hear me, Jack Tabor? If I learn of any further misbehaviour of this kind, I'll hand you over to Master Jude for chastisement and Kate will be sent home in disgrace. Don't ever give me cause to speak to you upon such a matter again. Go, sweep the workshop: every corner, every cobweb. I want it spotless as Mistress Em's Sunday cap. Now be gone from my sight. You tire me.'

'You let them off too bloody lightly, Seb. I might have known you would.' Jude looked annoyed.

'They know I am greatly displeased. I hurt too much at present to want to cause any hurt to others,' Seb said, lying back in the chair and closing his eyes. 'I couldn't contemplate it. They're so young.'

'Aye, just the age when they most need discipline. You're a fool, Seb. Before you know it, she'll be a slovenly 'green-gown' and he'll be a bloody rake about town. Then where will our good reputation be, eh? In the shit, I tell you.'

'Aye, but they promised me.'

'And you believe all that rubbish about it being the first time ever? Huh. Your head must be more damaged than I thought.'

'Did you never kiss a wench just to discover how it felt?'

''Course I bloody did but I never got caught, did I? Too careful for that. What of you, Seb, who did you first kiss?' Jude sounded playful now, his annoyance abated.

'Nobody 'til Em. She was the first.'

'Nah. Surely not. There must have been someone else afore her. You were what? A score of years in age by then. You tell me you never kissed a wench 'til you were twenty winters old? You tell bigger bloody lies than Jack.'

''Tis true. Who would ever have wanted to kiss a cripple like me, being as I was back then? Nobody. Em was and is my one and only love.'

'My poor, sad little brother,' Jude said, oozing mockery. 'But you made up for the lack ever since, no doubt?'

Seb shrugged. Such matters were a secret he wouldn't share, not even with Jude.

'Perhaps,' was all he said in reply.

Westminster

A NTHONY WOODVILLE felt he was steaming like a boiling pot, so great was his anger.

'You incompetent wretch!' he screamed. 'You killed the wrong man.'

'But my lord, you s-said he was in the bed closest to the altar. That was-s all I knew and I followed your ins-structions. How could I know the fellow was-s gone and the bed used by another?' The man refused to be intimidated by the earl. 'You never s-said what s-sort of man I had to dispose of nor how he looked.'

Anthony fumed silently, knowing the wretch was right. There had been no description of this Sebastian Foxley supplied by Lionel. Most probably, he had never visited the infirmary in person and hadn't thought to ask after Foxley's appearance. No matter: they knew the name. Enquiries could be made.

Later, in her bedchamber, he was forced to admit the failure of his would-be assassin to his sister. At first, Elizabeth said not a word but her eyes were eloquent indeed. Anthony's heart seemed to shrivel within his chest. The queen's gaze could reduce lesser men to quaking idiocy.

'Forgive me, sister. The matter is in hand, you may rest assured.'

'It had better be, Anthony, for all our sakes.' She petted the little dog that lay curled in her lap.

'Foxley will be removed by this time tomorrow. Fear not.'

'And if he speaks with Gloucester in the mean time? What then?'

Anthony shifted from foot to foot, rucking the exquisite carpet.

'I-I'll see that he does not.'

'How? Tell me.' She stood up, casting the dog aside so it fell with a yelp. 'How can you determine that a man you do not know nor recognise does not have privy speech with a duke over whom – above any man in England – we have least control? How can you prevent it? Gloucester is not a lapdog to be commanded like King Edward. If he learns of Clarence's secret – our secret – that is the end for us all.'

'I know, Bess. Foxley will be silenced.'

'See that he is and swiftly.' She sighed. The Woodville temper was ever a fleeting thing. She smiled at her brother. 'Come back later, sweet Anthony, when my ladies are all abed.' She caressed his cheek and he closed his eyes, adoring her touch and covering her beringed fingers with his own.

'My true soul-mate,' he whispered.

The Foxley house

SEB RETIRED early. Weariness had so overwhelmed him, he had eaten even less at supper than Jack and Kate were allowed as their punishment. He slept as soon as his head touched the pillow but not for very long. He awoke with a troubling thought in his head and slowly realised it had been there afore his mishap but lay forgotten for a while. It concerned Em and the babe: a terrible fear that the child would be born all awry and twisted, as he had been, and cause Em to die. Just as he had killed his mother. He felt sick at the possibility and knew he had carried that dreadful concern for a while now, ever since Em had told him she was with child.

He tossed and turned beneath the bedcovers until they were so knotted about him, he had difficulty fighting his way free of them. After Em came to bed and aided him in straightening the sheets and blankets, he drowsed a while only to be afflicted by that same hideous dream of yestereve, where he fled through everlasting blackness, chased by some unknown demon with wickedness in its heart. A demon that desired only his death.

After such a nightmare, Seb could do naught but lay awake, praying for the dawn that was oh so tardy in coming.

CHAPTER ELEVEN

Sunday the twenty-second day of February
St Michael's Church

LOW MASS was done. Seb was not usually among the congregation so early upon the Lord's Day but after a night so troubled and utterly without rest, let alone sleep, he knew something had to be done to ease his concerns for Em. Father Thomas had invited him into the vestry, where it was a little warmer and they could speak privily.

The old priest sighed as he removed his vestments, down to his faded, threadbare cassock. He stood with his rump turned towards the vestry brazier. The cold caused his rheumaticks to flare up and he was not happy, knowing young Sebastian wanted to discuss marital problems. Both men were aware of the perverseness of celibate priests being expected to advise on matters of which they were utterly ignorant – or should be. But Father Thomas would do his best. Who else could Seb ask?

'Take a seat, Sebastian,' Father Thomas said, waving at two stools, 'How is your Emily? You say this concerns her.'

'She is with child.'

The old priest beamed.

'That's wonderful news indeed. Bless her. I'm glad to hear such cheering tidings.'

'But I'm worried for her, Father,' Seb said, half lowering himself onto a stool but then unable to sit still.

'Of course you are, my son. 'Tis only natural.'

'No, Father, I'm not just worried in the usual way of things.' Seb was pacing the few steps the tiny room allowed, screwing his cap in his hands, 'til its blue felt looked like a wrung out dish-clout. 'You know how I used to be, Father: born a cripple with my hunched back and lameness and helplessness...'

'But you are so much better now.' The priest took the stool, though Seb continued to pace.

'But you must understand: birthing my disfigured form killed my mother. Supposing, like red hair or long limbs, such a trait runs in families? Suppose birthing the babe kills my Emily? I could never forgive myself. I love her so and may have condemned her. I couldn't bear it, Father.'

'Now, now, Sebastian, you and Emily have simply fulfilled God's instructions for those who are joined in holy wedlock. All women know the risks involved and, whatever the outcome, it is God's will. Emily understands that.'

'But she doesn't know that I killed my mother. I cannot bring myself to tell her but I feel she ought to be told the whole truth so she can, er, prepare herself for the worst. But I don't know how. Help me, please.' He wiped his eyes on his rumpled cap.

The priest watched him wearing the designs off his tiled floor, anguish radiating like heat from the brazier.

'Sit down, my son, I have something for you. I have come to a difficult decision – one I've been putting off for some years now. Your father left it to my safekeeping before he died, with instructions that I should give it to you, if ever I thought there was a need. I believe the time has come.'

Father Thomas took a heavy old key from his girdle and went to the great parish chest. The well-greased lock opened smoothly and the raising of the lid revealed bundles of papers tied with ribbons, parchment rolls and leather bags of coin, releasing the perfumes of ancient deeds, dust and sanctity. He knelt to delve into the contents, knees creaking. He found what he wanted, then struggled to get up.

'Let me help you.' Seb took the old man's arm, knowing exactly what it was like to have such difficulties.

'Thank you, Sebastian. Now here; this is yours.' He passed Seb a folded paper with a seal of red wax. The hand was so familiar, as was the fox's head on the seal: his father's. Seb's name was inscribed in perfectly formed letters, a fine book-hand. He used his knife to lift off the seal and opened the paper. It read:

Written by me, Mark Armitage, the scrivener
of Foxley in the County of Norfolk, now stationer
and citizen known as Mark Foxley of London, this
nineteenth day of December in the year of Our Lord Jesu
Christ 1473.
To my son Sebastian greetings
I write this upon the day of the twentieth anniversary
of your birth, knowing I shall not live to see you reach
the age of your majority a year hence. Forgive me that
I have never had courage enough to speak to you of these
matters though I should have and tried many times to do
so. I hereby confess to you my great guilt, the black stain
upon my conscience that none, not even the Almighty, can
forgive. But I beg you, nonetheless, to forgive me if you
can find it in your dear heart to do so.
All your life, I let you believe the birthing of your poor
misshapen body killed your mother, the woman I adored
above all things. That was not true. My dearest Agnes
died of childbed fever ten days after you were born. I held
you to blame. I have to tell you, my son, that you were
delivered straight of back and limb as could be wished.
For two months after your mother's death, you were hale
and whole but I hated you as I have never hated anything
before or since. One night, you were wailing, I was weary
and ill temper overcame reason. I threw you down the
stairs to silence you. Forever, I hoped. But you lived,
broken and feeble, damaged beyond mending. Yet, when

*I picked you up, you looked at me, trusting as ever and
I wept for what I had done.
The next day we left our home for the neighbours knew
you were a fine babe and I could not explain the change.
I brought you and Jude here to London to make a new
life. I have spent every day since trying to make it up
to you, caring for your every need, giving you as good a
life as I could. You are the best of sons and I learned to
love you deeply. It was fear of losing the love and trust
you bore me that held my tongue all these years. I am a
coward and can only tell you the truth from my grave.*

*Forgive your loving father his most terrible sin if ever you
may. Pray for me.*

Signed Mark Foxley

Seb awoke from a kind of daze to find he was standing beside
a wide river, its slate-grey waters hastening on their eternal
errand. It had to be the Thames. Yet he had no knowledge of
how he came to be here.

He felt as though his father's hand had reached from beyond
the grave to rip out his soul. Now, bereft; he had nothing left.
He could not feel the icy wind gnawing at his face and hands,
nor the chill dampness seeping into his shoes as he stood on
the muddy bank. His whole life had been mistaken. He had
believed in his father's near-saintly love and devoted care. But it
had been a charade… a lie from beginning to end. It wasn't love
but guilt and remorse that made his father care for him. The
father – the parent he revered – had caused his lameness, the
misshapen shoulder that had been like a hump upon his back.
He couldn't have believed it if the letter had not been penned
in the hand he knew so well.

He watched the seething waters of the Thames on a fast ebb
tide, knowing it only required a few steps forward to let the river

take him. It would not be a sin to endanger his soul, for that was gone already, leaving an empty, suffering husk. He took a pace so the water came over his left foot. Then another. The water lapped softly, caressing his ankles as he stared straight ahead at the colourless sky across Lambeth marshes. It would be an icy embrace but merciful, stopping his eyes, his ears, his breath… his immeasurable hurt.

'Master! Master, can we go home now? I'm cold.'

'What?' Seb staggered back from the water's edge. 'What in God's holy name are you doing here?'

'I follered yer.' Jack was pulling at Seb's mantle.

'I can see that. Now get you home.'

'But I waited for yer.'

'Why?'

''Cause I thought yer might need us, didn't I? Yer looked so worried, master, and then yer comed here. I don't know why. Did yer come t' meet somebody, 'cause they ain't come, if yer did?'

'No.'

Blindly, oblivious, Seb had walked all the way to the old ramshackle buildings of St Mary Rounceval, almost to Queen Eleanor's Cross at Charing. Then, for some reason he couldn't explain, he had turned down the narrow passage of Holy Tree Lane to the riverside. Bewildered, he felt as though wakening from another evil dream. Gulls squabbled over something stinking and unnameable washed up on the mud. The timbers of an ancient wharf were rotting away; collapsing into the river ooze as the tide retreated, leaving soft, sodden splinters of black wood mixed with the slime. Why had he come here? Had the whisper of lapping water in this abandoned place drawn him, enticing him with their quietude? But that was shattered now by the raucous gulls.

'Go home, Jack. I don't want you here.'

'Can't, can I?'

'Please, go away.' Seb glanced at his frozen hands, still clutching the dreadful letter. There was the threat of tears; an ache at the back of his throat. And all the while the sad grey water enticed him.

'Can't,' Jack repeated, 'Don't know the way, do I? 'Less yer show us. Beggar don't know the way neever, do yer lad?'

'That's absurd: it's a straight road back to Ludgate.'

Jack shrugged.

'Ain't never bin here afore; how do I know? Yer'll have t' take us home, master, else we'll get lost, won't we, Beggar?'

'You're not so dull-witted as that.'

Jack grimaced and Seb realised his intentions. No, he was a bright lad, wise beyond his years in some ways.

'I suppose we must go home, then.'

The lad nodded.

'Mistress Em'll be cross. We're that late fer dinner, master. She'll prob'ly box me ears, if she can still reach.' But he sounded quite happy at the prospect.

As they were about to leave the riverside, a barge, resplendent in gold and red livery with noble banners snapping in the sharp breeze that gusted across the water, passed by on the ebb tide, having left Westminster Stairs, no doubt. Something about it cast a light on Seb's muddle of memories that had yet to sort themselves into some kind of meaningful order. He had seen that barge recently but couldn't quite recall when or where. No matter, there was other more pressing knowledge to deal with at present.

He and Jack went back along the Strandway, passing the grand townhouses of bishops and abbots on the riverside and lesser dwellings on the left hand. The odours of stately Sunday dinners wafted on the chill breeze, setting Jack's belly rumbling. He was eager to be home but Seb dawdled.

Once, Jack steered his master out of the path of a galloping horseman: a danger of which Seb was quite unaware until the lad dragged him aside. The thought of having to explain to

Emily made him feel ill. What could a man say when his life had been wrenched in two by the vicious hands of Fate? The folk they passed in Fleet Street, going about their Lord's Day business, had naught in common with him. He was a man apart, a mere observer of a world in which he belonged no more. There was a terrible sense of loss, grieving for a past, none of which was truly as he remembered it. Bereaved. Betrayed by his beloved father.

The Foxley house

IN THE warmth of the kitchen, Emily fussed and scolded him about a dinner spoiled; wet shoes; icy hands and a forlorn demeanour he refused to explain. Even Jack, for once, said naught of where they had been or what had occurred. Not that he knew much to tell, anyway. Emily told Nessie to stuff Seb's wet shoes with straw and set them by the hearth to dry – not too close to the fire or the leather would crack. Seb pushed his dinner aside, untouched. Everyone else, whom Emily had made to await his arrival before the meal was served, did their best with scorched cod and cold dumplings gone hard as pebbles.

With a cry, Emily picked up her plate and threw the food into the fire.

'And don't pretend you can eat this,' she said looking around at everyone. 'It's his fault everything's burned. If I have to spend hours, preparing a meal, just to see it go to waste because he can't take the trouble to come home but would rather skip off upon some fool's errand that takes his fancy.' She jabbed the air across the board with her knife in Seb's direction, her breath quivering. For a moment she waited, expecting him to say something… anything, but he didn't look up, only went on gnawing at his thumb. 'It's all your fault! If I died tomorrow you wouldn't notice.' Sobbing, she turned and fled the kitchen, tears streaming. Her feet pounded up the stairs at a run, then across the floor above their heads and, finally, came the creaking protest of the bed as she flung herself down upon it.

'You've done it this time, little brother,' Jude said, going back to wrestling a bit of vaguely edible fish from the cold cinders of his dinner. 'She'll have you eating humble pie 'til Easter and beyond.'

Seb didn't respond. The uncomfortable silence resumed.

'I'll go to the workshop,' Rose said. 'Come, Kate. You too, Tom and Jack. We can look out the work to be done on the morrow. You coming, Jude?'

Jude abandoned the food and stood up.

'May as well; I'll get no good company here this afternoon.'

'Don't go, Jude, please. We have to talk.' Seb half expected his brother to protest but, surprisingly, he didn't, simply sat down at the board once more.

'You go; I'll come along later,' he said to Rose. 'Nessie. Go tend your mistress and give her company 'til I call you. Come on: get it said, for Christ's sake, little brother.' Jude leaned across the board to pull Seb's hand away from his mouth; his chewed thumb was bleeding. 'You haven't done that for years.' Jude wrapped his discarded dinner napkin around it. Seb hid his hand in his lap, staring at nothing. 'What's amiss? You look like the bloody Grim Reaper on a bad day.' He watched Seb. He would always think of him as his *little* brother, even though they were much of a height these days, since Seb's crooked back had been miraculously straightened. He had never got to the bottom of that 'miracle'. Seb never said much about the day he'd almost died, trapped in a warehouse fire, down by the Steelyard. Jude had been in gaol at the time and, upon his release, had found his brother standing tall, the hump of his misaligned shoulder blade reduced to no more than an unevenness that his jerkin disguised completely, even his limp was hardly noticeable, unless he was cold, tired or unwell. Jude saw lines of devastation scored in Seb's youthful face; suddenly seeming ten years older than his four-and-twenty.

'I spoke with Father Thomas after mass this morn,' Seb said, staring at nothing over Jude's shoulder, unable to look at him, else his courage would fail.

'I know.'

'I told him of my fears for Em… concerning the babe.'

'Why? What do you expect him to do?'

'I don't know. I thought he might pray for her especially, for her safe delivery.'

'You mean, you want another miracle? You've had more than your share already.' Jude hoped Seb might smile at his little jest but he didn't.

'Father Thomas gave me this.' Seb pulled the crumpled letter from inside his jerkin and passed it over.

Jude frowned.

'This is our Pa's hand; I'd know it anywhere. How come the old priest had it?'

'Just read it.'

Jude unfolded the letter and scanned the words, his brows drawing together in an ever deepening scowl. Finally, he put the letter on the board and pushed it towards Seb, so it sat betwixt them, threatening.

'Fuck,' was his only comment.

'Did you know of this?'

'I was less than three years old when you were born. How would I remember that?'

'Our father never said anything to you?'

'Pa told me the same as he told you: that you were born that way. I don't know what you bloody want me to say.'

They both sat silent, alone with their awful thoughts. Eventually, Jude roused himself enough to pour ale for them both, left from dinner. 'At least you won't need to worry so much about Em now.'

'I thought he loved me.' Seb's voice was strained, husky with unshed tears.

'He did.'

'No. It was just his guilty conscience.'

'He says he loves you in the letter.'

'He says he hated me... more than anything before or since.' Seb spoke softly, afraid something fragile might break.

'He changed his mind. He must have loved you, Seb: he treated you so well, cared for you.'

'He wished me dead.' Seb went on staring at some far distant thing, beyond the kitchen wall. He so wanted Jude to reach out, touch him, comfort him, but knew it might knock him from the knife's edge of emotion, so delicately poised.

Instead, Jude removed and refolded the offending epistle, tucking it out of sight in his purse.

'I'm sorry, Seb, so very sorry. I wish there was some way to undo this. That bloody interfering old priest should never have given you this damned letter.'

Seb sat utterly still, brittle as Venice glass, almost afraid to draw breath for fear his composure would shatter.

Jude drank his ale.

'There's naught to be done now, Seb. Pa's dead and buried these three years and more. Nothing has changed, not really. Come now, little brother.' Jude decided blunt common sense was the only solution here. 'Will you tell Em? In truth, I don't see the need now, do you? Pa did his best for you, whatever his opinions of you. You must grant him that much.'

'You defend him?' Seb felt so hurt.

'Aye. He was our father.'

'I wish he'd killed me as he meant to. How can I live with this knowledge?'

'Don't be an ungrateful fool,' Jude lectured him, leaning across the board. 'You have a pretty wife, a child on the way, wealthy patrons and work you love, a roof above you and a full belly,' he said, counting the items off on his fingers. 'What more do you want, eh?' He threw his hands in the air. Seb didn't move, simply stared at him. 'Look at me: what do I have to compare? Living in lodgings, still unwed, a one-time gaol-bird with naught to look forward to but decades of pointless scribbling, 'til I'm too blind to work any longer. I should be the one upset. Not you. You deserve no pity, so stop feeling sorry for yourself.' For reasons he couldn't quite explain, Jude wanted to preserve his father's untarnished reputation, at least with others; saw no reason to destroy his near-saintly image beyond the two of them.

Seb looked at him at last. His eyes were a shock; the hurt within them so deep even Jude could feel it.

'I'm sorry if my words sound brutal, Seb, but you must see reason. Drink your ale,' he said more gently, 'Things will seem better tomorrow. You're at Crosby Place again, aren't you, with your best patron? That will cheer you. I know you like Lord Richard. Two of a bloody kind, the pair of you: little brothers both. You must compare notes,' Jude laughed.

Seb managed a feeble smile.

'Aye.' He sighed, sagging with weariness now the emotion had drain away, like water flowing out of a holed bladder. 'I suppose I must prepare my stuff, get Tom to grind more pigments.'

'There! See? Something for you to mull over, more profitable than wallowing in misery.'

'Which I'm not,' Seb protested, though he dabbed at his eyes one last time with the blood-spotted napkin before dropping it on the board amongst the platters of half-eaten food. He squared his shoulders and breathed deeply. 'I'm alright now. And you're right, Jude: I should be thankful and count my blessings.' Finally, he drank his ale. 'I must go, make my peace with Emily: eat humble pie, as you say. May I have the letter?' Seb paused at the foot of the stairs. Jude handed it back, reluctantly. 'What shall I say to Em?'

Jude shook his head.

'About the letter? Nothing; she doesn't need to know, does she?'

'Not that: how do I persuade her to forgive my lateness and surliness, earlier?'

Jude chuckled.

'She's a woman, not some wicked-eyed, evil-tempered stallion. Treat her gently.'

Seb looked blank.

'For heaven's sake, little brother, go to her, put your arms around her, tell her she's more beautiful than Helen of Troy, kiss her, stroke her hair… you know the rest, surely?'

Seb nodded and went up the stair, taking his time before giving a tentative knock on the chamber door above. No doubt Jude was grinning over his ale, thinking how hopeless with women his little brother was.

A few moments later, Nessie came down to the kitchen, red-eyed and dishevelled – as her mistress, no doubt. She went and sat on her stool by the kitchen fire, turning master's wet shoes to dry the soles.

'Get this board cleared, Nessie,' Jude ordered, keen to forget what had gone before. Give these burnt offerings to the dog, if he'll have them. Then see to supper; we'll all be starved by then.'

The maid obeyed but the expression on her face – never a pretty one – was enough to turn butter rancid in the churn.

Jude found that amusing too. Women! A sudden hefty thump on the floor above sent dust falling from the beams, then came the sound of wood splintering.

'Get out, you spawn of Satan! You second cousin to the Devil!'

'But Em, please…'

'You misbegotten beast!'

Seb came stumbling down the stairs. A woman's shoe swished past his ear and landed on the kitchen floor. Next, the heavy pewter chamber pot hit him in the middle of his back and he would have fallen, if Jude hadn't caught him. The upper door slammed shut as the chamber pot rolled beneath the board, dented.

'I hope that was empty,' Jude said, turning away to retrieve the pot so Seb wouldn't see the laughter in his eyes, his twitching lips that threatened a smile. Seb's face was the image of unfathomable bewilderment. 'Didn't work out quite as you planned, eh?'

'I did exactly as you told me.'

'Ah, well, that's women for you: mysterious beings all; no two the same. You just cannot tell.'

Seb slumped on a stool.

'Don't take it to heart; she didn't mean what she said. They never do.' Jude poured more ale: his solution to most problems. 'Come on, Seb. You look like some green lad, messed up his first fumble with a skirt in a dark alley.'

'Jude!' Seb cocked his head to indicate Nessie, busy chopping a turnip for the pottage pot.

Jude only grinned.

'Nessie knows more of such matters than you do. Isn't that right, Nessie?'

The maid flushed redder than a poppy in a cornfield.

'Don't embarrass her, Jude; don't let's have another woman in tears.' Seb sighed, closing his eyes. 'What should I do now?'

'Do? As I said before: you eat humble pie from now until she forgives you.'

'In my own house?'

'Seb, a man may own a house but his goodwife rules it. Tut, tut, you have so much to learn, little brother. Now, Nessie: how about some bread and honey, eh? My belly's rumbling so loud, I can't hear myself think.'

That afternoon, with naught else to divert his woeful thoughts, Seb set to work on the 'Gawain' Manuscript, even though it was the Lord's Day and Holy Church forbade such activity. He justified it to himself by thinking of it as a medicinal remedy, needful to revive his still foggy memory, and an urgent distraction from the turmoil of feelings that assaulted his heart.

At first sight of the blank sheet of vellum that Tom had ruled up, he hardly knew how to begin. The urge to abandon the commission for ever was most tempting but he resisted.

'Tom, fetch me the exemplar,' he said, arranging his quills and brushes just so. 'I'll need to refer to the passages that are no longer legible on these spoiled gatherings.'

'Sorry, master, but the book isn't here. Remember, you sent it to Master Appleyard to affix a new clasp and make good the metal corners. It was so old and well used. You said you'd finished with it and could spare it to be repaired.'

'No, I don't remember and now I have need of it.' Seb sounded petulant. A rare thing indeed.

'Sorry, master,' Tom repeated.

Jude sat idle at his desk: not for him the sin of working on a Sunday. He was toying with a pair of dice he had lately acquired, their fall supposedly guaranteed. He intended to see how predictable they were.

'I'll go along to Appleyard and fetch the book back, whatever condition it's in,' Jude offered, out of boredom rather than kindness.

'My thanks, for that, brother. I appreciate it. This work being so urgent.'

The afternoon cloud was so thick and dismal that dusk was falling even earlier than it should. Jude pulled his mantle closer about him as a thin drizzle set in. Fortunately, the carpenter's place run by Stephen Appleyard, Emily's father, was just a short walk away, along Cheapside, by the Cross.

When Jude arrived, Stephen had but recently returned from Smithfield where, as Warden-Archer, he organised the weekly archery practice as the law required.

'Didn't see you at the butts this week, Master Jude,' Stephen said as he opened the door. 'That's four weeks in a row you've missed – not that I'm counting but there are those that do.'

'Aye, I know. Matters have been so upturned, what with Seb going missing and one thing after another falling all amiss, I barely remembered to go to church.'

'You'll take ale, master? How is young Sebastian? Recovering, I pray. He gave us quite a scare, going missing like that.'

'I would like ale but no,' Jude said, shaking his head. 'Seb is well enough to work and asked me to fetch the book he sent for repair. 'Tis needed in haste, unexpectedly. I wonder if...'

'Oh, aye. I finished it yesterday. Sit yourself by the fire whilst I get it from the workshop.'

Stephen returned carrying the heavy exemplar book. It consisted of an odd assortment of manuscripts, collected down the years and roughly bound together by Matthew Bowen, their predecessor at the shop in Paternoster Row and coming to them with the business assets as a fine source for copying. Seb had added a few more interesting manuscripts since then, including decent faithful texts of the *Siege of Troy* and *Sir Gawain and the Green Knight*. The book had seen considerable usage over time. Its bindings were fast failing. Hence, the need for repairs.

'Here, master. I hope that meets with your approval.' Stephen held out the great volume, requiring both hands, it was such an unwieldy weight.

'It looks very well,' Jude said. 'And new covers?'

'Aye, well, beneath the fraying leather, the oak had got the worm and was turning to powder, slowly but surely. So I took the liberty of making new ones. No point in putting new metal corners and a strong clasp on wood that was crumbling, was there? These oak boards are of the best quality and far stouter than the old. So many pages need thicker covers to hold them firm.'

'How much do we owe you for your labour and materials?' Jude asked, hoping it wasn't going to cost more than their meagre money pouch could allow.

'By rights, I should charge you at least a groat for the new covers and tuppence-halfpenny for the metal fixings, plus a good half day's work,' Stephen said but seeing the shocked expression upon Jude's face, he added: 'But since you're family and didn't ask for the covers to be replaced, I'll settle for sixpence, all found. How would that be?'

Jude unbuckled his purse and fished about for coins of the appropriate value.

'Fivepence-three-farthings. That's all I have with me. Will that suffice?'

Stephen groaned.

'You drive a hard bargain, master. Remind me to do business with your brother in future, rather than you. He always pays a fair price for my work. With too many customers like you, I'd be destitute within a month, begging my dole of the monks at St Martin's.'

Jude laughed but, in truth, he felt a little guilty. Such fine workmanship was deserving of better payment but they simply didn't have a penny to spare. And their parlous predicament was all his fault.

Out in Cheapside, the drizzle had become a steady fall of rain. Jude turned the brim of his cap down to cover his ears – an awkward accomplishment when both hands were required to hold the book, but he managed by balancing on one leg and using his knee to take the weight briefly while he adjusted his hat one-handed. Then he clutched the volume to his chest beneath his mantle, wriggling his shoulders and leaning forward a little so the woollen cloth fell in folds before him. It would not do to get the new bindings wet, endangering their precious exemplar. Head down against the rain, he returned along Cheapside, passed St Michael's church and into Paternoster Row. The sounds of merry-making behind the door of the Panyer Inn were enticing but he walked on.

'Hey, you!' someone shouted. 'You, Foxs-sley!'

Jude was almost at the door of the house but thinking a friend hailed him – though the voice was unfamiliar – he turned.

The glint of a blade in the half-light was all he saw before it plunged through his mantle, aimed straight at his heart. Jude stumbled back, shouting out as he fell upon the doorstep. His assailant paused just long enough to be certain blood was soaking the cloth around the protruding knife handle before running off, disappearing into the gathering night.

Rose opened the door, having heard his cry.

'Jude?'

'Help me,' he moaned. 'I am stabbed,' he managed to say before swooning at her feet.

Jack and Tom came hastening to assist Rose, lifting Master Jude within doors to safety before Rose sent them out, to hammer upon neighbours' doors, banging at window shutters, yelling to raise the hue-and-cry. Swiftly, the neighbours were on the street with lighted torches, eager to pursue whoever had attacked Jude but it was a hopeless cause. No one had witnessed the assault and even Jude – once revived with a cup of mulled ale – couldn't describe the fellow for he'd seen only the weapon coming at him. Whoever he was, the devil was long gone but the mystery remained: why would anyone try to kill Jude and make no effort to rob him. Though his purse was empty indeed, the thief wasn't to know that.

'It bloody hurts, that's all I know,' Jude complained in answer to Sheriff Colet's questioning. Surgeon Dagvyle was suturing the gouge on Jude's arm where the blade had caught him before being buried deep in the hefty volume so newly recovered. 'What a waste of fivepence-three-farthings,' he moaned, knowing the covers would need replacing – again.

'Forget it, Jude. It matters not a jot,' Seb said. 'I praise Jesu that your injury is no worse. The stout cover proved an excellent shield, else you would have...' He choked upon the words and fell silent. Instead he reached out and patted Jude's good arm.

'Do you have any enemies, Master Foxley? Anyone who might wish you dead?' Colet asked. He was a great hairy bear of a man, a mercer by trade. His appearance meant that as one of the two sheriffs this year, he was certainly a deterrent to would-be criminals but the citizens were swiftly realising that was his only contribution to the office. Like Coroner Fyssher, Sheriff Colet preferred a quiet life.

'No. Nobody,' Jude said. 'Ow! Careful with your bloody stitchery, surgeon.'

The surgeon tutted, the sheriff nodded but Seb frowned. His brother had answered far too swiftly. His reply did not sound overly convincing either – not to Seb's accustomed ear, at least. Jude was not being entirely truthful. Seb dragged forth from the back of his mind some partial memory. The Redmaine brothers. Could they be afraid Jude suspected one of them had killed their father? A possibility. Seb thought it through, uncertain whether he recalled the facts aright or if some aspects of the case might still be missing from his battered memory. By the time he determined to speak of it, the sheriff was gone, back to his fireside on such a wet and miserable eve, and Surgeon Dagvyle had packed away his needle and thread, promising to send the bill upon the morrow, and left.

'What of the Redmaines, Jude?' Seb whispered. There had to be a reason why his brother had not mentioned them.

'Who?'

'Roger and William Redmaine. Might they be concerned about your investigation of them?'

Jude flexed his fingers, making sure the bindings on his forearm weren't too tight. He winced dramatically.

'My poor lambkin,' Rose said, hastening to her man's side. 'Is your pain so great? What may I do to ease it?'

Jude could hardly conceal his grin. He could think of a few things. He had never been a beautiful woman's "lambkin" before and would make the most of it.

'Could your assailant be one of them?' Seb insisted on pursuing the matter.

'No, I'm sure it was neither of them.'

'They may have paid someone else to wield the knife.'

'Forget it. I don't want to think about it anymore. Rose will tend me, won't you, sweetheart?'

'Of course I will, willingly,' she said, kissing his forehead.

That was just as Jude hoped. He sighed long and softly. The pain in his arm seemed much improved of a sudden.

CHAPTER TWELVE

Monday the twenty-third day of February
The Foxley workshop

IT WAS still dark although dawn had broken by now. The rain had continued through the night and the louring clouds prophesied that it might be set in for the day. The little courtyard was awash – no linen could be laundered this day – the puddles lapping at the kitchen step.

Emily cursed the weather, hating the disruption of her ordered domestic tasks, but it couldn't be helped. Another difficulty was Jack and his wretched carving. The wood shavings made such a mess and the dust created could not be allowed in the workshop at this time, where it would adhere to the damp ink, sized parchment and wet pigments of the precious 'Gawain'. On such occasions, the lad was usually sent to do his work out in the yard but in such weather as this, none could be so heartless as to make him sit outside. Even beneath the lean-to, a large puddle would be soaking into his boots as he worked which meant he would have to be in her kitchen, under her feet, in the way and getting wood shavings everywhere. It really was too bad. If only Seb had got around to opening up the unused chamber above the parlour, they would have more space but of course, he hadn't. She had been nagging him for weeks, trying to persuade him that a larger bedchamber would be more commodious when the babe was born. Jack could then do his messy carving in their present, poky bedchamber. No doubt, it would be another job, left to the last minute, as always with any task that didn't involve Seb's precious books and manuscripts.

Rose came scurrying into the kitchen.

'Mistress Em, we have a visitor at the front door. Sir Robert Percy.'

'So early? Something must be amiss. Show him into the parlour.'

'But Jude is still sleeping in the bed we made up for him there.'

'Well, don't bring him into this kitchen when it's in such disarray with piles of dirty linen, unwashed pots, the floor not swept and myself all dishevelled. My cap must look a mess, indeed.'

'I'll take him straight into the shop then, shall I?'

'Aye. I'll serve him ale as soon as I may. And tell Seb to attend him. Nessie! Where are you, you idle wench? But apologise to Sir Robert for there are no wafers. I haven't had the time. Nessie!! Get in here this instant.'

Sir Robert waved aside Rose's apologies.

'I am the one who owes apologies, mistress, for disturbing your household at such an ungodly hour. This is not a social visit: I do not expect to be entertained. I am but a messenger and would speak with Master Sebastian, if I may.'

'I'll fetch him, sir.'

Seb hastened into the shop, flustered. He bowed low.

'Good morrow, Sir Robert. Am I late? Have I misremembered the hour that I should be at Crosby Place?'

'Not at all, Master Seb. Lord Richard sent me with a message to spare you the walk to Bishopsgate on such a filthy morning. He asks that you forgive him this sudden change of plan but my lord has been summoned to Westminster. The king desires that he should be the one making arrangements for the funeral of the Duke of Clarence.'

'Oh, of course. It had slipped my mind, as I fear much else has also, that Lord Richard must be in mourning.'

202

Emily came in with a jug of ale and cups upon a pewter tray. As always, she was neatly arrayed, her linen spotless. Seb smiled: she was always a credit to the Foxley name.

'My thanks, Emily,' he said as she set the tray upon the counter board.

She did not so much as glance at him but made a deep courtesy to Sir Robert before leaving Seb to serve their visitor.

'You wed a fine woman there, master,' the knight commented as Seb handed him a cup of ale.

'I did.'

'And she with child, so I hear?'

'Aye.'

'Well done. I congratulate you.'

'The result is not entirely my work alone.' Seb realised he was feeling much easier in his mind now, concerning Em's impending motherhood. His father's letter, devastating as it was, had allayed one fear at least.

Sir Rob laughed.

'Indeed not. But we men must then leave that most arduous of labours to the womenfolk. I believe Almighty God, in His ultimate wisdom, arranged it thus, knowing we poor sons of Adam would never be up to the task of child-bearing.' He laughed again but Seb was aware that it was more forced than genuine this time and recalled Sir Rob and his lady had but recently lost a longed-for babe. He decided it was best left unmentioned.

'Lord Richard also wished me to ask after your own recovery,' the knight went on, 'And whether you were able to do any sketches of the Duke of Clarence? If your commission was able to progress that far?'

'Thank my lord for his concern. I am much recovered and well enough to resume my work.'

'That is excellent news. We both feared you would take time to mend.'

'As for the sketches… I was bringing them to Crosby Place, to show Lord Richard and know of his approval of them afore I begin the portrait – if he wants it still?'

'Now more than ever, master. But I would also enquire – though not at my lord's bidding – how fared Duke George that day? If I may give Richard some crumb of comfort by telling him his brother was in good spirits, that he was well? Is that how it was?'

'I cannot say he was…'

'I understand and little wonder if he was in a bad way.'

'No, you misunderstand me. In truth, I cannot make report upon the duke's condition, whether good or bad. I fear, Sir Robert, I have no recollection whatever of meeting with his Grace of Clarence.'

'None?'

'None at all. I only know I must have done so because I have the drawings I made of him. I suppose they must be of him and not some other? I hadn't thought of that possibility 'til now.'

'If you will show me, I may judge them?'

Seb watched as Sir Robert examined the drawings in silence. Perhaps they were so unlike the duke as to be beyond comment. Maybe the subject wasn't the duke at all but some other unfortunate fellow. Somehow, Seb felt so far removed from what was supposedly his workmanship, he wasn't sure it would bother him if the knight said they were unrecognisable as Lord Richard's brother. He couldn't recall that he'd yet been paid for this second portrait, so no coin need be returned. The sketches could go onto the fire and be forgotten. They meant naught to him but the cost of the paper.

'Aye, for certain, Master Seb, you've caught a good likeness, as you always do,' Sir Rob said after much deliberation, drinking the last of his ale. 'Though it pains me to see how thin and wretched the duke had become. I fear these will deeply distress Lord Richard. I dare ask: could you alter them a little? Some subtle fullness in the cheeks would help, less harshness in the lines around the mouth, the look of despair in those eyes?'

'Perhaps.'

'I know both you and my lord prefer honesty and a true likeness in such things but it would spare Richard so much hurt if he sees but a gentler version of these drawings.'

'Aye, I'll do what I can but it may mean the subject becomes less like himself. You see, I don't remember how he looked in person. I only have these to work with and I might, in altering them, change the very essence of the subject. It may no longer look like him in some vital way; the integrity of the image becomes lost. Lord Richard could notice that, even if we cannot who knew the duke less well. Have I explained it clearly to you?'

'You have, but I would take the risk rather than add to my lord's sorrow at this sad time. I am relieved that I was able to see these before you showed them to him.'

'Very well, if you be sure.'

'I am and most grateful to you. I will bring word when Lord Richard has the leisure to see you at Crosby Place again. By week's end, hopefully. Good day to you, Master Seb, and my felicitations to your lovely wife.'

Seb bowed him out and closed the door on the relentless falling rain. It was not yet eight of the clock and he felt weary as though he'd done a day's labour already. And now there was yet more work to be redone. As if the 'Gawain' manuscript wasn't enough to fill the days, he now had to redraw the sketches to please Sir Robert. Integrity? Aye, well, perhaps that wasn't so important as Lord Richard's peace of mind.

'Made a sale so early, little brother?' Jude asked, wandering into the shop, yawning and stretching. His rumpled clothes with lacings and fastenings all hanging undone were evidence of a man who'd slept without undressing last night.

'No. That was Sir Robert, come to say I'm not needed at Bishopsgate after all,' Seb said as Emily followed Jude into the shop and began putting the ale cups on the tray.

'Good news. So you can spend the day with the evil Green Knight instead. That should please you. Got any ale left in that jug, Em?'

'Not when I have done and completed it once already, only to have my efforts ruined,' Seb said.

'And to answer your question: no, Jude, you'll get ale at breakfast, as will everyone else,' Emily said, elbowing him aside.

'Oh. Like that, is it? You had another argument, Seb, with Mistress Moody Mare, have you?'

'How dare you call me such names in my own house? I ought to fetch my broom to you, you insolent rascal.'

'Now, now. Please.' Seb stood betwixt his wife and his brother. 'No more of this, I beg you both.'

They ignored him.

'Well, don't take your ill humour out on me, mistress: I'm wounded, remember.' Jude held up his bandaged arm like a token of victory.

'Aye, but I'll wager it won't stop you raising a drink to your mouth at the Panyer Inn later, will it?'

'Fortunately, it's my left arm. My ale-quaffing hand is quite undamaged. See?'

'Good. So there be no reason why you can't help my husband with the 'Gawain' text, is there? He'll never get it finished by Wednesday if he has to pen the words as well as paint the miniatures. He says nine out of the dozen gatherings were damaged beyond saving.'

'Tut. I don't know about that, Em. I should need to copy from the exemplar and that great rent in the pages would so remind me of my brush with death, with the assassin's knife... why, I fear I might well swoon.' Jude put his good hand to his brow and feigned a sigh.

'Fine. He'll work. You'll swoon. If you fail to finish it then we don't get paid. Your choice, Jude.'

'Bloody hell, sister, you are in a foul humour this morn. I was only jesting. Of course, I'll help... no matter what agonies assail me, I shall suffer in silence.'

'Please, please. Cease this,' Seb said in a vain attempt to restore peace.

'Silence is beyond you, Jude Foxley, unless your mouth be full,' Emily shouted. 'We all know that.'

'Then let's go fill it,' Jude yelled back at her. 'I smell oatcakes scorching on the griddle and I'm starving.'

'Oh, no!' Emily abandoned the tray and rushed to the kitchen.

'Why do you bait her so, Jude?' Seb said. 'She is with child, yet you make no allowance. Humour her for all our sakes, please.'

'Why does she always pick a quarrel with me, eh?'

'There was no need for name-calling, either.'

'She called me an insolent rascal.'

'After you called her a moody mare.'

'Well, it's true. She is.'

'You are as immature as any apprentice, Jude, you know that?'

'Careful, brother. I'm an injured warrior. I could take a turn for the worse at any moment.'

Seb picked up the tray that Emily had abandoned in her haste to save the oatcakes.

'She's right about one thing though: I won't get the 'Gawain' finished unless you aid me.'

'Indispensible, that's what I am... but only after we eat, little brother. Do you bloody realise I missed out on supper last eve?' Jude said as they went along the passage to the kitchen. 'Dame Ellen had promised me a pickled oyster pie.'

'You were in no fit state to return to Cheapside. You required the services of the surgeon and tending afterwards.'

'Aye. Rose tended me well indeed,' Jude said, rolling his eyes and grinning.

'Tell me no more; I do not want to know.'

'But you could have bloody fed me.'

After breaking their fast on soused herring and sharing out the few unburned oatcakes, Seb and Jude set to work on the 'Gawain'. Seb was swiftly immersed in his work, oblivious to the comings and goings around him, unaware even of a quarrel betwixt Tom and Jack concerning an errand to be run on so wet a morning. Seb so enjoyed mixing pigments and applying them to his sparse line drawings, seeing the images come alive upon the page. A miniature of Gawain riding his horse, Gryngolet, through a summer meadow in his quest to find the Green Chapel, gave Seb the opportunity to paint a myriad of tiny blossoms, each one recognisably of its kind: poppies, field scabious and buttercups, moon daisies, cornflowers and spikes of yellow archangel. A family of playful conies frolicked in the lower corner.

Jude was less successful at giving the text his full attention with a deal of sighing and much reshaping of quills – more than was truly required even by the worst of scribes. He left his desk and came to peer over Seb's shoulder. After watching for a while as his brother used the finest of brushes, no bigger than an eyelash, to paint the smallest of daisy petals with a speck of white lead pigment, he tutted loudly.

'You might save a deal of time, little brother, if you didn't bother with the bloody flowers. A plain grassy sward would do as well for the tale.'

'But it pleases me to paint such details and would give less pleasure to the reader without,' Seb said without glancing up, rinsing the brush and taking up a pin-point of yellow ochre to colour the centre of another blossom.

'Pleasure be damned. This has to be done by Wednesday, or had you forgotten that?'

'No, I haven't forgotten but grant me the courtesy of knowing what I am about. Leave me to my work and it will be done the sooner.' Seb dipped his brush in azurite to begin the few delicate strokes that would create a blue cornflower.

'Have it your way, then, but if it's not finished...'

'It will be.' Seb smiled to himself: the azurite was the precise beautiful hue of Em's eyes.

Jude shrugged and returned to his own work, muttering about 'unnecessary bloody embellishment' and 'a waste of damned expensive pigments'. The truth was that he envied his brother being able to enjoy his work when, for himself, it was an unpalatable chore, just a means of making a living. Still muttering under his breath, he resumed his task of penning one letter after another, a tedious succession of black ink marks that could never be a source of delight to him until he wrote 'finis' at the end. Even then, it was more a matter of relief that it was done rather than any pleasure at accomplishment.

By dinnertime, Jude had completed the accompanying text just in time for the ink to have been sanded and dried, so Seb could begin work upon an autumnal scene with hues of yellow, gold, tawny and copper. Jude was a little more hopeful now that the manuscript might be completed within the two days remaining until the customer expected to view it. He was just setting out the ruled pages of the next folio ready for after the meal when screams and screeching were heard in the kitchen. He looked at Seb – still oblivious to all as he prepared a new pigment – and saw his brother was quite deaf to the sounds of panic so he would have to investigate the alarm.

Nessie was flapping her apron and squealing as flames licked along its hem.

'Be still, you foolish wench,' Emily shouted. 'Untie it. Take it off.'

Jude grabbed Nessie from behind and held her still while Emily undid the apron ties which had become knotted. As the burning garment fell away, Jude trampled on it to quench the flames but Nessie continued to scream as her woollen gown was now alight. A tub of lye water stood in the corner with linen shirts and shifts in soak, awaiting rinsing.

'Help me, Jude,' Emily instructed, taking one handle of the heavy tub.

Realising her intent, Jude took the other handle and lifting it, they tipped the contents down the front of Nessie's gown. The wench shrieked and spluttered but the fire was out. Her gown was blackened and charred, her stockings scorched but, apart from a blistered ankle, she was unharmed. However, the kitchen flagstones were now awash with lye, making them slippery underfoot and somehow the bread and cloth upon the table, in readiness for dinner, had become soaked with it. Wet linen lay strewn in heaps across the floor – a scene of disaster that had Emily in despair.

As the rest of the household appeared from all quarters, matters only worsened. Jack arrived from doing the errand – having lost the earlier argument with Tom – his mud-caked boots turning the water on the floor to a grimy liquid and staining the soaked linen anew.

Beggar ran through the mess, yapping like a demon, getting under everyone's feet. Rose and Kate came from the shop, having been busy using their feminine wiles in persuading a customer to make a sizeable purchase. Tom left off grinding more verdigris pigment for Master Seb and arrived in time to see poor Rose slip on the soapy flagstones and go down, landing heavily on her backside.

Jude hastened to help her to her feet, concerned that she might have suffered some hurt but Rose was laughing as he lifted her. Her skirts were wet now and her cap lay in amongst the grubby washing.

'Are you hurt, dearest?' Jude asked, holding her elbow to keep her firm upon her feet and lifting her loosened hair, brushing it back off her face.

'My dignity be bruised indeed,' Rose said, 'But naught that a kiss will fail to mend.'

Grinning, he took her in his arms and kissed her heartily, unmindful of the spectators around them.

'When you two have quite finished,' Emily said, taking up her broom and floor cloths to begin mopping up. 'Nessie, put the washing back in the tub and fetch clean water and put it to heat. Everything will need soaking over again.'

'But, mistress, my gown is ruined and my leg's so sore,' Nessie said.

'Cease your whining. How many times have I warned you to kilt up your apron when tending the hearth? But do you ever listen to a word I say? And as for you, Jack, get that wretched dog out of my kitchen and scrape your boots afore you come back in. Rose, when you be done with him,' she said pointing at Jude, 'You can strip the wet cloth off and reset the board. Kate, see what can be saved of that loaf. Tom, go ask your master for a penny then run to Cheapside for more bread. I fear there will not be enough otherwise.'

In the workshop, Seb was still painting.

'Master, mistress says you're to give me a penny for another loaf,' Tom said.

'What's that?' Seb was using his brush to outline the back leg of a horse. One twitch of the brush awry and it would look like a broom handle. He could not afford a mistake.

'A penny. We need more bread and I've got to go to Cheapside for it in this weather. It's not fair. Jack could go: he's wet and muddy already. I don't see why I have to do it. Or Kate. She could fetch it. Shopping is women's work.'

Seb leaned back from his miniature, observing the horse with a critical eye before making an additional brush stroke.

'There,' he said, sighing with satisfaction. 'That looks well.' He washed out his brush and shaped it to a good point, then put it to dry, tip uppermost, in a pot. He turned to Tom. 'Now what was it you wanted?'

'A penny, master,' Tom repeated, sounding irritable and scuffing his feet.

Seb unfastened the purse from his belt and handed it to the lad.

'Take what you need. Is it raining still?' Seb frowned up at the high window. Grey sky was all that was visible. It was difficult to tell if it was raining.

'Aye, master, like Noah's flood it is and the kitchen's just as wet.'

'Is the roof leaking then?'

'No, master. It's wet because of Nessie's clothes catching fire and they tipped the washing water over her.'

'When was this? Is Nessie injured? What came to pass?'

'I have to go. We need the bread for dinner, else Mistress Em will be taking her broom to me.' Tom left the purse on the desk and hurried out, grabbing his cloak and hood.

Seb thought it wise to investigate the happenings in the kitchen. Oddly, whatever had occurred, it must have been done so very quietly for he had heard naught untoward all morning. He found Em, skirts kilted above her knees, kneeling on the floor, mopping the flagstones with a cloth and wringing it out into a bucket. Rose was doing the same, working her way backwards towards the door where he stood, her neatly rounded buttocks catching his attention as her damp skirts clung close. Kate was emptying a bucket out into the yard where it only added to the huge puddle lapping at the back step. Nessie was hiding in the chimney corner where she slept, silently sobbing over her burned gown. Em couldn't spare the effort to drag her forth and set her to work, giving her up as a lost cause for the rest of the morning.

Em looked up from her labours when she saw Seb, leaning on the door jamb.

'So, husband, you breathe still. I feared you must have died at your desk since so much noise and confusion failed to rouse you.'

'I was working on the 'Gawain' manuscript.'

'Aye, and deaf to all else.' She wrung out the cloth with such vehemence the linen might have torn. 'Now you're here, you can help. See that puddle by the hearth?' She threw a spare cloth at him. 'It needs mopping.'

212

Jude came in with a jug of ale from the barrel stored beneath the lean-to outside. Even such a short step across the yard in the unrelenting downpour left his fair hair plastered to his forehead. Jack followed him through the door, an armful of firewood kept dry under his cloak. Both wondered at seeing the head of the household on hands and knees, toiling away, trying to dry the floor. Jude was about to laugh at his brother but upon seeing Seb biting his lip in pain, realised his hip must be causing him agony, down on all fours like that. Instead, he helped him up, took the wet cloth from him and tossed it back in the bucket.

'That's no bloody work for an artist. Come, little brother, you must be in need of some ale.'

Seb nodded, rubbing at his left thigh, trying to ease the stiff joint and cramped muscles.

'Forgive me, Em,' he said, accepting the cup Jude offered him, 'Washing floors is a task beyond my abilities, I fear.'

After a frugal dinner of vegetable pottage with a thin wedge of bread each, all that remained edible of the soggy, soapy loaf - Tom's errand in the rain having been in vain, the bakers having sold their wares and gone home long since – everyone returned to their rightful work, except Kate. She remained in the kitchen to help her mistress and the still-tearful Nessie in putting the place to rights and preparing a better supper. The lass could be spared from the workshop since Masters Seb and Jude and even Tom were fully employed on the 'Gawain' and couldn't take time to instruct her. At least Rose could take charge of the shop without supervision. Jack and the dog made themselves scarce and no one missed them.

In the workshop, Seb settled at his desk, directing Tom to prepare red and yellow ochres for the autumn shades required for the next miniature. His purse still lay open on the edge of the work board where Tom had left it.

Jude picked it up, thinking to fasten it closed before any coin spilled out but the soft clinking of silver drew him to look inside. There was a goodly number of groats, half-groats, pennies and halfpennies, too many to count without tipping them onto the desk. Was Seb aware how much his purse contained? Knowing his brother, Jude doubted it and helped himself to most of the larger coins before fastening the catch. He would be able to pay that bloody wretch Thornbury a little more.

Finally, God be praised, the rain had ceased and the sun, though already low in the western sky, cast a watery light on puddles and midden heaps, making even such filth sparkle. The rooftops of London were scoured clean, the gutters rinsed by tumbling waterfalls. Jack and Beggar were mooching around the alleyways of the city. If asked, Jack would say he was looking for – what did Master Seb call it? – 'insterperashun' or some such thing but, in truth, the workshop seemed overcrowded these days, since Mistress Rose and Kate had come. Too many women, he decided, and worse yet were the strange feelings they caused him. Why did he so want to touch them? Why did a glimpse of the ties on Rose's shift so bestir his prick, he knew not what to do with himself, in case folk noticed? Why was kissing Kate just not enough for him?

'Come, Beggar, race yer!' he yelled to the little dog bounding along beside him. They ran up one street and tore down the next, heedless of puddles and pools of mud until, breathless, panting and hot, Jack stopped, bent double while he caught his second wind.

Beggar flopped on his belly, tongue hanging.

'Where're we, Beg?' Jack looked around. Knowing the city so well as he did, it still took him a few moments to realise they were almost into Gracechurch Street which became Fish Street and led onto London Bridge.

Despite the lateness of the afternoon, folk were coming out of doors now, to conduct business put off earlier because of the weather. East Cheap was becoming crowded as he and Beggar began to make their way back across the city. Just at the end of the narrow way known as St Clements Lane, off Candlewick Street, they were confronted of a sudden by a fellow with a huge hound, a mastiff of some kind. Before Jack could drag Beggar away, the little dog – thinking to defend his master and never one to back down, however large his opponent – leapt at the hound's throat. The mastiff shook him off and, growling ominously, lunged at the smaller animal. Jack and the owner of the hound were both yelling at their dogs but dare not attempt to pull the pair apart, what with cruel teeth and snapping jaws.

A crowd gathered to watch this unexpected entertainment, some cheering on one contestant, some the other. Wagers were being laid – all of them on victory for the mastiff.

The contest ended as suddenly as it had begun. The crowd drifted away, coins changing hands according to the outcome.

'Sorry, lad,' the owner of the mastiff said, patting Jack on the shoulder. 'Your little un should know not to pick a scuffle he can't never win but he surely put up a game fight.'

Jack nodded, not hearing the words. He was staring at the bloodied mess, the scrap of torn fur lying in the mud. He bent down, went on his knees in the filth to cradle his little friend of so many years he'd lost count.

'Beggar, Beggar, yer daft dog,' he wept, tears dripping on the dirty fur. 'Why Beg, eh? Why d'yer fight 'im?' He stroked a soft ear and massaged a grubby paw. He wiped away the blood from the dog's nose and kissed the little leathery snout. Beggar made no sound and already his bright eyes were dimmed, clouded by death. Beggar was gone.

While Jude returned to his lodgings to eat, supper was a hearty affair to make up for a meagre breakfast and a dinner that was little better. Emily had made a pie, filling the pastry coffin with every edible scrap from the larder, whether vegetable, fish, fruit, herb or spice. It tasted surprisingly good for such a hotch-potch of ingredients.

'This is excellent, Em. You'll have to prepare this dish more often,' Seb said, spooning another mouthful and savouring it.

'I doubt I could ever repeat the receipt. I just put everything in together. Kate helped.'

'Well done, Kate. I pray you don't want to be 'prenticed to a cookshop instead?'

'Nay, master. I'm happy here.'

Knowing Jack was always the first to appreciate anything Kate had a hand in, Seb spoke to the lad:

'You be very quite this eve, Jack. Are you not enjoying this fine meal?' It was a rare thing indeed that the lad's platter was still full of food. 'What's amiss, lad? Are you unwell?'

Of a sudden, silent tears were pouring down the youngster's cheeks, dripping into his supper. Seb left his stool and went round the table to where Jack sat upon a bench beside Tom. Tom moved aside, as though fearing sorrow to be contagious. 'Jack, now, now. What has caused this?' Seb said, comforting the lad as best he could. 'Where is Beggar? He will cheer you better than I.' Jack's tears became a cascade and he broke down, sobbing against Seb's chest. Looking at the others over Jack's bowed head, Seb mouthed the question: 'Has anyone seen the dog?' Heads were shaken. 'Where is Beggar, Jack?' Seb asked softly.

The lad pulled free of Seb's embrace.

'He's bloody dead, ain't he? That's where he is. Bloody dead an' gone fer ever.' Overturning stools in his haste, Jack fled out to the yard, climbing the wooden stairs to the loft he shared with Tom in an attempt to seek solace beneath his bed covers. A comfort that was not to be found.

'Can I have his supper then?' Tom said, holding out his empty platter.

'Poor Jack,' Kate dabbed her eyes on her sleeve and sniffed back tears. 'He so loved his dog.'

'It was lively enough at dinnertime. I wonder what happened to it?' Rose wiped her spoon clean upon a napkin. 'No wonder Jack is upset.'

'I'll give him time to compose himself a little, then I'll go up to him, speak with him. I know not what else to do to aid him. Beggar was his dearest companion. He is certain to take the loss hard.'

'You will not take him his supper, husband. I forbid it. Pastry in the bedchambers will encourage rats and I'll not allow it.'

'No, Em. I misdoubt he will be thinking of food this one time at least but a shoulder to weep upon may help or a few words of comfort to console him upon his great loss.'

'What are you saying?' Em demanded. 'A stupid little dog, a damned nuisance at best, has died and you behave as though the lad is orphaned of a sudden. He'll be over it by morn and wanting to break his fast.'

'Oh, Em. Have a little compassion, lass. The lad be in sore distress.'

'Over a horrible dog, the bane of this household, ever making a mess, shitting in corners and I know not what else. It is a mercy.'

'Jack does not see it so. I will go to him.'

Sitting side by side on the edge of his bed up in the loft, Jack poured out the whole miserable tale to Seb, how Beggar had fought the far bigger dog, thinking his master was about to be attacked.

'He was a valiant little creature,' Seb said.

'Aye. Valerant. That was my Beggar and no dog wos never like him.' Jack paused, rubbing his wet eyes, thinking. 'Master?'

'What is it, lad?'

'Can I bury him, proper, like a Christian?'

'Aye. I be sure we can find a suitable corner of the garden plot.'

'No. I mean in St Michael's yard where folks be buried.'

Seb huffed a breath.

'I'm uncertain whether Father Thomas would allow it, Jack. Holy Church says animals have no souls so will not rise again come Judgement Day.'

'But Beggar wos one o' God's creatures, weren't he?'

'Of course he was.'

'Well then?'

'I admit, I do not know whether such loyal, knowing animals as Beggar can be entirely soulless but 'tis not my place to argue with church doctrine. But think on it, Jack, if every beloved horse, dog, cat, squirrel and tame bird had the right to be buried in sacred earth, there would be no room remaining for Christian folk when they die, would there?'

'S'pose not. But Beggar's so little, he won't need much space, will he?'

'Where have you put it – him – for now?'

'Under the lean-to, be'ind the ale barrel. I wrapped him in them floor cloffs Mistress Em used to mop the kitchen. He's safe there 'til t'morrow, ain't he? Rats won't get him, will they?' Tears were dribbling down his face again and he cuffed them away.

'No, lad. I'll make certain of that, fear not.'

Later, sitting by the kitchen fire, Seb looked at the sketches he had made of the Duke of Clarence. The rules of the guild forbade working after sunset for fear of poor workmanship and a lowering of standards. However, in this instance, Seb couldn't see that it would matter. After all, the original drawings were most likely done in the gloom of a prison cell. Not that he could truly recall the circumstances: that memory was shrouded in darkness still. Sir Rob was right in thinking the duke's likeness would distress Lord Richard. When Emily had glanced at them, they had brought a catch to her voice.

Clipping fresh paper to his board, Seb copied the face of Duke George in a few deft movements of the red chalk, but this time omitting some of the harsh lines of his furrowed brow, changing the curve of the cheeks and using less shading beneath the cheek bones to fill out the face a little. The tiniest line at each corner of the mouth was sufficient to change the image of deepest desperation to one of quiet resolution. A slight adjustment to the lower eyelids, to show a fraction more of the iris, removed somewhat the element of torment from those deep set eyes. The features were still recognisable when compared to the original but the expression was now... how could he describe it? Not quite lifeless but bland. Aye, that was it. Bland. Not a word he approved of but the drawing would serve its purpose and be less upsetting to Lord Richard.

'How's Jack?' Emily asked, daring to interrupt as Seb took up a new sheet of paper. She was stitching hems on a length of linen: swaddling clouts for the babe, her sewing as fine and neat as if for a rich lady's gown. Like Seb, Em always took pride in her work.

'Sorrowful at the loss of his close companion of years, as we might expect.'

'But he's not going to take to his bed for a week, as he did once before? And have you waiting upon him like a servant.'

'No, Em. But he does want to bury Beggar in the churchyard.'

'What! Where does he get such idiot notions? A dog's not a Christian.' She stabbed the needle into the cloth with more force than was required.

'I know, Em, but you find a way to explain that to a grieving child for I cannot put my tongue to the most appropriate words.' Seb leaned across and took up a fire iron to push an unburned log into the centre of the dancing flame. 'Oh, I meant to say, I've put the, er, remains into the grain bin to keep it from the rats.'

'You put a dead dog in with our food! Sebastian Foxley, I swear you are run quite mad. How can we eat it now?'

'Fear not. I put a folded canvas in first and the body be well shrouded in your floor cloths. It does not lie touching upon the grain. 'Tis just for this night and will be buried as soon as there be daylight enough to see to dig a grave.'

'And where will you bury it? In my garden, I suppose?'

'Aye, but well beneath the bramble hedge at the far end – nowhere near your leeks and worts and herbs.'

'It had better not be.' Em broke off her thread with her teeth and smoothed the linen across her lap. 'There. Fit for a king's child and certainly for a Foxley babe. Have you given any thought to naming our child, Seb?'

'No. Have you? I wouldn't want to tempt Fate in this concern.'

'What's that got to do with anything? A suitable name requires a deal of thought. Once he is born, there will be too short a time before the baptism for proper consideration of a name. I have a list in mind. Stephen – after my father – or Mark – after yours.'

Though Emily didn't see it, Seb winced at the thought. No, the child would not be named after his paternal grandsire.

'Or Adam as he will be our first born,' Em went on. 'Or Richard – after your patron. Or Edward – for the king.'

'It could be a little maid,' Seb suggested, brushing chalk dust from his fingers and setting down his drawing stuff to drink his ale.

'No. It is a boy child, I know. Dame Ellen thought so too when I asked her about it at church yesterday and Nell Warren agreed.'

'Well, I suppose those two be learned in such matters; they must have delivered half the parishioners of St Michael's over the years. No doubt they know a few things about babes that we men be wholly ignorant of.'

With the new drawings of Duke George completed and another swaddling clout neatly hemmed, Seb and Em retired to their bedchamber. She slept soundly. Seb did not. He was once again running blindly through those fearful black tunnels but, new to the nightmare, were the dogs. Ferocious mouths slavered at his back. He could feel their burning breath upon his neck and then he fell, sent sprawling over a corpse which, despite the stink of death about it, yapped at him piteously.

CHAPTER THIRTEEN

Tuesday the twenty-fourth day of February
St Michael's churchyard

THE SUN was barely risen from its cloudy bed but Seb and Jack were in St Michael's burying-ground. Simple wooden crosses marked the graves of the more recently deceased, each bearing a name inscribed, but countless others slept the sleep of death, unnamed, forgotten by the living yet known to God. As they had hoped, Old Clem, the sexton, was there with his spade, already at work. A new grave would be required at the vespers hour for a local tiler who had slipped from his ladder and fell to his death a few days earlier.

'Couldn't dig, yesserday,' Old Clem explained, 'Rain kept washin' it all back in so I be all be'ind meself. Lots t' do.'

'Jack has brought a spade. He can help with your task. The earth must be heavy after so much rain. He be young and strong,' Seb said.

'You sayin' I can't do me job?' The sexton looked affronted and leaned on his spade.

'No, not at all. He is prepared to assist you is all. Isn't that so, Jack?'

'And why would he want to, eh?'

'He has a favour to ask of you.'

'Oh, aye. Course, I knows yer wouldn't do it fer naught. What d'yer want, then?'

'I-I want, er, if I can, er...'

'Jack's dog was slain yesterday,' Seb explained. 'He wishes it might be laid here, in the churchyard.' The idea had come to him in the cold, wakeful hours of the night, after more unquiet dreams. He had made no promises to Jack but suggested they ask Old Clem, if he happened to be opening a new grave, about interring the dog, unofficially.

'How big?'

''Tis a little dog, master. Won't need much room. He could lie in the bottom of this grave wot you're digging, if I help yer dig it just a bit deeper, put him in and cover him over, then the next body can go on top, can't it? He's such a small dog, it won't notice. Please, master.'

'I'll pay you for your trouble,' Seb added. 'The cost of digging an extra grave, if you will?' He opened the catch on the purse at his belt.

'Aye, well I might be p'suaded.'

'How much? In addition to the lad's aid in digging, of course.'

The sexton scratched at his beard.

'How about yer pays us a groat, eh?'

Four pence! It was a high price to pay to bury a dog. Seb knew the old man was paid a halfpenny for every grave he dug and a farthing for filling it in again. Yet one glance at Jack's pleading eyes and Seb knew it was worth the cost. He opened his purse, his fingers questing for a groat coin. There had been at least three groats in it yesterday and some half groats but now he could find only pennies and halfpennies. Oh, well, maybe he had left them at home. He took out three silver pennies and two half coins and counted them into Old Clem's filthy hands.

'Aye, that'll do,' the sexton agreed. 'Come on, young un, get diggin', us ain't got all day. Any bones yer find, set 'em aside, t' go t' the charnel 'ouse. I'll be watchin' yer.'

Seb left the churchyard, certain that Jack was most likely going to do all the digging. Not that the lad would protest, so long as Beggar was buried as he wished.

Again, as he passed the Panyer Inn, Seb wondered about the groats and half groats he had thought to be in his purse. What had he done with them? He had spent no coin at all yesterday. Perhaps Em had needed money, a bill to be paid maybe, taken it and forgotten to tell him, but enough to buy an entire week's food and drink for the whole household seemed to be gone. It was a great deal to go unaccounted. No doubt, it could be simply explained even if, for the moment, he could not think what that explanation might be. Perhaps he had mislaid the coins somewhere. Aye, that was all too possible, what with his mind on so many other matters and still somewhat foggy concerning certain remembrances.

The Foxleys' kitchen

'IN THE churchyard!' Em said, spluttering into her breakfast pottage. 'We'll be having dogs canonised as saints next, churches dedicated to St Fido. What were you thinking of, Seb?'

'It pleases Jack; will give him comfort of a kind. What harm can it do?'

'How much did it cost?'

'A morning's labour from Jack.'

'And?'

'Well, I did, er, have to pay Old Clem for his trouble.'

'How much?'

'A groat,' Seb said softly, as if that somehow made it a lesser amount.

Em shook her head in wonderment.

'Your sanity becomes more doubtful, husband, with each day that passes but at least I won't worry about finding a dead dog when next I pull up leeks. But four pence... he could dig half a dozen graves for such a sum.'

'Speaking of pence, Em: did you take coins from my purse yesterday? As is your right of course,' he added hurriedly, seeing her brows draw down.

'I sent Tom to ask you for a penny to buy bread. As you'll recall, I was too busy in the kitchen to take time, fetching my own purse. But since there was no bread to be had – was there, Tom? – he returned the coin. 'Tis still upon the shelf there.' She nodded towards the shelf above the hearth. 'Why? Have you spent coin and forgotten what you bought – again?'

'I fear that must be the case, unless… Tom, when you took the penny, could any other coins have spilled out? Did you close and fasten the purse after?'

Tom shrugged and stuck out his nether lip.

'I'm not certain, master. I thought I did but I can't truly remember. I left it on your desk; I know that.'

'Ah, then that must be what occurred. In all likelihood, the heavier coins fell out and rolled away. No doubt, they lie upon the workshop floor somewhere. We shall find them soon enough.'

'Wouldn't you have heard them jangle on the floor, master?' Tom asked.

'No, he wouldn't,' Em answered for him. 'After all, he heard naught of the commotion in the kitchen yestermorn, being so engrossed in his precious 'Gawain' as he was. I doubt he would notice if the archangel sounded the Last Trump once he's there with his pigment pots and pens.'

'What wouldn't my brother hear?' Jude asked, coming in through the kitchen door in time to catch a snippet of the conversation. He helped himself to an oatcake despite having eaten breakfast at his lodgings with Dame Ellen, his landlady.

'The sound of money escaping his purse,' Em said, collecting up the empty bowls. 'I don't suppose you know anything about coins going missing, do you, Jude?' She gave him such a look.

'Me? I have naught to do with Seb's money. How should I know what he does with it? Don't accuse me, sister-in-law. Where is my beloved Rose? I haven't had my welcoming kiss yet.'

'Dusting the shop's display shelves, I expect,' Seb said. 'Kate's in the workshop, setting out our desks – or should be – and Jack is at St Michael's, digging a grave. Which reminds me: Em, save some breakfast for the lad, he will have earned it.'

'What's this? Jack taken up a new craft, eh?'

'No, Jude. He's burying his dog.'

'In holy ground? Is that permitted?'

'The sexton agreed to it.'

'What a bloody relief.'

'The burying?'

'Being rid of that stinking mutt. No more piles of shit or puddles of piss to step around. No more yapping at customers. No more dog hairs on my best hose. And whenever the lad requires a beating, I can do it without fear of feeling its bloody teeth in my leg as it takes its reprisal. 'Tis good news, indeed.'

'I beg you, Jude. Say naught of the kind to Jack. He be grief-stricken enough without learning of your pleasure at his loss.'

'Loss? As if there aren't a thousand better bloody dogs in London. Buy him another – preferably one with no teeth and a bung up its arse. Oh, and I shall be going out later.'

'What of the text for the 'Gawain'?'

'It'll get done, little brother. Fear not. When have I ever let you down in the past?'

'Mm. Well…'

'Don't answer that. Now, where's Rose. Can't begin a day's work afore I get my kiss.'

Redmaine Hall in St Pancras Lane

'I DON'T CARE what father wanted or arranged. I'm not marrying Alice Verney and that's my final word on it.' William Redmaine stamped across the exquisite Turkey rug upon the parlour floor as if he was trampling down nettles. 'I cannot bear that simpering, meek-and-mild way of hers. It would be like marrying a bucket of milk – all pale, insipid and tasteless. I want a real woman in my bed.'

'You could always take a mistress,' his elder brother Roger suggested.

'Well, you should know, you being a connoisseur of loose women. But no. Jacquetta will be my wife, not my mistress, and you can't insist otherwise. I don't care that you're father's heir. You can have everything: this house, the business, the counting house and the ship, all of it but I will have Jacquetta Haldane.'

'I've so misjudged you, Will,' Roger said, refilling his goblet with ruby wine from a matching jug of Venetian crystal glass. 'I thought you wanted the business. After all, what do I know of the grocery trade compared to you? Father taught you things he wouldn't even discuss with me. I have no idea how to go about running this enterprise. I believed you had naught to gain by father's death but I was wrong. His passing gives you the opportunity to avoid the betrothal he insisted should be arranged. All I want is this house and the money. I'm more than willing to pass the business over to you in exchange for a modest income from the profits. What do you say?'

'You know, Roger, there are rumours that you murdered our father, fearing he was about to change his will, in order to make me his heir.'

'Aye, so I heard.'

'That does not rest squarely with the fact that you don't want to inherit everything, does it?'

'No. So why would I have killed him? The truth is that I didn't. If he rewrote his will, so what? It mattered not to me.

And if you wanted the business, why would you kill him before he changed it? Except that you say now all you want is to wed the apothecary's daughter whom father forbade you to see. Tell me, Will, how did our father die?'

'You know how he died as well as I: he disturbed an intruder, a thief, who beat his brains out and made off with a few choice pieces of silverware.'

'And that's God's own truth, is it? You would swear upon the Gospels and say the same?' Roger sipped his wine and put his feet upon a velvet-cushioned footstool.

'As far as I can tell, that's what happened.'

'Sit down, Will, you make me nervous with all this pacing about. And what of the missing valuables?'

'What of them? Have any been recovered, have you heard?'

'Were they ever stolen, I wonder? If they were, they never travelled very far, did they?'

'What do you mean?'

'They went about as far as that cupboard beneath the buffet. I found them yesterday. Tell me true, Will, there never was an intruder, nor a thief, was there? What really happened that night?'

The Foxley workshop

'MASTER SEB,' Rose said, coming from the shop, 'I've been thinking of late...'

'Ooh, watch out, brother,' Jude said, catching Rose around the waist as she passed his desk. 'A woman thinking always means trouble, mark my words.'

Seb was painting the image of the fearsome Green Knight about to smite Gawain's head from his shoulders with a great axe. He needed to concentrate. The knight was gruesome enough with his long, grass-green hair swathed, cape-like, across his shoulders, as the text described, but Seb was having difficulty with Gawain's face. How to make the hero's features show just the right amount of trepidation – without appearing cowardly – but not so bold that he seemed to know beforehand the knight would fail to kill him: it was a problem. Then he recalled the sketches he had done of the Duke of Clarence, the changes he had made to the original drawings, achieving an expression of quiet resolution upon the duke's face. That was how Gawain should look, he decided. Having solved the difficulty, he looked up from his work to see Jude and Rose in a rather too intimate embrace.

'What was it you wanted, Rose?' he asked, even as the heat of embarrassment washed over him.

'Oh, aye – get off, Jude, you lecherous devil – I was wondering about that room upstairs; the one above the shop and parlour you never use. Mistress Em mentioned it and we discussed it.'

'What of it?'

'We were thinking: it faces south, like the shop, so it must have a bright, sunny aspect, unlike your bedchamber at the back which is always cold and never sees the sun. What with Em's babe coming, wouldn't the chamber at the front be more suitable for her lying-in and bigger too? More room for you both and the babe's cradle. I don't mind cleaning it and making it ready... if you'll allow?'

'Allowing has naught to do with it. We don't have a key for that chamber; never have had. Tell her how it is, Jude. I must finish this afore the pigments dry out.' Seb returned to Gawain, using a mixture of red ochre and burnt umber to paint the hero's hair in a fashionable style.

'Pour me some ale, Rose, and I'll tell you about the locked room,' Jude said, making it sound mysterious. Before long, Kate and Tom were listening too. Although Tom knew the circumstances already, it was as good a reason as any to cease work, grinding yet more pigments for Master Seb. 'It happened like this,' Jude began. 'When Matthew Bowen, the former owner of this house and shop and all that goes with it, was poisoned by his second wife, he left a will specifying that it should all go to his wife and his heirs should get nothing.'

'That's me and my sister, Bella,' Tom said.

'Don't interrupt. But because his wife had killed him – well no matter what happened to her – she couldn't inherit anything, so Bowen's executors determined to sell everything: house, business and all, for the best price they could get, and divide the money betwixt various charitable deeds for the benefit of Bowen's soul. God knows, his damned soul must be in need of it, the old miser.' Jude took a long drink of ale. 'Well, nobody wanted to buy the place. Rumours went round that it was cursed, that Bowen's vengeful spirit haunted it. Of course, that was rubbish, as me and Seb well knew. We'd worked here for years: me as an apprentice and then a journeyman-scrivener, learning the trade, and Seb as a journeyman-illuminator. Bowen was a swine to work for but paid well enough and regularly.'

'But what about the locked chamber?' Rose insisted.

'I'm coming to that. Now, when Bowen died, Seb had just been given a lucrative commission by Lord Richard and had money enough to buy this place, so long as it wasn't overpriced.'

'So you spread the rumours that it was haunted.' Rose wasn't asking and Jude's smirk was confirmation enough.

'Well, I might have said something to that effect.'

'Jude! Did you truly do that?' Seb broke in, horrified. 'I never knew.'

'You didn't want to pay the full bloody price, now did you, little brother? I saved you a good deal of coin when the executors agreed to sell it to you – us – at a knock-down price. My tales of ghostly apparitions and weird clanking and wailing sounds did wonders for our financial situation at the time. You should be grateful to me.'

'And the chamber?' Rose prompted.

'Aye, so the place was ours but that bugger Bowen had died, leaving his chamber locked and no sign of a key. In all our years working for him, we never went near that chamber. Even if an important client needed to speak with him, we weren't permitted to go along the passage to knock upon the door.'

'So you've never been inside?'

'No. Never. And we've never found the key. That chamber is a mystery to us all.'

'But aren't you curious about it? Couldn't you break the lock, get it open somehow?'

Jude pulled a wry face.

'Probably.' He drank more ale. 'But the room must be bloody filthy. Nessie was never allowed beyond the door to clean it and I'm certain neither Bowen nor his wife ever swept it or dusted in there. It could be heaving with rats for all we know. Whooo. It could be full of rotting corpses...'

'Shut up, Jude, you'll frighten Kate,' Rose said, giving him a nudge and spilling a few drops from his cup.

'Mind the bloody text, woman! I've been working on this for hours.'

'I'm not scared,' Kate chimed in. 'I'd love to see inside that chamber.'

'As would I,' Rose said.

'Too bad,' Jude muttered, wiping the sleeve of his doublet, cursing at the minute ale stain. The text was undamaged.

'As for that text, Jude Foxley, I doubt it took above a handful of minutes to do what little you've written there.'

'Don't nag me, you unforgiving wench, else I'll kiss you 'til your lips be numb and serve you right.'

'Enough, all of you! There be work for all to do to complete this 'Gawain'. Tom, where is that red lead I asked you to grind? Kate, wash out these brushes for me, if you please? Rose, I think I hear a customer in the shop.'

'Aye, Master Seb,' they said together, chastened. It was rare for him to rebuke anyone.

'Forgive me,' he said. 'I did not intend to speak so sharply but I be most anxious about the 'Gawain', getting it finished for the morrow.'

After a hurried dinner with no one taking the time to appreciate Emily's cooking skills – which pleased her not at all – everyone returned to their given tasks. Except Jude, who announced that he had urgent business, elsewhere.

'Jude, you cannot,' Seb protested. 'That final gathering is not yet completed. How can I do the last miniature when the text is not written? The subject is the feast at King Arthur's court and will need much fine detail to do it justice. I have set aside this afternoon to do it but if you have not done the text and let the ink dry, I shall be working at it by candlelight this eve, breaking the rules of the guild.'

Jude shrugged his shoulders and took down his mantle from the peg.

'I won't tell the wardens. Will you? It won't be the first time their petty bloody rule book has been ignored, I'm sure. Besides, I'll do it as soon as I get back, I swear upon my oath to you.'

'No stopping at the Panyer? What is this matter of such importance, anyway?'

'Never you mind, little brother.'

Jude left the workshop with a frown upon his brow. Seb had never asked questions afore and it didn't do that he asked now. Was the most trusting of men at last becoming suspicious? Taking those coins from his purse yesterday was, perhaps, a step too far. A mistake that should not be repeated, unless it couldn't be helped. Bloody Thornbury, that greedy bastard!

But at least the sun was making an effort this day. The first warmth of the year had Jude tossing the sides of his mantle back over his shoulders. Others were also making the most of the better weather. By Cheap Cross, a group of youngsters had turned a barrel upon its side and used a plank across it to make a see-saw. Their shrieks of laughter and smiling faces were very nearly sufficient to improve Jude's humour, but not quite.

'Ah, Master Jude, I bid you good day and a very good one it is, indeed.' Stephen Appleyard, Emily's father, stood by, outside his carpentry workshop, watching the little ones. 'Take care there, young Sam,' he called, starting forward to set a small lad back upright on the plank.

'Master Appleyard,' Jude said, touching his cap to the elder man. 'Aye, 'tis well enough for those with leisure to enjoy it. Some of us have to work for our living.'

Stephen grinned, taking Jude's sour words lightly.

'They be young for such a short space, seems a pity to waste it, don't you think? They'll be 'prentised and labouring afore they know it. I like to see them take time at play.'

'You provided the plank, no doubt? What of the loss to your business, if they break it?'

'They won't. 'Tis stout enough to bear so small burdens as they. Besides, good timber is more readily come by these days than fun and amusement, to judge from your expression, my friend.'

'Aye, well, as I said: I have to work. Farewell to you, master.'

The priest's house next door to the church of St Mary-le-Bow looked as dour as ever. Somehow, the sun failed to glint off its roof tiles and its windows only showed the greater gloom within. A dreary, dark den befitting the black soul that lived behind the unwelcoming door, scowling beneath the overhanging roof, Jude thought. With a deep breath, he knocked, as he had done too many times before.

'Oh, it's you.' Thornbury gave no hint of pleasure at the sight of one who was about to hand him unearned coins. 'You'd better come inside.'

Jude stepped over the threshold into a grubby passageway that stank of rats' droppings and decaying fish.

'Don't you ever have parishioners to visit, last rites to dispense? I've never come by and found you not at home. Do you ever perform your priestly duties or is it your sole occupation, extorting monies from decent, hard-working citizens? You're a parasite, Thornbury, you know that.'

'Watch your mouth, Foxley, or the price will rise again.'

'I've had enough of your damned threats, priest – or whatever of Satan's minions you be. Demand another bloody penny and you'll not live long enough to spend it, I promise you. Here! Take what I have.' Jude threw the coins he'd filched from Seb's purse the day before on the floor, among the stale rushes. 'That's all you're getting; the last payment. You and your bitch can be content with that. There is no more. One more menacing demand from you and it won't be silver in your hand you get but steel in your gullet. Understand?'

Simon Thornbury's face was unreadable. He made no attempt to pick up the coins but blinked slowly, almost as though he distained his visitor as too despicable to look upon.

'Brave words,' he sneered. 'Not that you'd have the nerve to carry out your empty threats.'

'You think not? Yours wouldn't be the first blood I've spilled and my conscience has always slept easy afterwards. They were both as bad as you in their own way. Bullies, extortionists, tormentors. Ask for one farthing more and you'll join those buggers in hell. If I ever see or hear from you again…'

'You don't intimidate me, Foxley. I'm not afraid of some piss-pot drunkard like you.'

'No? Then you're stupid as well as bloody greedy.'

As he walked back along Cheapside, Jude wondered why he didn't feel any better, having vented his rage at that wretch. Perhaps the bastard was right about them being empty threats. He'd killed before, years ago – once in anger; once deliberately with good cause and naught to lose – but would he do it again? Could he? Rose had softened his nature of late, he knew, but Thornbury stood betwixt them, preventing their happiness together. Was that not cause enough to carry out his threats, if this damned business was not at an end? Maybe. Maybe not. He truly couldn't say.

Seb was still at his desk when Jude got back to Paternoster Row, diligently painting as though he hadn't so much as looked up from his task. He didn't acknowledge Jude's return – probably never noticed.

'I need ale!' Jude yelled at no one in particular. He was desperate to wash away the taste of that sour conversation.

'I'll fetch some for you, master,' Kate said, leaping from her desk and rushing to the kitchen. Jude glanced down at the work she had abandoned. He raised his eyebrows.

'You know, Seb, you're right about that lass: she certainly has talent. Look here. This cat going a-marketing, complete with apron and cap, is nigh as good as anything you do.'

Seb leaned back upon his stool, sighing and flexing cramped fingers.

'Then she can aid me with this.'

'How much is still to be done?'

'Oh, this miniature is nigh finished but I'll be waiting on you to get the text done afore I do that final picture of Arthur's royal court. I told you, I need it this afternoon. With but a few hours of daylight remaining, it will be a race against the sun.'

'I'll copy out the folio with the space ruled for your precious damned miniature first. Then I'll do the previous pages.'

'But the text must follow on in the correct order.'

'Seb. Give me some bloody credit, can't you? I've been doing this longer than you have. I'm a scribe by profession and a damned good one. You think I can't write folios in any order and yet get them all to marry up afterwards?'

'Forgive me. This commission has been cursed from the start. I am that weary of it, having to do it a second time. I shall be glad when 'tis done, I truly shall.'

'Ale, masters! I brought cups for all. I hope that was right.' Kate set down the tray upon her stool and began to pour bright golden ale from the jug.

Seb left his desk, wary of drinking ale too close to the precious manuscript. He took up Kate's drawings and leafed through them. He began to chuckle at the sketches of various creatures up to all kinds of antics: a huge red frog leaping over a tiny Tower of London; a blue squirrel, wearing a feathered hat, climbing St Paul's spire and the mischievous-looking cat buying mice at a Cheapside market stall.

'These are merry, indeed, Kate. We'll have to find a use for them, won't we? Set them aside safely in the box in the storeroom for future reference. I commend you on such fine drawings and your lively imagination, lass. Well done.'

Kate beamed and skipped on the spot.

'I love doing them, master. The pictures just seem to pop into my head.'

'Aye, but at the same time the animals are well observed and lifelike. Excellent work, Kate. You can leave that now and assist Rose in the shop. Take her some ale, also.'

Come suppertime, Seb was at last working on the scene of King Arthur's court and Jude was still scribing away with one final folio to complete. Already the daylight had ebbed away into a gloomy dusk and tapers had been lit to aid their work. The household was sworn to secrecy to say naught of breaking the regulations of the Stationers' Guild in this way but it could not be helped, just this once. Emily delayed the evening meal accordingly, against her better judgement.

'God be praised: 'tis done,' Seb said as he took his place at table. 'I know not what mistakes we may see in the daylight, come the morn, but I cannot spend another minute at my desk. My eyes be blurry and my hands ache.'

'Eat your supper,' Emily urged, 'Afore it goes cold. You've earned it – for once. You too, Jude.' Well, that was an invitation indeed from Emily.

Jude had been concerned that, at nine of the clock by St Martin's bell, Dame Ellen – like all respectable Christian folk – would be abed and, thus, no supper available at his lodgings. The cookshops closed hours ago and a supperless eve had seemed likely. Without making any attempt at scrubbing the ink stains from his fingers, Jude sat on the bench beside Rose and tucked in.

'Once the customer has approved the bloody manuscript tomorrow morn, Seb,' Jude said, sucking gravy from his thumb, 'I think we should take time away from our desks and visit Redmaine Hall. There are still loose threads there I want to see trimmed off and neatened.'

'The demise of Giles Redmaine, you mean? Aye. That was a conundrum, if I remember it aright.'

'A con in drum, master? Wot's that then?' Jack asked, licking his platter clean.

'Manners!' Emily said, snatching the plate from the lad's hands.

'An enigma, Jack,' Seb explained, pleased that Jack was somewhat returned to his old self.

'Well, I don't know wot one o' them is neever, do I?'

'A perplexing problem not easily resolved.'

Jack was frowning. He hated it when Master Seb used words he didn't understand.

'A bloody mystery,' Jude said.

'Oh. Yer should a said in the first place. I'm goin' t' bed.' Jack climbed off the bench he shared with Tom. 'Come on, Beggar.'

There was a moment of awful silence. Everyone looked up at Jack. The lad's face puckered as he bit his lip and choked back tears.

'May the Almighty bless you and all His saints care for and console you this night, Jack,' Seb said.

The lad left the kitchen, wordless in grief.

'Poor Jack,' Kate said rubbing her eyes, though whether for tears or tiredness, it was hard to tell. 'We'll have to get him a new dog. He'd like that. My father's bitch had pups not long since. He might like one of those. We could ask my father next time we visit, couldn't we, Master Seb?'

'Perhaps. Now away to your beds, all of you. The hour be so late. Jude, will you stay or shall I light a torch for you?'

Jude glanced at Rose. They exchanged knowing looks.

'I may as well stay,' he said, doing his best to sound as though it was truly a matter of indifference to him, merely a convenience for all concerned. 'Best not disturb Dame Ellen, coming home at such an hour.'

Seb nodded, knowing full well that Dame Ellen, sleeping at the back of the house next door to the one where Jude lodged, would hear naught of his arrival and not be the least disturbed.

'I'll put the blanket in the parlour for you,' Em said.

'Thank you, sister-in-law, I'll be warm enough without it.'

Emily snorted in disgust.

'You'll turn my house into a house of ill-repute, will you? When you be wed, you and Rose may share a bed. Until then, under my roof, you sleep in separate beds.'

'We are bloody betrothed.'

'But not married. I'll fetch the blanket. Woebetide you, Jude Foxley, if I find it unused in the morn. Turning my home into a bawdy house… I won't have it, you hear?'

'Oh, very well,' Jude said with a great sigh, 'But I'll not sleep without a good night kiss. A long one, Rose – very long and heartfelt, if you be so kind?'

CHAPTER FOURTEEN

Wednesday the twenty-fifth day of February
Redmaine Hall in St Pancras Lane

'I'M SO relieved the 'Gawain' was all approved,' Seb was saying as he and Jude approached the grand portal of Redmaine Hall, with its golden lion knocker. 'I was afeared the work we did by candlelight last eve would not be of our usual high standard.'

'But it was, so you need not have worried. You know, you worry too bloody much, little brother.'

''Tis in my nature. I cannot help it. And I still believe the azurite pigment for King Arthur's robes looked somewhat washed out in the daylight. I used it too thinly in my haste to be finished.'

'It looked fine to me. The customer admired it particularly, didn't he, so cease bloody fussing about it. We got it finished in time. 'Tis done, all bar the stitching and binding. I'll do the first, then you and Jack can do the latter, seeing he wants a carved wood cover with gilding.'

'I fear the carving may take a while. Poor Jack be hardly of a mind to work since he lost Beggar.'

'Too bad. The idle young bugger'll just have to get on with it, won't he? Now, look to our present business with these Redmaines: they're up to something, I know.' Jude mounted the steps, lifted the heavy knocker and let it fall with a thud. No one came to the door, so he knocked again. After a long pause, he did so a third time, his insistence finally rewarded when the steward opened the door.

'This is a house of mourning,' he announced grandly.

'We know. Walter, isn't it? Are either William or Roger Redmaine at home?'

'What's this? Oh, it's you, again. If Master Coroner has yet more questions he can show more respect and come in person to ask them, instead of sending you and your lackey to do it for him. The masters are away, attending to business.'

The steward's claim was immediately given the lie when Master Roger came into the hallway.

'Who is it, Walter?'

'The coroner's assistant, sir. I told him you were attending to business but...'

'Go see to whatever it is that you do, Walter. I'll deal with this.' Roger Redmaine was tousled as a man roused from his bed untimely, his hair uncombed, swathed in a loose night robe, his unstockinged feet shoved into a pair of damask slippers. His drooping eyelid seemed more noticeable, as though still half asleep. He yawned and scratched his unshaven chin. 'Did I not make it plain enough last time when I forbade you bothering us again? We've told you all there is to tell, now be off, or I'll send for the sheriff and have you removed, charged with trespass upon our doorstep.'

'By all means, send for him,' Jude said, mild as mother's milk. 'It will save me the trouble of summoning him myself to have you and you brother arrested.'

Seb gasped. They hadn't come to do that, had they? Jude had said naught of such a thing.

'This is an affront to the name of Redmaine! On what invented charge would that be?'

'One of you two, or your steward – maybe all three – is guilty of murder and the others are accessories to the crime at the very least.'

240

'How dare you make such unfounded accusations!' Roger roared. Passers-by turned to watch and listen. 'You'd better come inside,' he said, lowering his voice and stepping back from the doorway. He closed the door behind them but did not invite them into any of the rooms. Clearly, he intended they should swiftly be gone. The interrogation would have to be conducted in the hallway.

'Where is your brother?' Jude asked.

'William?' Roger asked, as if he had many brothers. 'I have no idea. At the shop, probably. Why don't you go there and ask?'

'That would be the shop on the corner of Ironmonger Lane and Cheapside, would it? We asked there as we were passing on our way here. It seems your brother has granted himself a holy day. He isn't there. What have you done with him, eh, Roger?'

'Done with him? He's not my chattel. He's his own man and does as he will. What is this? Dear Christ on the Cross! You think I've killed him?' Roger stepped back, leaning against the wall for support. 'What are you saying? I could never…'

Seb moved in front of Jude.

'Master Redmaine, we are certain that's not the case,' he said. Roger's face wore an expression of such shock and horror, Seb was sure he must be innocent of so foul a crime. 'But we are – that is, the coroner – be concerned for your brother's whereabouts.'

'Why? What does he care about William?'

'He is concerned for all of you. What if the intruder returns to complete his business here?'

'What business?'

'Since he made off with so few of your valuables, 'tis possible he took them, such that we would suspect a thief in the night,' Seb said, composing his tale as he went. 'Supposing rather that he had some great quarrel with your father in the past and intends to be revenged upon all the Redmaine family?'

'What quarrel would that be?'

'Surely, you should know that better than we, sir?'

'Aye, well that's as may be but I still do not know where William has taken himself. You could try Haldane's apothecary's shop in Lothbury. He has a liking for the daughter of the house. Jacquetta, I believe is her name.'

'Thank you, Master Redmaine. We will try there. Good day to you.'

Touching his cap courteously, Seb nudged Jude towards the front door and they left Roger Redmaine to dress for the day. But the instant the door closed behind them, Jude turned on Seb.

'What in hell's name do you think you're about? I'm the coroner's man here; not you. I was asking the questions and might have had him upon the verge of bloody confessing his guilt and you butt in with your own foolish version of events and let him get away with it. For tuppence, I ought to knock you on your skinny arse. You messed up my plan completely.'

'He didn't do it, Jude,' Seb said. 'He is not our culprit.'

'And how do you know that, you bloody little genius?'

'By his look. He was shocked beyond reason when you hinted – less than subtly – that he might have killed his brother.'

'And no man could ever act such a part. Is that what you're saying?'

'There was no pretence in him, I'm certain. Let us go to Lothbury and find William there. I promise you, Jude, we will not let him off so lightly.'

'You believe he is our murderer? He killed his father?'

'If not, I suspect he knows who is.'

'When last we spoke to him, he was most helpful and readily answered all my queries,' Jude reminded Seb.

'Aye, but did you not feel he was being a little too helpful? It seemed to me he was guiding us away from the truth.'

Haldane's apothecary's shop, Lothbury

A S MATTERS turned out, Seb and Jude had no difficulty discovering the whereabouts of William Redmaine. His and Master Haldane's voices could be heard arguing long before they reached the shop doorway and an odd sort of argument it certainly was.

'I can't give her a dowry, no matter what. I can't afford it,' shouted Master Haldane from behind his counter board, all red in the face.

'I don't want your damned money,' William yelled back. 'I'll have Jacquetta to wife without a penny of yours.'

'She's fat and idle and useless in the house. Can't cook, can't sew, can't brew. I'd put her in a nunnery, if I could pay them to take her. Marry her if you will but there's no dowry.'

'I love your daughter. I don't care if she can't cook. I have money enough to have servants to do that. I will marry her, no matter what you say.' William ran out of breath and ceased his ranting.

Slowly, it seemed, the two realised they were arguing the same case.

'You have no objection if me and Jacquetta wed?' William said at last.

'None at all, if you don't demand a dowry.'

'Done!' both men said together and shook hands across the counter to seal the bargain.

Upon the instant, a jug of hippocras was produced and an assortment of cups set out. Seb and Jude found they were included in the impromptu celebrations, along with any customers entering the shop. Learning that wine was being handed out for no charge, the place was soon crowded with assorted passers-by: apprentices, housewives, craftsmen of various kinds, all grabbing cups or even bringing their own, that they might share the benevolence. When a large sow muscled her way in and jolted Jude's leg, such that he near spilled the drink in his hand, he decided they should leave. An interrogation was impossible in the circumstances. They would have to come back another time. At least they didn't need to fear for William Redmaine's safety any longer.

The Foxley workshop

JUDE WAS busy stitching the gatherings of the 'Gawain' manuscript together and Seb was sketching possible designs for the wooden covers. He wanted them to impress but was unsure how intricately Jack could manage to carve them. Lime wood would most likely be best with its fine grain. He would see Stephen Appleyard about it later; ask the carpenter's advice.

'Did you catch your murderer then?' Emily asked, coming into the workshop with a platter of cinnamon and saffron cakes. 'Try these. They're made to a new receipt I'm devising.' She handed the platter around to Kate, Tom and Jack.

'Not yet,' Jude said, stuffing a whole cake into his mouth, 'But we will. We're pretty certain now that William Redmaine killed his father – or at least, Seb thinks he did. We'll catch him eventually. Trouble is: we need evidence, don't we, Seb? These are good, Em. You're not such a bad cook, unlike Jacquetta Haldane, apparently.'

'Who?' Em asked, as Rose joined them from the shop and Nessie came from the kitchen with a second batch of little cakes. They were proving most popular.

'The apothecary's daughter. We went to Lothbury in search of William Redmaine for Seb feared his brother, Roger, might have done away with him.'

'I certainly did not,' Seb objected.

'Shush. I'm telling this bloody story. Now where was I?' He helped himself to another cake and took a large bite, demolishing more than half of it. 'Oh, aye, we found Will at Haldane's, arguing with her father for Jacquetta's hand in marriage. It was quite a bloody to-do, wasn't it Seb?' Jude told the tale, mimicking Will and Haldane and adding plenty of extra embellishments until they were all helpless with merriment, laughing 'til their ribs hurt.

'Don't go on, Jude,' Em begged, holding her belly. 'Else I fear my babe will be born untimely.'

'And then a bloody great pig strolled in to join the party,' Jude added, setting them all laughing anew.

The only person not laughing was Kate, who put down her cake, uneaten. She looked deep in thought as she took up her charcoal and continued with a sketch of a devilish monster with forked tail, horns and cloven hooves. But his face was recognisably that of a young man.

'Master Seb,' Kate said as they sat at dinner, 'Since we could not go to visit my father upon Saturday last, as you were still recovering, might we go this afternoon, now the 'Gawain' is finished? I'm sure, I recall you saying that we might.'

'Did I? I don't remember, lass, but truly a number of things have slipped my mind of late. If I said that, then indeed we shall.'

Kate cupped her hand around one side of mouth: the side closest to Jack, so he should not hear.

'Then we may look at the pups...' she whispered, 'For Jack.'

'Oh, aye,' Seb said, smiling. 'I'm certain your father will appreciate a report of your progress.'

For a moment, Kate looked worried. It was upon the previous Saturday that Tom had told his sneak's tale to Master Seb, about seeing her and Jack kissing behind the pig sty. Would master report that to her father also? But master was still smiling: perhaps he'd forgotten the incident.

'Why not take those joyous drawings you did yesterday,' he was saying. 'Your father will like to see them, no doubt.'

The Verney house in Walbrook

MASTER SEB was talking with her father in the parlour. Kate had so feared he might mention 'that kiss' but, so far, over ale and marchpane comfits, he hadn't. Instead, both men were discussing and so greatly admiring her humorous drawings, she knew she was blushing, could feel her cheeks burn.

'Master, Papa,' she said as her father refilled her master's cup, despite his protestations, 'May I go speak with Alice, please?'

The men exchanged glances. It was ever difficult in such an instance. Being an apprentice to Master Seb, he was her guardian, but in her father's house, *his* word was law. So who should she ask?

'Of course, my chick,' her father said, 'If your sister is at leisure. I believe she went upstairs. Your aunt has been advising her upon a suitable betrothal gown. All women's business, of course,' he added, turning to Master Seb.

'Remember the dogs, master,' Kate said as she left the parlour.

'Dogs? What about the dogs, Master Sebastian?'

'Oh, just Kate had an idea. Young Jack – I may have mentioned him in passing to you – his dog was lately killed. The lad is bereft and Kate – soft-hearted as she be – thinks one of your dogs might cheer the lad. She said you had a recent litter of pups?'

'Aye, so we do and they be just of age to leave their dame. Come through to the yard. We don't let them into the house. You can have the pick of the litter. They be fine guard dogs and not so bad at ratting, neither.'

Seb followed Master Verney through the house and outside. The dogs were kept in a stout kennel and looked well cared for. Master Verney called to the bitch and she came out and licked his hand.

'She seems friendly enough,' Seb said, tentatively stroking her coat. Her fur was long and black with white patches; her ears drooped over just a little. He let her sniff his fingers and was soon rewarded with a cold nose thrust in his palm and a lick from a rough, wet tongue. Seven pups, all similarly coloured, tumbled out of the kennel, plump and bright eyed.

'They're shepherding dogs. Take your choice, master. Was it a dog or a bitch you wanted?'

Kate had hastened up the stairs and found Alice frowning over three gowns spread out upon her bed.

'Kate!' she cried, opening her arms wide and gathering her younger sister into a fond embrace. 'How fortunate it is that you have come this day. I am so perplexed as to which gown will most suit me when Will Redmaine and I are betrothed. The date is all set for next week and even though Will's father died so recently, he has not put it off for a time of mourning. Does that not prove how much he longs to have me as his wife? I could be an Easter bride, Kate. Will that not be quite wonderful? Now, tell me: which gown will suit me best? I had intended to wear the crimson but now I'm not certain.' Alice offered Kate the hem of a pale blue gown. 'This is of the softest wool. Feel it. Aunt Bess says she prefers the tawny one but I like this better, except for the neckline. Is it unseemly low, do you think?'

Kate did not touch the fine cloth but sat upon the bed.

'Beware, Kate. Don't crease the gowns.'

'Ally. Please harken to me,' Kate began, twiddling her fingers in her dark curls.

'Of course. Just say which gown you prefer,' Alice insisted.

'It matters not.'

'But it does.'

'No, Ally, it doesn't because I know you will change your mind another dozen times or more, whatever I or Aunt Bess decide. But I have something to tell you. 'Tis important, so please listen.'

'I can't think what could be more important than my betrothal gown but go on. Tell me, sister.'

'I know something of Will Redmaine...'

'He's not taken sick, is he? St Mary forbid...'

'No, Ally, he is quite well but I overheard my master and his brother talking of him at dinner.'

'Do they know my Will? What did they say?'

'I know not why, but they visited Haldane's apothecary shop this morning.'

'Where is that?'

'I'm unsure. But Will Redmaine was there, discussing his betrothal with Master Haldane.'

'Does that not show how eager he is to tell everyone about us?'

'No, Ally, it doesn't. Oh, my dearest sister,' Kate said, putting her arms around Alice. 'He wasn't speaking of you. He was confirming his betrothal to Master Haldane's daughter. I'm so sorry, Ally.'

'That's just nonsense, Kate.' Alice pulled away. 'You're making it up. Will is my betrothed and nobody else's. Why do you tell lies about such a thing? You know full well how important this is to me.'

'It is no lie.'

'Then you must have misheard the story... or your master was making it all up. You are wrong, Kate. Will and I shall be wed come Eastertide and there's an end to it.'

'I'm sure it's true, Ally. My master wouldn't invent such news.'

'Then you're a liar... always have been,' Alice cried and slapped Kate across the cheek as hard as ever she could.

With a gasp, Kate held her hands to her face.

'I am no liar, sister!'

'Then I'll make the devil pay!' Alice screamed.

'No, Ally, please not that. Say you don't mean it.' Kate was begging, sobbing.

'Just get out of my chamber. Leave me!' Alice raised her arm to strike again.

Kate ran to the stairs and fled down, away from her sister's fearful anger.

The sound of laughter was coming from the parlour.

'You be quite a lively one,' she heard Master Seb saying.

She straightened her cap, smoothed down her apron and wiped the tears on her sleeve. She could imagine the imprint of Alice's hand, burning like a brand on the side of her face, but it couldn't be helped. With a pretended calm, she rejoined the men in the parlour, head held high.

Master Seb was receiving a thorough wash from a bundle of black and white fur, its pink tongue wetting his chin, his hands, even his ear.

'What do you think, Kate?' he said, handing her the squirming pup. 'Will Jack take a liking to him, do you suppose?'

Kate held the little creature against her cheek. Its fur was soft indeed and served to hide the damage Alice had done.

'He's lovely,' she managed to croak. 'May we take him back to Paternoster Row?'

'That's the intention,' her father said, 'But he's meant to cheer the lad, Jack, so your master tells me. He's not yours, lass.'

'I know but I think he likes me.' The hint of tears was there in her voice and it occurred to Seb that young Kate might be missing her family, even though they were divided by a few streets only.

They were nearing home, turning into Paternoster Row by St Michael's church, Kate carrying her drawings, Seb with the pup tucked inside his jerkin beneath his mantle for warmth. A chill wind was rising. As the wind tugged at Kate's hair, blowing it back, Seb saw the horrid weal upon her cheek.

'Kate,' he said, stopping and crouching down beside her in the street. He brushed her hair aside with gentle fingers. 'Whatever came to pass, lass? What is this mark?'

'It's nothing,' she told him, pulling her curls to cover it again and turning away.

'Who hurt you, Kate? Tell me.' He drew her into the porch of St Michael's.

'I quarrelled with Alice. She called me a liar and slapped my face. We used to argue all the time. It's nothing, I tell you. It will fade; it always does.'

'Is that how it is with sisters, quarrelling?'

'Did you and Master Jude never come to blows? Everybody fights. That's just how life is: quarrelling, arguing, bickering and lashing out'

Seb frowned. Kate did not speak as an innocent young lass of fourteen years should but rather as a world-weary old woman.

'Why do you think my father was so eager to 'prentice me to you?' she went on. 'My talent had naught to do with it. He wanted me out of the house afore... afore...'

'Afore what, Kate?'

'Afore either me or Alice killed each other. The day before you agreed to take me on, Alice had gone at me with a kitchen knife and I clawed her face with my nails. I know you all think I'm merry, smiling Kate but I'm not. Papa says there be bad blood in the family on my mother's side. You know where she is, my mother? Papa never told you, did he? 'Tis our family's awful secret. He lets folk think she's dead but she isn't. She's locked in Bedlam Hospital with the mad folk after she tried to burn our house down. Twice she did that. So now you know.'

'How fearful for you, Kate.' Seb was stunned and hardly knew what to say.

'You won't send me back to my father, will you? I can't live in the same house as Alice again. It's not safe for either of us. And you won't tell him I told you everything, will you? Please, Master Seb. I'm so happy at your house.' Kate was sobbing.

'No, lass. Our home be your home for as long as you wish. Now, dry your tears. Mistress Em will have supper ready and you know how she hates us being late at table.'

Arriving back home, the pup received welcomes of more or less enthusiasm. Emily was, for once, in agreement with Jude that the little dog was likely to prove a confounded nuisance requiring too much food, causing disruption and making a mess. Rose was won over upon an instant when it licked her hand, scooping it up, turning it upon its back and tickling its belly. Tom, likewise, approved the new arrival, at least until he was told it was going to be Jack's dog. Nessie seemed content, saying she hoped it would keep the rats at bay as Beggar always did. But what of Jack?

At first sight of the newcomer, Jack scowled and turned away.

Kate took the pup from Rose and went to him.

'Look, Jack. We've got a pup for you. Isn't he sweet?' Kate said, holding out the bundle of fur to Jack. 'Master Seb chose him.'

Jack folded his arms.

'I don't want the bloody thing. It ain't my Beggar, is it? Take it away. I never wanna see it agen, do I?'

'But he's lovely, look,' Kate insisted, tears threatening. 'How can you not want him, Jack?'

'He ain't Beggar!' Jack shouted and ran out to the yard, up the wooden stairs to his loft.

'No matter, Kate,' Seb said. 'Dry your tears, lass.'

'Looks like you got yourself a bloody dog, little brother,' Jude said. 'Serves you right. You'll have to do all the cleaning up after it.'

'It seems I have been somewhat over-hasty,' Seb said, sighing. ''Tis too soon for Jack to think of replacing Beggar. No matter. I expect the day will come. Until then, I suppose 'tis down to me to see to the pup. First, I'll take him to the garden that he may relieve himself whilst you womenfolk think of a name for him, such that he can learn to come when called.'

Seb took a length of binding tape, used to support the spine of a book, and tied it around the pup's neck. He didn't want it disappearing into the brambles, never to be seen again. Its little legs were so short, its belly so rounded that it became stuck upon the kitchen threshold and Seb had to lift it over and down the step, into the yard. Otherwise, it trotted along quite well though ever eager to sniff at each new scent. They'd hardly made it to the pig sty gate by the time the pup had done what was required and Seb made a fuss of him, to show approval that he had done the right thing. Hopefully, that might spare the kitchen and workshop floors from puddles or worse.

During supper, various names were suggested for the little dog which slept all the while beneath the board, curled betwixt Seb's feet. Rose suggested 'Hardy' after the pet she'd had years ago. Tom thought 'Hercules'; Jude suggested 'Bloody Nuisance'. It was Kate who proposed a name that had been on all their lips of late, so the pup became 'Gawain'.

That evening, with Jude gone to Dame Ellen's and the youngsters abed, Seb was content to sit by the hearth in the kitchen, attempting to get Gawain to answer to his name. Emily and Rose were at the kitchen board, armed with a large pair of tailor's shears, needles and thread.

'Em! What be this? That's my most favoured work-a-day shirt,' he said, alarmed at recognising the garment spread out upon the board. 'What are you doing with it?'

''Tis good linsey-woolsey cloth, Seb, but see how it is frayed at neck and cuff. And this ink stain on the sleeve will never come out.'

'I know, Em, but I be comfortable in it.'

'Comfortable? You mean downright scruffy. Rose and I are going to make two new shirts from it for the babe. Besides, you have better shirts than this. You be hardly a credit to my skills as a wife, wearing this old thing. I feel ashamed when I see you clad in it.'

'Oh. Then I suppose… Oh, well, if 'tis for the babe. Come, Gawain, let us see that the side gate be secured and you may do your business afore we retire. Come.'

Out in the yard, he was about to bar the gate for the night but saw a bright glow in the sky to the east. It was an ominous light all too well known to Londoners.

Fire.

He ran back into the kitchen. 'Em, there be a fire, somewhere along Cheapside, I think,' he said, putting on his mantle. 'I'll go see what may be done to help. I'll take the buckets, if I may?'

'Of course but be safe, husband. Don't do anything foolish.'

Seb made haste as best he might, being joined by others, likewise armed with buckets, pails and fire hooks as well, for pulling down burning thatch. Cheapside was crowded as market day, everyone with the same intent: to prevent the fire spreading and thus endangering them all. Seb had thought the blaze must be in Cheapside, he could see the flames so clear against the night sky. In truth, it was farther away in St Pancras Lane, yet the size of the conflagration had made it seem nearer. Folks were queuing at the conduit to fill buckets and wash tubs, brewing vessels and elegant jugs – anything to hand that might carry water.

Seb spotted Jude, dashing off down Soper Lane and turning into St Pancras with two full buckets. He looked wet and soot-stained. Clearly, he had been at the fire already.

'It's Redmaine Hall ablaze,' he shouted to Seb.

Seb filled his buckets and followed on.

In St Pancras Lane, a human chain had been organised and Seb passed his buckets down the line, receiving empty ones in their place which he passed back towards the conduit. The flames lit up the street as bright as a full moon. He could feel the heat, scorching one side of his face. The citizens worked together, determined to defeat London's oldest foe. Every now and then, a gust of wind sent sparks and smoke back at them, making their eyes water and setting them coughing. Occasionally, outlined black against the flames, the skeletal timbers of Redmaine Hall stood stark. It seemed the fine house was lost but the battle continued to prevent the fire spreading. Seb's shoulders were agonising as he handed water containers back and forth. Sweat ran in his eyes and he had discarded his mantle long since as it hampered his efforts. He did not know the men on either side of him in the chain but they were comrades in arms, like battle veterans. They took it in turns to rest for a few moments, the others stretching to fill the gap each time.

A woman came by with a jug of ale that was shared eagerly by the thirsty.

As Seb paused to drink and ease his aching shoulders, he stepped out of his place in the chain. Looking back towards Soper Lane, he espied someone, cloaked and hooded; someone who was making no attempt to fight the fire. A woman. A tongue of flame leapt high. She gasped and clapped her hands in delight. In the blaze of firelight, Seb recognised her.

When she saw him looking at her, she pulled her hood close about her face and ran off, into the night. Seb wondered about her as he returned to the chain and resumed the fight.

Gradually, the light and heat of the flames was diminishing, returning the street to darkness and the February cold. Drizzly rain began to fall, aiding the task of extinguishing the fire. The lane was awash, turned to mud; everything smeared with soot. The crowd was exhausted, flagging, but, into the small hours, they had the victory, even if they were too weary to celebrate it.

Their city was safe. Relieved, they began to make their way home. Daylight would reveal the extent of the damage.

Jude appeared as Seb was searching for his mantle. The sweat upon his skin was turning cold and he shivered in the chill.

'How be your injured arm?' Seb asked him.

'What? Oh, I had forgotten it 'til now. The bindings look to be loosened but it'll serve for tonight. Come back to my lodgings and you can tie it anew for me,' Jude suggested. 'It'll save you waking Mistress Moody. It'll be like old times, just you and me, little brother.'

Seb found his mantle lying in a sodden heap on someone's doorstep.

'No. Em may be awake and worrying. 'Tis better if I go home. Don't forget, the 'Gawain' manuscript requires binding first thing. Don't sleep late upon the morrow.'

'There will hardly be time to doze off. Hear that? The bloody bell for lauds already.' The bell at St Martin le Grand was summoning the monks to prayer. 'Who'd be a bloody monk, eh?' Jude said as they trudged back along Cheapside. 'Mind you, I didn't see any of them buggers out tonight, fighting the bloody fire, did you?'

'God keep you safe, Jude,' Seb said as they parted company outside Dame Ellen's house. He walked on alone now. Few others from Paternoster Row had gone to help put out the fire. It was, perhaps, far enough away so most of his neighbours had been unaware of it.

In the kitchen, Em was asleep upon her stool, leaning back against the wall. Rose had her head on the table board but both women roused as he entered, disturbed by the cold draught that accompanied him through the door. Em fetched him ale and tutted over the state of him but they were still half asleep and Seb was almost too weary to climb the stair. He vaguely heard Em say he was too filthy to go to bed without a good wash but then his head touched the pillow and he knew no more 'til daylight. Even the accustomed nightmares of recent times could not invade his sleep of utter exhaustion.

CHAPTER FIFTEEN

Thursday the twenty-sixth day of February
The Foxley house

'YOU STINK, Jude Foxley,' Emily said by way of greeting when he arrived, somewhat tardily, to begin the day's work. 'Come to that, your hair also smells like smoked hams, husband.'

'Bloody woman. What do you expect when we were up half the night, fighting the fire?' Jude retorted. 'If you've got any salve for my blisters...'

'Out to the yard, the pair of you. Rose and Nessie will bring you hot water and you may use a little of my good soap to wash your hair. Go on, both of you. I'll not have the stench of burnt meat at my table, if you want to break your fast.'

Like scolded schoolboys, the men obeyed. Stripped down to their shirts, they compared the ravages of last night. Being unused to manual labour, both had a fine crop of blisters on the palms of their hands from passing so many buckets of water. Having been closer up the line, nearer to Redmaine Hall, Jude's face was a little scorched and still reddened. His hair had been singed by flying sparks.

'The jerkin I was wearing is ruined,' he complained. 'Little burn holes all over it. Ruined, I tell you. What of yours?'

Seb shrugged but then gasped as Nessie poured a jug full of steaming water over his head. He almost cursed at its scalding heat.

'Don't know,' he managed to splutter, 'Probably not so bad as I was farther away from the blaze. Em will tell me, no doubt.' He began working up a lather on his dark locks with Em's best scented soap.

'I'll smell like a bloody courtesan using this stuff,' Jude said, doing the same. 'Have a care for my injured arm, woman.'

'Forgive me.' Rose was assisting him, saying naught of the ragged ends where his hair had been scorched away. She knew for Jude his fine head of pale hair was a vanity – how it would distress him if he realised its condition now.

Nessie obliged Seb with another cascade of water to rinse away the soap. Again he gasped, this time because it was icy cold. She handed him a linen towel to dry off but she had soaked his shirt as well as his hair in her carelessness.

Both men returned to the kitchen to dry off before the fire.

'Dame Ellen had news of the fire this morn – as ever, the first with the gossip,' Jude was saying as he struggled to pull a comb through his hair. 'She says there be rumours that a woman did it.'

'Did what?' Seb asked, trying to determine whether his shirt would dry out afore he caught a chill, or if he should change it for another.

'Set the fire at Redmaine Hall, of course. Ugh. I swear I can taste soap upon my lips. Aye, well, so the good dame told me, someone saw a woman smearing pig fat around the door and window ledges and – thinking it was some new way to keep out the rain – they said naught about it. Then, later, those very places were seen first ablaze. Of course, they're wrong: can't have been a woman, can it?'

'No? Why is that?' Seb poured ale for them both, to wash away Jude's taste of soap.

'See sense, little brother. It shows forethought and planning. 'Tis a fact well known that a woman's head is just a place to put her cap with not a bloody ounce of learning and deliberation within.'

'Do not let Em and Rose hear you speak such nonsense: they will make a penance of your life.' Seb realised Jude was jesting but then an alarming thought occurred to him regarding what Jude had said. 'If the doors and windows were the first parts of the house to take fire… Oh, Jude. What of anyone within? How were they able to escape? Did they manage to get out?' He sat down heavily upon the nearest stool. 'Is it a coincidence, do you think, that Em said our hair smelled of burnt meat? God have mercy, Jude…'

Breaking their fast would have been a sombre affair – and for Jude, a delicate one as he had particular trouble using his knife and spoon because of his blisters – but the youngsters wanted to hear of the excitement last eve.

Seb told them the bare bones of the story, enough to satisfy their curiosity, but said naught of the possibility of deaths resulting.

'Some are even saying – madmen all,' Jude said, laughing, 'That a woman started the fire. Did you ever hear any tale less bloody likely? They must have been drunkards, seeing things. It'll be sheep singing vespers and witches on flying broomsticks next.'

Everyone laughed. But not Kate. She sat, white as a swan's quill, shaking, with tears rolling like raindrops down her cheeks.

'Kate, lass. Whatever be amiss?' Seb left his spoon in his pottage and went around the board to her. 'Did my words so afright you, lass? Forgive me.' He put his arm around her shoulders and could feel her shuddering sobs. 'It wasn't so bad: the city be quite safe now.'

Kate pressed her head against his chest.

'It was my sister, Ally. She did it, I know,' Kate whispered into his shirt so only he should hear her words.

Seb stroked her dark curls.

'There now, Kate. Shh. Do not distress yourself.' He spoke soothingly but he was frowning. 'Be easy, lass. 'Tis over and done and all be well,' he said, praying silently that his words were the truth.

'You may help me in the kitchen this morn, Kate,' Emily said brightly. 'We could make more cinnamon and saffron cakes to perfect my receipt. What do you say?'

Kate nodded, drying her eyes upon her apron.

In the workshop, Jude was cursing mightily. Every action in attempting to bind the 'Gawain' manuscript tore at his blistered hands.

'I'll do no more damned stitching. Sod it all. My hands are too bloody sore: it'll have to wait.' He threw his tools down, catching his sleeve on the prongs of the binding comb. 'Shit! Now look: my bloody cuff be torn. Damn it, Seb. I'm done here for the day. I can't bloody work like this.'

'Does Em's salve not help?' Seb asked. He was at his desk, marking out the customer's chosen design onto the thick wooden board that would form the book cover, ready for Jack to carve. His hands were sore also but his task did not scrap the blisters as in Jude's case.

'I can't use it, can I, else I'll get bloody grease upon your precious damned folios?'

'Leave it, then. Use the salve and we can take a walk meantime. I'm not much of a mind to do this either.'

Jude was surprised: Seb not in the humour to work? Most unusual. He must have some pressing matter upon his mind.

Redmaine Hall

WITHOUT ANY discussion as to where they were going, the brothers retraced their steps of last eve, back to St Pancras Lane, each knowing the other needed to survey the fire's remains. The once fine house was a shell, its upper storeys seeming precarious. Charred timbers balanced upon little but other timbers in similar condition. A quirk of fate: the statue of St Giles was still in his niche above the door lintel, the marble blackened and cracked by the heat. The smell of smoke lingered like a fog over all and flakes of ash swirled like black snow with every breath of wind.

Coroner Fyssher was there talking with the sheriff and some neighbours, among them the priest of St Benet Sherhog – the church to the right hand of Redmaine Hall.

'If that lot comes down, it'll go straight through my church roof and who will pay for that, eh? Not the Redmaines, not now, that be certain.' The priest threw his arms in the air. 'And what of the shattered west window there? That cost a pretty penny three years since, I can tell you. I demand that I be recompensed for the damage!'

The priest and churchwarden from St Pancras church upon the left hand joined in, all shouting out, demanding that somebody should do something.

'The lord mayor will come after dinner,' Sheriff Colet said loudly, trying to make himself heard above the clamour of angry voices. 'He will assess the damage hereabouts, apportion blame and determine who should pay for repairs to which building. Now be about your work, all of you! That means you too,' he added, turning on Jude and Seb.

'This is my bloody work,' Jude told him. 'As Master Fyssher's assistant.'

Seb said naught but moved aside in haste as a woman with a stout hazel broom came along, sweeping aside debris to clear the gutter before her doorstep.

'Where is my William?' Jacquetta Haldane came rushing up. 'Where is he? I just heard of the fire...' Her voice trailed off, becoming a wail, like a tormented soul, as she gazed up at the blackened timbers.

As if in answer to her cries, there came an ominous creaking sound, as though the house was in pain. Timbers groaned and the crowd scattered in a panic as the building collapsed with a great roar, sending up clouds of soot and dust that set onlookers choking and gasping. As the cloud settled, they could see the grand house was gone, only the stout door with its saint above remained. Then, as they watched, the marble saint crumbled and crashed into the street, narrowly missing the woman with her broom, leaving naught but his sandal-shod feet in the niche. Slowly, that too began to lean and the oak door with its gilded knocker fell in upon the mountain of debris. Redmaine Hall was gone.

'Will! Will!' Jacquetta screamed.

The priests had no words of consolation for her, being too concerned for their own affairs and yet more damage done to their churches.

'Permit me to walk you back to Lothbury,' Seb offered. 'Your father will give you more comfort than this place, Mistress Haldane.'

Jacquetta shrugged free of his hand upon her sleeve.

'No! I want my Will. Where is he?'

'Seems to me you must know the answer, my dear.' The woman with the broom, despairing of getting her gutter swept, what with yet more debris blocking the lane, put an arm around the distraught wench. 'Come away in to my place. We'll get you some ale – both of you,' she said, nodding at Seb. Perhaps she thought they were acquaintances.

They were about to enter the woman's house a few doors along when a man, hatless and without a cloak, came rushing up.

'My house! Great God Almighty. My house.' He fell to his knees amongst the mud and burned wood in the gutter.

It took Seb a moment to recognise Roger Redmaine with his drooping eye.

'They told me there was a fire. They never said it was so bad...'

'I'm so sorry, Master Redmaine,' Seb said, helping him to his feet. 'So many of us did what we could to save it but we could not.'

'Where's William? This is most likely his fault: careless with a candle as ever.'

'It be thought, master...' Seb began, then shook his head, at a loss to find the words. 'None have seen your brother since, I fear,' he managed to say.

'Are you telling me he was in there? In the fire?'

'Master Coroner will know more than I,' Seb said, ashamed at his own cowardice.

Later, as they walked back to Paternoster Row, Jude suggested they should stop by at the Panyer Inn for some ale.

'My mouth tastes of bloody cinders,' Jude complained. 'I swear I saw grains of charcoal floating in the air. Come, you can buy the drink: I forgot my purse.'

Seb made no answer.

'Are you bloody ignoring me or have you gone deaf? Hey, Seb, I'm speaking to you.' Jude gave his brother's arm a shake. 'Stop day dreaming.'

'What? Oh, aye. I was thinking of last night. What you said about a woman setting the fire...'

'I also said that was a foolish thing for any bugger to suggest. Now, what about that ale you promised me?'

'Oh, Jude, I believe a woman may well have done it and, worse yet, I think I know who it was.' Seb was wringing his hands. 'I know not what to do for the best.'

'I'll tell you, little brother. You buy the ale and we can discuss this. I don't know how you come by these insane thoughts.'

'Insane. Aye, there you be correct, Jude.'

In the Panyer Inn, Seb paid a farthing and asked for a jug of small ale.

'Oh, come now, Seb. Proper ale, for God's sake. I need a decent brew.'

Seb sighed and changed their order, handing the pot-boy another farthing. They found a vacant bench by the window and waited for their ale.

'Let me tell you: last eve…' Seb began.

Jude held up his hand to stop him.

'Not until I've swigged my ale.'

The ale was served and, having filled their cups, Jude emptied his in a single draught. He refilled it and, finally, nodded at Seb to say his piece.

'At the fire, I saw a woman watching the blaze. She made no move to aid us in quenching it. Rather she took pleasure in seeing Redmaine Hall consumed by flame. As soon as she saw me looking at her, she hid her face and ran away.'

'There will always be some who enjoy the bloody spectacle, rather than doing anything to remedy it. So, you said you knew who she was?' Jude beckoned to the pot-boy. 'Bring us some bread and cheese, lad: I can see this being a long story. Pay him, Seb.'

'Aye, and how I wish I'd never seen her. This will cause such heartache, Jude.' Seb fished out a last halfpenny from his purse and put it into the pot-boy's sticky hand.

'For us? Just say the name, then we can tell the bloody sheriff and be done with it.'

'I fear, I made a foolish promise to one we hold dear: I said that I would say naught, but now… You be right, Jude. I have to tell what I saw… who I saw. It was Alice Verney. Kate's sister: she who is – or was – supposedly betrothed to William Redmaine.'

'Bloody hell, Seb. The jilted bride? That would explain so much, wouldn't it? But it's a bold bloody step for a woman to take. Are you sure?'

Seb nodded.

The lad brought a platter of maslin bread and ewe's milk cheese and put it before them. Jude set about the food.

'I would give anything to be mistaken,' Seb said, cradling his chin upon his hand. 'But young Kate confided in me: their mother did much the same. Why? I do not know but Kate said she tried to set their house afire on two occasions.'

'Is that how she died?'

'Nay. Mistress Verney lives yet but bides within Bedlam Hospital, so Kate said.'

'With the mad folk? Sweet Jesu's sake. No wonder Master Verney plays the part of a widower. Who would want to own to a bloody madwoman in the family? What are you going to do about it?' Jude spoke around a mouthful of bread, wiping crumbs from his lips with his sleeve. He swallowed and took another bite. 'As a respectable citizen, you can't let such a one remain loose in the city. She might burn us all in our beds. I don't care what half-arsed promises you made, you have to tell the bloody sheriff, or Ol' Fyssher, at least.'

Seb looked doubtful. Breaking a promise went against his conscience and he had been wrestling with the problem since the first light of dawn had pushed its fingers betwixt the shutters. Was his promise to Kate more important than his duty to his fellow Londoners? It seemed an easy choice upon the face of it but the thought of the distress it would cause to Edmund Verney – and dear Kate – if he told what he had seen, was far more personal. He could not hurt them so.

'There may be a way to solve this.' Seb finally took a sip of ale. 'It will not be pleasant for the Verneys but it may lessen the hurt somewhat and avoid the humiliation. But it can only happen if no one else recognised Alice last night. Have you heard her name mentioned?'

'Dame Ellen named no names this morn,' Jude said, smearing the last of the soft cheese on the remaining piece of bread. 'You want this?' he offered.

Seb shook his head. Food was the last thing upon his mind.

'She said someone thought they might have seen a woman,' Jude continued. 'Might have: mark you. Not certainly. It wouldn't surprise me if you were the only one to see her for definite. After all, most likely you were the sole fellow shirking his task in the bucket chain, you idle bugger.' Jude grinned and pushed the empty platter aside, having used a wet finger to pick up every last crumb. 'So what's your ingenious plan, young Aristotle?'

''Tis not ingenious: just a means of causing less sorrow, I hope.' Seb pushed away from the board and stood up. 'Will you come with me?'

'You haven't drunk your ale.'

'You may have it.'

Jude obliged, draining Seb's cup.

'Where're we going?'

'Walbrook.'

'To the Verney place?'

'Aye.'

'Bloody hell, Seb, I'm not sure I want to be the bearer of such ill tidings. There'll be tears and wailings, anger even. What if Mad Alice puts up a fight, or her father? We could find ourselves slung out into the bloody gutter.'

'Since when did being thrown off the premises worry you, Jude? You have been kicked out of more inns and taverns and ale-houses than most good citizens,' Seb said, suppressing a grin.

'That was before I met my sweet Rose. I'm a reformed character now, I'll have you know, little brother.'

'Until the next time…'

Jude was not in the best of humours as they made their way to Walbrook. In Watling Street, a laden dray trundling by forced them into the doorway of a saddler's shop to make way. The carter was cursing the pair of sorry nags harnessed between the shafts, making such excessive use of his whip, Seb winced in sympathy for the poor beasts. Amidst the scent of new leather and years' worth of polish, the saddler rushed over, thinking he had customers.

'Since we haven't got a bloody horse betwixt us, why – in Satan's name – would we want a soddin' saddle?' was Jude's response to the saddler's polite enquiry.

'I crave pardon for my brother's lack of manners, master,' Seb said. 'We were startled somewhat by the dray. I pray God shall give you good day.' He touched his cap and dragged Jude out of the shop doorway. 'What was the need for such rudeness?' he asked when they were outside.

'Got eyes, hasn't he? What fool would mistake us for horsemen in need of saddles?'

'We could have been grooms from some lord's stable,' Seb suggested.

'No we couldn't. We don't stink of horse shit and sweat. I for one smell like a belle-dame's bloody boudoir with all that soap your Em made me use. He was trying to force us into making a purchase. That's against guild rules, that is.'

'I be certain he had no such intent, Jude. Besides, at present, I couldn't afford an iron harness ring, never mind one of his beautiful saddles. Did you note the fine craftsmanship of his work?'

'No I bloody didn't. I was too concerned to avoid being run down by a damned cart.' Jude kicked out at a skinny cat that dashed from a side alley as they crossed Cordwainer Street. When a cookshop lad tried to accost them to come try his mistress's mutton pies, that was the final exasperation for Jude. He cuffed the youngster about the ear and knocked him off balance so he fell in the mud. 'Fuck off!' he yelled.

'Oh, Jude. What be amiss? Do not take your ill temper out on others.'

'Don't you bloody tell me what to do. I've had enough of this. You and your damned do-gooding. I'm not going to Verney's. If you have any sense, you'll just tell the bloody sheriff and make an end to it.' Jude turned to walk away but Seb confronted him.

'Be you afeared of telling Master Verney what we saw?' In truth, Seb was certain his brother could not be. Storms, lightning, God's wrath: those were things to fear. Jude had no fear of anything else, not tavern brawls, high places, the darkness, savage beasts. Not even the river that scared Seb half to death whenever he was forced into a ferryman's boat.

'What *you* saw, you mean. I never saw anything and o' course I'm not bloody afeared. I've got more important things...'

'You fear meeting Alice Verney, don't you, because she be most likely insane. Is that the case?'

'Course not,' Jude repeated but his words lacked conviction.

'Very well. I'll go alone.' Seb spoke the words quite sure Jude would change his mind and accompany him. Therefore, he was dismayed, shocked even, when his brother shrugged.

'Be careful, Seb,' he muttered and turned back along Watling Street, leaving Seb standing, somewhat at a loss. A madwoman had made a coward of Jude? He never expected that.

Seb trudged along Budge Row and turned up the hill on Walbrook. He was still attempting to decide upon the best way of broaching the subject of his speech when Edmund Verney opened the door to his knock, in person. Edmund did not invite him in but simply opened the door and stepped back. As Seb entered, the first thing he noticed was the unusual silence: no servants' chatter, no women's voices as he had heard upon previous visits. Even the dogs were silent.

Without a word, Edmund led him into the parlour. Refreshments were not offered. He indicated the chair where Seb should sit, then took the other himself. He sat, staring down at his hands in his lap. It was discourteous to speak first in another man's house but Seb realised as the quietude drew out in length that he might have to. Then Edmund spared him the offence.

'You've come about the fire,' he said softly. It was a statement, not a question.

'I have, Master Edmund.'

'You saw her, didn't you? You saw my Alice. She said you did.'

'Aye.'

'I've been expecting the sheriff any time. I suppose you have informed him?'

'I have said naught to anyone in authority, master. I wanted to speak with you afore I did anything.'

'Truly?' Edmund looked up from gazing at his hands. His eyes seemed strangely bright. Tears maybe? Or a glimmer of hope, Seb wondered.

'Rightly or wrongly, Kate has told me what occurred with Mistress Verney. She made me swear never to tell and I was prepared to stand by my promise.'

'Until last eve,' Edmund said, 'And now you find your promise to be untenable. I understand and am grateful for your courtesy and kindness in telling me first, before the sheriff.'

'Nay. You mistake my purpose, master. One glance at your elder daughter's face last night was sufficient to convince me that she was not in her rightful mind, even if Kate had not told me of what befell their mother. After learning her betrothed had cast her aside for another, was it any wonder her humours were much disturbed. She be in need of care and sympathy, not a gaoler's rough treatment and a turnkey's shout.

'Master Edmund, if I may take the great liberty of advising you, I think your daughter belongs with her mother, in Bedlam, awaiting recovery, not in Newgate, awaiting the services of the hangman.'

Edmund thought long upon the words, rubbing his hands over his face many times, as though to erase the pain.

'And if I arranged it thus, you would not go to the sheriff? You would spare my Alice such punishment for her crime? Despite the possible deaths of three men in the flames?'

'There were but two deaths. William Redmaine and the steward, Walter. Roger Redmaine was elsewhere. And that would be the way of it: the sheriff should hear naught from me. So long as your daughter was no longer a danger to anyone.'

Edmund moved from his chair, as though a great burden had been lifted from him. He clasped both Seb's hands within his own.

'You are the kindest of men, Master Sebastian, to let poor Alice evade the worst. You are correct: the lass is quite out of her head. She confessed all to me, told me what she had done, laughing madly and weeping with sorrow by turns. You have my heartfelt gratitude for the rest of my days. The Lord Jesu could not show greater mercy.' Edmund was smiling with relief.

Seb nodded, embarrassed by such effusive praise.

'Shall I send young Kate home to you?'

The smile was gone from Edmund's lips in an instant. He sighed heavily, releasing Seb's hands and stepping away.

'Aye. I should not expect you to be held by the terms of our indenture. You are wise not to want to keep in your household one who may well be tainted with madness like her sister. After all, their mother's blood flows in Kate's veins too. You would ever live in fear that she may harm you and yours. I understand.'

'That was not my meaning, master,' Seb objected. 'I thought you might welcome her company for a few days at this time of sorrow for your family. I have no intention of ending Kate's apprenticeship untimely. She has a disposition that cheers us like summer sunlight and a quite remarkable talent. She works diligently and willingly. I would not part with her from choice... unless you want me to?'

'Then you would keep her?'

'Aye. Of course, I would.'

'Then again, I am in your debt. Let me fetch ale and we can drink to our continued agreement.'

Seb smiled and realised how thirsty he was now.

Westminster

ANTHONY WOODVILLE, Earl Rivers, made a sweeping bow, removing his beaver hat, blocking the Duke of Gloucester's exit from King Edward's privy chamber.

'My lord earl,' Richard responded, courteously touching his cap – a gesture not required by etiquette in greeting one of lower rank but he did it all the same. It cost naught and avoided any suggestion of a slight. 'I trust you be in good health?'

'Indeed, your grace, and I thank you for your enquiry.' The earl's words were polite enough so why, Richard wondered, did he always feel the man was mocking him, sneering at him? Richard moved to pass by but Anthony did not step aside. 'I would ask after your business with the king. How are the funerary arrangements progressing? I offer my services if…'

'Well enough. The Abbot of Tewkesbury has agreed that ten days hence will suffice for preparations to be made for the Duke of Clarence's burial. My brother is to lie with his wife in the crypt, behind the abbey's high altar. The king's barge is to be decked in mourning to transport the-the body as far up river as Cricklade.' Richard paused and breathed deeply. He would not show this man how wretched was his heart with sorrow. He looked down, smoothing the soft black wool of his doublet with his hands – not because it was creased but because he would not have a Woodville see the tears in his eyes. Bad enough that he must have noticed the catch in his voice. 'Then the hearse will go by road to Gloucester and then, once more by water, up the Severn River to Tewkesbury. I have received word from the other religious houses along the way, where the hearse will rest each night, apart from the Abbot of Cirencester who is away from his abbey at present, so the letter from his prior informed me. As soon as that be confirmed, all is ready.'

'That must be a relief to you, my lord. And what of Clarence's portrait? I heard tell you had such a work in hand?' Anthony could not have cared less about any such foolishness. What he wanted so desperately to hear was that the artist was no longer available to do it. He should, in fact, be as dead as his subject matter, if the assassin had fulfilled his task, as ordered.

'Indeed. Master Foxley is coming to Crosby Place upon the morrow, if I have my wish, to complete his portrait of myself and to show me his d-drawings of G-George.' Richard coughed to clear his throat and failed to notice the earl's startled expression.

'And that is certain?' he asked.

'Aye. His goodwife told my messenger that he will be there as I requested. Is there some difficulty with that which I know not?'

'No. No, indeed, my lord. I bid you farewell.' Anthony Woodville hastened away at last, such that Richard could leave also.

The duke was relieved but somewhat mystified by the earl's strange response.

As for the earl: a certain lackey of his was about to regret that his mother had not strangled him at birth.

The Foxley house

'TWO OF the clock, on the morrow, at Crosby Place, the messenger said.' Emily passed Seb his platter of mackerel in a saffron sauce.

More saffron, he thought gloomily. Not only was Em's craving for the stuff costing them a small fortune, at this rate, they would all turn yellow afore Eastertide.

'Was it Sir Robert who came?' he asked.

'I would have said, if it was. No, but the fellow wore the Gloucester livery. You will go, won't you?'

'Refuse the duke? I would not dare. Of course I shall go.'

'That is fortunate then because I assured him you would. Now tell us about the fire. Can Redmaine Hall be saved?'

Seb shook his head and swallowed a spoonful of mackerel.

'It collapsed as we watched, did it not, Jude? More importantly, at least two lives were lost, it seems, which be a great sorrow. Any signs of William Redmaine and his steward, Walter, have not been found.' Seb noticed then that Kate's head hung so low, her hair trailed in her food. 'But enough of that,' he said. 'No more talk about the fire now. Kate, did you make any cakes for us this morn, as Mistress Em suggested? I be looking forward to tasting them.'

'Aye. I made some.' Kate sounded miserable indeed. 'But I forgot to watch them on the griddle pan.'

'Her mind was not upon her work. Was it, Kate?' Emily said, looking resigned. 'Cinders were all we were left with. So much spice wasted, both saffron and cinnamon, 'tis a crime. No matter: Seb, you can fetch some more from Haldane's. Lothbury will be but a short step out of your way when you go to Crosby Place tomorrow afternoon.'

'Oh. I suppose I could.'

'You would begrudge me, husband?'

'Of course not, Em.' He kissed her and whispered: 'We must speak privily, concerning Kate. I would have your womanly advice. And Kate,' Seb said as an afterthought. 'Could you take Gawain out to the garden for me? Play with him: he needs the exercise but keep him upon the leash so he cannot run off and be lost. Can you do that, please?'

'Aye, Master Seb.'

'You know, Kate, that it takes more effort to look mournful than to look happy. Will you not smile for me? Just a little, at least? That be more cheerful, lass. Rose, you'll see to any customers in the shop and Jack, you can begin tracing that design I made onto the boards, ready for carving. Tom, you will practise your stitching methods on those cheap students' pamphlets: those stitches need to be smaller and more even. What of you, Jude? What will you do? I trust the Panyer Inn will not occupy your afternoon?'

'Tut tut, little brother, as if it ever would.'

272

When everyone else was busy with their tasks, Seb spoke quietly to Em.

'I have to tell you, Em, last night's fire was begun by Kate's sister.'

'What! Surely not. How can you know that?'

'Hush, wife, keep your voice low, I beg you. I tell you this in utter confidence, such that you may aid young Kate. This will be hard for her, indeed. Tell no one else, however tempted you may be. I thought I may have seen Alice at the fire but was confused as to why she might be there. This morn, I called upon Edmund Verney and all doubt was erased for Alice had confessed to him, that she had burned the house about William Redmaine's ears because he had rejected her.'

'But that's awful. She deserves to hang...'

'That is not so, Em. The poor lass be quite mad. Insanity runs in her mother's family, so it seems. Master Verney will see to it that she be safely cared for in Bedlam. But we need to look to Kate. As soon as Jude mentioned that gossips were saying a woman did it, Kate told me it must have been her sister. The little lass knew straightway. Once the elder girl be moved to the hospital, Kate will return to her father, for a few days. I would have you explain to her that she is not being sent away in disgrace; that in no wise do we think to blame her because she bears the Verney name; that we love her and will welcome her back as soon as her father thinks fit.'

'You could tell her as well as I.'

'Aye, but you will do it with a woman's soft touch.'

Em raised her eyebrows.

'Me?'

Seb nodded.

'I know beneath that veil of stark efficiency, you have a heart as kind as any. Kinder than most. Please, Em. The words would mean more coming from you.'

'Because I'm usually the one who has to speak sharply and instil some discipline in this house, as you do not.'

He smiled, hoping to win her over to his cause.

'Very well: a woman's soft touch it shall be.'

'Thank you, Em. You be the best of women in London.'

She gave him a harsh look.

'I meant 'in the world', of course.'

'Mm. You'd better mean that. And you can reward me later for my kindness of heart.'

He kissed her upon her brow and stroked the curve of her cheek with the backs of his fingers.

'And don't think that will suffice, Sebastian Foxley,' she said with mock severity, wagging her finger at him. 'For it will not.'

CHAPTER SIXTEEN

Friday the twenty-seventh day of February
Westminster

BEHIND THE king's mews, three men were talking over their plans. The fellow with the lisp was not among them and never would be again. The churning waters of the River Thames were content to swallow up detritus of all kinds, including ineffectual servants who repeatedly failed their lord.

One of the three, a man with prominent lips looking somewhat froglike and wearing a green cap, chinked a purse in his hand.

'Easiest wages we'll ever earn, lads,' he said, laughing. 'Our quarry is some mincing artist fellow from Paternoster Row. He is due to meet Gloucester at Crosby Place two hours after noontide. Our task is to see he never arrives there. My lord was insistent: the artist must on no account have speech with the duke.'

'How will we know this, er, artist?' one of the others asked, snorting with derision at the thought of a fellow so pathetic, he must earn his living with a paint brush.

'We will follow him from Paternoster Row. The difficulty for us is that we must do this job in the daylight but there are dark alleys aplenty off Cheapside, Poultry and Cornhill. Another problem is the route he might take: after Poultry, he may turn up Broad Street instead of Cornhill and that street has few alleyways and its breadth means it is less easy to waylay our quarry there. But in Poultry, beside St Mildred's church is a narrow way: Scalding Alley. You know it?'

The other two men nodded.

'Aye. The Walbrook stream runs there, by the church,' the third man said. 'That would be as good a place as any.'

'Glad you agree. Now, listen: this is my plan...'

The Foxley house

'SEB,' SAID Emily as they dined on pickled mussels in – once again – a saffron sauce. 'You won't forget to go by way of Haldane's, will you? You promised to buy me more saffron and we have need of cinnamon also. Kate is going to attempt to make those cakes again. And we won't let them burn this time, will we, lass?'

'No, Mistress Em. I'll do my best with them.' Kate managed a smile. It was not her usual merry smile but it was a passable effort.

'Good, lass,' Seb said to encourage her, 'But that means Tom and I should set off for Crosby Place shortly. Tom. Go collect what we shall need from the workshop. And bring my scrip with the Clarence drawings.'

'But, master, I haven't finished my dinner yet.'

'You can eat the remains for supper. And I shall need money for the spices,' Seb added, scrabbling in his purse and finding a solitary, badly-clipped halfpenny – not enough, he feared.

'I'll fetch that,' Jude said quickly. The last thing he wanted was his brother finding their money pouch in the chimney nigh bereft of coin. It was going to take a miracle to refill the bag before Saturday and his own guardian, St Jude, being the patron of lost causes, hadn't yet seen fit to perform one. His prayers had been wasted, as usual. The holy saints were all stone deaf, he was sure.

'Here's your coin.' Jude tipped a few pennies into Seb's hand.

'Sixpence? Oh, well. That will have to serve. So, what shall you do?'

'Em and Rose have decided it's time to start making use of ol' Bowen's bedchamber.'

'And when was that discussed? We do not have a key.'

'Last eve, whilst you and I were fighting fire, apparently. As for having no key, that is my task for the afternoon: to break into the room, one way or another. I'll take a bloody axe to the door, if I must.'

'Take care with your wounded arm and those blisters, if you do.'

'What are you? My mother or my wet-nurse? Don't bloody fuss me, Seb.'

As Seb and Tom left the house and turned along Paternoster Row, towards Cheapside, three men watched them from one of the gateways into the precinct of St Paul's.

'That him? The skinny one with dark hair?'

'Aye. He looks the sort and see that? Rolls of paper in his scrip. Must be him.'

'We can't get this wrong. Remember what happened to Lispin' Laurie.'

'No one said there would be two of 'em. What do we do about the lad? He looks big enough to give us a bit o' trouble, if we don't do fer 'im quick.'

'Two wisps o' straw like them against us three. What you worried about? We can lick 'em like that.' The man with the green cap clicked his fingers. 'Come on. Keep 'em in sight but no crowding, else they'll spot us.'

Along Cheapside, the better weather had brought out a street entertainer, a stilt-walker juggling hoops. He was making much pretence at dropping a hoop and having the smallest children stretching up to pass it back to him, only to have him drop another instead. There was much laughter and merriment and a sizeable crowd for Seb and Tom to have to push their way through, if they were to reach Crosby Place on time. At the Cheap Cross, Seb turned up Wood Street, to escape the press of people. As they walked, he felt an itch betwixt his shoulder blades, as if he was being watched. When they turned to cut through to Catte Street, he glanced back.

Two idle fellows were behind them, looking as though they had but lately left some tavern or other. A third man, wearing a cap the precise hue of unripened apples, Seb noted, was tending to the lace upon his shoe. Something about his face seemed familiar but Seb was unsure what exactly.

A pair of goodwives puffed over their heavy baskets piled with vegetables. An elderly fellow carried a cock in a cage and a beggar called for alms from the shelter of a doorway. Upon a whim, Seb sent Tom running back to drop the clipped halfpenny in the beggar's bowl – he dare not spare more from his meagre purse. Perhaps upon their return, if Lord Richard paid them, he might give a more generous donation.

Tom barged past the man in the green cap and shouted an apology for almost oversetting him, to be cursed in return.

'This ain't working out as it should, is it?' one drunkard muttered to his companion. 'This way we won't be going by St Mildred's at all.'

'No, and we've got t' get in front of 'em, if we're t' grab 'em. How can we do that when we don't know which way they're going? I don't like this job at all. I don't reckon old Frog-face thought this plan through proper.' The pair hung back until the man in the green cap caught them up.

'Lothbury,' he whispered, 'Alley beyond St Meg's. Now.'

The drunkards seemed to sober up of a sudden and quickened their pace. They were singing some bawdy song at the top of their voices as they ambled past Seb and Tom. One gave them 'good day' and a gap-toothed leer.

Seb touched his cap to them, grinning, even as he hoped Tom had not heard the filthy subject of their song. Glancing at the lad, his flushed cheeks suggested that he had heard well enough. They stood to one side to allow passage of a cart loaded with barley sacks, going to the maltsters by the well where Catte Street joined Aldermanbury. A group of five mounted men rode by; the foremost pair in Gloucester livery. Where were they bound upon the duke's business, Seb wondered.

At last, they reached the apothecary's shop. Mercifully, it wasn't busy. Time was growing short. Master Haldane wanted to discuss the fearful fire that had claimed the life of his daughter's betrothed but Seb apologised, explaining that he was expected at Crosby Place and was not at liberty to linger. He made his purchases of saffron and cinnamon and put them in his purse, buying the smallest amounts possible which, even so, left him with but a farthing beside the spices there.

'He ain't comin', is he?' said one of the supposed drunkards. 'How can he get lost betwixt there and here?' The two were lurking in the narrow way beside St Margaret's, Lothbury that led to the churchyard behind. Both had drawn long-bladed knives from beneath their cloaks.

'Patience,' growled his fellow. 'They'll come.'

Across the street, the man in the green cap waited in the doorway of a disused shop.

As they walked, Seb was explaining to Tom the order of work he proposed for the afternoon.

'Will you get Lord Richard's portrait finished today?' Tom asked.

'I hope so. It depends how much time the duke spends looking at my sketches of his brother. If I do complete it, I'll show you – as I promised some while ago – how to bring life to an image by a most simple means. You did remember to bring the white lead pigment? That will be the secret...'

'Masters, excuse me.' The man with protruding lips, wearing the apple green cap was standing before them. 'I believe I saw you drop a roll of parchment from your bag earlier. If I may return it to you, my friend has it ready at hand nearby.'

The green cap; the oddly shaped mouth. Seb recalled those but had no memory of having dropped anything. His heart was thudding against his ribs. This was wrong, somehow.

'Tom! Run!' Those two words were all he had time to shout before he was tumbled to the ground and dragged into an alleyway beside a little church.

'Is aught amiss, masters?' Seb heard a woman's voice. 'Is your friend unwell?'

'Nay, mistress. Be not concerned. He is to be wed upon the morrow and this be his last day, free of wedlock.'

'Such merry japes,' the woman laughed. 'Enjoy yourselves.'

'Fear not, mistress; we will.' After a pause, Seb heard: 'Get him out of sight and finish this afore any other nosy do-gooders espy us. My lord Woodville would have this matter ended, once and for all.'

In the narrow alleyway, the two men who held Seb were hampered by their broad shoulders and wide, heavy-set frames, having little room and getting in each other's way. Their difficulties gave Seb the chance to undo the clasp on his mantle and let it fall away, leaving the fellows entangled in the yards of cloth as he made a break for freedom.

Never a runner, he could not hope to escape them by fleeing. They would swiftly overtake him. His only hope was evasion but he had no idea how he might do that. Needing a few moments to think, he ducked into St Margaret's church. He crouched behind the ancient stone font but they would soon discover him there. Creeping low, he made his way silently around the edge of the little nave, praying his hip bones would not click, as they often did, and betray him. He heard the door open behind him.

'Must be in here. Where else could he go?' one of his pursuers said.

'Buggered if I know. You see him?'

'Nah, but I smell him pissin' hisself wi' fear.' They both laughed.

Seb found the vestry door open and slipped inside. Without his mantle, he was so cold, his teeth chattered. There was nowhere to hide but a priest's vestments hung from a peg, awaiting the time of the vespers service. Thinking to warm himself, Seb took down the priest's cassock and wrapped it around his shoulders, if only to still his shivers. But he realised, worn thus, the cassock would hamper him if he had to fight off his assailants, so he put it on, over his jerkin. It was a little short but would serve. A coif and priestly hood lay ready upon a stool. Seb smoothed his longish hair into a tail and pulled it on top of his head, as he saw Emily do each morn. Then, not so deftly as she, he managed to get the coif on to cover his hair. It seemed to fit snugly enough that he hoped it would keep his unpriestly locks hidden without pins, as Em used by the dozen to the same purpose. He slipped the Lenten chasuble of pale wool, edged with grey fur, over his head, then placed the white stole around his neck and, finally, the hood.

'Sweet Jesu, forgive this sacrilege,' he murmured and, taking up a breviary book that lay to hand, he braced himself and left the vestry.

He looked neither left nor right but the fellows were noisy in their search. One sneezed gustily as he looked beneath the altar cloth in the tiny chapel dedicated to St Christopher, disturbing the dust.

'We don't get him, the earl will be usin' our guts to lace his boots.'

'Hey, father!' the other called out.

Seb almost froze to the spot.

'You seen anyone come in here just now? Skinny, dark of hair?'

'Only Almighty God has passed this way of late, my son,' Seb answered, lowering his voice to a sonorous tone. Walking very slowly – any haste and his limp became more noticeable – he approached the chancel steps and made a deep reverence before the rood, cloaked in its shroud for the Lenten season. He moved towards the high altar. Inside, he was trembling mightily but hoped it did not show. If only those wretches would leave. Suppose they questioned him further? They would surely recognise him if they looked closer. At least here, beyond the rood screen, laymen were forbidden and he hoped they would honour and respect that, even as he had not.

What could he do that might seem an appropriate action for a priest, something to command his full attention that they would be reluctant to interrupt? Seb stood before the altar and placed the breviary there, bowing low. Then he stood erect before the covered crucifix and, holding his arms high, palms lifted to embrace and welcome the Almighty, Seb sang the lines of the *Miserere*, solemn but beautiful. He sang as though his soul would burst, as if his life depended upon the music – which might very well be so.

'*Miserere mei, Deus!*' he sang. 'Have mercy upon me, O God!' As always, as he sang to the Lord, it was as if the world went away and he stood alone before his Creator. For the moment, there were no men behind him, intent upon doing him harm. And, as he finished the final angelic note, he felt calm, forgiven. If his end came now, he was at least composed.

Having bent the knee and crossed himself, he turned from the altar and walked back to the nave. All three men stood by the door. If he was to leave, he would have to walk by them.

'That's quite a pair o' lungs you got there, father. Not bad singing – fer a cleric. You'd do better in a tavern of a Saturday night: make a groat or two.' They laughed.

Seb knew he was going to have to be bold indeed.

'May the joys of the Lord Jesu be upon you and grant you peace, my sons. *Benedicite,*' he said, raising his fingers high to give the blessing. As he hoped, out of habit, the men bowed their heads to receive it as he passed by. 'A generous contribution to the alms box for the poor and destitute would do much to commend your souls to Almighty God,' he added. All three went to look in their purses and Seb walked out into the street, still wearing full priestly garb.

The Foxley house

THE REPEATED use of a well-placed boot had served to break the lock into Matthew Bowen's old chamber. Jude looked around. It was over furnished indeed with hangings and tapestries and rugs upon the floor, a chair, a *prie-dieu*, a buffet – in a bedchamber? – and a small altar with ornate gilded candle sticks and a crucifix. Above it there hung a painted image of the Virgin and Child. Jude shuddered: She was, without doubt, the ugliest Mother of God he had ever set eyes upon. He crossed himself for having so blasphemous a thought.

Rose would have a deal of work to do here. The dust lay thick upon everything and the hangings were festooned with cobwebs so impressive, he hoped he would not encounter the spiders that made them. Not that he was afeared of such creatures, of course. He sat upon the coverlet of the grand bed, sending up a cloud of dust which enveloped him and set him coughing, followed by a fit of sneezes.

Just what had the old miser kept hidden here, in his lair? Jude used to wonder back then, when he worked for Bowen. Now was his chance to find out. Beneath the bed, he found wooden boxes of clothes, every item utterly moth-eaten. A decent pair of boots might come in useful sometime, he thought, dragging them out from behind the buffet. Dear God, but they reeked, so maybe not.

Mouse droppings littered the shelves of the buffet but the displayed silver goblets would polish up well with a bit of effort. A large velvet doublet hung upon a peg – Bowen's Sunday best, Jude recalled. It had once been bright blue but the layers of dust turned it grey. He went to brush off the dust and the cloth fell to pieces in his hand and a rat scuttled out of the sleeve with an indignant squeak. As the rotted cloth lay in a heap at his feet, he was sure he saw it move. He stirred it with his foot and a tangle of naked, squirming baby rats was revealed. Horrified, he stamped on the damn things 'til they moved no more.

Glancing up, he saw the Virgin looking at him, watching him with cold, lifeless eyes. That image had to go; he couldn't put up with her gloating at his efforts. He tried to lift the picture down but it would not come, no matter how he cursed and swore at it. Then he saw that it was hinged, like the door of an aumbry. It swung open. Half expecting more rats or spiders to have set up home behind it, Jude peeked in.

For once, Almighty God must be feeling bountiful this day. He reached in. Two small chests and a number of bulging leather bags sat there before him. He could smell the metallic odour of silver. A smile spread across his face. Money. More coin than he could dream of – or rather hope for. He had dreamt of fortunes but never expected to find one. Yet here it sat, under the same roof for all these years. Silver, aye, and gold coins too, glinted in the palm of his hand. God be praised! His money problems were ended.

Jude emptied one of the wooden boxes from under the bed and packed the little chests and all the coin bags but one into it. The one pouch he slipped into his purse. Then he chose the least moth-eaten of the garments and arranged them to hide the riches, laying the stinking boots on top to put off others from looking too closely. He went downstairs, carrying the box.

'The door is open now,' he announced to the womenfolk working in the kitchen. 'Do what you will up there but I warn you: there be rats and spiders and the bloody Devil knows what else beside.'

'What have you got there?' Emily asked.

'A few bits that are too bloody revolting for us but might still be of use to some beggar or other. I thought I'd take them straight to St Michael's and put them in the alms box.'

'Why in such haste?'

'Sniff the boots and you'll see why.'

'Ugh! You're right, Jude. Get them out of my kitchen.' Emily flapped her apron to disperse the stink.

As ordered, Jude removed the offensive stuff right swiftly but not to the church alms box; not yet. First, he went home to his lodging in Dame Ellen's house in Cheapside and hid the money in the linen chest which served as a bench or table board, as required. A safer hiding place would have to be devised later, when he had the time to do it properly. He returned to Paternoster Row, leaving the box upon the doorstep of St Michael's as he passed. If anyone helped themselves, then they must be desperate indeed and welcome to it.

In the parlour, he took the greatest pleasure in tipping coins into the money box and pouch kept in the parlour chimney. There would no longer be any fear of Seb's Saturday Accounts or any discovery, by whatever means, of the too numerous times he had had to filch from their hard-won savings. Jude was a happy man. Better yet, he realised he could now afford to make Rose his true wife. Life was marvellous, wasn't it?

Crosby Place

B Y THE time he turned down Broad Street, by the Hospital of St Anthony, with no sign of his pursuers, Seb had felt nigh fainting with relief, his knees barely able to support him. He leant against the hospital wall to steady himself. He should return his borrowed vestments. No priest went about the streets in his chasuble. He might wear the cassock, but not the stole about his neck. But afore there was any opportunity to disrobe, he arrived at the gateway of Crosby Place.

Even as the guards raised their eyebrows at a cleric clothed thus, they bowed all the same and let him pass through. He was safe.

Still clad in the fine chasuble, Seb hurried across the courtyard, breathless. Tom was standing at the foot of the grand steps up to the great hall, speaking animatedly to Sir Robert Percy, waving his arms about and pointing towards the gate.

'Oh, sir,' Seb heard Tom saying, 'I pray we be not too late. They took Master Seb. Three of them. In Lothbury, sir.'

As Seb approached, they made way for him and both bared their heads in respect. He stopped beside them.

'May I be of service, sir priest?' Sir Robert asked, 'Only there is a most urgent matter...'

'Not so urgent, sir,' Seb said, grinning as he removed the hood and coif, shaking out his dark hair so it fell about his face.

'Well, bless me!' the knight said, blinking twice and staring.

'Master Seb! You're safe!' Tom shrieked. 'I was so scared for you.'

'So, you've taken holy orders and been ordained since last I saw you and there was I, believing you but a humble scrivener.' Sir Robert laughed heartily. 'And we were about to ride to your rescue. The lad said your life was at peril. Was that not the case, Master Seb?'

'It was, sir. I fear the lad spoke truly. I pray you, let me disrobe. I tire of the pretence and we be late for the appointment with my Lord of Gloucester. Ah, Tom. You save the day twice over: I see you have both the scrip and the drawings. Bless you, lad. I wondered where they might have come to rest.'

'I wasn't going to let those devils get their hands on our precious stuff, Master Seb. These were most important – after yourself, of course, master.'

'Aye, I dare say it was a close contest,' Seb said, smiling, giving Tom an approving pat upon the arm.

Once Seb had been relieved of the vestments, with assurances from Sir Robert that a servant would return them straightway to St Margaret's, he entered the solar where Lord Richard was waiting. The tale of the assault, aye, and the miracle of his escape had to be retold, in full, for Richard's benefit, although the duke had heard something of the danger to his favoured artist.

'Rob, ask them to prepare spiced wine for Master Sebastian and young Thomas, if you please. They must both be sore in need of refreshment and its soothing influence. As for you, Sebastian, I will fully understand if you wish to leave the portrait for today after your dire experience.'

'Thank you for your consideration, my lord, but there be naught amiss with me now, truly. And since I am here with all prepared, I may as well work as intended, if you consent?'

'Very well – after you have had your wine – but as you see: I am not wearing the usual robe but mourning garb. Although, if needed, the robe could be brought.'

Seb nodded.

'I understand but I have completed the painting of the garments, so there will be no need. I just have to put the finishing touches to your features, my lord, and I thought to alter the background a little. The view of the garden through the window looks so grey and wintery…' He gestured towards the expanse of barren earth beds and bare trees beyond the oriel. 'I think a hint of green upon the boughs and new shoots piercing the soil would suggest the approach of spring and a new hope for the future. By your license, of course, since the image will not then be entirely truthful. It will also contrast with the crimson robe and make the colour seem more vibrant.'

Lord Richard gave a sad smile.

'That would be well, Sebastian.' He went to the chair. 'I shall sit as you direct, as always. But first, whilst you drink, will you not permit me to see the drawings you did of my brother of Clarence? Sir Robert tells me they be as fine as I have come to expect of you.'

Seb took the paper sheets from his scrip and unrolled them, placing the wine jug at the top and a silver candlestick at a lower corner, to keep the drawings flat.

Lord Richard looked long at each image, saying naught – as was his way – until he had considered all, moving the jug and candlestick as required.

Seb studied his cup assiduously and nudged Tom hard when he saw the lad watching the duke. Tom averted his eyes also. The duke's quiet composure was a fragile thing, Seb knew of old. They should not bear witness to the glint of a tear, nor hear the shuddering uneven breath of emotion as Lord Richard gazed upon his sibling's image.

'They are as I would have hoped, Sebastian.' The duke spoke so softly. 'Any one of them would be suitable to be made as a portrait. I shall leave the matter in your capable hands. We can discuss the cost, later. I shall have the contract drawn up afore I leave London.'

'As you wish, my lord,' Seb said bowing his head in acknowledgement.

The duke took up his accustomed pose as Seb unveiled the portrait. Not having worked on it for a while, he was better able to judge a few small improvements to be made. However, observing his subject's face in detail and comparing it to the image, some changes were plain: beneath the eyes were dark shadows, like bruises, where none had been so noticeable before; strands of silver had appeared in the duke's raven hair. Seb could not think that he had failed to see them previously. And the vertical furrows betwixt the brows that had always been there were now extended and more deeply marked. Sorrow had fallen harshly upon Richard's features. Seb wondered whether the portrait should reflect these changes. He decided it should not.

'Tom. I would have the white lead and the finest brush. Then I will show you the secret of giving life to a likeness, as I promised you.' With the tiniest brush in his hand, Seb lowered his voice to a whisper. A master had to pass on the mysteries of his craft to an apprentice but the guild forbade that others should know its secrets. 'Now, Tom, observe the subject's eyes closely. Compare them to the painting. What do you see?'

'The colour is right, master, and the shaping. They are perfect, I think.'

'But what is not there? What is lacking?'

Tom looked blank and shook his head.

'Don't know, master.'

'Light, Tom: the light of life; the very presence of the soul. Look again. Do you not see how the light from the window reflects in the eyes, even taking the shape of the window? If you had ever seen the eyes of the dead, you would know that light dims within moments of death. I believe the eyes truly are the windows of the soul and when the soul departs, the light in the eyes is no more. Now watch...' In a few deft strokes, no bigger than the width of a hair, Seb used the white pigment to indicate the reflected light in the eyes of the image.

Tom was stunned to see what a difference those two pinpoints of paint made to the portrait. Lord Richard truly did look to have come alive.

'That's a miracle, Master Seb.'

'No, lad, 'tis artistry and naught more. I shall be needing the verdigris next and mix a little yellow and white with the green. I may also require a touch of brown ochre to soften the hue, so have that ready also. 'Tis, done, my lord,' he said, raising his voice. 'I have but to complete the view of the garden, as we discussed, so you may move as you wish.'

'I am eager to see the results of your labours, Sebastian.'

'It will be finished afore we leave, my lord.'

'That will be as well. Parliament has been dissolved and the arrangements for my brother's funeral accomplished, according to the king's wishes. There be naught to keep me in London now. I shall go back home. We leave upon Monday next. My household here will be packed away. Dame Crosby can let this house to some other tenant.'

'But, my lord, does that mean you will not return to the city?' Seb asked, somewhat shocked.

'I mislike the king's court at Westminster: too many folk who smile to your face, all the while just awaiting an opportunity to stab you from behind. Too much plotting and intrigue and dark deeds for my comfort. I cannot feel easy in such company. Never could. If Parliament be summoned, I shall attend, as duty requires, but I can bide at my lady mother's place at Baynard's Castle by the river. Otherwise, London will not likely see me again for some long while.'

Seb took up his brush and began to put touches of green to indicate the first inkling of spring in the garden in the background of the painting.

'Come, Boru!' the duke called to his great wolfhound that, as ever, had been lying by the hearth. The dog got up and loped over to its master.

Tom had no liking for the creature, whatever assurances Lord Richard gave that it was too old to be a danger to anyone. The lad watched the dog warily, giving its passing by all his attention, sparing none for his work in hand.

Of a sudden, a pool of green pigment was spilling upon the floor, spreading across the fine tiles until it embraced one leg of Seb's easel and flowed towards his left boot. Quite what happened next, Tom would never be able to explain.

He was trying to apologise but Master Seb stared at the mess, dropped his brush and staggered back, clutching at his head and crying out 'Jesu, save me!'

Lord Richard grabbed him as he fell, crumpling like wet paper. He assisted him to a bench.

'Easy, Master Sebastian. Rest here. I should never have allowed you to work after your ordeal earlier.'

For the space of some minutes, Seb was unable to form words. His mind had been overwhelmed. The sight of the green pigment spreading overall had brought a cascade of memories into his head, too many to cope with all at once. He was dizzy and nigh drowning in a waterfall of remembrances.

Someone put a wine cup into his hand and bade him drink. He obeyed.

'You are unwell,' the duke was saying. 'When you feel able, Sir Robert will see you home.'

'Nay, sir, I be well enough. I-I believe my memories of what came to pass at the Tower have all come flooding back. I remember so much of a sudden. I recall being with his Grace of Clarence. I know what happened that night. Fearful things...'

'Do not dwell upon such matters. Clearly, they trouble you over much.'

'No, my lord. In truth, I would tell you everything.'

'A burden shared is a burden halved, as they say, eh? Very well. You and I can speak in confidence.'

'That would be as well. I fear I recall some dangerous knowledge it would be unwise to share with others.'

The duke nodded.

'When you be ready, we may retire to my closet. We shall have utter privacy there.'

By the light of candles upon the little altar, Seb prepared to tell Lord Richard everything. The *prie-dieu* had been moved aside and two stools, two cups and a wine jug supplied. The duke closed the door. They were alone.

Richard poured wine for them both as a restorative. He seated himself.

'As you will, Sebastian,' he said and waited for Seb to speak.

'Whilst I was there, with your lordship's brother of Clarence, he was drinking wine. He said as how he could not eat the food for fear it was poisoned but he considered the wine to be safe since it came from his favoured vintner. The wine jug was emptied soon after but two fellows arrived, bringing a rundlet of malmsey. The duke was pleased and had me broach the barrel straightway but – here be a point to note – the men did not say it came from the vintner but from a well-wisher. The duke insisted that I too should share the wine, saying it was a sad thing indeed for a man to drink alone. I have never drunk malmsey afore so the taste was not one I knew but it had an after taste that seemed amiss. I only took a few sips. The duke too commented that it was not as he expected.'

'You suspect it may have been poisoned?' Richard asked.

'I think it may have. Not because of the taste – on which I have no experience to make a knowledgeable assessment – but because of what I heard said by the Watergate, as I was leaving.' Seb paused, closing his eyes whilst he put his thoughts into some coherent order.

'You be feeling ill again, Sebastian?'

'No, sir. The story be as if new to me. I must think it through; try to resolve something sensible from the strange collection of images that crowd my mind. I believe I have it now. It was nigh dark as I approached the Watergate but I heard the sounds of a scuffle. One was injured, I be certain, and a fellow asked: "Is this the man you saw with Clarence? You know what my lord did command: no witnesses." I think they were speaking of me. The fellow had a strange way of saying the 's' sounds, like a serpent hissing.'

'Did they name the lord who commanded them to leave no witnesses?'

'I fear not but, even so, I have a suspicion.'

'Who?'

''Tis not proof exactly but I recognised the shape of the prow of the barge moored there, awaiting the turn of the tide. I have seen it since more than once...' Seb hesitated. He did not want to implicate an innocent party, if he surmised wrongly. 'It was the barge belonging to Anthony Woodville, Earl Rivers. I be sure of it.'

Richard muttered under his breath, then nodded.

'Indeed, Sebastian, I have suspected for some time that the queen and her kin were behind George's imprisonment, though, upon my life, I could not – and cannot – think why they should be so intent upon destroying him.'

In that moment Seb realised with a jolt that he *did* know why: George's secret knowledge that King Edward was married already when he was bewitched into a marriage with Elizabeth Woodville. Thus, she was not his true wife and her children were bastard born. That meant Clarence was still Edward's heir to the crown. No wonder he had to die. Seb looked at Lord Richard's troubled face in the candlelight and understood that, with George gone, he was now sitting with the true heir to the throne of England. Yet, if he revealed the secret to this man, he would put Richard in the exact same danger as George had been. He dare not tell; not yet, at least. Perhaps the day would come...

'Tell me, how did you make your escape?'

'Quite by chance. I hid in a building in use as a grain store, though I suspect from the wood panelling, it had once been a far grander place. I was attempting to conceal myself from my foes and fell through a panel. I found a stairway which led down into a spider's web of ancient tunnels. At first, I had a torch to light my way but then, when they followed me, I had to dowse it, else they could see where I was. I knew I was running for my life. In the pitch darkness, I lost my way, I fell, I ran into walls, found passages blocked. One bad fall left me senseless, for how long, I know not. I believe it was that which robbed me of my memories for a time. All I knew was terror. Somehow, I reached the daylight by St Katharine's and they took me in.'

'I have heard tell of secret tunnels beneath the Tower,' Richard said, toying with the ring upon his finger, as was his way, 'But have never known there might still be an entrance and, indeed, a way out. The tale runs that the third King Henry, having fallen foul of the rebel, his brother-by-marriage, Simon de Montfort, sought refuge in his Tower of London, only to discover the citizens had joined de Montfort and he was now besieged upon all sides by his enemies. They even guarded the Watergate, so he could not escape by river. Henry ordered tunnels to be dug that he might get away from them. As it happened – so the story goes – a compromise was reached with de Montfort and the tunnels were never used but the first King Edward, son of Henry, during the construction of further curtain walls and new towers there, having learnt a lesson from his father's troubles, had the system of escape tunnels enlarged and completed. That would be two hundred years ago. Until now, I do not think anyone was sure if the tale was true and, even if it was, whether the tunnels had collapsed or been filled in long ago. But it seems they do exist.'

'Aye, my lord, and they would have been a deal less terrifying if I could have kept my torch.'

'And they treated you well at St Katharine's? You may know, Lionel Woodville is the master there.'

'No. I did not.'

'Unfortunately, the Woodvilles are the only people in England whom even I dare not bring a prosecution against. The king would never allow such a case. 'Tis a pity we cannot prove the wine was poisoned, not that it would help very much.'

'I have some evidence,' Seb volunteered. 'As I was in those tunnels, all the while my heart was pounding nigh fit to break my ribs. I blamed my fears and exertions for it. Then, when first I saw daylight again, everything looked green to me, as though peering through a mist of greenish hue. That effect lasted for days. I believe that be why, when Tom spilt the pigment, it jostled my memory and I remembered. Anyhow, I did not connect my violent heart palpitations with the way things looked green until Jude described my symptoms to an apothecary. He diagnosed poisoning by means of the juice of the foxglove plant; said I was fortunate to survive even so small a dose. Now I have recalled that I sipped some of that malmsey wine… I fear your grace's brother drank down far more.'

'Foxglove poisoning? Aye, that might well be the Woodville way of destroying their enemies.'

'Also, my lord, my attackers this day: one said "My lord Woodville would have this matter ended, once and for all." I fear the earl wants me slain and he has already tried more than once to have me killed. It all makes sense now. After Sir Robert helped bring me home from St Katharine's Infirmary, the story ran that the poor fellow who was put into my bed thereafter was smothered to death. And even Jude suffered a near miss from an assassin's blade that was likely meant for me. He said the attacker called out "Foxsssley!" That was all. He could have mistaken Jude for me, if he knew not my likeness. And with the hissed 's', I now recall to mind, it may have been the fellow at the Tower, one of the Woodville henchmen. They want me dead for fear that I may tell what I know... and now I have, may Jesu Christ aid me.'

Seb was shaking as he finished his tale. How could he, so humble a man, escape the wrath of the queen and her kinsmen? He wished those memories had remained elusive. Now he was more afeared than ever.

'Sit quietly by the fire, Sebastian. You and I have much to ponder upon afore we determine how best to deal with this weighty matter. I will discuss it with Sir Robert; see what can be done. Drink your wine and ease your concerns.'

Seb felt sick with worry. He did not touch the wine, for which he had little liking anyway, and half afraid it might be poisoned, like Clarence's malmsey. He returned to the solar and sat by the fire. The cold of the day seemed to be biting his bones, gnawing at his hip particularly.

'What's happening, master?' Tom asked. 'I've been here, doing naught for an hour or more. Shouldn't we be going home? Mistress Em will be angry, if we're late for supper.'

'Don't ask me, lad. 'Tis out of my hands now.'

'What is? I don't understand.'

'Nor do I, if I speak truly. We must wait upon Lord Richard a while longer. Be patient.'

'What was it that you remembered, master? Was it about the Duke of Clarence?'

'Aye, in part.' Seb held his hands out to the blaze. He had never felt colder.

'That must be why Lord Richard looked as if the sky had fallen down upon him.'

'Perhaps it has. Oh, Tom, lad, I fear what may become of us all. I have made powerful enemies and know not how we can be saved. What have I done?'

'But Lord Richard is powerful too, and he is your friend. He will save us.'

'I pray so, if he can even save himself. Clarence could not.' Seb stood up, straightened his jerkin. 'But do not harken to me, young Tom. I be melancholy, is all. You will see: all shall be well.'

The Foxley house

'TIS ALL in hand, Em. There is no other way.'

'Leave London! But I cannot. I was born here; my father and brother live here; all my friends... I will not go. I care not what you say. The matter cannot be so bad as that.' Emily was wringing her hands in her apron, her face flushed. 'Go, if you must but I won't have anyone – even Lord Richard – ordering me to leave my home. You'll have to go without me.'

'He is not ordering us, Em. He be aiding us. My life be in danger. Tom and I did not dare come home from Crosby Place without the duke providing an escort for us, not after what came to pass on our journey there. If we remain in London, I shall be glancing over my shoulder every minute; never have a moment's respite from fear of an assassin's blade.' Seb took her in his arms and held her close against his heart, uncaring that the rest of the household looked on and supper had been forgotten – even by Jack. 'Oh, my dearest Em: I don't want to die. I would not have you widowed with a fatherless babe. I love you, Em. Please...

I beg you. Come with me. It will be for a short while only, until my enemies see sense and realise I be no threat to them.'

CHAPTER SEVENTEEN

Saturday the twenty-eighth day of February
The Foxley house

SEB AND Emily had talked for much of the night and the dawn of a new day saw little resolved. Seb took the pup, Gawain, out to the garden afore first light, certain he had not slept at all. Em was still abed, worn out with tears and argument, and he would let her sleep on, poor lass. Was he being unkind in expecting her to leave London with him? It was a wife's duty to obey her husband, was it not? She had wed him, promising that they should hold fast to each other 'for better or for worse'. Aye, but this situation was far worse than anything they might have imagined when making their vows.

He watched the little dog – made visible in the half light by his patches of white fur against the black – snuffling along the weed-embroidered stones of the garden wall. Of a sudden, he took off after some tiny creature, a shrew or vole maybe, barking his high pitched puppy bark of pleasure as he attempted to drive the animal into a corner. The vole disappeared betwixt the stones, leaving Gawain wondering where his quarry was gone. His questioning look of puzzlement when he turned to Seb made Seb laugh. The pup then turned his efforts to herding Em's chickens.

''Tis good to hear you laugh, Master Seb,' Rose said as she came out to the garden, bearing two cups of ale. Like Seb, she wore her mantle, as though she intended to remain outside for a while.

'My thanks, Rose. There was no need to bring it out to me; I shall come in as soon as Gawain has refreshed himself with a little exercise.' Gawain appeared betwixt Seb's boots, having been sent on his way by a beady-eyed hen. Seb picked him up, smoothed his fur and set him down again as Rose handed him a cup.

'I wanted to speak with you where no other would hear. The youngsters be upset enough at the thought of you leaving. I know you have problems of your own but I must ask: what will become of the rest of us?' Rose leaned against the back of the old pig sty and sipped her ale. She was dressed for the day but had yet to secure her cap and her fair hair hung in its night-time braid over her shoulder.

Seb was distracted for a moment by the beauty of his brother's betrothed as the strengthening light unveiled her lovely face – one so worthy of a fine portrait. He was shocked at the feelings she aroused in him: feelings which had naught to do with art. The thought that he might not see her again for many months made his heart heavy. Without his conscious decision, his hand reached out and touched the softness of her skin, her hair.

'I would not have you suffer a single moment of distress because of what has come to pass, Rose. You are so dear to me, I will see that you be safe, no matter what.'

She laid her hand over his, to keep it against her cheek. Both knew what might have been, if Seb was not the most faithful husband on God's earth.

'You will never have to return to your old life, have no fear on that score.' He understood that to be the root of her disquiet for Rose had once been forced to earn her bread in a bawdy house. 'Even if my tardy brother never makes you his wife – and he be quite mad, if he does not – you will always have a home in this house, whether Em and I be here or not. As yet, I have told neither Emily nor Jude but Lord Richard has made generous compensation for his responsibility – as he regards it, at least – for my perilous situation and the need to flee London. There will be monies sufficient to keep the workshop going without taking on commissions for expensive illuminated works that only I can fulfil. Jude can make enough profit on plain Latin primers and cheap pamphlets for scholars and the like. If you will, I would beg you to stay and tend to the household. Nessie will require a good mistress to keep her in order and Tom and Jack will need a woman to mother them. Kate will be going home, for a while at least. As for Jude, I trust you will keep him within bounds and, when he marries you, you will be as master and mistress of the house, if that will please you?'

'If he marries me. Sometimes, I fear he has changed his mind but knows not how to tell me so. But I thank you for trusting me to do these wifely duties here and for putting my mind so much at ease. I shall not disappoint you, Seb, I vow it.'

'You have never disappointed me, sweet Rose.' He so wanted to kiss her, to have their lips touch. Would it do the least harm, if he did?

'Ah! What's this?' Jude appeared of a sudden, coming from the side gate. 'A secret tryst with my little brother? You'll be ploughing a barren furrow there, lass. He's more celibate than any bloody priest I know.' He laughed loudly, scattering the hens and setting Gawain whimpering.

'I be glad we amuse you so, Jude,' Seb said, a hint of testiness in his tone that Jude, fortunately, seemed not to notice. 'We were discussing future arrangements for the household, were we not, Rose?'

'Indeed we were,' Rose confirmed, ''Tis all determined that...'

Jude smothered her words, giving Rose a hearty kiss of greeting that turned tender, then lusty as his large hands cupped her buttocks and pulled her close against him.

Seb walked away. No need to pour vinegar into the newly inflicted wound. He wondered if Jude had witnessed more that he let on. How long had he stood there, watching? Not that there had been anything improper to see – not really. Yet Jude's possessive behaviour with Rose might have been intended as a warning to him, not to trespass.

Over breakfast, the talk was all about leaving London. Emily, who seemed ever upon the verge of tears, was still torn betwixt her husband and her beloved city.

'If we must go, you have to tell me where we are bound, else how can I tell my father and Dame Ellen? I demand to know. How can I decide otherwise? I will not be dragged to some far distant corner of England and no one knows where I am.'

Seb reached for a heel of bread.

'Em, how many times have I said: our destination is better kept secret. I promise to tell you ere we leave but no sooner. You are not to inform your friends.'

'You're a cruel heartless man, Sebastian Foxley. If we are going all the way to Yorkshire – wherever that is – with Lord Richard, then tell me!'

'We are not going to Yorkshire; not so far as that. Remaining with Lord Richard's household would be nigh as dangerous as staying here. We did discuss the possibility, briefly, but he says every noble household has its espiers – I did not know that – and he fears my enemies would come to hear of my presence, if we went to Middleham with him.'

'Middleham? I never heard of such a place. God be thanked we're not going there,' Em said, smearing honey on her bread.

'Middleham Castle is his lordship's favoured home in the North Country.'

'I might like to see a duke's residence. It must be very fine.'

'But Em, you just thanked God we're not going there.'

'I can change my mind, can't I?' She threw down her bread, uneaten, and dissolved into tears again before hastening off to the parlour. To weep unseen, Seb suspected.

'I'll go to her,' Rose said, 'But Master Seb, if you could tell her where you be bound, I'm sure she would be easier in her mind. She can keep a secret, you know. We've all of us done that before, over the matter of Master Gabriel. We've never told a soul.'

'Aye. You may be right, Rose, but comfort her in the meantime, if you be able, for I cannot. Every word I utter seems to make matters worse.'

When the women were gone from the kitchen, Seb sent the youngsters, including Nessie and Jack – whether he would or not – out to the garden to play with Gawain. Alone with Jude, he broached the problem that vexed him more than the danger to his own life:

'What should I do, Jude, about Em? Do I drag her all unwilling from her home, to face a daunting journey and all the hardship that entails, to a place where we shall be homeless strangers, without friends and acquaintances? Am I truly being cruel, if I do this? Or should I leave her here and go alone, forsaking my wife? Help me, brother, for I know not what to do.'

'I'm hardly the man to ask, am I? Me? I'd be gone without a second thought and damn the bloody woman.'

'Would you truly? If you and Rose were man and wife, would you leave her?'

'Rose could fend for herself. Whether I'd trust her honour in a city full of lusty males, that's another matter. I'd turn my back and the lass would be pursued by every bugger with a prick before ever I'd left the city gates. So, no, perhaps I'd make her come with me.'

'That is not very helpful, Jude. You don't know either, do you?'

'In truth, I don't think there would be any difficulty for me. Remember, Rose made her own way to London from Canterbury. She has travelled farther than any of us, apart from Jack, perhaps, and God only knows where that young devil came from in the first place. So, Rose would not be afraid of leaving the city.'

'Do you suppose that is the trouble, that Em fears travelling further afield?'

'Has she ever left London before?'

'Not that I know. I suppose there was never cause.'

'And if I agree to go,' Em said, returning, red-eyed, from the parlour and continuing the conversation as if there had been no pause, 'What then do I take with us?'

'Only as much as you may carry that be truly needful,' Seb said. 'You may have a new travelling cloak, any colour you wish, fur-trimmed...'

'But what of things for the babe? Do I take those or shall we be returned before my time comes?'

Seb stared blankly. Any such thought had not occurred to him and he had no answer. He shook his head.

'There! Isn't that just the way of men: no thought of anything beyond the morrow. Have you the least of plans for what we may do; where we may go?'

This time, he could make an answer:

'Aye, lass. I wrote a letter to the village priest where we be going. Lord Richard's messenger set out with it yester eve, seeing the matter was most urgent.'

'A village? Oh, Seb, how will we survive in a village? How may we find enough custom for my silk work and your scribing? I thought we would be going to Canterbury. Rose says Canterbury has a thriving market and is not so far away but a village? We won't know anyone...'

'Do not be concerned for making a living, Em. The duke insists he will provide us with money enough which, if used prudently, will keep us a year or more.'

'A year!' she screeched. 'Never. I will not go. A few weeks... a month maybe. I should be a grey-haired old woman ere we return and all my friends will have forgotten me.'

'Do not be afeared,' Seb said, attempting to soothe her. 'Think on it as a venture. It will be exciting to see new places and meet with new folk.'

'I am not frightened. Do not dare accuse me so.' But her words were belied by the terror reflected in her eyes.

Seb tried to take her in his arms but she slapped his hands away and ran out into the yard. Seb dropped his arms in despair.

'Just tell her to prepare for the journey and be done with it,' Jude said, taking up his mantle and preparing to go out. 'Every time you open your mouth, you do but make matters worse. I'd keep silent, if I were you.'

'I doubt you would, Jude, but 'tis sound advice all the same.' Seb sighed and sat back at the table again. He rubbed his brow where a headache threatened. In a single day, his life had become a waking nightmare. Perhaps it would be easier if he went alone.

Jude walked through the bustling Saturday market crowd in Cheapside. His brother's life might be in tatters but Jude was happy. That damned priest, Simon Thornbury, had been quiet of late, since he had threatened him, but there could be no peace of mind until the devil was finally paid off. And this was the day that would have the wretched business ended. Seeing the priest's house beside St Mary-le-Bow gave a Jude a moment's disquiet, as it always did; a cold feeling deep in his belly but he put on a bold face. That miserable bloody priest wasn't going to spoil his good humour this time.

Simon Thornbury opened the door to his knock.

'If you've come to threaten me again, Foxley, I'll summon the sheriff,' the priest said by way of greeting.

'No you won't,' Jude said. 'You are the wrong-doer in this case, not I. But I've not come to make trouble. Won't you invite me in? This would be better done without prying eyes looking on.'

'If you intend to harm me...' The priest seemed to shrink inside his doublet of baudekin – far too fine for a humble cleric, it broke every sumptuary law. The gold threads in the weave caught the light and sparkled against the green silk. King

Edward himself could not have been more grandly clad upon a Saturday morn.

'I'm here to pay off the debt, once and for all.'

'Honestly?'

Jude laughed at the irony.

'As if you know the meaning of the bloody word? Aye. In good faith. In exchange, I want a written agreement, signed by you, to the effect that I never promised marriage, or so much as a bent farthing to that woman of yours – whoever she is; if she even exists. That I never met her, spoke with her nor gave her good day. If you do that, I'll pay what you claim I owe and three marks beside for the contract. Agreed?'

'Very well but I insist we do this in the church, before the high altar, that God will be my witness, if you try anything underhanded.'

'You would make the Almighty a party to your filthy little schemes? How do you bloody dare?'

'I am His priest and He has seen me safe thus far. Have you brought writing materials for this contract, or do you expect me to supply them?'

'I've come prepared,' Jude said, patting his scrip.

Thornbury looked so doubtful, Jude opened the leather bag so he might view the quills, ink pot and parchment within: there was no dagger nor cudgel to do him hurt.

Later, with the debt discharged and a document to that effect signed and sealed, Jude had another call to make. Whistling a tune and light of heart, he entered St Paul's. But he hadn't come to worship nor to buy more writing materials from the stationers' stalls in the nave. This was another matter entirely: he would speak with the dean and arrange for the banns of marriage to be posted. Master Jude Foxley, bachelor of the parish of St Michael le Quern, and Rose Glover of the parish of St George in Canterbury were to be wed at last, as soon as Lent was ended. He would cast off his bachelorhood forever within the grandeur of the mighty cathedral, as was his prerogative as a citizen of London.

Rose was dealing with a customer in the shop, parcelling up a Latin grammar book and a thin soft-covered version of a book on manners, the latter proving popular of late. She accepted his coin and counted out the change – twice – to be certain there was no mistake.

Jude could hardly contain his impatience, waiting for the customer to depart. When the man paused at the door to leaf through a selection of pamphlets weighted down with a pebble upon the counter board, it was all he could do to stop himself shoving the fellow out into the street. Then, when another possible customer approached, Jude shut the door on him.

'We're closed. Can't you see? Come back next week.'

'Jude. That was so rude,' Rose objected. 'We'll lose customers that way.'

'I don't bloody care!' He lifted her up and swung her around the shop, knocking a pile of cheap students' glossaries on Aristotle off the shelf and scattering them like leaves in an autumn gale.

'Jude. Jude, put me down, you foolish fellow,' Rose cried out, though, clearly, she was laughing.

'Don't call me foolish, you heartless jade. I won't have you calling me names when we are wed.' He kissed her hard upon the brow, the cheek and then the lips.

She tried to disentangle herself from his fierce embrace.

'Wed? Oh, aye, and just when will that be?'

Jude ceased his kisses and stood back, grinning hugely.

'Monday the twenty-third day of March, if that be convenient for you? Of course, if you have more important things, like peeling bloody onions or washing linen, to do that day…'

'Jude? Do you mean it? Oh, Jude Foxley, I love you so!' Rose flung herself into his arms with such enthusiasm the pair near overbalanced. Then they went dancing a jig around the shop, laughing and giggling.

'I see I be interrupting,' Seb said. He stood in the doorway from the workshop, sombre as a spectre at the graveside.

Rose left hold of her soon-to-be husband and ran to him.

'Master Seb, such joyful news: we are to be wed at last. At last!'

Seb blinked like a man astounded by a blow but he managed to force a smile.

'Marvellous indeed. When will that be?'

'The day after Easter Day,' Rose said. 'I am so happy.' She twirled on her toes, spreading her skirts and skipping like a little maid. 'I must tell Emily.'

'I wish you every joy of the day and a long life together. I shall be sorrowful not to be there to see you make your vows.' He clapped his brother on the shoulder. 'Well done, Jude. It has taken you so long.'

'I never thought you'd miss my bloody wedding, Seb. I forgot about you leaving. Maybe you'll be back by then. 'Tis nigh a month away, well, three weeks, at least.'

'Nay, I shall be gone longer.'

'We could delay it,' Jude suggested, though he plainly did not want to.

'After all this time? Rose would never allow it. You be wed as planned, Jude, and I shall pray for you both especially upon that day.'

Over a dinner of leek and parsnip pottage, all the talk was of the wedding. Emily seemed more like herself: not a hint of tears, as she and Rose discussed what needed to be done: a new gown for Rose, obviously, and a flower garland.

'Primroses and violets will be blooming by then,' Emily said. 'You could have a gown of the same hue as one or other flower. That would become you so.'

'Pale yellow?' Rose queried. 'Will that not make me look like a wan and frail maid? I would prefer violet.'

'Mm, perhaps. And I shall see to the wedding breakfast for you. It can be set out in St Michael's, as it was for our wedding, can it not, Seb?'

Emily looked to him to confirm and saw his face was as a carven image. He did not speak but lay down his spoon beside his bowl of pottage. It was his turn to withdraw to the parlour for solitude. But unlike Emily, he would not waste time weeping. Instead, he would face his Saturday trial: the Accounts. However meagre their income for the week, it could hardly make him more downcast than he was. Also, since Jude had done the figures last time, there was no knowing how much sense he had made of them.

Seb took down the pouch containing the week's takings from behind the loose brick in the side of the parlour chimney. Surprisingly, it weighed somewhat heavier than he had expected. Hopeful, indeed. He set it down upon the table beside the fat Accounts ledger and went to lift out the coin box. That was strange: he could hardly lift it. It must be caught up somehow. He fetched a stool and climbed on it. From a greater height, he might see why the box was stuck but could make out no obvious reason. Had Jude decided to make it more secure by gluing it in place, such that a thief might not take it? He pulled with both hands and the box came away but was so heavy he almost dropped it and nigh fell off the stool. What on earth had Jude put in there for safe keeping? Iron horse shoes by the weight of it.

Lifting the lid revealed coins – a small mountain of them: not only silver groats and pennies but gold nobles also. As ever, Seb was scratching his head over the Accounts and yet again, this week they did not tally. But for once it wasn't a short-fall. It was the most miraculous surplus of money. And a miracle it must surely be – unless Jude had robbed the Goldsmiths' Guild.

Seb put his head into the kitchen.

'A word, Jude,' he said, 'In the parlour, now.'

THE COLOUR OF MURDER

By his brother's stern tone, Jude knew what had come to pass and rose from the board where the rest of the household were sat, eating apple fritters. He pulled a face which set the others laughing and raised hands all a-tremble.

'You done wrong agen, master?' Jack said, for this one time feeling a kindred spirit with the man who was more usually his nemesis.

'No doubt.' But Jude was chuckling as he went down the passage.

'I shall have a truthful answer, Jude: from whence came this money, these gold nobles?' Seb pushed the little heap of glinting metal discs across the board. 'Are we to be in trouble because of it?' He was sitting in the chair loaned by Lord Richard for his recovery and his frown looked every bit as forbidding as any royal duke's.

'You think I stole it?' Jude feigned horror, leaning on the chimney.

'How else did it get here? A charitable donation?'

'I found it.'

Seb snorted in disgust.

'I truly did,' Jude went on. 'In ol' Bowen's chamber. You recall what a bloody miser he was? Coins lay here and there in little piles, so I put them in our coin box. They're come by honestly, I swear.'

'If that be the case, should the coin not more properly go to young Tom as Bowen's son and heir?'

'I don't see why, Seb. You bought this house, workshop and business in good faith, including all appurtenances, fixtures, fittings, furniture, rats, mice, mildew and bloody fleas. For certain, any good things within the place must belong to you, as well as all the problems? 'Tis just a few coins.' Jude shrugged dismissively. He wasn't going to mention the rest of the hoard now safe hidden beneath the floor at his lodging.

''Tis quite a lot of coins, Jude. In total, they amount to twenty-four pounds, seventeen shillings and eleven pence.

More than a year's wages for most craftsmen and a fortune for a labourer. But if you swear that you found it thus...'

'You don't trust me, little brother? I'm deeply hurt.' Jude clutched his hands to his heart dramatically.

'I know not. If you said you won it at dice or cock-fighting...'

'As if I ever would.'

'That I might believe, though it would have taken a marvellous run of good fortune.'

'The money is there in our coin box. Believe that much and cease worrying about how it came to be there. We are now prosperous citizens of consequence. Be content, little brother, and enjoy your new found wealth. Now, I am going to the best tailor in London, to be measured for my wedding clothes and damn the bloody expense. We can afford it. I have a mind to wear green silk baudekin and an osteriches plume in my hat, like the lord mayor. Will you come with me to give your approval?'

'I cannot. Sir Robert is coming here to go over the final arrangements for Monday morn. Besides, Lord Richard advised me not to go out without an escort.'

'You'll have me. Or am I no longer sufficient escort for your most noble high-and-mightiness?' Jude made a mocking bow, sweeping the floor with his cap.

'You know the danger I be in. Do not jest about it, please.'

Everyone assembled in the kitchen to bid Kate a fond farewell as she was to return to her father's house for the present.

Kate and Rose were both cloaked and hooded, prepared to face the drizzle that had returned to add to the misery and tears of the day. The younger lass had a basket packed with her few belongings and her best pieces of work. These were wrapped against the weather in a loose waxed leather binding Seb had given her as a parting gift. It bore a gilded letter 'K' upon the front which had delighted her extraordinarily and it greatly pleased Seb to have given her joy. He held the lass close and kissed the top of her head.

'Be of good cheer, Kate. Give your father my sincere wishes that your family may find contentment once more. I have explained all in the letter and made my apologies for not taking you home in person. I be sure Rose will be an acceptable lieutenant for me. Take care, lass. Be good. You shall return to us once I be back in London.' He kissed her again as others stepped forward in turn to do the same. Jack held back until the last.

'Don't see why she has to go at all,' Jack muttered. 'She could stay here wiv us, same as before, couldn't she?'

''Tis for the best, lad. Her father be bereft and in need of her company for a while.'

'But I'm berrested too, ain't I? First Beggar goes and now Kate. It ain't fair.'

'You have Gawain, if you want him?' Seb said in a gentle tone, nudging the little dog with his foot as it lay curled in sleep beneath a stool. The pup stirred and yawned, showing a rosy tongue and tiny points of teeth, before settling again. Babes slept a great deal, Seb was coming to realise.

'Well, I don't, do I? He ain't my Beggar, now is he?'

Kate, forgetful of propriety, hugged Jack tightly.

'Don't be downcast, Jack. I'll be but a few streets away. I'll ask my father if you may come visit me.'

'You will?' Jack's face brightened like the sun breaking through cloud, his voice leaping from a gravelly bass note to a childish squeak within those two words.

'Aye. I'm sure he will approve – if I ask him sweetly.'

Seeing her bewitching smile, Seb wondered if any man – least of all a doting father – could ever say nay to Kate. He was also relieved that Jack's sorrows would not be increased on her account. The lad was moody and miserable too often of late.

Sir Robert Percy arrived promptly at three of the clock and was shown into the parlour. Seb offered the knight Lord Richard's chair.

'I must arrange to return it directly to Crosby Place,' Seb was saying, as Em served them ale and her now-famous saffron and cinnamon cakes before leaving the men to talk. 'The duke will want to take his chair with him, back to the North Country.'

Sir Rob shrugged and helped himself to a second cake.

''Tis but a piece of furniture. My lord is more concerned to transport you and your goodwife to safety. She certainly makes very fine cakes.' The knight licked his fingers. 'May I?' he asked, reaching out for another.

Seb nodded. He wondered how best to admit that the maker of such delicacies had no intention of travelling anywhere.

'In the meantime,' Sir Rob continued, 'Richard has sent this money as compensation, such that your business shall not fail during your enforced absence.' He handed Seb a heavy purse.

'This be unnecessary, sir. The duke has been over generous to us already. Unless this be payment for the portrait of Clarence? Does he still wish me to proceed with that commission? There be more than enough coin here to cover both materials and labour with money to spare.'

'In truth, I can say only that Richard hasn't mentioned it. Too many more urgent matters have distracted him, as you can imagine. But keep the drawings safe; the day may come when he has leisure to recall the project. As for the journey: you and your wife will need to be ready to leave at dawn. I shall come to escort you across the city – we don't want Woodville's henchmen getting you at the last, do we?' His voice sounded amused at the jest but his eyes spoke otherwise. 'Bring as few belongings as need be for although there will be wagons and horses to take your stuff as far as Godmanchester, once you part company with us, you will have to carry it. Now, how do you feel about riding a horse?'

'I've only ever done so once, behind you in your saddle, you may recall it? I've not ridden since but my backside bore the memory of that excursion for weeks after.'

Sir Rob chuckled.

'Aye, that day made my hair stand upon end too.' He ran his fingers through his fine hair, the colour of fire. 'And what of your wife? Richard would provide you both with the most docile of palfreys. Their gait gives a more comfortable seat for a long journey. What do you say? The only alternative would be to travel in one of the baggage wagons, else how will you keep up with the rest of the party? On foot, you would soon fall behind.'

'We cannot walk?'

''Tis a mounted household. We can reach Yorkshire in seven days – six, if the roads aren't flooded and the bridges are in good repair. Five, if we don't wait for the baggage train to keep up. We should get to Godmanchester on the third or fourth day, depending upon the weather. So, you will both be ready by dawn?'

Seb drew a breath and watched the knight devour the last cake.

'I shall be waiting but... well, Emily is not coming with me.'

Sir Rob paused, mid-bite, and put the cake down on the platter.

'But she's your wife. Of course she must come. Who can say how long you will be parted elsewise? It wouldn't be right. This isn't like going to war, Seb, where men leave their womenfolk behind.'

'I know.' The words sounded so pathetic.

'Is it the babe? Is that the problem? Does she fear to travel whilst being with child? If that be the case, assure her that many women journey far in that same state and much closer to their time of deliverance without suffering for it. My first wife rode her horse daily until but a few weeks before and my son was born safely and whole – a lusty little fellow, indeed. She need not worry and may sit in a wagon, if bestriding a horse becomes uncomfortable for her.'

'She says she would be friendless. Besides, there be a wedding to prepare for now.' Seb sighed. 'You know how women be concerned over such matters as gowns and flowers and food.'

'Who's getting wed?'

'Jude, at long last. He will finally make Rose his wife.'

'Just as you turn your back and leave London? Is there some reason for that?'

Seb frowned and shook his head.

'I do not believe so. It will make it easier for him to take over here, running the workshop. The guild prefers a master to be wed, such that his wife may provide a mother's tenderness and care to the apprentices. Rose will do that very well and assist my Emily too. They have become firm friends – a blessing, indeed.' He pulled a face. 'In truth, I think she will be the one to keep the business in good order. My brother is not the most reliable of men and has admitted to being somewhat reluctant to take on such responsibility. My hope be that marriage may change him, though I misdoubt it.'

'And your wife is not to be persuaded to accompany you?'

'Not by me, that be certain. I have tried reasoning, pleading, even bribery. The offer of the purchase of a new travelling cloak with fur trim was insufficient to tempt her. I fear I must content myself to live solitary for a while. I pray, it will not be too long a while.' He forced a laugh: 'Else I might starve to death, if I must do my own cooking. And what of clean linen? How may a man survive without a fresh shirt and nether clouts?'

'Lord Richard will be much concerned to think he has split a man from his wife. He will be sorry for it, as am I.' Sir Rob stood up and brushed the last few cake crumbs from his doublet. 'One last thing, Seb: your household – all of them – do they understand the need for utter silence concerning your forthcoming departure? They must never speak of your destination.'

'As yet, they know it not. I have not named the place, even to Emily or Jude.'

'A wise decision.'

'But I will tell my brother afore I leave. Someone needs to know.'

'Aye, I suppose so. Oh, and one piece of news has come to our notice – by what means, I shall not say – that Anthony Woodville is also leaving, as of Wednesday next, taking the little Prince of Wales back to Ludlow, where both will remain for the foreseeable future. King Edward has appointed him as the prince's governor and tutor – may the Almighty help England – so London will be a safer place for your household, if not for you at present. Perhaps your time away shall not be over long. Woodville will have the prince's education to think of and less opportunity to trouble himself about a certain young artist.'

'That be welcome news. I shall tell Emily. She may even change her mind and come with me, if I may assure her 'tis for a few weeks and no more. My thanks, Sir Robert. I shall be waiting come Monday at dawn. Whether my wife shall be there...'

CHAPTER EIGHTEEN

Sunday the first day of March

PERHAPS IT wasn't the wisest thing to do but, since it was the Lord's Day, Seb determined he would attend mass in St Michael's church, despite the danger of going abroad when Woodville must know by now that he lived still. It seemed right to give due thanks for his recent fortunate escape from his assailants, to make apologies once more for having dressed like a priest to practise deceit and to beg for divine protection upon his forthcoming journey to a place he knew little of, apart from its name. Lastly, but by no means the least reason, he wished to pass a final hour or two with familiar folk: his friends and neighbours, most especially Em's father, Stephen Appleyard, and Dame Ellen. Of course, he could not bid them a proper farewell, nor make over much of parting company with them after church since his departure must remain a secret. Yet he felt the need to be in their company – though he would not admit the thought, even to himself – for what might be the last time.

Thus, he dressed with more care than usual in his Sunday best doublet – the blue one with fur trim and fashionably slashed sleeves that he had worn when he and Em were wed in St Paul's – tying the points neatly. He took the trouble to comb his hair properly with a comb, instead of simply raking it through with his fingers, as he usually did. Looking out at the weather, he knew the effort with his dark hair would not be wasted: for once the sun shone and the wind was no more than a whisper of air, so no hood need be worn and disarrange it. There was even a hint of spring warmth in the sunbeams that spilled through the open window of the bed chamber when he pushed the shutters wide. It was a sight to be welcomed with a smile – almost.

He assisted Em with the complicated pleats of her going-to-church veil, handing her the pins, one at a time and approving when she got the folds even and matching on either side of her face. That beloved face. Those sapphire eyes: pools of colour so deep he used to feel he might sink into them and drown in pleasure. Nowadays, there was little time for such lovers' nonsense but he pulled her close and gazed long upon her face. Perhaps there was still a glimmer of that beguiling blue – he liked to think so. At least she did not push away from him and he could feel the growing roundness of her belly pressed against him. Of late, she said she could feel the babe kicking but he had yet to experience that joyous promise of a new life. He lay his hand there, hoping the babe would move against it but, if it did so, he was unable to feel it.

'Take the best care of yourself and our child, Em, whilst I be away. Promise me?'

She nodded and he watched as a tear formed at the edge of her eye. As it poised to drop, he wiped it away with his thumb, then sucked it, tasting her salt. 'Do not weep, lass. All will be well. Just say that you love me and I can face anything the world might throw at me.'

'I love you, Seb, more than my soul, more than my life. You will come home safe to me, won't you? Promise?'

'Anything for you, sweetheart.'

'Promise me.'

'Aye. I shall swear upon the Gospels in St Michael's this morn to return to you, as soon as ever I may. You are my lodestone, Em, you will draw me back wherever I may be. I cannot do otherwise.'

'If only you had never gone to the Tower in the first place...'

'It cannot be undone now.'

'No.' Emily stepped away from him, straightened her apron and held her head higher. 'We should go. The others will be waiting. It will not do to be late at church.'

As they walked the short distance to St Michael's, Seb had to clutch Gawain under his arm since the pup could not keep up. They were joined by their fellow parishioners, many of the men and lads carrying their bows. What with February having been such a wet month, the lawful Sunday archery practice at the butts over in Smithfield had been set aside. No bowman worthy of the name would get his weapon wet by choice. Jude, Tom and Jack all carried their longbows to church. Jude and young Jack were skilled archers; Tom not so much. Emily was the best woman in London with a bow and had proved it more than once but, as a goodwife and soon-to-be mother, she had let the weapon alone of late. As for Seb, he had never loosed an arrow in his life. His crooked shoulders and lameness had excused him from the weekly archery butts in his youth and now, though so greatly improved it was nigh unto a miracle, it was too late for him to grow the strength of muscle and sinew to draw a bow properly. A pen was ever his choice of weapon.

Emily's father, Stephen, met them by the church door. He had brought a dozen bow staves. As Warden-Archer of the City, it was his task to arrange the butts and take note of any able-bodied male who failed to attend. Not having a suitable bow was no excuse.

'Ah, what a day this is,' Stephen said, catching Jude by the arm, 'Even Jude Foxley has deigned to bring his weapon. Haven't seen you at the butts for... let me think... aye, afore Christ's Mass, I believe it was.'

'That's a lie,' Jude said, nudging the elder man's elbow. 'I most certainly attended in January, once at least. You weren't thinking of fining me, were you? I'll protest most loudly, if you are. I have been gravely wounded of late.' Jude pulled up his sleeve to show the bindings still tied about the knife wound on his arm, though it was healing well.

'Get away with you,' Stephen jested. 'I'll wager it didn't hinder you raising your ale cup, eh?'

'My brother said exactly that but 'tis my left arm, see? I can drink one handed but drawing a bow needs two.'

All weapons were laid behind the font, being too precious to leave unattended outside the church.

Seb made the effort to greet everyone, even those with whom he was not on especially close terms. Every face was familiar and a welcomed sight for its own sake. He found it impossible to sing the responses as he usually did. The lump in his throat could not be dispelled and tears pricked his eyes more than once as he wondered if he would ever stand here, in St Michael's, surrounded by folk he knew again.

He hoped no one would espy his sorrowful humour but Dame Ellen certainly did, asking after his health and giving him such a knowing look, he feared Em might have told her something. But no.

'I'll maybe have a small commission for you, Sebastian,' she said. 'I have a mind for a horn book as a gift for little Janey, my granddaughter over at Deptford, as you'll recall? I'll come to your shop next week to discuss it with you.'

Seb nodded, relieved she had no inkling that he would not be there.

'Indeed, Dame Ellen,' was all he said, smiling and leaning forward to kiss her old cheek, soft as a plum's skin.

As they left the church, Father Thomas drew him aside.

'You were not singing, my son. 'Tis unlike you. Is aught amiss? Your father's letter still weighs heavy upon your mind?'

'No, father, I thank you for asking. All is well. I ask only that you will pray for me, please. I have coin...'

'You have my prayers every day, my son, *gratis*. I do not require payment for loving and serving my parishioners as Our

Lord Jesu instructs. You are a good Christian man, Sebastian. Hold fast to the Almighty and He will see you safe at the last.'

'Aye. I know it, Father Thomas, and thank you for all you have done for me.' Did that sound too much like a farewell? Seb knelt for the priest's blessing – not an unusual thing of itself but did others see how hard he pursed his lips and bit down upon them, trying not to weep as the old man's hand lay gently on his hair?

Outside, the menfolk had their bows to hand and were joshing each other as to who would be buying the ale later: whosoever was the best shot. They all turned up Bladder Street, towards Newgate and Smithfield beyond, or most of them at least. The women lingered, chatting with their friends, so Seb waited also, watching whilst Emily and Rose told them about the wedding – those who hadn't been informed before mass. The details had to be trawled through, trimmed, stitched and examined to the last minutiae. This might take some time, he thought as he compiled in his head the list of tasks he had yet to complete afore the morrow. Gawain squirmed in his arms and he set the pup down. It capered over to the nearest bush and did the necessary. Seb was pleased the dog seemed to be learning its manners but it did not do to waste time here. Em could speak with her fellow gossips another day. He went over and took her hand.

'Em, I need to go home.'

'Aye. I must just speak with my father. It won't take a moment.'

Stephen Appleyard was also there, talking to a fellow who was listing his excuses for not going to the butts. Stephen had heard them all before a thousand times but he patted the man's arm and they parted company. Em went over to him, Seb still clutching her hand.

That was when he saw the bowman, one who had not yet gone along to Smithfield. His weapon was raised, held at full draw and the arrow was aimed straight at Seb's heart. He cried out, though whether a word or some animal shriek, none could say, but all heads turned. Stephen had his bow up, a shaft nocked and loosed afore anyone else drew breath. No time to aim, but the warden-archer's skills were legendary and the arrow caught the fellow in the throat.

As he fell, his companion was there, likewise aiming at Seb, who seemed as one frozen where he stood.

Emily dragged her husband away, running along Cheapside. His hip, disobliging as ever, had him stumbling, only Em's grip upon his arm keeping him from sprawling on his face.

'Run, for pity's sake, Seb. Keep up.'

They fled past Dame Ellen's place and Em glanced behind. The second bowman was coming. There was nowhere to hide. Folk were spilling out from St Peter's in Cheap as their mass service ended but Em elbowed a path through the crowd, by the Eleanor Cross. She was breathless and had a stitch in her side. Seb was panting, not used to running.

Their pursuer had been hampered by the churchgoers but was catching up. They had made it nigh as far as the Stocks Market when Seb fell headlong in the gutter.

'Get up!' Em screamed, pulling on his arm but then she saw it: the fletched shaft protruding from his shoulder. 'Seb! Oh, Holy Mother.' She bent down and tried to lift him, only daring to breathe again when he struggled to his feet. 'Lean on me. Come, we daren't stop now.'

His breath came in gasps of pain but he said not a word, putting all his remaining strength into keeping going.

Cornhill seemed never ending as they laboured, one slow, encumbered step after another. Em looked back, saw the bowman stopped and taking aim. She shoved Seb into the nearest alleyway. He tumbled in an ungainly heap, down among a tangle of brambles and she landed atop him, just as an arrow thwacked into the wooden paling fence above their heads. It was still quivering there as she clambered to her feet. But the bowman loomed before her, now knife in hand.

'Got yer.' He grabbed her but Em wasn't done yet. As streetwise as Jack when needs be, her well-placed Sunday best boot landed just where a man would take most hurt. With a howl, the fellow dropped the blade to clutch his privy parts. No time to rest, she pulled Seb from the thorns, put his good arm about her neck and half-carried him onwards, turning into Bishopsgate Street, at last. A few yards more.

'Don't give up now,' she panted, though whether encouraging Seb or herself, she didn't know. Sweat was stinging her eyes. 'Almost there, Seb. Just a few steps. Then you can stop and rest. Keep going.' Another arrow shaft swooshed past their heads and impaled itself in someone's front door. Seb was becoming heavier by the moment. A sound – a whimper – escaped him as he slipped to the ground. She could keep hold no longer, else he would drag her down beside him.

'Help us, here!' she cried and saw the guard standing by the gatehouse of Crosby Place turn to look. Whether he recognised Seb or else was Christian enough to aid anyone in need, he came running, shouting to others to follow. Swords were unsheathed, bows drawn but the archer behind them was already falling forward to land face down – dead. Stephen came running up.

'I'm getting to old for this,' he puffed. 'How's Seb? Is he badly hurt?'

'I don't know,' Em sobbed, clinging to him. 'You saved us.'

'That's what fathers do, lass. Hush now. Tend to your husband.'

Other friendly hands reached out to her. Lord Richard's men surrounded them. Then, with the greatest care, Seb, limp as wet linen, was lifted up, off the street, borne to the gate and taken within.

For the second time in three days, he would find a safe haven at Crosby Place.

'Hold still, Master Foxley,' the duke's surgeon instructed.

Seb was lying face down upon a trestle board, the fletchings of the arrow stuck upright from his left shoulder. The instruction was hardly required: Seb hadn't moved since they laid him there.

The surgeon took up a large pair of shears.

'Merciful Mother!' Emily cried.

'Calm yourself mistress. These are but to cut through the doublet and shirt. 'Tis not an amputation. Not yet, at least. Take her away, someone. I cannot work with a wailing woman at my elbow.'

'Come, Emily,' Sir Robert said, 'He is in good hands. You cannot help him at present. Besides, a woman with child should not see such things.' The knight led her away and handed her into the care of two serving women who supplied ale, kindly words and encouragement concerning the surgeon's undoubted skills.

Sir Robert, another burly fellow in Gloucester livery and an assistant surgeon stood ready to hold down the patient, should it prove necessary.

The shears snipped the cloth, cutting away Seb's one and only doublet. As the surgeon peeled back the wool, the arrow shaft leaned and, as the blood soaked linen shirt was cut through, it dropped to the floor.

'Well, that has spared us a deal of work,' the surgeon said. 'The wound is but a gash, not a penetration. The arrow was held in place only by the thickness of cloth.'

By the time Em was allowed to see him, Seb was sitting up, propped upon a bench by the fire, swathed in a blanket. His face looked grey as hoar frost; a mist of sweat glistened greasily upon his brow.

'Your man was most fortunate, mistress,' the surgeon was saying as he folded away his instruments in their leather pouch. 'In the main, he is suffering from the shock of it. He will be sore for a few days but the arrow gouged the flesh, rather than piercing it. I have washed the wound with wine and smeared it with honey. He will mend soon enough, God willing.'

'How are you feeling, Seb?' Em asked, stroking his right hand: the one not resting in a linen sling. His hand was too cold. She pulled the blanket closer about him.

'He says I was fortunate.' Seb's voice was no more than a husky whisper. 'Not so. If I was, I should not have had men attempting to kill me at all. I have never been shot at afore. When I saw that arrowhead, Em, pointed straight at me... I thought it was the end.'

'But it wasn't, so cease fussing, husband,' Em said, trying to make out it was but a slight mishap. 'A night's rest and you'll be as good as new.' The pretence was not working. She watched as he winced, easing the arm in the sling. 'You're not much of a hero, are you, Seb Foxley?' She kissed his forehead. It was chill and damp beneath her lips.

'I have never tried to be,' he said. 'I am what I am and naught more. I was not meant to be a Gawain, nor even a Sir Robert Percy. I leave the heroic actions to their kind. I want a quiet life, Em. No knife-brandishing assassins at my door, nor poisoners, fire-setters or killers with longbows. Just us. You, me and our child.'

'Our son, you mean.' Em pulled his free hand to her belly. 'Feel him kick? He is dancing a merry jig this eve.'

Seb rested his hand there. Then he felt it. For the first time, he felt the babe move.

'I felt it, Em. It kicked against my hand.' He smiled, forgetting the pain in his shoulder. ''Tis moving about.'

'Aye. You think I don't know? Every time he does so, I have to rush to the privy.'

They laughed together.

''Tis a wonder, Em. A new life. 'Til now, it was not quite real to me, being told you were with child. But it lies in your belly, growing and moving: a living soul. And 'tis ours; a gift from the Almighty for us to cherish and care for. Oh, Em...'

'How's our injured warrior, then?' Stephen asked, coming in, unannounced. 'I trust you're taking good care of him, Em?'

'Of course, father. I thought you must have gone home by now, or to the butts. How will the archery go on without you?'

'Well enough, I dare say. How's the shoulder, Seb?'

'It will heal, so they tell me. Apparently, I was fortunate.'

'That is good. Is there anything I may do to help you?'

'Aye, there is,' Em said. 'The surgeon hacked Seb's clothes to get them off: his wedding doublet is ruined. Could you go to our house and ask Rose or Jude to bring all that we need, please, father?'

'And what is it you want, Em? Your clothes look to be all of a piece.'

'Just say that I need my things for tomorrow. They'll know what I mean.'

As Stephen opened the door to go, a small bundle of black and white fur tottered in and fell, exhausted, at Seb's feet.

'Gawain!' Seb said, surprised, 'How ever did you find me, lad?'

'He must have followed your scent.' Emily scooped up the little creature and gave him to Seb. He just fitted within Seb's sling, as if it was meant for his bed, and was sleeping within moments. 'He's very loyal and has walked so far just to be with you, at your side,' she said, scratching the pup's soft ears. 'I wish I could tell my father, Seb. He saved your life this day. We are in his debt and I feel badly, deceiving him.'

'Tell him what, Em? That I be leaving?'

'I want to tell him where we are going.'

'We? But I thought…'

'Of course: we! You don't suppose I'm letting you go alone, do you? Not when it is so plain that you can't manage without me. Who will tend your wound, if I'm not there to do it for you? I thought I'd lost you too many times of late.' There was a catch in her voice. 'I'm not losing you again.'

'You will come with me? Oh, thank you, Em. I did not want us to be apart.'

'On one condition: that you tell me where we are bound.'

'Very well.' Seb looked about the little chamber in which he had been told to rest quietly until a bed could be prepared for him. The duke had ordered it so, deeming it too dangerous for him to return to Paternoster Row. They were alone but past hints that walls listened and espiers lurked everywhere made him cautious. 'The county of Norfolk,' he whispered, drawing her close. 'To the village of Foxley, where Jude and I were born and our father afore us.'

'And you have family there?'

'Ssh, keep your voice low. In truth, I know not. My father spoke so little of the place. Things came to pass there which he preferred to forget: our mother's death was not the least of them. I believe he mentioned one time, that he had a sister. Whether she be still living, I cannot say. I may have cousins. My father's family name was Armitage. Once there, we cannot go by the name Foxley, for that could apply to every villager. In writing to the local priest, I signed myself as Sebastian, the son of Mark Armitage – that will be remembered from my baptism – so he might tell my relatives – if any there be. Will you mind having a new name? Mistress Emily Armitage?'

'I suppose it sounds well enough. So long as you are safe and we be together, I don't care what name we must use. I love you, Seb Foxley-Armitage, whatever your name, whatever you call yourself. I hope you have a dozen handsome cousins.'

'Some may even be women, Em,' he said, smiling at her. 'Others may be ugly.' He kissed her. 'None will be as wonderful as my Emily.'

She kissed him in return. This time, his skin felt warm.

AUTHOR'S NOTES

It is the case that there were contemporary rumours of the Woodvilles dabbling in witchcraft – how else to explain King Edward's infatuation with Elizabeth Woodville-Grey, a near penniless widow of the enemy to the point of marrying her in 1464? There is probably a very human explanation: an attractive, sexy, older woman pleads poverty and vulnerability to a young, lusty fellow, drunk on the power of kingship, who thinks that whatever he desires is there for the taking.

However, there were those who found it unbelievable that Europe's most eligible bachelor, who could have had the pick of wealthy princesses, had married instead a woman so unsuitable, who brought no dowry, no prospect of a valuable political alliance but a plethora of unwed siblings. No wonder that in 1469, when Edward fell out with his powerful cousin, the Earl of Warwick, Warwick blamed the now-influential Woodvilles and must have been delighted when someone claimed they had found lead images which Elizabeth's mother, Jacquetta of Luxembourg, had made and used for the purposes of witchcraft. In those days, sorcerers and witches were very real and provided an explanation for Edward having wed Elizabeth – obviously, she and her mother must have employed the Black Arts to bewitch and enthral the king.

Both Jacquetta and Edward refuted the allegations and the charges were dropped – but not forgotten. After Edward died unexpectedly in 1483, his brother, now King Richard III, revived the accusations. Although Jacquetta had died in

1472, Parliament declared that she had brought about the king's marriage to her daughter by means of witchcraft. Whether people believed it or not, it was a convenient explanation and served to further blacken the Woodville name. One thing is certain: Richard had little liking for them and had avoided coming to the king's court as far as possible after his brother George's death in the Tower of London by 'drowning in a butt of malmsey wine'. If anyone knew the true cause of the Duke of Clarence's demise, history has failed to note it and I felt at liberty to fill the gap.

Foxglove poisoning – an Agatha Christie favourite – truly does cause the symptoms of a painful, irregular heartbeat and oddly coloured visual disturbances, as described in my tale, along with a few less appropriate and messy side effects that I have omitted. Even a small dose can be fatal and all parts of the foxglove plant contain the poison. The plant was known by this name since at least the fourteenth century. For readers who may be interested, *A is for Arsenic – The Poisons of Agatha Christie* by Kathryn Harkup reveals all in the chapter 'D is for Digitalis' (Bloomsbury, 2015). Just don't try this at home, as they say.

As for those mysterious tunnels beneath the Tower of London, years ago, I got chatting in our local library to an elderly lady who, in her youth, worked for the Vintners' Company of London. She told me how, during the Blitz bombing in World War II, the company was granted royal permission to store its barrels of vintage wine in the tunnels under the Tower to keep them safe. She said that she and her friends and colleagues often used to shelter there too during air raids and the fun they had daring each other to brave the cobwebs and darkness of the unexplored passageways. I always meant to ask her for more details but she died suddenly, taking the secrets with her. I expect those tunnels must be known to someone – certainly to the Vintners – but guidebooks and websites about the Tower make no mention of them. I could probably have done further research into the subject but, in the end, I decided not to. I reckoned the less I knew for certain, the more I could allow my imagination to create the horrors of the unknown.

With thanks to my valiant other half, Glenn, and Tim and Claire Ridgway at MadeGlobal, I dedicate this book to my much-missed Mum and Dad, Joyce and Albert 'Lofty' Botting. They told such marvellous tales around the fire on cold winter evenings, it is no wonder I have inherited their love of story-telling. I like to think they would be happy to know I have kept up the family tradition.

Toni Mount
28th August 2017

READING GROUP QUESTIONS

Thank you for taking the time to read my novel. As with all novels, there are a number of themes which run through the narrative. I hope that you enjoyed the book and that the following questions help you to get a deeper understanding of the novel.

1. The prologue has a dark, sinister and supernatural feel. Did it make you want to read on and discover who these two people were and how the incident fitted into the narrative or did it give too much away?

2. As an author, I have tried to make Seb, Emily and Jude believable and human characters. Do you find that you can relate to them? Which secondary character did you feel added most to the story?

3. How important do you think the setting of medieval London was to the novel and did the historical elements of the narrative draw you in or put you off?

4. What were the main themes of the story in your opinion? Do you think that these are timeless themes, or things that could only happen in the medieval period?

5. Have you been reading along with the whole Sebastian Foxley series? We've seen the main characters develop through the books. Do you think that characters like Seb, Emily and Jude have developed in the way that you would have expected?

6. Thinking about Sebastian, what do you think are his main strengths and weaknesses. Do these help him in his life, or do they hold him back?

7. Who is your favourite character in the book, and why?

8. Are there any characters you particularly admire or dislike, and why?

9. There are strong emotions throughout the book. Can you pick out a passage that you found particularly profound or interesting? Did it make you think about your own life?

10. Personal reactions – what did you enjoy (or not!) about The Colour of Murder?

If you enjoyed *The Colour of Murder*, please consider leaving a review at Amazon, Goodreads or the place where you purchased the book. I read every review left online and really appreciate the time you have taken to read the book and comment on it.

TONI MOUNT

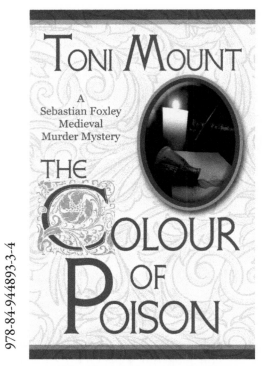

TONI MOUNT

A
Sebastian Foxley
Medieval
Murder Mystery

THE

COLOUR

OF

POISON

978-84-944893-3-4

**The first Sebastian Foxley
Medieval Mystery by Toni Mount.**

The narrow, stinking streets of medieval London can sometimes be a dark place. Burglary, arson, kidnapping and murder are every-day events. The streets even echo with rumours of the mysterious art of alchemy being used to make gold for the King.

Join Seb, a talented but crippled artist, as he is drawn into a web of lies to save his handsome brother from the hangman's rope. Will he find an inner strength in these, the darkest of times, or will events outside his control overwhelm him?

Only one thing is certain - if Seb can't save his brother, nobody can.

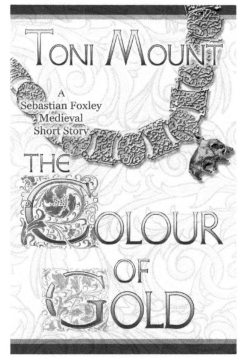

978-84-946498-0-6

**The second Sebastian Foxley
Medieval Mystery by Toni Mount.
A short story.**

A wedding in medieval London should be a splendid occasion, especially when a royal guest will be attending the nuptial feast. Yet for the bridegroom, the talented young artist, Sebastian Foxley, his marriage day begins with disaster when the valuable gold livery collar he should wear has gone missing. From the lowliest street urchin to the highest nobility, who could be the thief? Can Seb wed his sweetheart, Emily Appleyard, and save the day despite that young rascal, Jack Tabor, and his dog causing chaos?

Join in the fun at a medieval marriage in this short story that links the first two Sebastian Foxley medieval murder mysteries: *The Colour of Poison* and the full-length novel *The Colour of Cold Blood.*.

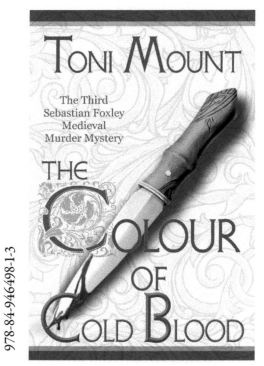

978-84-946498-1-3

**The third Sebastian Foxley
Medieval Mystery by Toni Mount.**

A devilish miasma of murder and heresy lurks in the winter streets of medieval London - someone is slaying women of the night. For Seb Foxley and his brother, Jude, evil and the threat of death come close to home when Gabriel, their well-liked journeyman, is arrested as a heretic and condemned to be burned at the stake.

Amid a tangle of betrayal and deception, Seb tries to uncover the murderer before more women die – will he also defy the church and devise a plan to save Gabriel?

These are dangerous times for the young artist and those he holds dear. Treachery is everywhere, even at his own fireside...

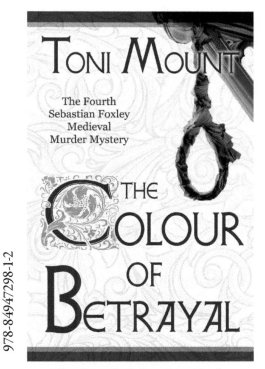

TONI MOUNT

The Fourth
Sebastian Foxley
Medieval
Murder Mystery

THE COLOUR
OF BETRAYAL

978-84947298-1-2

**The fourth Sebastian Foxley
Medieval Mystery by Toni Mount.
A short story**

Suicide or murder?

As medieval Londoners joyously prepare for the Christmas celebrations, goldsmith Lawrence Ducket is involved in a street brawl. Fearful that his opponent is dying from his injuries, Lawrence seeks sanctuary in a church nearby.

When Ducket is found hanging from the rafters, people assume it's suicide. Yet, Sebastian Foxley is unconvinced. Why is his young apprentice, Jack Tabor, so terrified that he takes to his bed?

Amidst feasting and merriment, Seb is determined to solve the mystery of his friend's death and to ease Jack's fears.

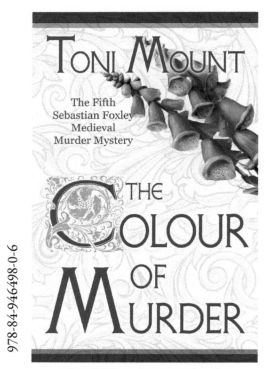

**The fifth Sebastian Foxley
Medieval Mystery by Toni Mount.**

London is not safe for princes or commoners.

In February 1478, a wealthy merchant is killed by an intruder and a royal duke dies at the Tower. Neither case is quite as simple as it seems.

Seb Foxley, an intrepid young artist, finds himself in the darkest of places, fleeing for his life. With foul deeds afoot at the king's court, his wife Emily pregnant and his brother Jude's hope of marrying Rose thwarted, can Seb unearth the secrets which others would prefer to keep hidden?

Join Seb and Jude, their lives in jeopardy in the dangerous streets of the city, as they struggle to solve crimes and keep their business flourishing.

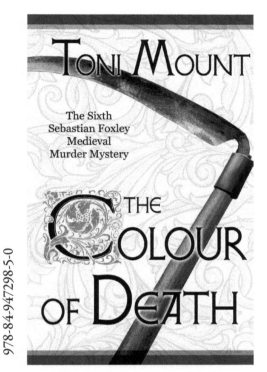

Toni Mount

The Sixth
Sebastian Foxley
Medieval
Murder Mystery

The Colour of Death

978-84-947298-5-0

**The sixth Sebastian Foxley
Medieval Mystery by Toni Mount.
A Short Story**

Seb Foxley and his wife, Emily, have been forced to flee medieval London to escape their enemies. They find a safe haven in the isolated Norfolk village where Seb was born. Yet this idyllic rural setting has its own murderous secrets and a terrible crime requires our hero to play the sleuth once more.

Even away from London, Seb and Emily are not as safe as they believe - their enemies are closer than they know and danger lurks at every twist and turn.

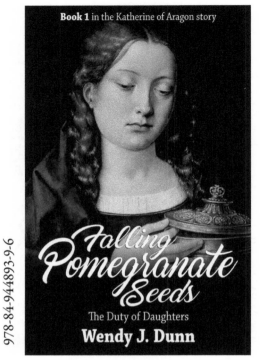

Book 1 in the Katherine of Aragon story

Falling
Pomegranate
Seeds

The Duty of Daughters
Wendy J. Dunn

978-84-944893-9-6

Book 1 in the Katherine of Aragon Story

Doña Beatriz Galindo.
Respected scholar.
Tutor to royalty.
Friend and advisor to Queen Isabel of Castile.

Beatriz is an uneasy witness to the Holy War of Queen Isabel and her husband, Ferdinand, King of Aragon. A Holy War seeing the Moors pushed out of territories ruled by them for centuries.

The road for women is a hard one. Beatriz must tutor the queen's youngest child, Catalina, and equip her for a very different future life. She must teach her how to survive exile, an existence outside the protection of her mother. She must prepare Catalina to be England's queen.

A tale of mothers and daughters, power, intrigue, death, love, and redemption. In the end, Falling Pomegranate Seeds sings a song of friendship and life.

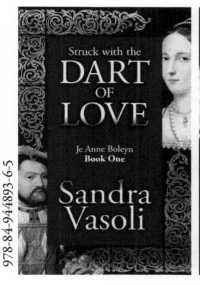
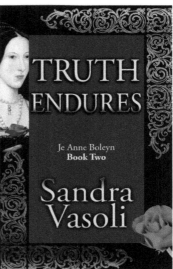

The *Je Anne Boleyn* series is a gripping account of Anne Boleyn's effort to negotiate her position in the treacherous court of Henry VIII, where every word uttered might pose danger, where absolute loyalty to the King is of critical importance, and in which the sweeping tide of religious reform casts a backdrop of intrigue and peril.

Anne's story begins with *Struck with the Dart of Love*: Tradition tells us that Henry pursued Anne for his mistress and that she resisted, scheming to get the crown and bewitching him with her unattainable allure. Nothing could be further from the truth.

The story continues with *Truth Endures*: Anne is determined to be a loving mother, devoted wife, enlightened spiritual reformer, and a wise, benevolent queen. But others are hoping and praying for her failure. Her status and very life become precarious as people spread downright lies to advance their objectives.

The unforgettable tale of Henry VIII's second wife is recounted in Anne's clear, decisive voice and leads to an unforgettable conclusion...

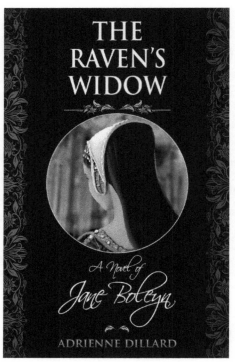

978-8494649837

"Only a few moments more my lady, the Tower is just ahead."

Jane Parker never dreamed that her marriage into the Boleyn family would raise her star to such dizzying heights. Before long, she finds herself as trusted servant and confidante to her sister-in-law, Anne Boleyn; King Henry VIII's second queen. On a gorgeous spring day, that golden era is cut short by the swing of a sword. Jane is unmoored by the tragic death of her husband, George, and her loss sets her on a reckless path that leads to her own imprisonment in the Tower of London. Surrounded by the remnants of her former life, Jane must come to terms with her actions. In the Tower, she will face up to who she really is and how everything went so wrong.

Why not visit
Sebastian Foxley's web page
to discover more about his
life and times?
www.SebastianFoxley.com

Historical Fiction

Falling Pomegranate Seeds - **Wendy J. Dunn**
Struck With the Dart of Love - **Sandra Vasoli**
Truth Endures - **Sandra Vasoli**
Cor Rotto - **Adrienne Dillard**
The Raven's Widow - **Adrienne Dillard**
The Claimant - **Simon Anderson**

Non Fiction History

Anne Boleyn's Letter from the Tower - **Sandra Vasoli**
Queenship in England - **Conor Byrne**
Katherine Howard - **Conor Byrne**
The Turbulent Crown - **Roland Hui**
Jasper Tudor - **Debra Bayani**
Tudor Places of Great Britain - **Claire Ridgway**
Illustrated Kings and Queens of England - **Claire Ridgway**
A History of the English Monarchy - **Gareth Russell**
The Fall of Anne Boleyn - **Claire Ridgway**
George Boleyn: Tudor Poet, Courtier & Diplomat - **Ridgway & Cherry**
The Anne Boleyn Collection - **Claire Ridgway**
The Anne Boleyn Collection II - **Claire Ridgway**
Two Gentleman Poets at the Court of Henry VIII - **Edmond Bapst**

Children's Books

All about Richard III - **Amy Licence**
All about Henry VII - **Amy Licence**
All about Henry VIII - **Amy Licence**
Tudor Tales William at Hampton Court - **Alan Wybrow**

PLEASE LEAVE A REVIEW

If you enjoyed this book, *please* leave a review at the book seller
where you purchased it. There is no better way to thank the
author and it really does make a huge difference!
Thank you in advance.

Lightning Source UK Ltd.
Milton Keynes UK
UKHW011826290319
340174UK00001B/108/P